# COLUMBUS:  MERCY
## Project Columbus, Book 5

By J.C. Rainier

Columbus: Mercy
Project Columbus, Book 5
Copyright © 2014 by J.C. Rainier
Published: 22 April 2014
ISBN: 978-1-939817-08-2
Publisher: Oakenbrand Press

In conjunction with Oakenbrand Press

## Currently Available by J.C. Rainier:

*Columbus: Flight*

*Columbus: Ashes*

*Columbus: Demeter*

*Columbus: Winter*

## Other Projects by J.C. Rainier:

*The Sorcerers* - Web Comic by J.C. Rainier and A. Kochetova – http://sorcerers.manyhatsonline.com

Please follow J. C. on Facebook or Twitter (@JCRainier), or check http://jcrainier.com periodically for blog updates and sneak previews of the Project Columbus series.

>BEGIN PLAYBACK|

CONCORDIA

DUM VITA EST

SPES EST

Cool, damp mud slithered from the ground under her knees, wrapping them in a gentle embrace. Her feet tingled and tiny pinpricks stabbed at her feet. Gabi shifted her weight off of her shins and onto her left hip, swinging her legs to her side and rubbing her thin calves.

"How many times, Gabi? How many times do you have to come back here?"

Her gaze slowly lifted to meet Will Vandemark's harsh features. His shaggy brown beard only accentuated the slits of eyes that peered back in judgment. Gabi sighed and dropped her eyes back down. The wooden stake in the ground leaned slightly to the left, just out of the reach of Gabi's fingers. A thin band of slightly darker wood a couple inches from the top marked where the cross piece had once resided on the grave marker. It had fallen off months ago, and blown away in the storm that followed a few days later. Yesterday's rains had drenched the wood, but every detail was burned in her memory from the repeated visits she had made to the site.

"Leave me alone," she muttered just above her breath.

His right foot made a soft scuffing noise as he swept the ground in a circular pattern. "It all started with her, you know."

"That's what they say."

"It's the truth. I was there. She was the first one from Camp Eight to fall to the scourge. For us, the Sorrow started with her. She couldn't fight it off if she tried."

Gabi let loose an exasperated sigh as her eyes darted to the blue skies above. "She wasn't the first. You know that. Karen said that…"

Will stepped into her line of vision and his brow furrowed. A snarl crossed his lips as he interrupted. "Karen said a lot. You'd think that they were almost proud of the scourge, that they had survived it. Look where it got them." His arm shot out stiffly and he pointed to a patch of ground where several more grave markers lay. Some were cairns of stone, others were simple wooden crosses, newer than the one that Gabi sat before, yet still battered by the elements.

A flicker of flame rose within Gabi, and she clenched her teeth together for a brief moment as she gazed at the dozens of graves that Will called to her attention.

"Why are you bugging me, Will?"

"We're waiting for you. It's time to go."

*Time to go*, she thought. *Time to leave behind everything that I know. For the second time in my life. Time to leave home for somewhere I've never been to live in a place no one knows for sure exists.*

"I don't want to."

"You don't have a choice," Will said as he wandered to the base of a nearby palm tree and retrieved their vinewood bows. He casually jerked his thumb at the grave in front of Gabi. "She says so."

"She's been dead for years. She can't say anything," she retorted, the heat of anger spreading to her cheeks.

"She said enough to me when she was dying. And it's a good thing she said it to me and not someone else in the room when she went. Otherwise I'd be leaving you on this dirt pile to die." A cruel sneer twisted his beard and nose upward. "Then you could be with her forever. Imagine that."

"You wouldn't do that."

"No, I can't do that. You know it too. So just save us both the trouble and come with me so I don't have to carry you like a sack of pepperines."

Gabi's eyes dropped to the dirt in front of her as a heavy sigh escaped her lips. The welling anger ebbed from within her, and she shook her head. Rising to her feet, she said, "Fine. Just… just give me another minute, okay?"

"You've given her enough minutes."

Gabi ignored him and swiftly picked her way through the graveyard to another equally old marker. Though heavily weathered, it was still bound together, bearing the unmistakable shape of a cross. She put her knees to the dirt next to it and traced her fingers along the faintly visible name chipped into the crossbar: LUIS SERRANO.

"I'm sorry, Papa," she whispered, nearly choking on the words. "You're not alone. We're just leaving this place behind. I know you're with all of *Raphael*, and we need you all with us now. Please, Papa… watch over us. Sing us to sleep, and keep a watch for us through the night, from now until forever."

Gabi's lips quivered and she could feel tears roll down her face as a slight breeze kicked up. She sniffed and wiped away the tears, taking in a deep breath to force away her loneliness. When she felt she was calm enough, she rose and faced Will.

"I'm ready."

"No more Sorrow," he grunted. "We move on. We put the past and our losses behind us. All of us."

Gabi nodded in hollow agreement. As Will handed Gabi her bow and turned from the cemetery to make the trek to the sea, she retrieved her battered, muddy backpack. It was a drab green color, torn in several places and sewn back together with thread made from the palms that shaded the now silent Camp Eight. It had been patched by a dozen hands over the years, but like all supplies in the village, it was never thrown away as it could still be used. A loop of fabric from another torn pack had been sewn into the right edge, serving as a quiver for her six rough-fletched arrows. A similar but smaller loop adorned left edge; in this she had stowed her tomahawk.

Will had given her the axe on their fourth hunting trip. It was fashioned from a cut down and lightened hatchet, the original wood handle had broken long before and been replaced by jaguar bone wrapped in worn, salt crusted leather. The first thing that Will had taught her was how not to cut off her own limbs on accident. The second thing that he had taught her was how to hone the blade to a razor's edge, making the first lesson all the more valuable.

Will moved swiftly along the overgrown foot trail, brushing blue green vines and shrubs alike from his path. Gabi had to stay on his heels to keep the rebounding plants from whipping her face and body, but she had grown used to doing just that on their many hunting trips over the past year.

They reached a snarl in the trail formed by nearly a dozen palms, twisted and thrown across the hillside by the most recent hurricane to slam into the island. As Gabi scrambled to the top of the pile of splintered timbers, she glanced up at the hill that Camp Eight rested on. The heights were not so far away that Gabi couldn't make out signs of fresh damage in the decaying village. The roof of the once comforting Palm Palace had peeled back again, and now flapped slowly in the wind as a vivid reminder of the colony's failure. Burned and collapsed shells of cottages accentuated the now ruined village, and the farmland on the adjacent hill was an overgrown mess of pepperine and vinewood.

Gabi hopped down from the logs and formed up behind Will one more time. They made their way into the valley and past the makeshift tents that lined the once bustling shoreline. The rotting, rusted hulk of one of the old sleeper pods lay heeled over and half buried in the sand, now only usable as emergency shelter during storms. Dark red rust stains streaked every surface of the pod, and where they met the white sands, they spread like trickling blood. She scanned the horizon in vain for signs of the second pod, but the salt, storms, and surf had ripped it to shreds two years earlier, leaving only the barest trace visible at the lowest tides.

On the sands at surf's edge rested the contraption that Will swore would be their saving grace. It looked ridiculous to Gabi; it was merely a few fishing canoes strapped together with palm rope, with another log sticking straight up with a few woven fronds strapped to it. Stout logs jutted from both sides of the boat to other clusters of logs at their ends. Will had called these things 'outriggers', though it looked to her almost like a giant gull laying its wings between two trees on the water. The whole boat looked to her like something Aidan would have thrown together as a toy when he was bored.

Gathered around the boat was a sight just as ludicrous to Gabi. Several figures waited idly by, some standing with their hands shielding their eyes, others hunched over the sand in a semicircle, drawing figures on its surface. Gabi brought a hand to her eyes to shield them from the sun. Once her eyes adjusted, she identified them as Kristin Vandemark, Gina Bryant, and the two surviving teenagers from the Baker family: Caleb and Karina. Karina was a hair older than Kristin, and more solidly built as well. Caleb was a bit of a bruiser for a thirteen-year-old; he was both nearly as tall and as stout as his older sister.

"Damn it," Will cursed. "The other boats left yesterday, and we're losing the tide. We need to go now, or we'll be another day behind them."

He sprinted across the sands ahead of Gabi, whose legs struggled to cross the span at a rate even close to Will's. He tossed his bow into the boat; the soft clatter of vinewood against palm wood met her ears. A few seconds after she caught up, she hopped aboard and presented herself in front of her companions.

*Damn it,* she cursed to herself.

Gabi's eyes locked on Marya Brennan. Now thirteen years old, Marya stood several inches taller than Gabi, though over a foot shorter than Will. Her hair was bleached by the sun, and her skin had a deep bronze quality to it. Marya covered herself with a loose jaguar fur vest and shorts. In her palm cord belt she had secured two battered fur sheaths. The angular hilts that jutted out were easily recognizable as two of the last completely intact steel knives in the colony: a pair of bayonets.

Gabi shook her head and brushed past the older girl, hopping onto the boat and plopping her backpack down into the center canoe, just below the mast. Haphazard stacks of canteens and scavenged supplies in packs lay within the makeshift hold. At the bow of the boat she caught sight of Aidan Brennan, his back to her, staring out at the sea. By his side was Gabi's younger brother, Diego, and Gina's half-sister, Daphne, who were busy kicking their legs in the sparkling surf.

"Hey," Marya called out. "We better not have a problem out there, Gabi."

She ignored Marya and continued making a nest for her pack amongst the cluttered supplies. She cleared a small space between the hold wall and several canteens, and slid her pack securely in the space. As she did so, she spotted the stock of a rifle, buried under the supplies. Her heart skipped a beat as her finger traced over the cold metal.

*What? Where did this come from?*

"I'm serious," Marya harped as she walked onto the small ship. "Are you going to be able to handle this without flipping out?"

Gabi hid the weapon quickly and stood up. She narrowed her eyes and walked to within inches of Marya, flinging her bow carelessly to the deck. "I don't want to be here with you either, so just shut up."

For a moment, the two were locked in a duel of stares, slowly breathing in and out through clenched teeth as their eyes danced and darted at each other. Despite the older girl having a decided height advantage, and Gabi being unarmed, she did not back down. Will stepped in, gently pushing on each of their shoulders and stepping between them.

"Enough. If you two cause problems, I'm throwing you both overboard," he growled. "Marya, get to the back of the boat and get ready to push. Gabi, grab a paddle and get ready."

With one last burning glance, Gabi turned away. She grabbed one of the wooden paddles from the deck and made her way to the port side near the bow.

"Diego," she yelled at her brother. "Get down in the center of the boat and wait there."

He rolled over and looked at her through his tangled locks of sandy blonde hair. The very sight of him made her blood boil; he was the living embodiment of everything that had gone wrong for her since her family landed on Demeter.

"I don't wanna," he protested.

Gabi hoisted the paddle above her head in a grand swinging motion. Diego saw this and his eyes widened as far as they could as he let out an ear piercing shriek. His short arms and legs clawed at the logs of the deck, and he quickly scurried to the edge of the cargo hold and rolled inside with a thud. Gabi smiled smugly and dropped her knees onto the rough bark of the deck.

She felt a hand on her shoulder and looked up. Kristin Vandemark stood above her, oar in hand. Her dark brown hair was woven in a single, long braid, and she wore a grim look of disapproval on her face.

"That was horrible. He's your brother. Don't even think of hitting him," she glowered.

"Fine, I'll drown him then," Gabi retorted.

"You even try it and I'll throw you over myself."

Gabi's cheeks flushed and her temper flared. It was all she could do to stay quiet; she did not want to anger Kristin or her brother. The journey ahead was going to be very long, and she knew that any one person on the boat could make her life miserable. Three of them were almost certain to, no matter what she did.

She watched as Aidan took the oar from Kristin and took a position on the opposite side of the boat. At ten, he was just barely younger than Gabi and two inches shorter as well. He was a very quiet and withdrawn boy, and fiercely guarded by his older sister. He used this to his advantage and would antagonize Gabi when he felt like it, then run and hide behind Marya.

Gabi glanced over her shoulder at Marya. Though she could barely remember the actual incident, Gabi knew that Marya had broken her arm years earlier. Likewise, she knew that at some point she had retaliated and almost drowned the girl, and for years the two had been at each others' throats. Before, there were plenty of adults to break up any squabbles. But as the Sorrow wore on, the population dwindled as villagers succumbed to disease and fighting. Then the hurricane came, and wiped out just about everyone else. Now only Will and Kristin were left to keep the fragile peace, as the other twenty survivors had already left on their own ships the day before.

Her eyes wandered under the mast and caught sight of Diego. She clenched her teeth and her hands wrung tightly around the handle of the oar. Diego was the first child born in Camp Eight, just over five years earlier. He was also one of only two Demeter-born children to survive the Sorrow. He shared blood with Gabi, but the bond was not full. With her dark brown hair and almond skin, a casual observer would think she was a mismatch for Diego's sandy hair and pale, sunburned skin. But the resemblance in their faces was unmistakable. Looking at him reminded her of the mother they lost, and she hated him for it. Her anger was fueled further by the fact that their mother died when he was just a baby, so he was living with no memory of her.

After their mother's death, Gabi and Diego were cared for by Chief James Vandemark for four years until his demise during the great storm. The two surviving Vandemarks took in the Serrano children as foster siblings.

The deck of the boat lurched forward and Gabi heard the stern scrape along the sand as it was pushed into the water. She waited for Will to yell "Now!" and then plunged her oar into the water and pulled hard against the roiling surf. The bow of the boat rose up and crashed down, almost knocking her to the deck.

"Dig deep," he shouted from the rear. "Pull!"

Gabi focused on the waters just ahead as she thrust her oar into the waves over and over. Cool water sprayed her face as the vessel slammed into another roller. There was a momentary sensation of backward movement, and Gabi clutched her oar tighter.

*We're never going to make it.*

"Get ready… DIG!"

Her oar splashed as she caught the top of the next wave. Again the boat lurched, but Gabi kept rowing as hard as she could. Another wave approached a few seconds later, but this time it barely lifted the bow, and did nothing to slow their momentum. She looked down over the side and saw the mottled floor of the sea well below. A glance back revealed that the shore was well behind them. Something seemed off to Gabi. The pod wreck on the shore was too far off to the left. As she turned forward, a glimpse of a dark form out of the corner of her eye made her heart plunge into her stomach.

Her arms reacted as quickly as her mouth. She thrust the oar out has hard as she could just off the bow to fend off the black mass and yelled, "Pod wreck! Turn right!"

A split second later, Will's voice powered over the droning of the sea. "Aidan, Marya, Gina, back paddle now! Everyone else dig!"

Gabi's oar caught the corner of the jagged steel hulk that lurked just under the surface, which ripped the oar from her grasp, slicing her left hand open. Searing pain gripped her as she fell back to the deck, grabbed her wrist, and screamed. Then the whole ship rose on the port side and a terrible crack pealed through the air. Gabi tumbled backward into the cargo hold and hit her head on the mast. She rolled to her side, sucking in a huge gulp of air and letting it out in a loud moan. Her eyes closed and her fingers and toes began to tingle.

Shouts from her companions came from all around her, and then the deck shifted again with a loud splash and the scrape of wood on metal.

"No! Kris!" Will's voice was near panic and Gabi could hear his long strides moving across the deck. "Hang on!"

Gabi struggled to her knees and opened her eyes. Her vision blurred from the pain of her injuries, and her hand nearly slipped from its perch from the blood that poured from it. Will was flat on his belly over the port side of the boat, drawing his oar slowly closer, with his hand fully extended. Their other companions, Caleb and Karina, were hunched over his shoulders.

"I've got her. Keep paddling, we need to get deeper."

Caleb and Karina scurried to their positions on the port side and began rowing furiously. The outrigger thumped again on the side of the pod, but cleared quickly once they gained forward momentum. Will heaved with all his might, and pulled his sister out of the water and onto the deck, where she coughed and spit up a mouthful of water.

Will left his sister where she lay and hurried over to Gabi. "Let me take a look."

He spun the top of a canteen open and grabbed Gabi's hand, then gave it a quick rinse of water. The warm splash stung and she was unable to stifle a yelp. Will muttered and swore under his breath, then took Gabi's head in one of his massive hands and turned it to get a better look.

"Your head's fine. We need to fix your hand up."

Gabi sucked in a deep breath and then cycled it out. "Where's the med kit? I'll take care of it."

"The hell you are," he said as he rummaged through a row of packs laid on their sides. "It's pretty bad, I think it needs stitches."

"Fine," she grumbled and winced. Though sharp, the pain was not as severe as when she had broken her leg three years earlier.

Will fished the battered metal case from its pack and opened it on the deck, careful not to let the extra supplies stuffed inside fall out. His hand found a bottle of peroxide, which he splashed on the wound after Gabi nodded that she was ready. She bit her lip hard and took a deep breath to force the sudden wave of pain from her mind. Will stopped for a couple minutes until the ship was in deeper, calmer waters. He selected a suturing needle, wiped it in alcohol, and threaded it.

Gabi stopped him just as he was about to plunge the needle into her flesh. "Where did you get the guns?" she whispered.

He looked around to ensure no one was listening. "I've been hiding them for years in a cargo pod out in the jungle. I thought Dad was nuts to order them all destroyed, so I kept a few for myself."

"Why? We can hunt just fine with bows."

Will shrugged. "Thought they might come in handy someday. When we get to the other colony, they might be good for trade. Keep us from starving, you know?"

"If we get to the other colony," she corrected. Gabi nodded her readiness for him to begin.

Pain throbbed in her hand with every suture that Will wove, but she took care to breathe deeply as he worked, and made sure she did not make any sudden moves that could make the damage worse. Any mistake might not only delay her recovery, but stiffen her hand once healed. Once the sutures were tied, Gabi applied a salve of thorn root, packed gauze on the wound, and dressed it. The last part took several tries since Gabi was left-handed, and the necessary motions were awkward when working with her right hand. When her work was finished, she flexed her fingers. The bandage made her hand stiff, but she could still curl her hand enough to crook her nock fingers.

*Good. I can still use my bow.*

"Paddles in," Will cried over the wind as he turned his attention to the sails. "We've got good wind."

Glancing around, Gabi saw all of the voyagers pull in and stow their oars. They were far from shore now, with the tall palm trees in the distance looking more like blades of grass, the orange globe of Bravo hanging above the land. A bald hill just to the right of the river's mouth marked where the now abandoned Camp Eight sat in repose. Out to the horizon, the ocean extended without end. Kristin came over to the hold and sat next to her. Diego curled up at Gabi's feet, hugging them and whimpering. Gabi curled her lip at him. Will lashed the rigging and joined them.

"You okay, Kris?" he asked. His sister nodded. With a relieved sigh, he flopped onto his back. "That was close. You saved our bacon, Gabi. If you hadn't seen that, we'd have ripped off the port outrigger."

"Thanks," she muttered as she picked at the dressing on her hand. "Remember that the next time you want to throw me over."

"Right," he said as he sat up. "Let's get the maps out."

"I've got them right here," Caleb said as he knelt next to them.

Caleb handed Will a leather folio bound with thin cords. He freed the strings and pulled a stack of yellowed papers from within, setting them gingerly on the deck. His fingers traced the distinct coastline of Raphael Island, over the dot representing Camp Eight.

"We need to keep an eye on the coast for prominent features. That will help us figure out how far we're going each day. When we make it to the strait, that's when we need to decide how we get to the mainland."

Will tapped his fingers on the map just over a large dot a little inland from the northern coast of a nearby continent. Gabi's eyes fixated on the dot, and the lines flowing next to it that represented a river.

*So that's where we were supposed to land when I was younger, huh?*

. . .

Sweat dripped from Cal's brow as he checked the batch of crude glycerin. Satisfied that the speed of the mixer was correct, he adjusted the shut-off timer for his equipment and walked out from under the cover of the outdoor shed attached to the rear of his shop. He loosened his vapor mask and let it sit slack against his chest, then stripped off his goggles and stowed them in one of the inner pockets of his leather apron.

A stiff breeze kicked up, blowing down the Fairweather River from the hills. The winds cooled the sweat on his skin, giving him pleasant relief from the midday sun. He glanced across the river to its southern banks. A small log jam in the excavated cove beneath the mill just downstream and across the river told Cal that his friends had just received fresh materials for their work, although the silence in the air led him to believe that the mill was idle at that moment. In the distance, Cal could hear the deep chime of the Civic Hall's clock toll once.

*Another beautiful day, Concordia.*

Cal retrieved a blue handkerchief from his apron and swiped it across his forehead, then walked through the shed past the rows of stills, heating plates, and cauldrons. He moved past the staircase to the upstairs apartment and through the storage room that dominated the bulk of the building's lower floor, and into the small storefront. Alexis sat behind the modest counter on a high backed wooden chair. Her swollen, pregnant belly was prominent under her long green linen dress. When she saw Cal enter, she quickly withdrew her arm from a basket that sat on the counter and popped something in her mouth, and gave him a playfully guilty look; her slight smile giving away any hint of innocence.

"Hey now," he chuckled. "Don't eat it all before we get to the park. Kind of spoils the idea of a picnic."

Alexis stuck her lip out in a dramatic pout. "I'm just having a little nibble."

"Alright," he said as he stole a kiss from her. "Just a nibble."

"That's what I thought."

"I'm serious, babe. I don't want you to spoil your appetite before we get there."

"Hey, don't deny the pregnant lady."

"Wouldn't dream of it. I know the consequences," he grinned.

Cal walked around the counter to a pair of tall wooden shelves along the side wall. He tidied up the displays, and fussed for a couple minutes on how he would best face the bottles of soft soap on the shelf.

"C'mon, Cal. Quit being anal and let's go."

"Just straightening up. I've got five more minutes before I have to move the batch along. I can't leave before then."

Alexis rolled her shoulders and sighed heavily. "I don't want to be cooped up all day, hurry up!"

The front door swung open with a soft creak, and Dr. Taylor emerged with her grandchildren Steven and Hannah in tow. The doctor and Hannah were dressed in long dresses and their hair was bound in matching pigtails. Steven wore loose trousers and a short-sleeved shirt that had a pair of broad, muddy swipes down the front, and his left cheek was tinted tan with mud that his grandmother had not quite been able to scrub away.

Cal took one glance at the grimace on Dr. Taylor's face. "Again?"

"Again," she replied.

"Steven, are you being a hassle for your grandma?"

The young boy shuffled his feet. "I wasn't trying to. I saw a frog down by the river and went to go catch it. Only I slipped."

"Face first into the mud," Dr. Taylor added. "It's a wonder you didn't break a tooth or an arm the way you took a dive there, kiddo. It's a wonder that your mom lets me take you out at all." Cal chuckled and retrieved a bottle of laundry soap from his shelf, flipped it in his hand, and offered it to her. "I also think sometimes you set up shop here on the river just so I can fund your retirement."

Alexis laughed from her chair near the corner. "No, just a happy coincidence. We'll do this bottle for just one favor so you know we're not taking advantage of you. I'll put it on your tab. Say, you're all dressed up today, where are you guys going?"

"Thanks for the discount. I *was* going to take the munchkins to Benedict Square, but now it looks like there may be a detour home to clean up a certain mud monster."

Alexis's eyes lit up. "Hey, we're just about to go there too. Cal's making me wait forever for his work though. Do you mind if I tag along?"

"We still need to get Steven cleaned up."

"Oh, don't worry about that. It's not like Darius is going to call the mud police on us," she pled with a wry grin.

"Just be patient, my dear. I'm sure we'll see you there."

"Well. I guess you leave me no choice," Alexis said as she lifted herself slowly from the chair and grabbed the basket. "My dear husband is going to sit here and work all day, and my friends are all going to ditch me. What's a pregnant girl to do on a hot summer day but walk down the street with this heavy basket?"

Dr. Taylor groaned. "Is she always this stubborn and dramatic?"

"Only on days that end with y," Cal replied as he winked at his wife. "C'mon, no one will care if Steven has a little mud on him. Besides, you know he's just going to get dirty again if you change him. Might as well bathe him once instead of twice. I'll be along in just a few, okay?"

"Alright, alright. Goodness, if having to deal with one McLaughlin isn't bad enough, what chance do I have when they gang up against me?" Dr. Taylor smiled and took the basket from Alexis. "Come on, kids. Let's go."

Alexis planted a kiss on Cal's lips on her way out. "My hero. Don't make me wait, okay?"

"I promise."

After the party left, Cal went out the back door to the open-sided shed. The mixer and heating plate had turned off automatically. He detached the mixer attachment and set it aside, then covered the batch and moved it near the wall, double-checked that all of the plates were off, and went back into the storage room. He checked on the progress of a couple of batches of biodiesel and a batch of bar soap, tidied up, and went upstairs to the modest apartment that he and Alexis called home.

He ran a hand across the top of the crib that sat empty and waiting at the foot of their bed. The light color of the Demeter fir that it was crafted out of made it almost glow from the sunlight that shone through the open window shutters.

*I still can't believe it. I'm going to be a father.*

The thought still gave him butterflies, both of excitement and apprehension. The closer it got to the due date, the more intense the knot in his stomach became. Cal was starting to think that any day he might explode from the anticipation. For the past two weeks he had trouble sleeping. He thought his tossing and turning at night might clue Alexis into his worries, but she always slept soundly.

Cal smiled and grabbed a package that he had carefully hidden under the compacted mattress. His fingers ran along the folded, waxy paper and coarse flax string. He set it down on the bed long enough to remove his oil splattered apron and drop it to the ground, then he picked up the parcel and tucked it in his pants behind his back. He quickly made his way down the stairs and out the front door of his shop. He began to whistle a familiar tune as he walked down the packed dirt span of River Way, turning left onto Benedict Boulevard.

The boulevard was the widest street in Concordia, and preparations were well underway to make it the first paved street in town. Benedict was also the western edge of the market square, a section of town built after the first winter. Like his own dwelling, the structures that comprised the market were made from layers of coarse river stone and rough-hewn timbers mucked together with native clay. All were two stories tall, with apartments constructed above shops. Though doors had been planked and installed in the subsequent years, the structures lacked glass windows. Instead, similar to his home, large, open windows were equipped with wooden shutters that swung outward to let light and air in.

There were several passers-by as he made his way toward Benedict Square, and businesses along the row appeared to be readying for the afternoon rush. He smiled as he spotted Frank, the butcher, laying out a selection of meats in the front display of his own store, which was little more than an oversized set of wooden shutters on the ground floor that retracted to reveal the tables and hanging meats beyond. He exchanged quick pleasantries with Mr. and Mrs. Walker as they strolled into the clothing shop operated by Saika Kimura. He even exchanged a courteous nod with Traci Josephson. The years had not made their relationship any less awkward, though at least now it was civil.

The prominent gable of the clock tower at Civic Hall jutted up from the street far ahead in the distance, against the backdrop of the battered and aging hull of *Michael*. Benedict Square stretched out in a "U" shape behind it. A hundred acres of fields, native shade trees, a fledgling apple orchard, and even a few picnic areas drew families and romancing couples alike. Every year, nearly everyone in Concordia would come at some point or another to pay their respects at the Rafael Disaster Memorial.

For Cal, there was a measure of awkward pride whenever he stopped to view the Project Columbus Monument. The miniature statues of *Michael* and *Gabriel* still gave him a chill when he saw them together. The memories of what almost happened six years ago, just a few hundred feet from this very site, were still as fresh as if they had happened a mere week ago. And yet, any time a member of either crew would take him aside and congratulate him for his role during the Unification, he would still blush and fidget. He knew that somehow he had helped, but he was just an awkward kid back then, rushing in without thinking. Cal shook his head and took a moment to read the clock in the distance, then doubled his pace.

*Lexi's going to kill me if I'm any later. Hell of a way to start off an anniversary. Note to self, work can wait.*

Cal was nearing the end of the boulevard when his legs seemed to bow under him. He wobbled for a moment, lost his footing, and his head smacked the packed earth. In an instant he rolled to his back and yelled for help, but a terrible grumbling noise had risen up. The buildings swayed all around him, and he could hear the terrified shouts of the nearest townsfolk. Disoriented, he tried to scramble to his feet and assess the situation, but could barely regain his knees.

The world wouldn't stop jarring and shaking, and his stomach felt like it was in free fall. Cal took a deep breath and forced the pain to the back of his mind. His eyes caught the form of Traci running toward him at full steam. Her lips were moving, but his ears were ringing, and he couldn't hear what she was saying. Then in an instant, he saw fear in her eyes as she pulled up and skidded to a halt fifteen feet from him. He heard and a few loud, rapid cracks. Cal was hurled to the ground from his blind side, and the world went dark.

Stabbing, agonizing pain ripped through the left side of his body and he came to with a loud moan. He felt like he was being pressed into the ground. There was a voice, feminine. He was looking at the smooth, packed dirt of Benedict Boulevard. He tried to push his body upright but flopped back down. Blood stained the pavement where he had momentarily risen from. The voice called out to him again.

"Calvin, are you alright?"

He tasted blood and spat a glob of red saliva onto the ground.

"Calvin, answer me. Are you alright?"

"What… what the hell just happened? Why can't I move?"

He heard the clatter of rocks and wood against the ground, and the nearly crushing weight began to subside.

"Hang on, I'll get you out of there. Oh God… stay with me."

Another voice caught his ears. Sharp. Commanding. "I've got him. Go get your truck, Sergeant."

"Yes sir," Traci snapped back.

*Sergeant,* Cal thought as he closed his eyes and swallowed, trying to force back the pain. *Captain Devereaux?*

The weight gradually released as the din continued. It seemed to become quicker, more frantic. He felt hands on his shoulders, and someone rolled him into his back. The burning orange ball of Bravo hung high in the blue sky, and then was quickly eclipsed by the dark form of a man kneeling over him. Feeling him. Checking him.

"Where are you hurt? Can you move, Cal?" There was a pause. "Cal, are you with me?"

Cal put his right elbow under him and lifted his head off the ground a few inches. The movement sent a fresh wave of pain through his abdomen and he winced, but it did not stop him from peering at his rescuer.

"Frank? What the hell was that?" he croaked.

His brow was wrinkled in concern and Cal could tell that even the veteran ex-Marine was doing all he could to remain calm. "Earthquake. We just got hit by an earthquake."

Cal turned his head to each side and saw rubble strewn throughout the street. To his left side, the entire wall of a shop had sloughed away; its trail of debris led into the street to where he lay.

*Oh God... Lexi!*

He rolled to his knees and forced his body to rise. Cal stood for a moment. He saw Frank Devereaux utter one word that he didn't hear, and his knees came out from under him. Frank lunged forward and caught Cal in his arms, easing him down to the pavement.

More words flowed from Frank's mouth, though as the man turned around to bark at anyone nearby, Cal's focus began to fade and his vision blurred. At the same time, something from within him screamed at him to get up and find his wife. He tried again to right himself, but Devereaux planted his meaty hand firmly on Cal's chest and kept him still.

"Let me up," Cal mumbled. "I have to find Lexi."

Though the ringing in his ears was more intense than ever, Cal was able to read Frank's lips as his intense stare locked on him. "We'll find her, don't worry. Just lay still."

"No," he protested weakly.

Frank did not relent, holding Cal steady and doing what he could to control the bleeding from a wound on the back of his head. A minute later he could smell the pungent scent of exhaust as Traci backed her city-issued truck to within a few feet of him. Frank hoisted him as if he weighed nothing, then carefully loaded him in the bed of the conveyance. The militia captain then jumped in the rear of the truck and slapped his hand on the roof, prompting Traci to move out down the street.

Cal winced and closed his eyes as the wheels bumped over the debris that littered the streets. He sucked in a great breath of air and held it, hoping that the pain would ebb. The truck lurched to a halt at the end of the street, far sooner than he had expected, and most certainly not anywhere near Concordia's modest hospital.

They did not move right away as Cal had expected. As the time passed, his head started to spin, and what little will he had left to get up and search for Alexis soon faded as he realized that he was in no condition to do so. Instead, the urge to rest replaced it, surging stronger with every dizzying revolution of his mental malaise. Cal could hold out no more, and he slipped into the black.

. . .

"Tom!" he sputtered as loudly as his dust-choked lungs would allow. A chilling silence answered his call. His heart pounded furiously, and he coughed as he sucked in another breath of contaminated air. "Tom, where the hell are you?"

This time he heard a faint groan from just beyond his stout desk. Darius rolled his body around to see where he had just been sitting moments earlier. A snapped timber had fallen directly into the seat of his chair, flattening it and splaying its legs and back like a shattered flower. Light poured in from beyond, where the wall of his office had stood just prior to the sickening sway of the building.

Darius craned his neck out timidly from under his hiding place. A six-foot swath of the roof had fallen away as the roof timber had snapped; the other two beams that he could see were still intact, though the whole building seemed to creak with every breath he took. The floor seemed solid enough, and it still ran intact all the way to where the wall had peeled away. Though he feared that the action of standing might cause the structure to collapse, Darius knew that it would not be prudent for him and his deputy to stay inside the structure.

"Tom!" he called out as he rose and swiftly rounded the end of his desk.

Dayton lay sprawled in front of the great bureau. He was bleeding from a laceration at his hair line, and his legs were pinned under the bookshelf that had toppled during the temblor. Darius rushed to his side and checked for a pulse, even as shouts began to rise from outside the damaged building.

*Good, he's still alive.*

Darius heaved at the shelf, grunting and straining under the weight of the solid furniture. He was able to hoist it and pivot just enough to lean it on the top corner of his desk. Darius rolled up Tom's pants legs to check for obvious trauma, of which there was none. He then wrapped his cohort's arm around his neck and rose up, bearing both of their weights as he dragged the limp, semi-conscious man through the open office door and down the hall toward the stairs. His relief at seeing the stairs intact was tempered with rising apprehension at the loud creaks emitted from the wood with every tread they descended.

By the time they reached the bottom of the flight to the ground floor, Darius's legs were burning, and his chest heaved with every gasp of air he drew in. With the imminent danger of falling down the stairs gone, he gently took a knee and set his deputy on the floor, rolling him onto his back.

"C'mon, wake up," he said, gently shaking Tom's shoulders. "Wake up!"

The flow of blood had not slowed much, and it covered much of the left side of Tom's face. Still the man did not open his eyes or give any sign that he was about to come around. Darius took in his surroundings. The lower level of Civic Hall was mostly dominated by a meeting hall that ran the width of the building, and the staircase leading to the offices above was tucked behind this room. The few decorations that had adorned the meeting hall were strewn about, and the flagstaff that stood in the corner of the dais near the stairwell had toppled over and rolled off of the platform.

Darius again collected Tom, proceeding toward the front door of the building. As he passed the fallen colors, Darius cast an anxious gaze at them. The blue and silver banner of Concordia was folded in half over the flag staff, which made the angel look as if she were pleading for mercy. The eerie symbolism gave Darius a moment of pause, and suddenly he felt very small.

*Lord have mercy on us all. Protect us from this disaster.* He paused in the middle of his thought. *Give me the strength to see us all through this trial.*

They reached the door, which stuck slightly before giving way. As he threw a hand up to shield his eyes from the midday sun, the sounds of chaos reached his ears. Shouts of confusion and screams of terror echoed from everywhere. Debris from the crumbling wood-and-stone facades of buildings littered Foundation Street as far as he could see in either direction. Moments later, Traci Josephson's white pickup–the only one on the north side of the river–barreled out of Benedict Square Park and turned sharply onto Foundation, in the direction of the town's hospital.

"C'mon, Tom," Darius muttered as he helped his companion down the street after them.

Less than a block later, at Benedict Boulevard, Darius received welcome assistance from Frank Devereaux, who had emerged from the Square only moments after Traci had left. Devereaux swiftly moved in and linked his arms with Tom on the other side, taking half of the load off of Darius.

"What happened, Governor?" asked Devereaux. Though Darius didn't care whether the citizens of the colony addressed him by his title, he knew Frank always would. In addition to being the finest butcher in the city, he was the commander of the Colonial Volunteer Militia, and one of only a handful of Marines that had hitched a ride with the sleeper ships after the attack on Earth.

"Not completely sure, Captain. The quake hit and I took cover. Tom wasn't able to get clear fast enough. Bookcase fell on him, and I think he hit his head, too. We need to get him to the hospital."

"Let me give you a hand. Sergeant Josephson has Doc Taylor with her, and they're headed to the hospital with a couple injured."

"Good," Darius nodded as he shifted his load slightly to account for the balance that Devereaux provided.

They moved as quickly down the street as they safely could with the injured deputy between them. By that time the streets had become choked with the citizens of Concordia. Some were wailing or panicking while others called out for their friends and neighbors. Several began to venture into the wreckage of buildings in search of those who might be trapped.

"Get to *Michael* and make sure the reactor's safe," Darius boomed at Vince Hartley as soon as he saw him lingering in the crowd. He then singled out his liaison, Roger Miller, who was directing a search. "Get across the river and make sure Quinn checks out *Gabriel*."

A young teenage girl with tears streaming down her cheeks ran up to Darius, shrieking almost at the top of her lungs. "I can't find my mom and dad. Please, you have to help me."

"Governor, we've got people trapped in the grain mill," Don Abernathy stated as he approached just a moment later. "The building's collapsed on them."

*Damn it.*

Darius scanned the crowd and picked four gawkers, ordering them to follow Don to the mills. He dispatched another two to help the frantic girl with the search for her parents.

Frank turned to Darius. "I'll take Tom to the hospital. You're needed here," he boomed in a firm voice.

Darius nodded once in acknowledgement. "I'm activating the CVM, Captain. Put your command center somewhere near the hospital. I want a second post near the south side clinic. Coordinate searches for missing persons, and assist the doctors in any way they need."

"Yes, Governor."

Captain Devereaux continued down the road with the injured deputy governor. Darius rubbed his shaved head as he surveyed the destruction around him. Besides the damage to Civic Hall, at least four shops along Benedict and three on Foundation had lost at least one wall. From what he could see of the burgeoning crowd, it looked like most of the townsfolk had escaped serious injury.

"I need a runner," he bellowed. Jamie Taylor, son of Dr. Taylor, stepped forth. "Go to one of the farms. Any of them. I need horses. At least three."

"Of course." He nodded and headed in a full sprint through Benedict Square.

Urgent shouts rose from where Kimura's Clothiers stood. Two men were waving frantically and pointing at a pile of rubble. Darius's legs moved without thought, carrying him at full speed over the broken debris. His nerves began to unravel as he dreaded what he might find under the mess. Still he plunged forth, attacking the pile with his bare hands. He cast rocks aside and heaved at heavy timbers. He could hear cries from those trapped within. Though wrenching to hear, it was at least reassurance that whoever was buried was still alive.

Moments later he and the other citizens had freed the Walkers from their tomb of wreckage. Matt favored his left arm and howled in pain. Leah sobbed and wobbled into the street, where she collapsed in Saika's arms. Darius took the time to let out a relieved sigh; the Walkers were injured, but at least they were alive.

He then turned his attention to the crowd in the street. "All members of the Colonial Volunteer Militia are to report to Captain Devereaux at the hospital as soon as you are available. The rest of you citizens, please try to stay out of the buildings. If you find anyone trapped, get help. Don't try to get them out alone, especially if they are inside a building. If you are asked for assistance by the CVM, please do so immediately and to the best of your ability."

Darius doubled back toward the Square, and was met by Jamie, who was astride a horse, leading two others in full saddle at his side. Darius climbed on top of the familiar paint gelding, then took the reins from Jamie.

"Take these other two horses to Captain Devereaux and have him put them to use. Tell Sergeant Josephson to get down to the mill with her truck. We're going to have casualties there, and we need her help transporting the victims."

"Yes, Governor."

Darius spurred his mount onward to the grain mill, steeling his nerves for what lay ahead.

. . .

Darkness enveloped Cal. It was the sort of darkness that could not be penetrated, and even his arms seemed constricted by the inky void. His fingers wiggled, though the numbness of his dark embrace made them feel somehow disembodied, at least for the fleeting moments that he thought he could feel them.

It took Cal a moment to figure out that he was asleep, though the revelation didn't make it any easier for him to awaken. Every part of his body was too heavy to move. Even his eyelids could not be coaxed into opening. He began to wonder if he was in fact dead, and not asleep. He then considered why this concept didn't terrify him, even though, by every right, it should.

*Lexi's going to be so pissed if I'm dead.*

He waited alone with his thoughts for quite some time before another realization hit him.

*I'm thinking. But there's no light. No flames. Nothing at all.*

Cal's churning thoughts shifted once more as he considered the possibility of something else being the cause of his imprisonment. He wondered if there was something wrong in his head. He pondered what it might take to revive his senses, or if this was something he would just have to wait out.

*I've heard that people in comas can hear the voices of their friends and family when they talk.* If he had been able, he would have shrugged at that moment. *I guess it's worth a shot.*

There was still no control over his body, so all that Cal could do was relax his mind. Pushing away his worrisome thoughts, he calmed himself with thoughts of Alexis's brilliant white smile and bouncing auburn locks. Through the dark he was able to conjure a ghostly glimmer of his wife, cradling her swollen belly and laughing. He held on to the image as long as he could, but it faded after mere moments, replaced by a soft, almost imperceptible glow before him.

Cal tried again to bring her into his mind, but the image eluded him. Instead, the dull, diffuse light before him grew brighter, and he could discern a slight flicker in its intensity. The sensation of light was not the only thing that came to him at that time. Barely more than a throb, his left side and head did indeed ache, giving him the first real sensation he could confirm.

*The dead don't feel pain, do they?  No, that wouldn't make sense.*

His eyelids twitched as a sudden, sharp sound came to his ears.  It was far louder than he expected, but by no means painful or terrifying.  It did evoke another emotion in him: concern.  He wasn't sure why, as the noise was shrill and broken.

*Crying?*

As his eyes fully opened, he looked to his left, searching for the source of the noise.  Cal's head was swimming, making his field of vision feel oddly tilted.  He was in a dimly lit, unfamiliar room, lying on a bed.  Along the far wall were a narrow wooden table and a single chair.  A storm lantern sat atop the table, its flame flickering and swaying as it drew air into its minute combustion chamber.  A dark figure moved in front of him, reaching down into a bassinet at the side of his bed.  The man picked up the child from its resting place, soothing it as it screamed nearly at the top of its tiny lungs.

*My God…*

The man then walked to the chair and sat down.  Pale light washed across Hunter's face as he adjusted the crook of his arm to better support the baby.  Cal's child.

"Hunter," he croaked through parched and cracked lips.

Hunter looked up at Cal.  Exhaustion was scrawled all over his face.  His eyes drooped, making him look a decade older, and the shadows gave him an almost haunted look.  His forehead was smeared with dirt and dust.  Hunter smiled, though weak and fleeting.

"You're awake," he noted.

"Where am I?"

"The hospital.  You were in pretty bad shape when Traci brought you in.  She said a building fell on you.  Doc says that you lost a lot of blood, and that you're lucky to be alive."

He looked under the sheets.  The lantern cast just enough illumination that he could see the bandages wrapped around his torso, stained slightly where they caressed his left side.  Another bandage was wrapped around his right hand, extending halfway up his forearm.

*Maybe she won't be so pissed.*

Cal returned his attention to the child in Hunter's arms.  "Is that… that's our baby, isn't it?  Mine and Lexi's, I mean."

Hunter nodded, rocking ever so gently.

Cal exhaled with relief, his mouth widening into a smile. Tears immediately came to his eyes, and he brought a fist to his mouth, fighting back his urge to both whoop and cry at the same time. "What is it?"

"A girl."

"A girl," he parroted. He paused for a moment, both stunned and elated. The vertigo he felt suddenly shifted, swinging in the opposite direction. Cal closed his eyes for a moment and took a deep breath, steadying himself. "Can I see her?"

"Of course."

Hunter crossed the room, gently cradling the baby girl as he knelt next to the bed. Her skin was wrinkled and folded, and her cheeks were bright red. Her eyes closed as she cried out. Only a couple wispy strands of hair adorned her crown. Cal reached his hand out and stroked her cheek. It was unexpectedly soft; he had heard that babies were, but he had not expected that degree of softness.

"Can I hold her?"

Hunter sighed and drew back slightly as he shook his head. "Doc said that if you wake up you're not supposed to touch her until she says it's ok. With how doped up you look right now, I agree with her. I'll hold her for you, though. Give me a sec to get the chair, okay?"

The world again shifted, reversing course. Cal had the sensation that he was being driven into his bed, though he knew that he had not moved at all. He ignored this, desperately wanting to hold his daughter. "I'm fine," he bluffed.

"Orders are orders, Cal."

Hunter placed the girl back in the bassinet, prompting a fresh round of squalling. He retrieved the chair and placed it next to Cal before collecting the girl once more and sitting next to her father. Cal reached out to stroke her, and immediately her tiny hand clenched his pinky. Chills ran down his spine, and another grin washed across his face.

"Wow. Look at that!"

Hunter mirrored the smile on his friend's face.

"Did she do this for Lexi?" Cal asked.

The smile evaporated in an instant.

"What?" The pit of his stomach began to tremble, and he felt as if his head did a barrel roll. "What's wrong?"

Hunter slid the chair back along the noise, its legs scraping and stuttering along the floor. The newborn clutched her father's finger for dear life before the reach became too far.

"Hunter?"

Hunter's broad shoulders slumped as he heaved a great sigh. "Lexi didn't make it." The words tumbled out of his mouth as if he was biting off his tongue at the same time. "She passed away right after your daughter was born."

Cal's stomach churned at once, and his fingers went numb. His jaw slacked, and the edges of his vision blurred. A moment later, he began to hyperventilate. Loss and despair coursed through every pathway in his mind and soul.

"No…" he croaked feebly.

Hunter's silence and weary eyes dispelled any hope Cal held that this was just a cruel hoax. That Alexis would jump out from the dark shadows and scare him. Instead all that returned from the gloom was his own sobs, echoing back to him.

"No!"

"Cal, I'm so sorry."

Cal screamed an obscenity at the top of his lungs, arching his back and throwing himself onto the bed, fists clenched and arms taut. Pain shot like lightning down his side as whatever drug Doctor Taylor had given him could not dull the tremendous surge from his nerves. He cried out again, this time as much in agony as anguish. His daughter joined in the wailing, screeching as loud as her tiny lungs could manage.

"Take it easy," Hunter said in a hushed tone as he bolted out of the chair and placed his free hand on Cal's shoulder. The door burst open, and Kayla Reid hustled in, her protective apron smeared with blood.

"God damn it, Hunter, *why*?" Cal seethed.

"Because you'll tear yourself up and I don't know if Doc can put you back together again."

"Calm down, Cal," Kayla soothed as she deftly checked his bandages.

"No," Cal choked on his tears. "Why her? Why not me?"

As soon as Kayla finished her checks, Hunter passed the wailing baby off to her, sending them both out of the room and away from Cal's toxic emotional outburst.

Hunter sat on the edge of the bed. He pressed his hand against Cal's shoulder firmly enough to pin him, but not so much that it hurt. Alexis had been his friend as well, and the pain of her loss was clearly evident in his blue eyes. "There wasn't anything we could have done. She went into labor right after the earthquake. Traci picked her up on the way to the hospital. I guess you were passed out in the back. Lexi was freaked because she couldn't wake you up."

"No…" he whispered again.

"Doc and Kayla had their hands full when they got here. Doctor Granger was injured so he couldn't help at first, and I guess Carla was on the other side of the river when we got hit, so she was over there helping out at South Clinic." Hunter sighed and bit his lip. "Doc was patching you back together when Lexi started bleeding out fast. Corporal Swift saw her pass out and carried her into the OR."

"God no," he rasped hoarsely. "Please."

Hunter's fingers dug into Cal's shoulder, the knuckles turning white as snow as they clamped hard enough to make the pain shift from his side to his clavicle. "Doc did everything she could."

"She should have let me die instead."

"What?" Hunter gasped and pulled back for a second. His momentary confusion melted away, and he shook his head vigorously. "No, it wasn't like that. Doc knew you were stable enough for her to work on Lexi. But she went real fast. I mean, it was just a couple seconds after Swift brought her in. Doc couldn't save her. She was barely able to save your daughter."

Cal's gut wrenched tight, and his voice failed him at last. Torrents of tears rolled down his face, dropping onto the mattress beneath, which absorbed and held them fast. He wanted to scream again, but didn't have the energy. He wanted to curl up and sleep, but he was too furious. He wanted to do something, anything at all, but his shattered heart would not let him move.

"I'd like to say that I know how you feel," Hunter said softly. "But I don't. As much pain as I feel over her loss, I just can't fathom what you're going through right now. I'm here for you though. Whatever you need from me, it's yours. Just give the word."

Cal rolled over onto his shoulder, turning his back to his friend. The offer seemed somehow hollow to him, though he wished he could feel anything in that moment.

• • •

J.C. Rainier

Darius awoke with a start and a snort. His skin was pimpled from the chill of an early morning wind that lifted and curled the edges of his blanket. He straightened up in the creaky chair and yawned, examining the thin linen sheet. It was the kind used in the medical clinics, but Darius didn't recall at first when he had procured the blanket. He was thankful for the small amount of protection it provided as he found himself sitting in the park, just a few feet from Foundation Street. The sun was on the eastern horizon, rising out of the ground like a brilliant, multi-hued marble.

In his groggy state, the mystery of the chair took a moment to decipher. He vaguely recalled entering the unstable Civic Hall in the dark of early morning to retrieve it from the lower floor. He remembered being so tired that his feet dragged, and he wanted so desperately to be comfortable when he finally sat down for some rest. He couldn't figure out why he had decided to risk going into the building, though much of the hours leading up to his eventual collapse from exhaustion was a blur.

The last time Darius had looked at his watch, it was two in the morning. He had been digging through rubble for over ten hours straight, searching for survivors. What had started as a frantic dig through timbers and stones at the collapsed grain mill ended up as a methodical street by street search expanding outward from the river, finally ending well into the night as the last piles of rubble were turned upside down. Amazingly, only eighteen townspeople had been found in the rubble, including the four mill workers. Unfortunately, most of those who were trapped suffered significant injuries, and Darius knew that the tiny hospital was stressed beyond its capacity.

Worse was the staggering news that Darius was given as he arrived at the hospital with two of the wounded: there were three reported fatalities.

*Dan Forrest. Luka Kedrov. Alexis McLaughlin.*

The list weighed heavily on Darius. Each person who had passed was someone important to the colony, and one was a close friend. The loss of Luka's reliability would certainly be missed once the mill was rebuilt, and Forrest had proven himself to be a talented tailor, learning the trade under the guidance of Sarah Kimura.

But the immediate shock of Alexis was something that would be a bitter pill for the entire community, and Darius felt it keenly. As he stared through the gaping hole in the upper story of Civic Hall, he recalled that the McLaughlins had invited him for dinner tomorrow evening. He imagined what tantalizing dish Alexis would have served, and what stories Cal would have told at the meal. He let the image slip away on the wind, knowing with a heart as heavy as lead that such dinners would never happen again.

Darius stretched once more before climbing to his feet. He draped the blanket over the chair and walked the short distance to the intersection of the two major streets of North Concordia. As he surveyed the scene in the early morning light, the damage to the town somehow didn't seem as bad as the previous day. Perhaps it was the immediate panic in the wake of the temblor, or the search for survivors that ensued, but his perspective seemed to have changed with the all too brief night's sleep.

A half a dozen or so buildings had lost a wall, and three others in the market square were leaning precariously. The grain mill had shown the most spectacular damage when it had caved in on itself, and the destruction of Darius's office was probably visible anywhere on the north side of the Fairweather.

He grimaced. *Well, we can rebuild,* he thought as he turned toward the hospital.

The familiar walk along Foundation gave him time to scrutinize two structures more closely. Darius determined that both would need to be torn down and replaced. Four dwellings were destroyed in those buildings, with none to spare in town. He sighed heavily, realizing that a new problem had cropped up; where would the displaced sleep? He made a note to have the sleeper ships checked for structural damage, as their berths might once again become home to some of the people.

Darius arrived at the medical clinic several minutes later. Corporal Swift was slumped against the outside door frame, fast asleep. Darius imagined that he had been assigned to stand guard, but the fatigue must have taken its toll on the young volunteer. Swift was only twenty-two, hybrid age, which meant that he wasn't old enough before leaving Earth to have joined any of the armed services. Darius stepped around him and opened the door as quietly as he could so as to let the young man rest.

Darius's eyes took a brief moment to adjust to the lack of light inside. The entire north side of the city was powerless, and someone had extinguished the candles that rested on top of the various furniture scattered throughout the waiting room. He checked one; the wax had hardened and cooled completely. Every seating surface in the room was occupied by a relative or loved one of one of the injured. Even the floor was seeing more use than ever before, and Darius had to carefully navigate around a sleeping man and his young son on his way deeper into the hospital.

He made it just beyond the door that separated the waiting room from the medical facility itself. Six patient rooms, a common recovery area, two examination rooms, and a small operating room made up the entirety of the small community's hospital. The common room, which Darius had just stepped into, was choked with portable cots. A patient occupied every one, save for a single cot butted against the wall to the OR. On this one slept Kayla Reid, one of the nurses. A lone chair sat next to her cot, and Captain Devereaux rose from this seat to greet Darius.

Though haggard and weary looking, the captain had kept his post dutifully. He snapped a smart salute at Darius before placing a firm hand on his shoulder and leaning in to whisper his report.

"Doctor Taylor is asleep. We didn't lose anyone else overnight. Roger stopped by to report a few minutes ago."

"Good. What did he find out?" Darius whispered. He wanted to hear about the situation on the south side of the city, but at the same time, he was gripped with a feeling of anxiety.

"One dead, nine injured. No collapsed buildings, just a lot of fallen debris. The River Islands bridge is still up, but Roger said that it needs a closer look before we clear it."

"And the reactors?"

"Quinn and Hartley report no leaks. The reactors on both ships are online and within parameters. They have power on the south side, but the grid interface is jacked up on *Michael*. We won't have power here until that's repaired."

Darius nodded. Hearing the source of the power failure gave him an odd sense of relief. He had helped build that power grid, and knew that he could repair it. He wanted very much to take his mind off of the tragedy and focus his attention on that instead, but the cleanup and search would require coordination. He rubbed at the short stubble on his scalp.

"Your orders, sir?" Devereaux whispered.

Darius looked at the ceiling and sighed as he thought for a moment. "I want the CVM to oversee distribution of emergency supplies to the town. Form a team of civilians to work on clearing the streets. We still have the horses, right?"

"Yes sir."

"Good. Use them to help. Find Baker and have him get together some men to look at the damaged buildings. Anything that can be rebuilt, I want it done as soon as possible. Then set them to work on demolition and replacement of the other buildings. Mill first, got it?"

"Yes sir. What about the power?"

"Get me Novak and Barajas. We'll get it up and running by tomorrow at the latest. Also get Roger to do another inspection on *Michael*. I want to know if it's safe to sleep people in there for a little bit. If so, move anyone displaced into the mid pods for a bit. I also have a job for Josephson, if you can spare her."

"I can. What do you need?"

"Send her to Rust Creek. See how badly they were hit, or if they need any help."

"Yes sir. Though if I might give you an order myself, go get more shut eye. You look like you're about to fall over."

Darius shook his head. "Got too much to do. I'll get some rack time when I restore power or night falls, whichever is first. I promise."

Devereaux nodded, his stone expression never flinching once. He left the hospital to execute his orders, leaving Darius surrounded by almost a dozen wounded. He sighed and crept to the door of the third patient room, exercising every bit of control he had over his hand to twist the door knob in near utter silence. Darius swung the door open just a couple inches and peered inside.

Cal was fast asleep on the bed, curled up into a tight ball. Against the far wall, Hunter leaned back in his chair, his snoring barely perceptible. His arm was curled around a tiny swaddled bundle that squirmed every ten seconds or so. A single, soft coo from the wiggling and bundled baby gave rise to more mixed feelings.

*I'm damn glad she's here. I just wish she could have met her mother.* Darius sighed as he closed the door quietly. *At least she has her dad. And the rest of us, too.*

. . .

Dr. Taylor passed Cal a tiny glass jar with a thin, screw-on lid. With one hand he opened it up to inspect the thick, white contents, cradling Andrea gingerly in his other arm. The pungent salve inside, a mixture made from native white milkweed stems and prairie mint roots, made his eyes water and his nose wrinkle.

"That's nasty," he complained as he tightened the threads on the cap.

She returned an indifferent shrug. "I don't make the rules for how pleasant a medicine is. I just find the resolution to the problem. This cream will help keep your wounds from getting infected." She rattled a tiny plastic pill bottle before handing it to him. His thumb rubbed over the label, still curled and moist from the glue that affixed it over a half dozen older labels. "This is for the pain. One pill, twice a day. You've got four pills in there. You can have plain old ibuprofen if you need it once those are gone. I only have a little left, so if you're okay without it, I don't want to waste it."

"Thanks," he mumbled as he stuffed the medication into his pants pocket. Dr. Taylor leaned forward and gave him a gentle hug. He knew the embrace was meant as a show of sympathy, but it just felt awkward to him.

"I'm sorry, Calvin. If there's anything I can do for you, just let me know."

"Thanks, Doc." The words tumbled out from numb limps, a hollow echo that he had reflexively uttered dozens of times over the past two days.

The front door to Concordia's hospital squeaked as Dr. Taylor swung it open. The bright evening sun poured in, and Cal instinctively threw a hand up to shield his eyes while they adjusted. The white and yellow wash changed and sharpened in detailed focus to reveal the packed dirt of Foundation Street, and the timber-and-stone apartment buildings on the opposite side. He cast a quick glance back at the empty waiting room, which was pristine, all of its furniture placed back in precise formation. A ghostly calm had settled over the hospital. There were still two others who were injured in the earthquake resting in rooms in back; all others had been discharged before Cal. But the front of the house was different. At some point, it would be full again, and the town's doctors would be cast into another struggle against death.

Like the one that suddenly took his wife.

He shuddered and walked through the door. Andrea squirmed and squealed softly. It was the first time he had taken his daughter outside, and she was clearly disturbed by the sunlight that had interrupted her fleeting rest. There was little Cal could do to shield her for the first portion of the journey; he would carry her for several blocks directly into the sun. Though Bravo kissed the very tops of the mountain ridges beyond, it would not be dark for over an hour still.

He trudged along, taking in the destruction wrought by the temblor. He had heard about the damage, but not seen it for himself. He passed by the gutted remnants of the apartment building that housed Traci Josephson and the Kuenz family. Their personal belongings were conspicuously absent, as was most of the debris that Cal expected to find. Someone had to have cleared the building, he figured. Pieces of earlier drug-hazed conversations with Hunter began to click, and he remembered something about Darius focusing the entire workforce of Concordia on cleanup and reconstruction.

Andrea's whimpering gradually escalated until they rounded the corner onto Benedict, where the shadow cast by the tenements above the marketplace finally shielded her from the offensive sunlight. She squirmed and snuggled, unable to find a comfortable spot, until Cal hoisted her warm body against his shoulder. She settled down quickly. Cal swallowed a lump in his throat; the reality that this tiny baby was his child was still a fresh revelation. The shock, joy, and love that he felt were tempered by the deep gulf of loss that he felt with keen awareness when he looked into her eyes.

Hunter, Dr. Taylor, and Kayla had all agreed that Andrea had Cal's baby blue eyes, but he always saw just a hint of green in them whenever he looked. A green that he had spent many nights gazing into. A green that had consoled him, admired him, and even at times seared his soul with their anger. And it was for that tiny imperfection, which Andrea could not help, that Cal hated her in that moment as much as he loved her. Because of who she reminded him of.

Every step he took toward home seemed to flow into a blur. He barely noticed the gaping hole where Kimura Clothiers once stood, and shuffled past the pile of rubble where the grain mill once graced River Way. A dozen men and three horses were hard at work clearing away the wrecked remnants of the building, but Cal continued on without acknowledging them. This was a departure from his routine; normally he would at least nod as he passed by other townsfolk if he didn't stop to talk to them.

J.C. Rainier

Cal knew that his home and shop still stood, though passing by the mill sent an image through his mind of his abode as a pile of stones and kindling. This was dispelled quickly when the two story building came into view from around the side of the warehouse that stood on the lot adjacent to his shop. There was a mild sense of relief when he saw no obvious damage to the exterior. The front door was wide open, however, and he paused for a moment to listen. From within he could faintly hear the unmistakable tinkle of broken glass.

He stepped inside, only to find that the outside of his shop was in far better condition than the inside. Hunter was busy sweeping the small shop floor; jagged shards of glass littered nearly the entire surface of the floor, mixed in murky, bubbly goo. One of the two display shelves lay in two pieces in front of the sales counter, one of the uprights fractured on impact as it toppled onto the stout counter. Hunter stopped his laborious task as he caught sight of Cal. He wiped glistening sweat from his brow, leaving a smear of soap in his arm's wake.

"Welcome home, Cal," he said, still short of breath. "I didn't think Doc was going to let you go until later."

Cal grimaced as he took in the damage. It looked like both shelves had tipped and spilled their contents onto the floor. Two small jars of hand soap sat on the counter, apparently salvaged by his friend's clean-up efforts. Otherwise, every ounce of product in the displays had been destroyed, now smeared all over the floor and mixed with dangerous shards of glass. His stomach began to jitter; his business now looked as if it was in jeopardy.

"Don't worry about it, man," Hunter continued. "I'll get this cleaned up. You just take it easy and get settled in."

*No.*

Cal carefully maneuvered over the slippery boards and toward the back room. He opened the door, dreading the mess he knew would be just inside the stock room. To his surprise, the floor was immaculately clean, and his remaining stock was still neatly crated and shelved. Only a couple crates were missing, both from the top shelf. The unmistakable tang of alcohol—albeit cut with floral scents—assaulted his nostrils, so he took a step back.

Hunter sidled up next to him, leaning gently on the handle of his broom. "It wasn't that bad back there. A couple crates of soap, and maybe two bottles of vodka. I pushed everything that was loose back onto the shelves. You'll probably want to go through and sort it all out again anyway when you're ready."

A relieved exhale rushed past Cal's lips. *At least it's not all gone.*

"Thanks."

"No problem. Oh, that reminds me." Hunter snapped his fingers and reached into his front pocket. He produced a small, crudely wrapped package, wrapped in coarse twine. In an instant, Cal recognized it, and his heart sank. "Doc said this fell out of your clothes when she put you on the table to patch you up. I kept forgetting to give it back to you when you were at the hospital."

Hunter's long arm stretched out, offering the gift that had been intended for Alexis. Cal stood for a moment, numbed. Within the folds of the paper was a mere trinket: a simple wooden cross on a leather cord, with six bone beads. One for each year that they had been married. When he had asked Saika to make it, Cal had envisioned years passing, anniversaries that would be marked by slipping another bead onto the cord, until he and Alexis had turned old and gray. Hunter seemed to recognize the importance of the package, and how much it meant to Cal, even if he didn't know what exactly it contained.

"It was for Lexi, wasn't it?"

"Yup. Didn't get a chance to give it to her myself." Cal sniffed. He was getting better at suppressing the emotion in his voice, and got the impression that he would become a master of this masquerade in just a few days.

His friend drew back the gift, clutching it gently under his chin with both hands. "Want me to hold onto it for a bit?"

Cal shrugged. "Maybe you should just toss it." He didn't actually want this, but couldn't bring himself to take possession of it either.

The package crinkled as Hunter returned it to his pocket. "Maybe I'll just hang on to it for you for a bit. I'd hate for you to change your mind later and for it to be gone."

"Whatever."

Hunter twisted the end of the broom in his hand. The bristles danced in a nearly perfect circle on the floor as it made two complete rotations before Hunter snatched it up. "Alright, well I'm going to finish cleaning the front room. I'll be up in a minute to help clean your apartment."

"That's alright. You can go now. I'm sure you've got better things to do."

"Not really."

Cal scoffed. "The mill's still a wreck. Shouldn't you be out shoveling up debris or something?"

"That's not my concern right now."

"I bet Darius just loves that." Cal was starting to get impatient, and he didn't bother masking his sarcasm this time. He had enough to absorb, bringing Andrea home for the first time. Hunter's lingering presence was bordering on unwelcome.

"He knows what I'm doing, and he's fine with it. Actually, he wanted to come help too, but I told him that he needed to tend to the bigger matters first."

"Fine. I get it. Could you just… just finish up and leave me alone?"

Hunter frowned and nodded. "Well, Traci should be by in a bit with a can of baby formula. Let me know if you need anything else," he said as he walked back to the sales floor.

Cal grumbled under his breath as he climbed the flight of stairs to the apartment. The rise of the treads seemed much steeper than before. Andrea wiggled at an inopportune time, and Cal nearly dropped her. He cursed and finished the ascent.

The simple apartment was a mess. Clothing baskets had rattled on their shelves, a few toppling outward and spilling their contents on the floor. The ceramic wash basin had fallen from its perch and shattered into four large chunks and a dozen or so small, razor-like splinters. The latch that secured the slatted wooden shutters closed had broken loose, and the left shutter creaked softly, bouncing off the wall and swinging back toward center, before the wind would catch it and repeat the process. Only the crib and bed seemed undisturbed, except for a modest coating of dust.

Cal ignored the jumbled chaos and maneuvered to his side of the bed. He snapped the top blanket back and forth a couple times, catapulting the dirt into the air and onto the floor. He then lay down, still cradling Andrea in his arm. She adjusted out of instinct, but was soundly asleep. Cal unscrewed the medicine bottle with his free hand and popped a pill into his mouth. It felt as if it caught in his throat as he swallowed, and at once he wished he had washed it down with a swig of water.

He sighed heavily and stared at the ceiling. Minutes passed with nothing more than the rhythm of the loose shutter and the erratic breathing of his daughter to remind him of existence outside of his thoughts.

*So what the hell do I do now?*

*What you're supposed to do,* his familiar voice echoed from within. *What you've been doing for the past six years. Only now you get to figure out how to do it without frying or suffocating that little girl there.*

It had been years since Cal had heard from his inner tormentor on a regular basis. One of the colony's botanists had discovered that the bark of an otherwise ordinary, albeit brightly colored, flowering shrub contained compounds that could be extracted and refined into a low grade anti-psychotic. Cal had been taking it regularly since its discovery, though it had slipped his mind to ask for some when he was recovering at the hospital. Now the voice, who he called "Jerk", only spoke to him when he drank, or during the winter when the medicine was not available.

*How am I supposed to do that without Lexi?*

*I assume that whack to the head didn't make you forget how to brew hooch or diesel. I don't remember Lexi helping you with that part. So what's the problem?*

*What's the problem? She took care of everything else! Selling it all. Bookkeeping. Cleaning the shop. She was supposed to watch Andrea!*

*Well I guess you have a couple options here,* Jerk snarked. *Find a way to do it all yourself, or hire someone to watch the shop.*

*I can't afford to hire anyone, and you know it.*

*Well, there's the third alternative. Close up shop and try to find other work. Let's see here, what can you do while you're toting around that little bundle of joy of ours?*

Cal blinked his eyes hard for a moment, trying to ignore the pluralization.

*Well, construction's out,* the voice continued. *So's exploration. Probably shouldn't have sharp things around her, so the mill and the butcher shop are out. Can't work in the foundry or the smelter, she might get cooked. Oh hey, I know! You can go teach.* Cal swore he heard cackling in his mind. *Oh wait, not you can't. You don't know anything worth teaching.*

*Hey, that's not fair. I know how to make fuel and soap.*

*Great. Take on an apprentice. That'll solve all your problems.*

"An apprentice," he scoffed out loud. "Yeah, right."

*Why don't you worry about feeding the kid first, huh? Sort out the little stuff later.*

*Yeah, you're right.*

*As usual.*

*Shut up.*

*Make me.*

Cal pinched the bridge of his nose and made a mental note to visit Dr. Taylor in the morning for the medication that would do exactly that.

. . .

Gabrielle Serrano
17 June, 6 yal, late morning
2 miles northeast of tropical archipelago
>|

The bow of their ship dipped as it passed over a large, rolling wave. Daphne and Diego squealed as a spray washed over the ship, while Marya and Aidan huddled together at the stern. Kristin sat at the tiller, staring almost blankly into the distance. The air carried a bitter chill in it, and distant thunder trembled with a low growl. Memories stirred, and Gabi shuddered as a sudden uneasiness gripped her.

*That better not be a hurricane,* she thought nervously.

Will muttered a curse as he leaped from the outrigger to the starboard cargo hold, making the ship rock slightly side to side even as it ascended another wave. The wind shifted direction, and their forward momentum stopped.

"It's no good," he grumbled to Kristin, jerking his head at the darkening clouds that had swallowed the land mass far ahead of them. "We'll never get there in one piece if we try to cross now."

She sighed and nodded. "Where do we go then?"

"Double back. There was a cove at that last island where we can put in and let the storm pass."

Gabi shook her head and tucked her slender frame into the cargo hold, nestling among the sacks of dried vegetables and jerked meat. The boom of the sail would soon sweep above and the safest place for her, though full of conflicting odors, would be below deck. Diego joined her, adding to her apprehension. She turned away from him when he tried to cuddle up to her. Diego squealed in protest, but didn't press the issue any further.

*Stuck on this damn boat with him and Marya. Nowhere to run to. And now we have to turn back.*

Will would have them on their way again as soon as the storm passed—assuming it didn't turn on them, of course—but making up for the lost time was not an idea that Gabi cherished. If their cobbled-together boat had walls, they would have been closing in on Gabi, squeezing the very life and breath from her.

The boat rocked and pitched as Will adjusted the sails to compensate for the shift in the wind, and Kristin had the vessel pointed back toward the modest island they had passed less than an hour earlier. It was about eight miles long and two wide, Gabi guessed. Lush vegetation formed a verdant crown over the wide sandy beaches. The sight of familiar salt palms and vinewoods as they closed in gave Gabi a small measure of relief. She would be able to hunt, and hunting meant relief from her constant companions, even if for only a brief time. Will might object, but she knew that the others would appreciate the fresh meat, and Gabi would win out on the argument.

It took an hour and a half for them to reach the cove and secure everything in case the storm changed paths. Gabi collected her bow, quiver, and an empty sack, and excused herself to hunt. Will didn't object; he didn't even seem to hear her, his attention firmly on the distant tempest. She was almost disappointed by this reaction, and the lack of ensuing argument. As she disappeared into the jungle she took a long look back. Karina was overseeing the setup of camp, and the younger children took to their duties without hesitation. Even Daphne, at four years of age, kept herself busy collecting pepperines from the shrubs at the edge of the beach.

*Good,* she thought. *Keep them out of my hair.*

She found fresh tracks all over, and began to sort them out. A wide variety of smaller animals were present in abundance, but it didn't take Gabi long to figure out that the dreaded jaguars were nowhere to be found. Nor were the wild boars that were common around their old home. Her mouth widened into a pleased grin. There would be no predators today, or at least none that were a danger to her.

*Easy pickings.*

She spent hours hunting brush rabbits and fat birds of all colors. She only returned to the beach when the grumbling protest of her empty stomach escalated to the point where she couldn't ignore it any more. By that time she only had three arrows left that she hadn't broken or lost altogether. Gabi didn't want to waste any more ammunition, so her last kill was made from close range with a thrown tomahawk. The damage done to the miniscule rabbit by the heavy axe was grotesque, and she had to leave the mangled, unusable corpse behind.

Gina and Caleb were tending to a fire, boiling water that they had found somewhere nearby. Most of the others were hanging around a makeshift shelter at the jungle's edge. Will was alone, sitting on the bow of the center hold, eyes still fixed to the stormy east.

*That's weird.*

Gabi hauled the game sack to Caleb and handed it over. She didn't linger long enough to help her elders prep her kills for cooking. Instead she took a purposeful line for the crew's leader. Will didn't pay her any mind as she approached.

"Too bad we're stuck here," she said, taking a seat on the outrigger opposite him. "But at least we'll eat well. Who knows, maybe we can stock our supplies a little."

Will gave her a brief, dead glance before his gaze returned to the stormy seas.

"What's eating you?" she scoffed.

"It's such a long way," he muttered.

"Huh?"

"Through the strait. It looked so tiny on the map, but it's really quite far."

Gabi furrowed her brow and narrowed her eyes. "What are you talking about? You said it would be like twenty or thirty miles from the last island to the mainland. That's a half a day, maybe."

"Could have been the wrong half of the day." His piercing eyes finally turned to make contact with hers. "We could have been early, or the storm could have been late."

"So you turned us back. So what? It's a good thing." Gabi smirked. "It means I don't have to kill Marya yet."

Her morbid humor was lost on Will. He did not rise to his usual reaction or threats to forcibly remove Gabi from the crew or complain about her constant feuding with Marya. Instead he looked back across the sea and sighed heavily.

"I hope they made it. Before the storm hit."

"Who?"

"The rest of them," he growled. "Nick and Daniel's ships. How far ahead of us were they? They left the day before we did. Did they catch better winds? Were they moving faster than us? Did they make it across before the storm?"

"You saw what I saw," Gabi countered. "That storm came across this morning. We could see the mainland before it crossed our path. It wasn't there yesterday."

"What if there was another storm yesterday? Or the day before?" he snapped back. "What if they were out in the middle of that strait, exposed? None of the ships could stand that kind of wind or waves. Hell, I'm really not sure if this thing will make it all the way across the strait on a *good* day."

Gabi hopped down from her perch and took a seat next to Will on the bow. Hesitantly, she put her hand on his shoulder. "Nick's not an idiot. Neither is Daniel. If they saw the storm coming they would have run for shelter."

Will shrugged her hand off. "Shelter would have been this cove. This island. See any other ships here, Gabs? Cause I sure as hell don't."

"Or it could have been on the other side. If they made it most of the way across, they wouldn't turn back. Like I said, Nick's not an idiot."

"Well, I am."

"For what?"

Will's attention turned to her suddenly, and the hard scowl on his face put Gabi's nerves on edge. "For letting you delay us. For not letting the past go. For thinking that letting you walk through the wreckage of our lives one last time, or to worship Captain Kimura's grave one more time might possibly make you a civil being. If we hadn't lost time waiting for you to come around to the fact that it was time to go…"

"What, Will?" she cut him off. "What would you have done differently if we had sailed with the other two ships? I mean, you seem to think they got caught shaking their asses at a jaguar. That they're all dead. You have no idea."

"I know they're dead," he bellowed. "Every one of them."

"You don't know that. You didn't see the storm roll over their masts. We haven't seen a trace of them since we left the Sorrow behind for good."

He rose up from the bow and took three steps away from her, then paused. "You're right. I don't know for sure. But I have a feeling. It's something I can't shake. Like instinct. When I'm hunting and… and my eyes are lying to me." He spun around to face her. "You of all people should appreciate that. Especially after all we've been through."

"The only thing I see right now is our chief freaking out. Either they're safe and you're worrying about nothing, or they're dead and you should be thanking me for being such a pain." She hopped down and curtseyed sarcastically. "You're welcome."

Will laughed and shook his head, though it was hollow. The bitterness of his words drove that point home as soon as they came out.

"If you could, for one second, feel an ounce of anyone else's pain but your own, you would see the world a whole different way. I hope someday you get a chance to look back on yourself and see what a prickly little bitch you are." As he walked past, he drove home one final thought. "But I know I shouldn't expect that kind of self-awareness from someone who can't even open her heart to her own flesh and blood."

Her temper erupted in an instant. Gabi picked up a handful of wet sand and flung it at Will, hitting him in the back. He ignored it and continued walking toward the camp. "He's not my brother. He's just the reason my mom's dead."

Before she could hurl any more words or sand, Will was out of range. Though she held contempt for him, she did not want to pursue him. Isolation called to her, luring her into the hold of the boat with its song. In the bottom of the former fishing canoe she would be free from the judgment that she constantly faced, or the enemies within the crew. She would be left alone for the night, and that was all she could hope for.

. . .

Darius counted the doors that passed to his left as he walked Benedict Boulevard. The exercise was more mental than a navigational necessity. Still, it had been a long, laborious day, and he needed to do whatever was necessary to keep exhaustion at bay. Assuming that his efforts to repair the colony's power grid had succeeded, the two remaining errands would take him only a few minutes to complete. But no matter how short they were, he would still be returning to his temporary home on *Michael* in the dark. In the dying twilight, the details of the market square began to fade into one massive, dark shadow.

The fifth door on the east side was his target, preceded by a pair of benches that jutted out from the building in a wide 'V' shape. Frank Devereaux's shop was a popular gathering point that, for the past week, had been eerily silent. Devereaux had been busy directing the Colonial Volunteer Militia in cleanup and repair efforts, and his clients were scattered to the wind. Some tended to friends and family injured during the earthquake, others stood shoulder to shoulder with neighbors in an incredible effort to repair and rebuild damaged buildings all over the city.

Darius stepped up to the door and rapped hard with his bare knuckles. It was only a moment later that he realized he might not be presentable. In a fit of self-consciousness, he checked his attire. His pants were dusty, and several frayed fibers marked where a new hole was beginning to form at the knee. His once-white tank top was a dingy gray, and huge, dark sweat stains ran down the sides.

*Well, that's professional,* he thought, irritated at his presentation.

The heavy door swung open, and Devereaux rubbed his eyes and blinked. Darius's only consolation was that the Captain of the CVM looked even worse for wear than he did. Devereaux's clothes were equally dirty, though with more rips. An angry, red welt on his forehead spoke of some recent construction mishap.

"Yes, Governor?" he rasped, his voice nearly gone.

Darius straightened up and smiled. "Just wanted to check to see if you've got power back."

"Let me check." Devereaux disappeared into the darkness of his shop. Darius could hear his feet drag along the floor.

*He's as tired as I feel.*

It took Devereaux three minutes to return, which Darius found to be oddly long. When he did, he nodded. "Yeah, it's back. Had to reset the breakers for the refrigerators."

"Ah," Darius nodded. "Well, that's good to hear. That means we can reopen the lumber mills and the foundry tomorrow."

"And not a minute too soon. We used up all the back stock of building supplies."

Darius rubbed his scalp and neck. "Well, I'll have to remember for the future to keep around spare poles for the power grid. If we didn't have to go out and cut down new ones by hand, we could have got everything up and running a lot faster."

"Hindsight is perfect. Seeing into the future… well, that's a different matter. See you tomorrow, Governor."

Darius bid him goodbye and continued down Benedict to River Way. His final stop would take him on a more personal errand, to visit a friend whose life had been torn asunder by tragedy. Cal McLaughlin had barely been seen by anyone in the colony following his release from the clinic. Hunter and Dr. Taylor were the only two who had contact with him since then. Darius didn't begrudge him one bit. But sooner or later he would need to give his condolences, and checking in on Cal and Andrea could not wait any longer. In his mind, Darius was already well overdue for this visit.

As he approached, Darius could hear Andrea wailing from the second story of the small shop. She was clearly in distress, her piercing cry laden with an urgency that even a childless man such as Darius could interpret. Faint light flickered from the lower level, though the apartment above was dark.

*Preparing a bottle?* Darius wondered.

He knocked on the door, then cast his eyes at the night sky. The first pinpricks of light were beginning to emerge from the murky darkness. No constellations were yet visible. Even if they were, Darius couldn't yet identify more than a couple of the newly defined clusters. Most familiar constellations as viewed from Earth were grotesquely skewed by their position on Demeter. Others no longer could be defined cohesively. If he could find the same constellation two nights in a row, he considered it a personal victory.

After knocking once more and waiting a couple minutes, Darius noticed something peculiar. Andrea was still screeching upstairs, but the light hadn't flickered, nor had Cal come to greet him. Darius had a moment of second-guessing as to whether or not his knock was heard over the baby. Something was definitely amiss, so he tried the door knob. It turned easily, and the door swung slowly open with a labored groan.

The shop floor was dimly lit. The display cases on either wall were upright, though sparsely stocked. Cal was leaned back in a chair behind the sales counter, with his feet kicked up on the counter itself. A green bottle sat within his reach, its swing top wide open. Cal glanced at Darius, his hair wild and unkempt, his hand swirling an enameled cup.

"I was hoping you'd go away," he muttered as he downed the contents of the cup. One eye closed in a pained wince, and he wheezed loudly as he exhaled the first time.

*God damn it.*

Darius slowly walked up to the counter and leaned sideways against it. He took the open bottle in his hand and took a deep whiff.

*Whiskey.*

Cal grinned. "Been dying to try out my new product. It's been sitting in the ship for so long. Now it's finally ready for sale." His speech was slow, and he stumbled over the words. "Pretty good if I do say so myself. Want some?"

Darius smiled as he flipped the top closed and sealed the bottle. "Another time, perhaps."

Cal heaved his long body upright. His feet fell to the floor with an unnerving slap, but he didn't seem to mind. Nor did he pay any heed to the escalating screams from his baby daughter. He set the cup down and reached for the bottle, which Darius quickly pulled from his reach. Cal looked up at him with a scornful glare. His breath reeked of alcohol and decay. It took a great deal of willpower on Darius's part to suppress the instinct to cover his own mouth and nose in the face of such stench.

"I think you've put in enough work for one day, Cal," he soothed. "Let's go see what Andrea wants, alright?"

"Give it back," Cal growled. "I wasn't done."

"You are. It's time to tend to your family now."

Cal laughed and shook his head. "That's rich. You're going to tell me how to run my family. You. Who hasn't had a date since he was on Earth."

The accusation, though true, stung Darius a little bit. But he shrugged it off. "I don't need to tell you what to do. You know what to do; you know what's right for your family. This just isn't you," he said, dangling the bottle of whiskey just outside of Cal's reach.

"What's right is letting me get a little sanity around here." Cal lunged for the bottle, but misjudged the width of the counter and ended up tumbling over the other side and onto the floor. He let out a loud expletive. Andrea seemed to sense her father's anger, and her crying intensified once more.

Darius took on a firmer tone this time. "You think this is sane? Ignoring the cries of your daughter while you try to find yourself at the bottom of a bottle? When's the last time you've ever heard of that particular plan ending well?"

"Screw you," Cal shouted, his voice cracking as he fought back his emotions. His sky blue eyes glistened with tears, and the pain that raged within him was written in every twitch of his mouth, heard in every stifled sob and stuttered breath. He scrambled to his feet, swaying for a moment before he gained his legs back. "You don't know what it's like. You didn't have anyone left to lose. You just locked yourself in that ship away from all the problems. Away from us. From the starvation, the sickness, the death. You don't know half the shit that I've been through since we've been here. And you will never know what it's like to have your soul ripped away from you like I have."

"You're right," Darius snapped. "I don't know what you've been through any more than you know what I have. It hurt when I found out that Lexi had died. I can't fathom the kind of pain you feel from that. If I didn't respect you as much as I do, and if you didn't have a child to take care of, I might just consider letting you find out the hard way that there's no relief in drinking. It doesn't take away the pain. It doesn't make you strong enough to face it."

"With all due respect, *Governor*, when you look at Andrea, you see a colonist. A baby. Maybe a future contributor to your cause here. Do you know what I see?"

Darius shook his head.

"Her. I see my wife. The woman I was meant to love and protect for the rest of my life. I see my failure," he screamed, his armor cracking as the tears flowed freely.

"She's your daughter."

Cal lunged suddenly, catching Darius off guard. He grabbed the bottle with one hand, spun around, and hurled it into the door. Hundreds of tiny shards of glass glittered in the light of the lamp as they fell to the ground. The room was filled in seconds with the pungent tang of whiskey. Cal turned his back to the counter and slid down until he was sitting, tearing at his hair as he sobbed. Darius took a knee next to him.

"You don't have time to figure this out," he sniffed in disdain. "You have someone who needs your protection and love, and you're ignoring her in favor of self-destruction. Now, I'll sit here with you for one hour. If she's still crying after that hour, I'm taking her with me for the night. Maybe longer."

"Good, she'd be better off."

Darius crossed his arms as he stood up, burying his clenched fists under his armpits. "Any man who thinks his own child is better off without him isn't fit to live in this colony. Now I'm going to chalk that up to the alcohol and pretend I didn't hear it. Stand up. You've got fifty nine minutes, and I suggest you use them wisely."

It didn't take Cal fifty nine minutes to feed and calm Andrea. Darius was rather shocked by how quickly Cal was able to prepare and feed her a bottle, as well as settle her down. Whether from her exhaustion or Cal's, both of them were asleep after only forty minutes. Darius quietly stole out of the shop to make his long overdue journey to his own bed.

. . .

Gabrielle Serrano
21 June, 6 yal, early afternoon
Mainland coast, est. 70 miles from archipelago
>|

Progress was a funny thing to Gabi. Though it was clear they were on the path that Will had drawn out, turning north along the continental mainland and away from the tropics, the scenery didn't seem all that different. The coast was still lined with lush jungle canopies towering over white sand, and the mountain peaks were a little taller. Though in this place there were a few more jagged rocks jutting up from the otherwise pristine beaches. The only real change was that the landmass was one huge, unbroken ribbon that extended as far as the eye could see. No chains of islands to speak of.

Will had told her to be patient, but that was becoming more difficult by the day. They hadn't set ashore since they left their home islands; Will proclaimed this was necessary for safety, though wouldn't explain any further. He had withdrawn nearly into a shell after they found a torn sail and part of a mast in the water the day before, wreckage from one of the other two ships. In his contemplative state, Marya's presence had grown nearly intolerable, and had Gabi contemplating the wisdom of leaving the crew behind and swimming to shore. If she had thought she had a chance of surviving either the swim or the wilderness alone, that chain of thought would have lasted more than a couple minutes.

Gabi scurried across the woven netting between pylons and climbed onto the starboard outrigger. She stretched out in its dugout hull, taking in the warm sun as she dangled her left leg over the outrigger, dipping her foot into the crisp water. Diego shouted something barely coherent about wanting to join her, and began whining when she ignored him.

*I'm out here to get away from you,* she thought, irritated by the nuisance.

Someone eventually quieted him down, most likely Kristin. It was one of the things she was good at. That, and being a peacekeeper. But with her brother out of the game mentally, Kristin had difficulty keeping Marya from antagonizing Gabi. Worse, it seemed that Kristin didn't always believe Gabi that she was innocent, that she had no part in their squabbles. Marya could convince her now and then that an argument was Gabi's fault, even when she was clearly to blame.

Gabi pushed aside the thoughts of her rival. She found herself dozing off as the boat rocked hypnotically. Dreams of the future came to her, flowing in an ephemeral dance. She pictured a tiny town, not much smaller than the one she was born in on Earth. The landscape was far greener than she was used to, however; this was something that came from Will's description of what the other colony should look like. Tall trees shaded the village, though she always had difficulty reconciling Will's stories with the palms that she was so familiar with. They always ended up oddly top-heavy in her dreams.

Then there was a shift in her subconscious theater. She was in the wilderness, stalking along a stream that climbed rapidly into the mountains. She knew her quarry had gone into the stream itself, and she was examining shifting patterns of silt to determine where it had gone. A twig snapped from somewhere behind her, and she wheeled around. Slowly padding forward in a crouched position, a very fat black-and-white cat with blue eyes faced her. Gabi drew her arrow back and took aim. But when the creature yawned and lay down, she hesitated.

"Pelusina?" she asked.

The cat let loose a throaty growl that was half purr. It shifted to its side and stretched out lazily.

Gabi smiled and took two steps forward. "Pelusina! I've missed you."

Pelusina flexed her paws, baring her claws for a brief second before they retracted. Her voice uttered something almost human.

"What is it, girl?"

Without warning, Gabi slipped and fell into the creek. She gasped for air and bolted upright, thrashing around her. Her bow was missing, and searing light forced her to squint. She coughed, spitting up a tiny amount of salt water. Her confusion mounted quickly, and her heart began to race as she scanned her surroundings.

She was awake and on the ship. She was also drenched, as was the inside of the outrigger. Marya stood over her and grinned, tossing a bucket back into the cargo hold of the ship.

"Stop dreaming of your stupid stuffed cat. You've got work to do," she sneered.

"Marya! No!" Kristin shouted from her seat at the tiller.

Gabi's confusion quickly evaporated as her rage tore through. She gained her feet and sprang at Marya in one fluid motion, carrying both of them backwards. Gabi landed awkwardly in the emergency netting, and her arm stung as a loose palm frond sliced her skin. She bit her lip and forced the pain aside. Gabi lunged again, jamming her shoulder into Marya as she tried to get up. They each landed glancing blows on each other as they wrestled for advantageous position. The battle was short-lived, however as one of Will's powerful arms slipped between the two girls, and Gabi was hoisted and slammed into the cargo hold as if she was nothing more than a doll.

"That's enough, you two," he bellowed, fire burning wild in his eyes.

"She's the one who hit me," Marya complained.

*That lying little…*

"She started it!" Gabi protested. "I was…"

She didn't get to complete the sentence. Will reached down and grabbed her by the arms, then hurtled her into the air. Her stomach went tight, and it felt like a knife had been thrust into it. She knew instantly that she was not going to land in the netting. Will had thrown her hard astern.

"NO!" she shrieked.

She barely had time to suck in a breath and close her eyes before she hit the surface of the water. The wind was nearly knocked out of her as she landed face-first in the sea. Gabi thrashed and shot through the surface, coughing and spitting. A moment later she was treading water, spinning around to gain her bearings. The cut on her arm burned like fire. When she came about toward the ship, it was still moving off. Kristin was arguing fiercely with Will, though he demanded that she keep course.

"You ass, get back here," Gabi screamed.

She could see Kristin push on the tiller to change course, which prompted Will to yank her from her seat and take over. Gabi's stomach knotted even tighter than she thought possible, and her fingers began to tingle.

*No. No… No, you can't leave me here!*

"Will!" she shrieked as she started to swim after the ship. "Will, I'm sorry! Please, come back!"

Her effort was futile. There was no way she could catch up. Even though the ship was just a few salvaged canoes lashed together and patched up, under full sail it could still make five knots. A quick glance at the shore told her she was probably too far away to make it. She pressed on, desperately clinging to the hope that Will would change his mind and come back for her. But as the seconds passed and Will shoved Kristin away from the helm again, that hope began to fade.

"No…"

Gabi stopped her pursuit and resumed treading water. Her heart hammered furiously in her chest, and the world at the edge of her vision seemed to darken. The nerves that once kept her calm in the face of predators failed her in that moment, reducing her to a trembling, sobbing mess.

"You promised to protect me!" she screamed at the top of her lungs, coughing as she nearly swallowed a mouthful of seawater. "Will! You promised!"

Either he could no longer hear her, or her plea fell on deaf ears as he kept his course true. She was out of options, and nearly out of time. Her strength would not last much longer. Gabi turned for shore, trying to pace herself to conserve energy. She prayed desperately that the tide was coming in, and would carry her to shore. Alone, unarmed, and without food, but alive.

A minute later she caught sight of the ship once more. The sail was down, but the bow was pointed toward her. Four oars were in the water, pulling in near perfect synchronicity. Gabi turned again, swimming again for the ship. Will scowled at her from the bow, arms folded across his chest, unmoving. Her crewmates stopped rowing when they got close, and Will knelt down to hoist Gabi into the ship. She found herself again in the hold, though this time placed gently. Diego was crying, and immediately flung his arms around her. This tiny gesture, which otherwise would have disgusted Gabi, felt welcoming under the circumstances. For the first time in years, she hugged him back.

"Are we clear now?" Will asked coldly, enunciating every syllable.

Gabi nodded quickly.

Marya hopped to the center canoe and wrapped her hand around the mast, leaning outward from it with a smug grin on her face. "So she finally got what she deserved, huh?"

Will spun around to face her, and in the same chilling voice, issued another warning. "I was making a point to both of you. So help me, Mar, if I have to throw *you* in, I'm not coming back to fish you out. Are we clear now?"

Marya's grin vanished in an instant and the color drained from her scorched cheeks. She nodded, and scurried away to her duties.

Diego's sobbing faded away, and he whispered in Gabi's ear. "Don't leave me. I don't want you to go away ever."

Gabi stroked his sandy hair and held him closer. His words tore at her heart. She had said something similar, once. And then she had been betrayed.

*I'm not... am... am I doing that to him?* She asked herself in horror.

• • •

*Huh, well this is harder than I thought,* Cal reflected.

He stirred the slurry that would eventually become biodiesel and glycerin. Both were major products of his business, though the glycerin required additional processing to become soap. The stage of cooking that he was at required his full attention. Error would certainly render the fuel useless. That is what made Andrea's protest aggravating.

"Daddy will be with you in a second," he cooed, glancing over his shoulder at her bassinet, which was just underneath the corner of the shed.

She was not in danger; Cal had made sure that he placed her well away from any active equipment, and had even salvaged a fan from *Michael* that he used to blow any potentially hazardous fumes away from her. More than likely, she was hungry, as she didn't settle down upon hearing his voice.

*Great timing, kiddo.*

As much as it pained Cal to hear her cry, he had to let her do so for a few more minutes. Balancing her care with his work was a delicate act that Cal was only beginning to understand the complexities of. The biggest issue he faced was her erratic eating and sleeping schedule. There was no guarantee that any given time of day would be clear for work. The only thing that was certain at this point was that her schedule was never the same two days in a row.

Cal finished his work and double-checked the burner, assuring that it was off. He then collected his daughter, who was still crying insistently, and went inside the shop to make her a bottle of formula. Once ready, he sat behind the counter, cradling her gently and watching her blue-green eyes flick open and fade shut as she ate her fill.

"You look so much like your mother," he whispered and sighed. "You're going to be a heartbreaker. Just don't break your daddy's heart, okay?"

Andrea yawned and squirmed, burrowing closer to him. Cal gently stroked her nose. He watched as her eyelids finally closed, surrendering to slumber.

A gentle knock at the front door preceded Hunter, who entered cautiously. Cal brought his finger to his lips to indicate the required silence, and his friend nodded, closing the door as quietly as the rusty hinges allowed. Hunter padded to the counter and grinned.

"I think I've solved your problem," he whispered.

"Oh great," Cal replied in kind. "Which one? Because you know I've got a few."

"That needing to do three things at once problem. Brewing, selling, and parenting."

"Right. Which part are you fixing?"

"Selling. I had a discussion with Devereaux about your situation. He thinks it might be a bit of a hassle for you to hire someone for your sales floor, so he's considering a permanent supplier agreement for just about everything you make."

Cal readjusted in his seat to lean forward, making sure not to disturb Andrea. "What do you mean by just about?"

"He's going to write up a contract and bring it over. You'll still sell your fuel to the government, that part doesn't change. He won't be selling your laundry soap, someone else wanted that. But everything else he will take. Exclusively. Good terms, too."

"Why not the laundry soap?" Cal asked, confused as to who else would want it.

Hunter grinned and reached into his pocket. When he withdrew his hand, he held a folded piece of paper between his fingers. He flicked his wrist forward slightly, offering it to Cal. Cal took it, eyeing it suspiciously before unfolding it and reading.

"This is from Saika," Cal whispered. Hunter nodded, his grin growing wider. "It's a contract." Cal's lips began to move as he read the words. "…exclusive purchase rights to all production of McLaughlin laundry soaps, to be marketed and sold by Kimura Clothiers."

"Step one. Step two is when Devereaux's paperwork shows up."

"…Purchase of the entire production is guaranteed by Saika Kimura, and Calvin McLaughlin is entitled to retain a reasonable amount of product for personal use. This contract is valid in perpetuity, subject to the legal standing of both businesses, blah blah blah, price per unit, more legal mumbo jumbo…" Cal looked up at his friend and beamed. "You mad genius. I could kiss you."

Hunter chuckled under his breath. "Saika's giving you better terms for your soap than Devereaux would have. She doesn't care as much about the profit, she just wants a respected product to put on her shelves. Smart of her to snake it from him, in my opinion. It'll keep people walking in her door in case interest in her clothes slumps off."

Cal grabbed a pen and signed the contract. "Hope Devereaux's not too upset about that move. Speaking of, when is he bringing his offer?"

"Whenever is convenient for you. Tonight, if you want. Just give the word and I'll let him know."

"Yeah, tonight sounds fine. Six PM? Hopefully Andrea will be settled in by then."

"Sure," Hunter nodded.

A low grumble echoed through the air. Cal looked around, not sure of what would be causing it. Hunter looked equally confused. The racket escalated quickly, and Cal felt like his chest was being rattled. The pen he had just used jumped around on the counter. With one last glance at each other, Cal and Hunter shot through the front door as quickly as their legs could carry them. Andrea squealed in protest, trying to bury herself in Cal's chest. Cal's neighbors were equally in the dark as to the source of the noise. Many of them had taken to the street, looking around wildly.

Just as the noise was reaching painful levels, the street was eclipsed in shadow for just a couple seconds. Cal looked up and his jaw immediately dropped in surprise. There, overhead, was a sleeper ship. Its chemical thrusters burned furiously as it tried to slow for landing, and their shockwaves knocked Cal and Hunter off their feet. Just as quickly, the ship was gone, its deafening thrum fading into the distance.

Cal scrambled to his feet. He checked on Andrea, who was screaming in terror but otherwise unharmed. Hunter dusted himself off and mouthed something, though between the ringing in his ears and Andrea's ear-splitting cries, he couldn't hear for several minutes.

"Was that what I think it was?" Cal gasped.

"That couldn't have been another ship," Hunter said in utter disbelief. "There were three. Two are here, the other burned up."

*Raphael?*

"We never found wreckage, Hunter."

He shot Cal an incredulous look. "Six years, Cal? You can't tell me that thing's been up there for six years and we had no clue. We would have had radio contact. We would have seen them. No, that's not the other ship. It can't be."

"Well then just what the hell was it?"

Hunter couldn't answer him.

. . .

"Will you quit pacing, Governor? You're making me nervous," Tom complained.

Darius paused only a moment to shoot a look of disapproval at his deputy. "You should be nervous, Tom. You know damn well that was another sleeper ship."

"Right, but wearing out Foundation Street isn't going to change that. Plus you're making a spectacle of yourself."

Corporals Barajas and Inouye rushed past Darius on their way to Benedict Square. Their M4 carbines were slung over their shoulders, and the men wore expressions of worry on their faces. The governor had called up the CVM as soon as the mystery ship flew over, and most of them had assembled as ordered, with the last of the stragglers only now finding their way. But as another three of their rank and file passed by, Darius was struck by how inexperienced most of them were.

The Colonial Volunteer Militia only drilled a handful of days a year. Much of their officer corps was made up of the former ship crews, but the rest of the force was green. The CVM had a capable commander in Captain Frank Devereaux, but some of the newer volunteers were only in middle school when the ships left Earth. Darius had deep concern about their ability should combat arise. For that matter, he was concerned that the Militia might not even expect combat at all.

Rumor quickly spread through the colony that the strange ship was *Raphael*, and that their crew had somehow found a way to keep the ship alive for years, until they could make it back to the planet. Darius and the ship crews knew this wasn't the case. Even if *Raphael's* reactor hadn't gone critical, the ship that flew over Concordia was much smaller, perhaps only a quarter of the size of *Michael* or *Gabriel*. Someone else had to have the technology to build that ship.

*We could not allow for the possibility that another sleeper ship could be built,* Dr. Kimura's voice echoed deep in his mind. *If so much as one sleeper ship were to follow us, carrying soldiers…*

"They would easily conquer the colony," he muttered under his breath. A conversation from decades earlier. A horrifying possibility in the present.

*Does Tom understand this? Does he know what I know?*

Darius closed his eyes and cycled two deep breaths.

*Now you understand why Dr. Benedict stayed behind,* Dr. Kimura's explanation continued. *To destroy all plans and records for Project Columbus.*

*I guess you failed, Doc,* Darius thought.

Darius opened his eyes and folded his hands behind his back. Benedict Square was right in front of him. The CVM was mustered, and had fallen into parade rest. As Captain Devereaux walked toward him, Darius counted the number of Militia present. Not a single uniform was to be found among them. There was no time for them to get dressed, only to grab their rifles and report for duty.

*Seventy six. Seventy seven, counting Devereaux.* He sighed and saluted Captain Devereaux upon approach.

"Governor Owens, sir," Devereaux addressed him. "The Militia has heard your call, and stands ready. What are your orders, sir?"

"Captain, I'm sure you are aware of the reported sighting of an unknown sleeper ship," Darius began. "You are to march with the CVM and find this ship, determine its origin, and report back. By my orders, you are hereby given authority to seize up to six horses from the surrounding farms, to be used in this action at your discretion." Darius glanced at Tom, then jerked his head and cleared his throat. Tom nodded and walked away. When Darius turned back to the captain, his voice was hushed. "If this ship is from Earth, we have no idea who or what she holds. I don't want you walking into a trap. Pray this is a group of survivors, Captain, but assume they are hostile unless they prove otherwise."

"Yes sir."

Darius leaned in close to Devereaux's ear. "If they appear military, or if you're outgunned, you ambush them. You take them all down, no prisoners. Do you understand, Captain?"

Devereaux didn't display a hint of emotion or surprise. He merely saluted and said, "Yes sir."

Darius watched as Devereaux hustled back to his command, barking orders. In less than a minute, all seventy seven men and women were out of sight. Darius rubbed the stubble on his scalp. His deputy returned a moment later.

"When it rains it pours," he remarked.

"It would seem that the deluge never ends, Tom."

Tom nodded as he chewed his lip pensively. "Well, we've learned to swim pretty well around here. Maybe the river rises a little from this, but we'll find a way to shore."

*Only if we didn't just open the floodgates.*

. . .

Gabrielle Serrano
6 July, 6 yal, mid afternoon
Mainland coast, est. 600 miles from tropical
archipelago
>|

"I don't know, Will," Caleb said apprehensively. "It looks like that storm's ashore. We should be fine for another couple hours at least."

Another day of debate over storms and maps. Another argument about supplies and timeframes. Gabi barely paid attention to them anymore. One way or another Will always got his way. Well, nearly. A week earlier, he almost had a mutiny on his hands when he didn't want to pull ashore and let the crew off for the night. It was one of the exceedingly rare times that Marya and Gabi were in agreement, and working toward a common goal. It probably helped that each of them needed a break from the other's presence, but neither wanted to be the one to make Will snap and finally drown them.

Today was an exception, though. Gabi was in tune with the conversation, and this time it was Will who wanted to go ashore, but Caleb was pressing the case of sailing onward. He argued that the storm ahead was no threat, though the whole sky was overcast, and Gabi couldn't tell if the dark gray squall in the distance was even moving.

"Look," he jabbed a thin finger on the crude map the young chief inherited from his father. "You're sure we're here, right? But that long spit of land over there is probably this," he touched another point further along their projected path. "If we can get on the other side of that, there's this big bay here that should be very sheltered. We can make our repairs there."

"You're assuming that we're that far ahead," Will countered. "I see that bay and it's tempting. Lord knows we need a resupply, and having shelter like that would be incredible. But we're back here," he emphatically tapped on the original mark. "You're talking two days' sailing there, not a couple hours."

Gabi lobbed a nearly empty water skin at Caleb, which he caught with little effort. "There's your water for the next two days," she glowered. "Don't drink it all at once."

"Very funny, Gabi," he tossed it back.

"I'm serious. We'll be dying of thirst by the time we make it there."

"No we won't. Will's wrong about where we are."

This prompted another vigorous round of debate between the two young men as to what features on the map each of them had seen, and when. Will's argument almost always came back to the point that the map provided by the orbital probe didn't have proper topographical demarcations, and that he was the only one who could read them properly. This time Caleb wouldn't let the argument go, insisting that the landmass that sliced into the sea was a long, thin hook only a couple days from the river delta that was the ultimate goal of their sea voyage. From there the plan was simply to follow the river upstream to the landing site.

"So if we're only a couple days away from landing, why is stopping now to resupply such a big issue, Caleb?" Will asked, not giving an inch.

Caleb threw up his hands. "Jeez, you can't even give us two hours. Two stupid hours, Will. That's all I'm asking."

"We don't have that anymore, Caleb," Marya interrupted as she bounced from the outrigger to the main hull. "We're getting a lot of chop out here, and the bow is bouncing funny. Like it's twisting or something."

Will sprang from his seat and hurried across to the outrigger. He knelt down at the front and peered intently at the bow.

"Damn it, she's right. Number three is separating from the others. We need to put ashore right away."

Gabi cringed at the report. The main hull was essentially three fishing canoes lashed together. Separation of one of the segments could mean their supplies getting swamped, or worse, the ship sinking. They had already once been forced to deal with the third canoe—which was the rightmost—separating from the others. Repairs took most of the day and much of what spare rope they had left. Gabi silently questioned whether or not they'd have enough left for another repair.

Almost unconsciously she checked her bow and the remaining arrows, then devoted similar attention to both her pack and tomahawks. As Will and Kristin steered the ship toward a tiny cove, others in the crew prepared to pull the ship out of the water. But as they neared the shore, that task grew much more complicated.

As they had ventured farther from their tropical homeland, the vegetation had grown much more sparse, and the species of trees—where they even existed—were now mostly what Will called 'fir' trees. Sandy beaches had given way hundreds of miles ago, replaced by gravel shores, then increasingly large rocks. This particular cove seemed to be mostly coarse gravel interspersed with jagged boulders almost as large as the ship. It would take all of their skill just to pull the ship in close enough to unload. Repair looked like it might be impossible.

The crew maneuvered around the hazards just offshore. Their landing was less than smooth, however. The hull scraped loudly on the gravel, coming to a stop with an abrupt lurch that had Gabi checking her balance. She hopped over the gunnels and gasped in surprise from the ice cold water that lapped at her shins. She heaved on the pylon in rhythm with the others, and a minute later the ship was completely on the shore.

There was a narrow margin of stony beach flanked by steeply rising banks. Giant timbers loomed over the cove, with occasional gnarled, stunted timbers growing awkwardly at the edge of the banks. They looked as if they might fall over at any moment, yet their roots clawed deeply into the dirt and wrapped impossibly around massive boulders. The spectacle was quite unlike anything that Gabi had ever seen, and it was only after Will roughly shoved her pack and bow into her hands that she realized that she was gawking. Shaking her head, she slipped on her pack and returned her focus to the task at hand.

"No time for sightseeing, Gabs," Will barked. "Get Diego and go with Gina and Kris. We need you guys to set up camp. No way we're going out again today. Get a fire going, look for water, and hunt if you can. We'll be up as soon as we've patched up the boat."

Gabi retrieved a few sections of mobile shelter, which consisted mostly of large woven mats that could be folded down for storage or tied together to expand and shape their sleeping space. Kris had already gone ahead, but Gina was easy to catch; she had to handle an awkward toddler in Daphne, and Diego had followed her out of habit. Gabi deposited her supplies at the top of the bank, then helped Gina get the children up the slope. Diego giggled and grabbed two of the shelter panels.

"Where we going?" he grinned at Gabi.

She was about to snap at him and grab the pieces from his hands, but she had bigger issues on her mind. She collected what was left and led them into the thick undergrowth. Kristin had left a faint trail of broken branches and trampled bushes; Gina probably couldn't have picked out the path without Gabi's assistance. They walked for several minutes and over a short rise before they encountered the lone remaining Vandemark sister. She was hard at work clearing a patch of relatively flat ground. Gabi stashed her supplies at the base of a tree and set to work helping her. After a couple minutes, Diego joined in, grunting and tugging at the branches of a bush at the edge of the clearing. Gabi had to laugh just a little at his struggle. Diego was always eager to help, but an enthusiastic six-year-old was barely useful when it came to survival.

*I hope the people from the other ships think he's cute,* she thought. She paused and reflected for a moment, as a dark idea clouded her mind. *Will better be right about the other ships.*

Diego redeemed himself when it came time to finally set up the shelter. Even as the winds picked up, swaying the tops of the trees and bringing the first drops of rain, he followed all of Gabi's directions without complaint. The wind swept bitterly through the camp, slicing Gabi to her core. While she shuddered and her fingers fumbled, Diego didn't seem bothered.

Karina and Aidan arrived a few minutes later with more supplies. Gabi was relieved of her duties, and she loaded up on empty water skins. Diego must have sensed that she was about to leave, and he immediately latched on to her, throwing his arms tightly around her.

"Don't go," he complained.

Gabi grimaced and pried him off. "I'm just getting water. Go make yourself useful. Find some kindling or something."

Diego paused for a moment before nodding. Gabi slipped from the camp and took stock of her surroundings. The fir trees gave off a pungent smell that she hadn't expected, though it was pleasant. Thick tangles of undergrowth reminded her in many ways of the home they had abandoned only weeks earlier. Though the land was unfamiliar, the basic concepts that Will had taught her over the years came back quickly. She was able to find a small creek only a few hundred feet from their campsite that was more than sufficient to fulfill her needs. Laden with water, she climbed victoriously back to the others.

When she returned she was shocked to see Will and Caleb. She had expected them to be on the beach well into the evening. They wore grim expressions on their faces, and Will shook his head as he conversed with his sister. Gabi shrugged off the extra equipment from her shoulders and hurried to him.

"Will? What's wrong?" she asked.

"A little setback," he replied quietly. He sighed heavily and motioned for the rest of the crew to gather around. Gina herded the younger children to the front of the circle as they formed around him.

*This isn't little.* Gabi gulped and steeled herself.

"Our journey just got a bit longer," Will said. A subtle stumble in his words led Gabi to believe he was struggling to hold back his frustration. "We can't fix the ship. We're going to have to hike overland from this point."

"What?" Marya gasped. "How much longer will that take?"

Will shrugged. "That depends on how much progress we can make and how far away we are. The hike from our planned landing spot was probably going to be longer, but the terrain a lot easier. I guess this depends on how easily we can get over the mountains in our path."

"Why don't we just follow the sea?" Karina asked.

"Because that'll take about four times longer. I'd like to get there some time before winter."

"Do you even know where we're going?"

Will folded his arms across his chest. "I'll figure it out at first light tomorrow. We don't really have a choice here. The ship would never make it around that peninsula, not in the shape it's in now. She's been good to us, but it's time to leave her behind." Will glanced over at Gabi and gave her a slight nod. "Gabi, I need you to go hunting now. Kris and Gina need to tend camp and watch the little ones. Everyone else with me. It's time to salvage what supplies we can."

. . .

As Darius turned the palomino mare around he swiveled his head, locking his gaze on the ship that rested just a few hundred feet away.

Its hull was a dark gray that bore striking resemblance to the Project Columbus sleepers. Its design was a near copy, but in reduced scale. The bridge canopy was a little high, and protruded a little more like an early fighter's cockpit. The sleeper pods themselves were the exact same size and shape as either of the other ships, but only two graced either side, compared to the six per side on *Gabriel*. The cargo pods were much smaller; they looked like intermodal containers that had been reinforced and refitted with thrusters. Upon initial inspection, Darius wasn't even sure that they opened to the inner hull, or were airtight for that matter.

The cargo ramp on the strange vessel was on the front, tucked underneath the bridge, in place of the crew pod. It was wide open, and gave the impression that the ship was startled by something. The support and drive section were much smaller than the original XCS series design, which was consistent with its significantly reduced mass.

It was impressive in its own right, though the hardware itself didn't shed any light on its origins. That information came from its occupants. In the field to the ship's starboard side, dozens of men, women, and children huddled together in the light drizzle. They had been forced off of the ship by the CVM upon initial contact early in the morning. Most were unarmed. Those who did have weapons surrendered without a fight. The Militia conducted a sweep of the ship while Staff Sergeant Josephson rode back to Concordia to summon Darius. She was tight-lipped on the journey.

"You've got to see this," was about all she would tell him. That, and, "They're ours, Governor."

*American*, Darius thought as he slowly rode closer. *Civilians*.

Captain Devereaux took the reins from Darius as he dismounted.

"How many of them are there, Captain?" he asked, unable to peel his eyes from the eager, nervous faces that watched him.

"Six hundred forty-two. Every single berth on the ship must have been occupied. They had two up on the bridge, I'm guessing for crew."

*Two from the bridge, six forty behind. Divide by four pods*, he did the math in his head. *The pod layout must be exactly the same as ours. That's odd.*

"No trouble with them?" Darius asked as he looked around. The ship had landed in the middle of a wide grassland, with only the shortest of rolling hills for concealment. It was a great place to land a ship, and a horrible place to attempt an ambush. Darius was suddenly very thankful that the CVM didn't need to engage in battle here.

"No sir. They saw us coming and popped the hatch. Surrendered without any incident. It's like they expected us."

*Of course they were expecting you, Captain. They shouldn't even be on this planet, and they flew right over our city. They knew we'd come.*

"Have you figured out who's in charge yet?"

Devereaux motioned to a young private, who nervously marched his prisoner toward them. The man was not imposing by any means. Average height, slightly overweight, dressed in faded jeans and a t-shirt with a battered sport coat over it all. His dark hair was slicked back and streaked with gray, and he had what looked like a week's worth of stubble on his face. His features weren't particularly striking, and he had a definite 'everyman' look about him. But something about him was familiar to Darius. He couldn't pinpoint what or why, but he had the feeling he'd met this man before.

"Are you the leader of these people?" Darius asked.

"Y-yes, I am," the man replied timidly.

Darius brought a finger up to his pursed lips. Hundreds of questions flooded his mind. Questions about the ship, where they got it, and who they were. Their intentions, abilities, and cargo.

"I'm sorry to ask, sir," the man interrupted his thoughts. "But my people are tired and scared. We've been out here in this field at gunpoint for hours. We're hungry, and it's starting to rain. Can we please go back on our ship now?"

"I don't mean to be rude, but I've got some issues right now." Darius watched the man's eyes widen and his throat tighten as he gulped. "The biggest one is that you came here in something that's not supposed to exist. Now, I don't even know how to interpret that. So in the interest of taking things easy and deescalating what I see as an unimaginable threat, let's start with the beginning. Does that sound fair?"

"Threat?" the man choked on the word. "Look at us, we're no threat. We barely landed in one piece."

"From the beginning," Darius reaffirmed emphatically. "Are we clear?"

J.C. Rainier

"C-crystal, sir."

"Alright then. What's your name?"

"Harcourt Young. The Third."

Darius's eyebrows arched and he was momentarily at a loss for words. He glanced at Devereaux, who was likewise taken by surprise.

"The billionaire venture capitalist?" Darius asked incredulously.

Young looked down at his clothes, his arms open slightly. "I know I don't look like one, but yes. That's me. Was me, I guess. Broke as a joke now."

"And your people? Employees? Friends?"

"I guess you could call them my family now," he explained. "We were all refugees on Earth. After the Laramie Incident, the Chinese stopped pushing inland. We never really found out why. But things went from bad to worse for the rest of us. No government. No army. No law. People were starving in the streets. Some folks formed new towns and started new lives, others began raping and murdering. Mostly they raped and murdered those who had just started fresh." He trailed off, his eyes cast downward, but recovered after a moment. "They all found their way to me in one way or another. Before the world went to hell, I only knew two of them. Now we're a community."

Darius looked again at the refugees huddled next to their steel home. Children as young as five looked back with wide eyes. Their parents held them close, their expressions pleading their case for freedom. The images of what they must have seen sickened him. Some of the children must have grown up knowing only a world of violence and fear, and that stirred the embers of rage within him.

"Captain Devereaux," he said.

"Yes sir?"

"See to it that these people are fed and rested." Darius held up his hand to pause the order, and turned to Young. "I trust, in the spirit of building trust, you don't mind if we disarm your people for the night?"

Young grimaced. "I don't like the thought of my people being defenseless."

"Oh, they won't be. You're under my protection starting right now."

Young hesitated for a moment, then nodded.

"Take their weapons for the night, Captain. Post Josephson and half of the CVM here for protection."

"Yes sir." Devereaux saluted then spun on his heels to enact the governor's orders.

"A fine soldier, that man," Young grinned slightly.

Darius dismissed his comment. "I have about a thousand more questions for you."

"I can appreciate that… Governor, was it?"

"Correct. I am Governor Darius Owens."

"Well, Governor Owens, it would be my pleasure to answer any questions you have. But I'm very tired and hungry. I'd like to settle in just for one night. I promise you can interrogate me all you want tomorrow."

Darius frowned. "I need answers," he insisted.

Young sighed and pinched the bridge of his nose. "To what?"

"Well, first of all, how did you get a sleeper ship? Or the people to run one? And how could you even hide…"

Young cut him off, albeit politely. "That's a longer story than I can tell you tonight. Again, I promise that I will explain it all. Tomorrow."

Darius furrowed his brow, but kept his frustration in check. He dismissed Young, watching as he returned to his people. As they waited in line for Sergeant Josephson and her team to distribute food from the ship's stores, Young was smiling and hugging his friends, laughing at some conversation that was beyond Darius's ears.

*Perhaps a change of scenery will give these people the respite they've needed for so long. They could have fought us, but didn't.* Darius sighed as he wandered off in search of his horse. *Maybe I'm the one overreacting here.*

. . .

Gabrielle Serrano
7 July, 6 yal, early morning
Mainland coast, far from Camp Eight
>|

*Now we really can't go back.*

Gabi's heart sank at the sight before her eyes. Will's jaw clenched so tightly that she could hear his teeth grind, and Kristin let out a soft gasp before covering her mouth. The only other sound was that of waves lapping against the hull of their ship. Or, at least, what was left of it.

Between the cold and the wind, Gabi had a fitful night of sleep. But at least she could claim she survived her first storm on the mainland. Waves and wind must have risen up sometime in the night, dashing the fragile boat onto the rocks over and over. The nose of one of the outriggers bobbed in the middle of the cove, barely visible over the waves. Two large chunks of the mast floated nearby, tangled in the punctured green sail. Chunks of debris and waterlogged sacks of supplies dotted the gravel shore. Beyond that, nothing remained of the makeshift vessel that had carried them so far.

"Damn it," Will cursed. "We should have kept working. We should have dragged every last bit up to camp."

"Should we go take a look?" Kris asked.

He shook his head. "No, there's not going to be anything left that we can use."

Gabi turned in disgust and headed back to camp. The Vandemarks followed close behind her. The small clearing they had made was bustling with activity. Diego was busy helping Karina and Aidan take down the makeshift shelter. Gina was feeding Daphne her breakfast, as the youngest member of the crew was the last to wake up. Caleb and Marya were busy sorting supplies into stacks, based on each person's strength.

It didn't take Gabi long to figure out that, despite Will's protests to the contrary, they had already salvaged more from the ship than they could possibly carry. Not surprisingly, the two rifles and two pistols that Will had squirreled away for so long were among the supplies that he had taken the time to recover. It was then that Gabi realized that was why the older survivors were so quiet; they shared the same uneasiness in the presence of these weapons.

After the plague massacre four years earlier, most guns had been ordered destroyed. Only the chief and a few subordinates were allowed to have them. Over time, every single one of those weapons had ceased to function. Guns were thought to be extinct in the village, and bows were the tool of choice for hunting. No one knew that Will had stashed a few away inside a crashed cargo pod not too far from the village until he loaded them onto the ship just before they left. Even that act left Gabi with a question that she couldn't hold back.

She sought him out and pulled him aside for the second, then whispered, "Do the other crews have guns?"

His eyes darted around for a second, making sure they were clear of prying ears. "Of course they do. For the same reasons we have them."

"How did you get Daniel to take them? You know he hated…"

"I didn't give him a choice," he cut her off. "We can't afford choice. Not now. Not until we join up with the other colony."

"*If* there's another colony."

"Again, we have no choice. If we stayed home, we would have died. If there's no other colony, we'll probably die. But assuming the other ships made it, there should be a city. A big one, compared to Camp Eight."

Gabi scoffed. "I'll believe it when I see it."

"I'm sure you will."

They gathered their assigned supplies; Gabi double checked her arrows and tomahawk out of habit. Will looked at what was left and shook his head.

"Leave half of the shelter panels behind," he ordered. "We need these extra water skins."

"How can we build a tent with only half the panels?" Marya protested.

"Leave them," he repeated as he unrolled his map.

Marya grumbled as she executed his order. Gabi felt a tiny glimmer of satisfaction with the exchange. She knew from experience that there were other ways to create shelter, and that Will was right. There was no point in rubbing it in, though. Further conflict would only serve to anger Will, who was already on edge. And now armed with a gun.

Gabi helped Diego don his tiny backpack. He complained for a moment about its weight, which earned him a grumbled rebuke from his half-sister. The others were ready, and Will finished with his study of the map.

"We're on the wrong side of the mountains. We need to go inland. Head south or southeast." He looked in that direction, though only the thick forest canopy could be seen. "There should be some fairly high mountains over there. Once we cross it, we should be able to find a creek and follow it."

"A creek?" Caleb blurted. "Care to be a little more specific?"

"Don't need to be. At least not yet. If what I'm seeing is correct, most of the streams in the area about fifty or sixty miles southeast all converge into that river that we need to find. We just need to get over the divide and follow one of them."

"Oh, is that all?"

Will smirked. "Why, were you hoping for something a little harder?"

"Than blindly stumbling through the woods, praying we find the right stream?"

"There are dozens of correct streams. Just need to find one."

"Seriously, Will. How is this any better than…"

"I didn't ask for your opinion, Caleb. You want to march along the sea? Go ahead. You'll be doing it alone, without the map." Will scowled at each survivor for just a moment, then growled, "Let's move."

*And you thought he'd give you a choice, Caleb. How stupid.*

. . .

Darius stretched slowly and rubbed his back. He ached from spending so much time in the saddle over the past couple of days. Sergeant Josephson took the reins of the mare and walked her off.

The atmosphere around the sleeper ship was much different than the previous night. Though half of the CVM stayed behind on guard duty, the refugees from the ship were far more active today. They wandered around outside the ship, eating and conversing with each other. Darius glanced at his watch, which reminded him of the fact that it was lunch time. Sun filtered through high clouds, creating a patchwork of shadow and light across the plain. The scene was reminiscent of the day after *Gabriel* landed, though more relaxed.

*Maybe it's because their leader isn't a power hungry nutjob.*

He strolled casually toward the load ramp at the front of the ship. He was met there by Harcourt Young, who smiled broadly and welcomed him onto the ship.

"Governor Owens," he said, offering a firm handshake. "Welcome back. I'd like to thank you for the protection you have offered so far."

*It's as much for me as it is for you.*

"You're welcome."

Darius took keen note of the ship's construction as he boarded. The lower level was much like *Gabriel's*, and he was somewhat surprised to find that the cargo pods did indeed have access to the interior of the ship. The grand stairwell leading to the upper deck was much smaller. There were other small differences here and there. But most everything, down to the details of the deck plating and structural braces, was almost identical to the Project Columbus ships.

Young led them to the bridge, where lunch was delivered to them in the form of ration bags. Darius took the food out of courtesy, despite its unappealing nature. He took a seat at one of the two side-by-side terminals, with Young sitting at the other.

"So I owe you some answers, Governor," Young started.

"That would be correct."

"I'm guessing the first is how I got *Mercy*."

"That would be a good start."

Young set his food aside and folded his hands in his lap. "Project Columbus wasn't always a secret. It was somewhat obscure, and it was looked down on by my fellow investors as being foolish. I didn't quite share their feelings. Maybe part of it was that I was young and optimistic at the time, or maybe it was that I saw something in the project that no one else saw."

Young had a slight grin on his face, like he was proud of that fact. It was meaningless to Darius, who just stared blankly back. The smirk disappeared from the investor's face, and he continued his story.

"Over the years I've been part of hundreds of companies in dozens of industries. From agriculture to computers, communications, even construction. Some of these companies were contracted to create individual components of the Columbus sleepers. Since the late nineties, I've had access to bits and pieces of the ships."

"Which you shouldn't have," Darius remarked. "The parts themselves were to be available exclusively to the Project, no one else."

"A technicality." Young waved dismissively. "It shouldn't really surprise you that someone could buy the parts, or at least the design. Every man has his price."

"That still doesn't explain this ship."

"If I need to satisfy your impatience, fine. *Mercy* was constructed by a company I owned. At my direction." He leaned back as Darius blinked incredulously at him. "Oh, don't be so surprised. You already knew that I could get parts of the ship. What makes you think I couldn't just build my own?"

"Because no one was building another ship!"

"That you were aware of," Young corrected. "We started building her spaceframe around 2002. Of course, when I filed her registration paperwork and build plans, I may have… inadvertently… filed the plans for a deep sea research vessel instead. My bad, but at the time it was necessary. The government was not as receptive at the time to the idea of privatized space ventures as they were at the end."

"So why not just announce your plans when the winds changed?"

"For the same reason that the government didn't unseal their Project Columbus records. *Mercy* was far too valuable, and would have been a target for every kind of espionage you could think possible. As a non-militarized submarine, she was forgettable. But Project Columbus still played a role as a decoy. Every government in the world was interested in getting their hands on those ships. The Chinese were the only ones to make a move."

"I see. And how did you get around the issue of systems that were developed and built in-house at Laramie? Like the biostasis systems?"

"Like I said, Governor, every man has his price. It was just a matter of finding out where the crack in the Project's armor was, and who to bribe."

Darius felt his contempt rise. He couldn't blame Young for wanting that technology. After all, it saved his life and those of a few hundred others as well. But he was right that someone inside the Project would have to betray them in order for Young to get his hands on those secrets. Darius wanted to know who; this threat from within might still need to be dealt with.

"It's true. No man is an angel, Mr. Young. You're in possession of technology that you shouldn't have. I have every right to seize it and have you tried. That doesn't interest me so much right now. It might sow discontent in your people, and cause all kinds of trouble that neither you nor I can predict. On the other hand, if you told me who you bought off, you would be helping to gain my trust. That can do nothing but good. For you and your people."

Young took a sip of coffee from his rations, nodding as he swallowed it. "If we had been on Earth I might have done something to protect my contact. I'm exposed out here. All I have left is my people, and whatever mercy and acceptance you can give us." He sighed, as if finally lifting a heavy weight from his chest. "It's Doctor Benedict."

Darius's jaw nearly hit the floor.

*No. No, that can't be.*

"You're lying to me."

"I have no reason to…"

"Yes, you do," Darius snapped. "You're a very intelligent and creative man. That drove your success on Earth. So why would you out your mole in our midst when you can just as easily blame a dead man?"

Young's eyes widened. "D-David… is dead?"

"Of course he's dead. He died back on Earth. Blew himself up with a dirty bomb, trying to stop the Chinese from killing us all."

"The Laramie Incident?"

Darius sighed and slumped back into his chair. "More than likely. That was the day we left Earth. We don't know anything that happened after that day."

"Summer of 2014," Young said softly, his gaze drifting out into the distance. "There was a nuclear attack in Laramie. For a while we assumed that it was the Chinese that did it. That they were pissed because they failed to take the sleeper ships. Then rumor spread that it was actually an American who detonated the device. I couldn't believe it at first." His attention came back to Darius. "And you said that Doctor Benedict was the one who set it off?"

Darius nodded. "To give us time to escape. And to keep the Chinese from taking the plans for the sleeper ships. For all the good it did, since you seem to have the ability to make them yourself."

"I only made the one. Though I can't say that there won't be other ships. Even smaller ones."

A chill ran down Darius's spine. "More ships? How could there be more?"

"Because I gave people a chance at life," Young calmly replied. "Anyone with enough technical ability and material can build a single-pod ship and fly it here, as long as they've got a halfway decent computer." He must have sensed that Darius was at a loss for words, so he continued. "I couldn't just leave people to die. You don't know what it was like after the governments fell. To say it was hell would be an understatement."

"And you let these plans fall into the hands of our enemies."

"We had no more enemies in the end. Even the Chinese social structure broke down. Many of their troops were killed by insurgencies before they could go home to try to stabilize their own country." He laughed nervously. "Besides, it would take nothing short of a miracle for someone to use the sleeper plans I sent out to take over your colony."

"And why's that?" Darius growled without hesitation.

"Because they're designed to hold a maximum of forty people. One of your ESAARC pods with a self-guiding computer and a tiny reactor. That's it. No cargo. No emergency contingency. If something goes wrong with any one of the systems, it's a dead hulk drifting in space. If the guidance computer is just a little off on approach, the pod will burn up or skip off the atmosphere."

"I still can't believe you'd do such a thing without vetting those who would benefit from the technology."

"I didn't really want to, Governor. But I had an obligation I had to meet. It was part of the price I had to pay for the technology to begin with."

*What?*

"That's right, Governor. Doctor Benedict wasn't interested in money, cars, or fame. He was interested in the salvation of humanity. The design was his. I was to distribute it freely if the world was coming to an end. I didn't want to at first. Believe me, I'm with you. This technology shouldn't be freely available. But then the world went to hell, and I saw just what people were going through. So I honored my contract with David."

"And what was the rest of the price?"

"Newer computer equipment. Most of the computers on your ships were built by one of my holdings and delivered two years before launch."

Darius sat silent for several minutes, digesting the information. The man who he considered a hero seemed to have a dark side, if Young could be believed. The intent may have been pure, but his methods were questionable at best.

"Have I answered your questions, Governor?"

"All but one. What are you planning to do now that you're here?"

Young's wry smirk returned. "To live. We can establish ourselves here if we have to, but we'd like to become part of your colony. Will you take us in, Governor?"

Darius rose and paced back and forth a couple times on the bridge.

"I can't say I'm pleased to hear anything that you've told me today, but that shouldn't weigh on your people. You may do either or both. Those who wish to stay on *Mercy* and create their own town may do so. Anyone who wants to come live in Concordia may do so. I will have temporary quarters prepared on *Michael* for anyone who wishes."

"Thank you, Governor. We appreciate your help."

Darius's brows arched in concern. "I'm not sure how much actual help we will be able to give. We were hit by an earthquake less than a month ago. I can't guarantee that anyone who comes to town won't be pressed into labor right away."

Young nodded in acknowledgement. "We're ready to do our part."

"That is appreciated."

*Though I hope you know what you're getting into.*

• • •

*Unbelievable,* Cal thought as he placed another crate of laundry soap in the back of the wagon.

Even as shocking as it was, Cal knew that the ship that had flown over was another sleeper ship. But the news that Hunter had brought was what blew his mind. The ship wasn't built by a government. It was built by a billionaire, and full of refugees from Earth. People who had been left behind to fend for themselves during the later stages of the War.

"Whole families," Hunter said as he slid the last crate into place. "Can you imagine? Some guy just plucking you out of darkness, shoving you on a ship, and sending you off to a new life away from the War."

"It's not that far-fetched, Hunter. Well, at least not to me."

"Right. I forgot about that."

"Still, it *is* pretty incredible."

"Have you met any of them yet?"

Cal shook his head. "I've been too busy working and taking care of Andrea."

"Well, I'm sure that you'll get the chance sooner or later. Really nice people, the whole lot of them. Did you hear that Darius gave them the choice of building up around their own ship or coming to live in Concordia?"

"No, I hadn't. Have they chosen?"

"It's split. About half of them want to come live with us, the other half in their own community. There's good farming land out there, and not too far from town. I think that'll work out for everyone in the end." Hunter closed the tailgate on the wagon and locked its retainer pin in place. "Well, I've got to go. Saika's waiting for this. Her shop has been busier than normal this morning. New faces in town, you know?"

"I know. Oh hey, that reminds me. Any word on when Devereaux is going to send over his contract?"

"He just got back from Militia assignment, and he's got a few days' work to catch up on. I wouldn't expect anything for a week at this point."

*Another week of doing three jobs.* Cal sighed. *Guess I have no choice.*

"Alright. Well, give my thanks to Saika."

Cal waved at his friend as the wagon pulled away. Returning to his shop, Cal took a moment to sweep the floor of his shop and straighten his displays. He could hear Andrea begin to squeal sleepily upstairs, so he prepared a bottle of formula. By the time it was ready she was fully awake and crying. He brought her back down and sat in his usual chair to feed her. She quickly ate her fill and settled in, cooing in contentment. Cal got up and did a quick mental inventory of his products while he rocked her in his arm. He had barely finished that task when three people walked through the door, and his heart nearly stopped.

The two men were complete strangers. One was a hair taller than Cal, with a chiseled face and sculpted muscles threatening to burst out of his tightly woven shirt. The other was a good head shorter. His receding hair was cropped close and spiked, and a pair of thin-rimmed glasses rested on his nose.

But the blonde woman who accompanied them was familiar. Her eyes were slightly sunken, her cheeks were gaunt, and she had a jagged scar across her eyebrow. Laugh lines were beginning to form at the corners of her eyes. She had not aged nearly as gracefully as Cal. And if the rumors of post-launch Earth were true, it was no wonder why. Yet the woman who stared back at him, mouth agape, looked so much like the girl he had known all those years ago.

"B-Brittany?" he stammered, almost losing his grip on Andrea.

"Cal?" Her eyes widened and her lips curled into a smile. She gently threw her arms around him in a friendly embrace. "Oh my God, Cal. You're here!" She looked down at Andrea. "And you have a kid? Wow, what happened to you?"

"I ah… it's a long story. But I guess you know that. Yours is probably just as long."

She stepped back and looked down at the floor for a moment, then nodded.

"So, you two know each other?" the taller of her companions asked, saving them from an awkward silence.

"Yeah. We went to high school together. Hung out a lot, ran with the same friends. You know how it goes," Cal replied.

*I fell in love with her, she stabbed me in the back. You know how it goes.*

"Nice for you to get to see an old friend, huh Britt?" the man asked boisterously.

"Yeah." Her response was oddly terse.

"So what brings the three of you in to my shop today?"

"This is your place?" she asked.

"Yes ma'am. I sell only the finest soaps and hooch north of the Fairweather."

"Soaps and hooch?" the man asked. "What the hell kind of combination is that?"

"One of luck and necessity."

Brittany's friends looked at each other in confusion for a moment. "Well, we heard that you had booze. Think you could hook us up? It's been a really long trip."

"Of course." Cal walked to the display shelf adjacent to the counter and inspected the labels. He grabbed a bottle of whiskey and pulled it from the rack. "Unless you've got whiskey stashed away in that ship of yours, this is going to be the finest you'll find around here. Maybe not as refined as some of the stuff you could get back home, but it'll get the job done. Plus it's even drinkable."

"Whiskey, huh?" The newfound customer took the bottle and inspected it closely. "Why's it in a green bottle? Is it Irish?"

"That's the only color of bottle that was available at the time. No, this is a Kentucky-style bourbon. Barley and wheat sour mash. Aged three years in charred Demeter blue elm." Cal received a glossy eyed stare in return. "It's the closest thing we've got to white oak."

The man nodded. "We'll take it. What else have you got?"

Cal smiled politely. "Of course. I hate to ask, but do you have any money?"

Furrowed brows answered him. "Money? We just stepped off our boat after forty years asleep and you're asking about money?"

"Relax. I just had to ask. We have a system around here. No coins, no paper. We trade in goods and favors."

"Favors?" Brittany asked, a hint of apprehension in her voice.

"For future goods or services," Cal explained. "For instance, say you buy ten favors worth of whiskey from me, and don't have anything for me up front. I can ask you to give me that same amount in other goods. Let's pretend you hunt. I could cash it in for game that you killed."

"But we don't have anything," the shorter of her companions protested.

"Yet," Cal corrected. "It's not a big deal." He glanced at Brittany and nodded slightly. "Listen, I'll give you a discount on the bottle, and one of vodka. Six favors for the two. You've had a long trip, and I'm sure you want to unwind a little before you tackle your new lives."

"Hey, thanks, man," the taller man smirked as he took the second bottle from Cal. "Just let us know how we can repay you in the future."

The men headed for the door, though Brittany stayed behind.

"You coming with us, Britt?"

She startled a bit, as if she was coming out of a daydream. "You guys go ahead. I'm going to catch up with Cal for a little bit."

As soon as they were out of sight, she walked up to him again and hugged him. This time she lingered longer, long enough to upset Andrea and set her off. When she pulled away, a single tear rolled down her cheek.

"God, Cal."

"Shh," he soothed, as much for her as for Andrea.

"I thought you were dead."

"I can't say I haven't thought the same," he admitted. "I thought about you all the way here. I've thought about you since then. I wondered what happened to you. Whether you made it or were killed in the War. It's been almost fifty years."

She choked on her tears as she tried to laugh. "And you look pretty damn good for such an old fart."

"You don't look a day over twenty," he laughed nervously.

Brittany dried her eyes on her sleeve and took a deep breath. "And here you are. Alive, holding a baby." She leaned over for a closer look. "She's very pretty."

"Like her mom," Cal added, trying to mask that her compliment pained him very much.

"What's her name?"

"Andrea."

Brittany looked up at Cal. She bit her lip and nodded knowingly. Of all the people on Demeter, she was one of only a handful that would know that Andrea was named after Cal's father. She wouldn't need an explanation.

"How old is she?"

"Three weeks."

Brittany grinned wide. "Wow, look at you, stud. Taking care of such a tiny girl and not freaking out. You hiding any other kids back there?"

Cal felt his heart sink. The realization that Andrea was his only link to Lexi began to creep in. He wanted to run away, to curse himself for not having more children with her. "No," he mumbled.

"Well, where's mom? Can I meet her?"

"No," he turned away, holding Andrea even tighter.

"Well that's just rude. I thought we were friends."

"She's dead, Britt," Cal snapped. "You can't meet her because she's dead."

Silence engulfed the room. Cal walked around the counter and plunked down into his chair. Brittany was aghast, her color drained. Her mouth trembled as if she were stuttering words that wouldn't come out.

"I'm sorry," he sighed. "You didn't know. It's just that…"

"It's too recent," she finished his sentence. "Childbirth?"

"Not exactly. Lexi was badly hurt in an earthquake. Falling debris, I'm told. She didn't make it." Cal shifted slightly, prompting Andrea to burrow into him for warmth. "It was all that Doc could do to save Andrea. I wasn't there for it, either. I almost died that same day."

"I'm so sorry." She stepped forward but Cal waved her off.

"Thank you. Just making it happen one day at a time now."

"Bad luck all around, huh?"

"It comes and goes. But you said it before, alive and holding a baby. I can't ask for much more."

"Yes you can. You deserve more."

Cal sighed and stretched slightly. "No, I've seen what happens when I try to get more. No need to force it."

Brittany smiled softly. She couldn't figure out what to do with her arms, so she folded them in front of her. In that moment she didn't look like the brash girl he knew. Instead she was so much more vulnerable.

"Well, I guess I'll see you around then?" she asked.

Cal nodded. Brittany took her leave, glancing over her shoulder one more time as she walked through the door.

*Bad luck all around indeed,* he sighed.

. . .

*It just doesn't make sense,* Darius thought.

He slowly rubbed at his temples as he hunched over a portable metal table. He had been sitting this way so long that his back finally hurt more than his head, though that was the least of his concerns.

The presence of *Mercy* and her survivors still had his head spinning. But the idea that Dr. Benedict had betrayed the Project and sold its secrets was something that he still couldn't fathom. Darius could understand the sentiment behind such an action, if Young was indeed telling the truth. But it didn't seem right that Benedict would then stay behind to destroy the plans for the Project Columbus sleepers if he had already leaked the technology. Or another ship design.

*If Young was telling the truth,* he reminded himself.

So much hinged on that little detail. But there was little evidence to either support or refute the investor's story. There were only a couple people in the colony close enough to Dr. Benedict who might be able to shed light on the situation. Unfortunately, Deputy Governor Dayton was just as shocked and clueless as Darius. Other high-ranking crew members from the ships knew nothing, or accused Young of lying, but couldn't debunk his tale with any solid facts. Worse, Dan Forrest, one of the original Project Columbus conspirators, put forth the notion that Dr. Benedict could have sold their secrets. Though he didn't know one way or another, he pointed to the fact that Benedict was the leader of the original plan to steal the ships.

Darius needed answers. He was running out of options for getting those answers. The prospect of a stream of small sleeper ships dropping onto Demeter left him very uneasy. Even forty people, if desperate and armed, could inflict serious damage on Concordia. And Young's assurance that they couldn't be used by an organized invasion force was not as comforting as the investor probably hoped. Any nuclear power on Earth would probably have the capability of making fleets of them. Darius estimated that fewer than a half dozen, properly organized, would be required to take over the colony.

Roger cleared his throat. Darius looked up at him; he stood at the top of the bridge stairs, politely waiting for the governor's attention.

"Pardon me, Governor, but he's here."

"You don't have to…" Darius caught himself about to tell Roger not to use his title. He sighed, as the effort was always futile. "Send him in."

As Roger went to retrieve the visitor, Darius slid his chair closer and stretched out. His back popped a couple times, which was both painful and oddly relieving. He folded his hands on the table just as Dr. Kimura ambled onto the bridge. Darius motioned for him to sit down. Dr. Kimura complied, though over the years he had lost the spring in his step, and his posture had become slightly hunched.

"You wanted to speak with me, Darius?" the elder man asked.

"Yes, Doctor. I've got a lot to sort out here, and I wanted your help."

"Is this about the other ship? What did they call it, *Mercy*?"

"It is."

The doctor nodded as he sighed. "I'm not sure how much I will be able to tell you."

"Maybe more than you think. Tell me, does the name Harcourt Young mean anything to you?"

Kimura shook his head. "Should it mean something to me?"

"Maybe. Think back, Doc. I need to know if you ever heard Doctor Benedict talk about him. Whether it was to you directly or something you overheard."

"David? No, he never mentioned anything."

Darius pursed his lips and leaned back slightly. "What about problems with equipment? Perhaps a couple years before launch?"

"I remember him complaining about the navigation computers and data servers being too old and slow. He said they could cause problems when we approached the planet, and wanted to get them replaced."

"Tell me more," Darius pressed.

*This might be the key.*

"I don't know what to say. He complained about it for two or three years. He was having problems getting funding from Congress. But eventually he got the funding to replace them, two years before launch."

"Where did he get the funding?"

Dr. Kimura hesitated in a moment of confusion. "Congress," he insisted.

"Are you sure?"

"Yes. We got appropriations directly from them."

"So it suddenly changed? I bet Dr. Benedict was pleased with that."

The scientist was lost in a moment of thought. "Now that you mention it, he kind of glossed over the details. In hindsight, it seemed a bit suspicious."

*Could it be?*

"Was there anything else odd that happened around that time? Something that you can't explain when you look back?"

"There was something that I couldn't even explain at the time, Darius. Two months before David got his new computers." Kimura closed his eyes as he recalled. "Colonel Fox had me detained for a while because of an access breach on one of my workstations. I had no idea what she was on about. She claimed that I had downloaded specifications for the biostasis systems from the workstation to a flash drive." His eyes snapped open, and for the first time, Darius saw Kimura seethe with frustration. "I've never owned a flash drive in my life, Darius. And what would I need to do with the specifications of my own invention? All of that is stored in my mind. I don't need to consult a computer to recall it."

*Biostasis specifications. Shit, Young might have been right.*

"So what happened?" Darius asked. "And why didn't I know about this?"

"I was cleared after an investigation. David swept the whole incident under the rug. He felt it would be detrimental to the Project if it was perceived that one of the lead researchers might be trying to steal from the Project."

*Ironic, since you planned to steal everything with his help.*

"Who conducted the investigation?"

"Lieutenant Shipp."

*There's the cleaning crew. Someone under Benedict's sway.* A dark thought wormed its way into the tangled thread that he was already dealing with. *Shipp was assassinated. Were these two conspiracies connected? Benedict and Shipp played a part in both.*

"Darius, I have to ask," Kimura interrupted his thoughts. "Is there a reason for these questions? This all happened so long ago, and David is dead now."

Darius leveled his gaze squarely at his friend. "What if Doctor Benedict was playing more than one game? We know about the conspiracy to steal the ships. But what if he was involved in more?"

"I would say that is not possible. David only did what he did for the preservation of mankind."

*The preservation of mankind. Giving everyone the best chance they could.*

"Stacking the deck," Darius blurted. Kimura's eyebrows arched. "Stacking the deck, that's what you told me when we left Earth. We had to stack the deck to give ourselves the best odds of survival."

"Yes, it's what David said when he convinced me to help him steal the ships."

"What if he found a way to stack the deck even more? Give more people the chance to survive if the worst should happen?"

"That sounds like something that he would do if he could."

"He just might have, Doc. I've been inside that ship. The stasis pods are exact replicas of ours, right down to the latches. Your sleeper pods. No modifications that I could see." Darius rose and looked to the northeast, at the landscape beyond. "And the man who brought that ship here claims that he purchased the design from Doctor Benedict."

"That's insane, Darius," Kimura protested. "He wouldn't have sold the design. He stayed back to *destroy* all project data, including the designs."

"Designs he saw as a threat to the security of Concordia, right?"

"Of course they were a threat. If so much as one ship was built by…"

"I know, Doc. But what if there was a ship design that didn't pose a threat, at least individually, to the colony? A ship that could only carry forty people and almost no support cargo? Something that was designed to seek out and join an existing colony?"

"We had only two ship designs. The XCS and the XCS-R. We didn't design small ships because they wouldn't be sustainable on their own."

"Exactly. On their own. But what if, Doc? What if he designed another ship?"

"No," Kimura growled. "Darius, I don't know what's gotten into you, but you seem to be losing your grip on reality. Perhaps it is the stress of all of the recent events. You should consider letting Deputy Governor Dayton take over for a while."

Darius turned around and leaned over the table, putting his weight on his arched fingertips. "Doc, we've been friends a long time. Have I ever lied to you?"

"No," he admitted.

"And I'm not about to start."

"But you weren't there, Darius. All you can do is speculate."

Darius nodded and stood up. "You're right, it's speculation. But I've got some pretty good evidence now. Thank you, Doctor. You're excused."

Dr. Kimura took his leave, exiting the bridge as slowly as he entered. Darius walked to the forward bridge railing after he left, casting his eyes into the bright blue sky.

*Young was right, then. And Doctor K had no clue.* He sighed and tightened his grip on the railing. *What are we in store for if someone actually manages to build these escape ships?*

. . .

Gabrielle Serrano
11 July, 6 yal, shortly before dusk
About 25 miles inland, southeast of wreck site
>|

"We should get back soon," she whispered to Will.

"Just a little longer," he hissed back, his eyes squinting at something upslope.

The mainland continent posed strange new challenges for hunting. While creatures were out and about throughout the day, the transition that occurred around sundown seemed to be the busiest. Possibly owing to the short days on Demeter, there seemed to be a significant overlap between the diurnal and nocturnal creatures. There even seemed to be at least one creature that was always active: a strange hawk that glowed in flight during the night, yet still hunted during the daytime.

Prey of all sorts could be found in abundance. They had not lacked for fresh meat since coming ashore, though a couple times they had eaten solely from their supplies in order to make better time.

Gabi peeked over the rock that she knelt behind, trying to catch a glimpse of what Will was stalking. There was not much she could see through the dozens of branches that obscured her view. She sighed, resigning herself to wait for just a few more minutes.

*Better kill it quick, Will.*

She rolled over and tried to get comfortable. She tried to ignore the swaying tree tops above and instead concentrated on the sky. Fir trees were still an alien concept. In darkness they looked like towering giants, ready to snatch and swallow her with a hundred gnarled arms. It would be dark soon, and her insecurities would soon grip her again. The trees couldn't hurt her, she knew, but the vision of giants still lurked in her dreams. Her sleep was fitful, and she wasn't the only one.

Diego cried out in his sleep sometimes, and when he woke up he always sought comfort next to her. The first time he curled up next to her, she wanted nothing more than to shove him away. But she allowed him to share the space, and her own dreams that night were less intense. They shared some common bond, one that she never had fathomed possible. And while it served them both to take the edge off of their nightmares, Gabi hated herself for it. It felt like she was losing her grip on just what Diego did to their mother, and the pain of that betrayal gnawed at her as they marched. The crew barely conversed anymore. Hunting was the only distraction she had left.

She glanced over at Will. His focus had changed from the distance to something nearby. He slowly unslung the rifle from his shoulder and leaned it against the trunk of a felled spruce tree. Whatever he was tracking must have been small, as he then readied his bow and straightened his back. He raised the weapon high, and Gabi caught sight of his prey an instant before his bowstring let out a muffled twang. The small bird took the arrow through its chest and wing, toppling out of the tree and landing in a bush about twenty feet away. Will wandered away, returning a minute later with his prize in one hand and the bloodied arrow in the other.

"That should do it," he smirked triumphantly.

Gabi opened the mouth of the woven bag. He stuffed the bird inside, adding it to the three others that they caught earlier. She then cinched the bag and slung it over her shoulder as Will went about collecting his gear.

They were soon on their way. Will began to prattle on about the success of their hunt, but Gabi's attention was elsewhere. Dusk was upon them, and her anxiety started to edge in again. The forest floor was enshrouded by the shadows of towering ridges on either side. The bushes that carpeted the ground were potential hiding spots for predators. Though she hadn't seen any yet since landing, Gabi couldn't help but remember the jungle jaguars on Raphael Island.

*The sooner we get back to the camp and the fire…*

Her thought was interrupted by a loud boom that pierced the air. Her heart stopped for a moment. It took her second to realize what the noise was. She had heard it before, years earlier. Will had no such hesitation; by the time Gabi realized that one of the rifles had been fired, he was already twenty feet in front of her, tearing his own rifle from his back. His arms and legs seemed to work in fluid independence. He racked a round in the chamber even as he flew over the uneven ground. Gabi sprinted after him, casting aside the game bag after only a few steps. She fell even farther behind as her fingers struggled to find an arrow in her quiver.

More shots rang out from camp. Gabi finally got hold of an arrow, which she immediately clenched in the same hand as her bow's grip. With the distraction aside, she pumped her legs furiously. Smoke from the campfire curled in this wisps below the high branches ahead of her. Screams drowned out the sounds of her panting. Diego and Daphne's shrill shrieks could be made out, as well as the fierce growl of a large animal. Her heart beat furiously in her chest, and her stomach tied in a knot. Gabi had just a couple seconds to steel herself for whatever awaited beyond the brush line. Her nerves were nearly shattered as

Will's rifle belched out two shots just before she burst through.

The sight stopped Gabi dead in her tracks. A massive, snarling creature was reared up on its hind legs, blood and entrails dripping from its mouth. Wounds in its chest weeped, though it didn't seem to be slowed by the damage. If anything, it was enraged. It swept its massive paw low to the ground, casting aside Gina's shredded, lifeless body. The corpse skidded to a stop at Gabi's feet, splashing gore on her boots. In an instant Gabi felt dizzy, and her stomach threatened to turn. Even the chaotic sounds that surrounded her seemed to fade.

Another two shots from Will's rifle brought her attention back to the rampaging animal. It dropped low and aimed its body directly at Will, ready to charge. Gabi quickly let loose an arrow. It found its mark in the side of the animal's chest, but it didn't sink in as deep as with other prey. Her eyes widened and she gasped. Her weapon was useless against the great beast. The wound didn't even seem to register; she wouldn't be able to distract it.

Emitting a deep growl, the beast lunged at Will. He darted out of the way, just barely ahead of the eight-inch claws. On the far side of the camp, no longer obstructed by the animal's solid body, Gabi could see the rest of the survivors. Caleb was bleeding from a gash in his leg. Even at a distance, Gabi could see that his skin was ghost white, and he was having trouble focusing his eyes. Karina had a grip under his shoulders, and was trying desperately to drag him to cover. Diego and Daphne's heads were peeking up over a felled log, and they were still shrieking in terror. Aidan hopped over the same log, ducking next to the small children, while Marya scrambled to retrieve Caleb's rifle. Kristin covered their escape, her trembling hand pointing a pistol at the creature's haunches.

"Shoot it, Kris!" Will bellowed, narrowly dodging another swipe from the animal. He couldn't bring his gun to bear. It was all he could do to dance away from the wall of claws and fur that was trying to eviscerate him.

Gabi loosed another arrow, but this time her shot deflected harmlessly off of the beast's shoulder. Out of the corner of her eye she caught movement.

"Get out of here," Marya ordered as she circled to Gabi's side. "You're not going hurt it with that thing."

"But Will's…" she protested, but was cut off.

"I've got Will. Get the kids. Go!"

Gabi broke into a run straight across the campsite. The beast growled, and for a moment she could feel its breath on her skin, its gaze piercing her soul. She put her head down and closed her eyes. Another shot rang out, this time from behind her, from Marya's position. In an instant the sensation of the animal's breath was gone, and it bellowed out in pain. Gabi's eyes snapped open again three strides from the log, and she vaulted over it in one swift motion.

"Aidan, get them out of here!" she snapped at the younger Brennan.

He nodded wordlessly and scooped up Daphne, then grabbed Diego's hand and started dragging him away. Kristin still stood a few feet away, screaming Will's name over and over, her weapon still trembling. Gabi dropped her bow and quickly wrested the Beretta from her, then spun around. Marya had circled back a few steps. She fired again, but missed completely. The beast swiped its paw, and Will was flung aside like he was nothing.

"Will!" she shouted.

Gabi aimed and squeezed off a single round. She was taken by surprise by how the weapon kicked her arm back, and the blast made her ears ring. But her shot hit the mark, tearing into the animal's knee. It howled and wobbled for a second before regaining its footing. But that brief interruption of its rampage was enough. Marya trained the sights of her rifle on the beast's head and delivered the fatal shot. It collapsed instantly, without another noise.

Gabi slowly crept forward, pistol trained on the creature the whole time. It was probably close to fifteen feet long, and had a body very reminiscent of the bears she used to love watching at the zoo back on Earth. Marya joined at her side, and they circled around to where Will had fallen. He was dazed, but otherwise apparently unharmed. He collected his weapon and approached the beast cautiously. The barrel of his rifle dipped, and he stopped cold when he saw Gina's body.

An unearthly curse rose from his chest, and he marched purposefully forward, punching round after round from the rifle into the felled bear's skull until the rifle's mechanisms just clicked uselessly from the absence of ammunition. He then raised the stock to bash in what was left of its head, but stopped. His grip loosened, and the gun clattered to the ground. Will sunk to his knees and tore at his hair with his bare hands. Gabi approached slowly, and her heart sank and her lips trembled as she heard his anguished sobbing.

She knelt next to him, setting the Beretta down in the dirt. She hesitated a moment before throwing her arms around him from behind, trying in futility to keep her own sorrow in check.

"Will," she choked.

"It's not fair," he sobbed. "We… we were supposed to have a life together. It's not fair."

Gabi swallowed back her tears. Nothing about Demeter was fair. No one's death had ever been fair, except for those executed by James for bringing plague and death to Camp Eight. Her mother's death hadn't been fair. Diego's existence hadn't been fair. But it had all happened. Gabi knew that leading the last band of survivors taxed every nerve in Will's body, and he had already experienced his fair share of death and sorrow.

*This isn't fair. To any of us.*

"I know," she soothed.

"I loved her. I loved her and we…" he trailed off for a moment. "We were going to start a little farm together, you know? When we got there."

*If we got there,* Gabi corrected mentally, though she made sure not to express her doubts verbally.

"And Daphne," he added. "She was going to help take care of the chickens." Will lost what thin control he had left. He tried to suck in air as he cried for his lost love. His cheeks turned red, and he leaned his great weight on Gabi's shoulder, almost knocking her over. She cradled his head and stroked his hair for a long time. She couldn't find the words to soothe him. She didn't see the point; words had failed to help her so many times in the past.

It was after dark before Will cried himself to sleep. The others had come back to the camp, rekindled the fire, prepared their shelter, and dragged Gina's body out of sight. All of the others, except Karina, that is. When Gabi was finally able to shake herself from Will, she was pulled aside by Marya. Her rival's face did not bear the usual scorn or arrogance that Gabi was used to seeing. Instead, her head hung low, as if looking Gabi in the eyes was a terrible sin.

"Caleb didn't make it," Marya whispered. "He bled out in Karina's arms."

Gabi simply nodded, swallowing back the hard knot in her throat. She numbly stumbled her way to the shelter. Once inside she sat down and fixed her gaze on the dying light of the campfire. She couldn't say how long her stare was fixed like that; contemplating the new form of death that Demeter had brought them. All that she could say with any certainty was that, on this night, she would seek the reassuring comfort of Diego's presence.

. . .

```
Gov Darius Owens
11 July, 6 yal, 18:05
Michael, North Concordia
>|
```

Darius stretched and yawned, then rubbed his eyes. His eyelids felt like fine sandpaper; staring at the mainframe terminal for hours had left his eyes as dry as the air inside the computer core. While the strip lighting overhead illuminated the room enough to where he could navigate without running into equipment, the reflection off the terminal's screen blinded him momentarily when he shifted in the seat.

He sighed and got up. Darius paced down the rows of server racks, only letting his mind take a brief break from the task at hand.

*There's got to be a clue here,* he considered. *If what Young said is right, there would be evidence.*

Darius rubbed his neck as he rolled his head from side to side. His eye caught the manufacture label of the closest server.

*March, 2011. They're new enough, alright. But that's it. I've been over every bit of data on these things. Nothing out of the ordinary. Navigation systems, com routines, emergency reactor monitoring. All of it normal. Without any bugs or...*

His attention snapped back to the terminal mid-thought.

"Bugs," he muttered aloud. "The com system bugs."

Darius swiftly returned to the seat and brought up his old sandbox program. The corrupted com software files were still in there. He pulled one up and started to page through the garbled data as quickly as his tired eyes would allow.

*How could I have forgotten these? These were the only changes from the original program.*

The fragments of the assassin's program were heavily corrupted. Years of disuse had taken their toll; the bulk of the ship's computer storage was on magnetic media. Old-school hard drives. Not the most advanced technology at the time the ship's systems were finalized, but they were abundant, cheap, and durable, particularly when systems were built redundantly. But after forty years of use in space and another six on the ground, many of the drive arrays had begun to fail, and the redundancy along with it.

Darius wasn't sure if he should be thanking the drives that held his sandbox for remaining functional, or cursing them for making his job harder by damaging the files even further. Frustration set in, and his fingers tapped harder on the virtual keyboard with each page of garbage that passed.

"Damn it!" he cursed, swiveling about in his chair and clenching his fists until the nails bit into his palms.

*Get a grip,* he told himself. Darius cycled two deep breaths, and as his shoulders relaxed, his head dropped. *You don't have to do this all tonight. You've got time.* He then looked back at the terminal. *Five more minutes, then it's time to crash in a berth. Pick up again tomorrow.*

Darius turned back to the terminal and took another deep breath. He was about to cycle to the next page, but something caught his eye, and his finger froze just above the screen. A minute, but mostly intact subroutine. Something he had dismissed before as being a feedback loop.

*It's not a feedback loop. It's a redirect. A simple cloak.*

He brought up a smaller window in the upper right corner of the terminal, which displayed the repaired com system code. Carefully, he matched the expected location of the redirect routine to what he had repaired.

"Son of a bitch," he said. "I fixed it because I thought it was part of the diagnostic code."

Darius spent several minutes analyzing the redirect, comparing it to the patch he created to hold the com system together. Bit by bit, he deconstructed both bits of programming. After fifteen minutes, the debugger popped up with a complaint. Darius dismissed the warning, and immediately the schematic of the com system popped up.

*That's weird.*

He was about to dismiss that as well when he noticed something out of place. The schematics were something Darius knew well; he could trace them in his sleep if he had to. But a short Ethernet spur that ran from the second server bank indicated the presence of a fourth bank of machines. Darius counted the three rows, just to be sure that his mind hadn't played tricks on him for the entire journey. He then double-checked his work. There was no mistake. The redirect was designed to mask the presence of a fourth server bank.

*That's insane. Unless…*

"Voice interface activate," he commanded.

"VOICE INTERFACE ACTIVATED. AUTHORIZED USER LIEUTENANT DARIUS OWENS," the computer replied through a weathered speaker. Darius had never bothered to update the titles of anyone who had security access, so it still referred to him by his military rank. "COMMAND?"

"Integrity check, primary reactor monitoring."

"STANDBY." The gap was filled by the soft whirring of server fans. "SOLID STATE SYSTEM INTEGRITY VERIFIED. PRIMARY REACTOR MONITORING SYSTEM ONLINE."

"Shut down secondary reactor monitoring system."

The terminal spat back a disapproving bleat. "SHUTDOWN OF REDUNDANT REACTOR SYSTEMS INADVISABLE. PLEASE INPUT OVERRIDE SEQUENCE."

Darius typed the twenty digit authorization sequence into the terminal screen.

"CONFIRMED. SECONDARY REACTOR MONITORING OFFLINE."

The background noise softened slightly as server bank three shut down, its fans and drives spinning to a stop in a matter of seconds.

"Transfer emergency controls to bridge engineering stations and shut down remaining server banks."

Again the computer protested. "SHUTDOWN OF COMPUTER CORE INADVISABLE. COMMAND LEVEL OVERRIDE REQUIRED."

*Good thing Tom gave me his overrides, then.*

He quickly input the former colonel's login and command override into the mainframe.

"CONFIRMED. MAINFRAME RESTORATION MUST OCCUR FROM THE BRIDGE. TRANSFER COMPLETE, SHUTDOWN IMMINENT."

Five seconds later, the remaining two banks of servers, as well as the mainframe terminal, powered down. Darius was struck by the near utter silence in the core. It felt utterly alien. This was a place he used to come for solitude, and the now silenced white noise was his constant companion during those times. He slumped in his chair, sighing.

*Well, that was a waste of time.*

He rose from his perch and walked to bank two. He put his hand on one of the blades in the first rack. The aluminum casing was still warm to the touch. A fine coating of dust covered just about everything. Darius rubbed his fingers together, shedding the grit from the tips. The ball of dust slowly floated downward. About six inches from the deck plating, it took a sudden turn, floating nearly horizontal to the deck, as it was carried a few feet away from his feet.

*Huh?*

Darius got on his knees to check the lower levels of the rack, making sure the mainframe didn't forget to turn something off. All lights were out, but Darius detected a definite draft when he waved his hand over the deck. He got even closer, lying on his belly. There, right at deck level, he was able to detect the faint sound of drives.

*No way.*

He retrieved his tool kit and hastily loaded the cordless drill with a screwdriver bit, then threw the drill's motor into reverse. He traced the plating lines until they flared out, which was where the screws held the plates down to the framing. Underneath the core's floors were bundles of Ethernet cables, flowing into conduits that ran throughout the ship. Darius never had cause to open the deck plates before, but there was no doubt that something else was hidden down there.

A couple of minutes later he had taken up the first of the deck plates. He shined his flashlight into the cavern, and almost immediately saw the familiar rear end of a server rack. It was small, probably a quarter of the height of the other racks. Darius's flashlight clattered as it slipped from his fingers into the compartment below.

*Damn it. Young was right. Doctor Benedict was hiding something. But what?*

He fished the light out from the depths and closed up the plating, sealing the secret servers back under the deck. Whatever secrets it contained would have to wait for the morning, Darius determined. His head was swimming, and exhaustion had driven him to the brink. He was in no condition to pull drives from the machines for analysis.

Darius took a moment to put his tools back in his kit. He stretched and yawned before leaving the core in the direction of pod twelve. Thoughts raced through his tired brain as to the purpose of the servers.

*What was it, Doc? What was so important that you had to sell secrets to Young?*

· · ·

"She's doing quite well," Dr. Taylor smiled softly, stretching her wrinkles on her face. She swaddled Andrea back up in her blanket, then handed her to Cal. "Her development seems completely normal for a baby her age."

Cal sighed, relieved. "Thanks, Doc."

*So I guess I'm not a complete failure at this fatherhood thing. Not yet, anyway.* He thought for a moment as he looked down at his daughter. *Still got plenty of time to screw it up. Plenty of ways, too.*

"Do you have any questions about care or what to expect developmentally for the next few weeks?"

He tried to stifle a yawn as he nodded, though the effort was futile. Cal was amazed some days that he could stand, let alone function well enough to care for Andrea and interact with others. "Is she going to start sleeping soon? You know, through the night?"

The smile disappeared from the doctor's face, and she sighed softly. "I can't really answer that definitively. In the short run? No. She needs to eat every couple hours, so she's going to keep waking you up. As she grows, she'll be able to go longer between bottles. But I wouldn't expect her to start sleeping through the night until she's at least twelve months…" She trailed off for a second. By the way she was twitching her lips, Cal could tell she was counting. "My apologies, fourteen or fifteen months old."

"Still having trouble adjusting to time on Demeter, huh Doc?" he poked impishly. "It's only been six years."

"Right," she said flatly. "And I had sixty on Earth before all of this." She sighed, then sat down on the wooden rocking chair in the corner of the clinic exam room. It squeaked as she lowered herself into it, and more so when she rocked back and forth. "I think I'm too old for big changes like that, Calvin."

"C'mon, Doc. You're not that old."

"I am." She leaned forward, bringing the chair to a stop. There was sadness in her eyes when she looked up at Cal. "The next time you bring Andrea in, my replacement will be in the room with me. He will be giving Andrea her checkup. I will merely be observing."

"What?" Cal gasped. "Your replacement? Where are you going?"

"I'm retiring. I should have done it long ago. I was never fit for this journey. It was always the intention of the Project only to send those who were young and healthy enough…"

Cal cut her off. "No, you're fine. I mean, look at you! How many people have you patched up over the past six years? Heck, since the earthquake?"

"That's just it, Cal. I can't keep up anymore. Without access to the medications back on Earth, my arthritis is getting the best of me. It's hard for me to get up and walk to the clinic anymore, and my fingers, well…" she laughed nervously. "Look at me, talking to you like you're *my* doctor. I think that's another sign right there."

"C'mon, it can't be that bad."

"I'm afraid it is." An awkward moment of silence passed between them. "Tadashi was right about one thing."

"Yeah, what's that?" Cal asked.

"The pain was worth it. If I had retired before launch, I would have been left behind. Jamie, Beth, all of us. Whatever discomfort I've endured these years, it was worth it. To save them."

Cal squirmed as he nodded in affirmation. He knew all too well the cost of his ticket to Demeter. That ticket was a luxury only a few thousand people had gained, and most of them through an algorithmic lottery of sorts. His passage cost double: his father's life, and the life of someone who could have been chosen in his place.

*I wonder what the cost was for those who came on Mercy. For Brittany, and her friends.*

The exam room door groaned open, and the nurse, Sandy, poked her head in. "Doctor, we've got a nasty laceration that just came in. Pretty deep, I think you should look at it."

Dr. Taylor nodded and stood up. "Is the O.R. clear?"

"Yes, Doctor."

"Put the patient there. I'll be back in a second." Dr. Taylor waited for Sandy to close the door. She smiled faintly. "Duty calls."

Cal nodded solemnly. "It won't be the same. Coming back here and having someone other than Doctor Taylor look after us."

"Well, you won't have to worry about that. Doctor Taylor will still be your physician. Just a different Doctor Taylor, that's all."

"So Jamie's taking over for you?"

"He is." Dr. Taylor looked at Andrea one more time. She let Andrea grab her pinky for a moment before adjusting the swaddling blanket. "Keep doing what you're doing, Calvin. I look forward to seeing her grow."

Cal swallowed hard and nodded as he left the room. He passed down the hall and through the lobby. The clinic seemed deserted, though Dr. Taylor and Sandy were somewhere in the back working their healing arts on another patient. He paused for a moment, reflecting on the bittersweet memories that the clinic building had brought. It was in this building that he found out he was going to be a father. The joy that he and Alexis had experienced that day was soon drowned out by the sorrow of her passing in the very same building, just under a year later. And soon, the clinic would no longer be run by his close friend. Jamie was a competent doctor, and a friend as well, but the connection just wasn't the same. He felt his chest tighten, and he knew that he had to get out of there.

He needed something to clear his mind. Cal began to walk, with no place in particular in mind. He paused at Benedict Boulevard. The market square was between him and the river, and it hummed with unusual activity for such an early hour. While some merchants hadn't even opened up for the day, others seemed to be doing business at a brisk pace. Cal wandered along in front of the shops, glancing in their windows as he passed. He came to a halt outside Kimura Clothiers, where a crude hay-stuffed mannequin had been set just outside the door. It wore a long, light linen dress that curled and teased in the wind. Cal smiled and stepped inside.

"Too early for you to go shopping?" he asked Andrea, offering his finger to her. She cooed and latched on with her tiny hand.

"Cal!" Saika beamed as she sidled up next to them. "How are you? It's been so long since I've seen either of you!" She made a funny face at Andrea, followed by some nonsense baby-talk, eliciting a grin from the baby.

Saika was wearing a dress nearly identical to the one on the mannequin, except for color. While the mannequin sported a bright red garment, Saika chose a muted brown dress. Something along her neckline glimmered, which caught Cal's eye.

"There's… something new about you, isn't there?" he asked.

Saika grinned even wider, sliding her hand briefly under her modest-cut collar. She fished out a thin silver chain with an aluminum ring dangling from it. "He finally did it!" she squealed. "Tyler asked me to marry him!"

Cal managed to keep his smile, though the sight of the spacer ring had him instinctively clutching at the rings hidden under his own shirt. Three in total: his wedding ring, and Lexi's engagement and wedding rings. There was emptiness for Cal in Saika's revelation. He knew he should be genuinely happy for her, though he felt a sense of loss and jealousy.

"Congratulations," he replied, masking the hurt.

"Thanks! So do you want to go through sales figures for your soap today?"

He waved his hand dismissively. "Not today. Believe it or not, I'm actually shopping for once."

"Great. What are you looking for?"

"I'm looking for a dress for Andrea."

Saika made an exuberant squealing noise, which made Andrea startle. She then apologized and explained that she had been looking forward to 'dolling up' Andrea. Though amusing, this led Cal to wonder what other plans his friends had in store for his daughter already. Cal unbundled Andrea, who shivered and whimpered against his chest as Saika took measurements. Once completed, Cal wrapped her up and let her burrow against his body again. They discussed various fabric swatches for a moment, ultimately settling on light blue. Cal suggested linen for the material, but Saika pointed out that she wouldn't be ready to wear it for a couple months. The two agreed on a middle ground, which was light wool. Saika then excused herself to make a sketch of the garment.

Cal wandered around the store for a moment, eyeing the variety of men's shirts that were on display, and ultimately ending up at Saika's display rack that was stocked with his laundry soap. He reached out and brushed a bottle with the tip of his finger.

"Hey, stranger." Brittany's voice startled him. He spun around, causing Andrea to cry out in alarm. "Sorry, didn't mean to scare you there."

"Shouldn't be sneaking up on me then, Britt."

"Sorry. I didn't mean to." She hugged him, lingering a little longer than he expected. "How've you been?"

"Alive and holding a baby."

"So it's a good day, then?"

*Depends on what you consider good.*

Cal shrugged and smiled. "Just doing a little shopping on a nice day."

"Mind if I tag along for a bit?"

*A little.*

Cal shook his head. He wandered around the store with her as she admired the items for sale.

"Whoever made these is really good. Everything's so unique," Brittany commented.

"Saika's very talented. Her mom's even better. She taught Saika everything she knows. But she doesn't make much anymore."

"Why not?"

"Because she can't anymore. Her hands just aren't as steady or quick as they used to be." It was only after Cal said this that he realized that Doctor Taylor wasn't the only one preparing to retire.

"That's too bad. But I guess if Saika's this good, I guess it doesn't matter too much."

*Sarah doesn't matter? Maybe not to you,* he thought bitterly.

A minute passed in silence. The time must have weighed more heavily on Brittany, as she was the one who broke it.

"So, what was she like?"

"Hmm?"

"Your wife. What was she like?"

Cal sighed and closed his eyes. For a fleeting moment, he saw an image of her brilliant eyes, heard her echoed laughter. "She was smart, beautiful, and funny. Fierce when she needed to be, tender when I needed her to be. She was perfect. My everything."

He felt Brittany's gentle touch on his shoulder. "I'm sorry, Cal."

His throat tightened, and his voice wavered. "Thanks. It's just... I barely know what I'm doing anymore. I just feel like I'm going through the motions, that I'm not really living my life. Like this is someone else's life, because this much shit can't possibly happen to one person."

"Trust me, I know."

Cal shrugged off her hand. "How could you? You don't know what all has happened to me."

"That's a two way street, buddy." She raised her voice as he began to walk away. "Seriously? You're just going to shove me away like that?"

*You did it to me first. How does it feel now?*

He called toward the back of the store loud enough for Saika to hear. "Take your time, Saika. I have to go. I'll be back later to go over the sketch."

"Cal!" Brittany growled.

He didn't look back.

. . .

Gabrielle Serrano
12 July, 6 yal, shortly after nightfall
About 25 miles inland, southeast of wreck site
>|

Sweat ran from Gabi's brow in torrents. Her eyes burned from the mixture of salt and grit, and the moisture blurred her vision. She couldn't afford to stop and wipe her eyes. She could smell the stench of the beast that chased her. Its foul breath was warm and damp against her neck. Gabi reached deeper and threw herself headlong into the forest. She could see her way clearly, as if it was morning. But she couldn't focus on anything but the path ahead, for fear that the beast would overtake her.

"You can't run, Gabs," Will taunted from astride the hideous, distorted bear. "That's what this planet does, you know."

She darted left, plunging into the brush between two trees. Branches whipped her in the face, but she felt nothing. Only urgency and dread. There was a crash from behind her, and she cast a sideways glance. Will's mount had skidded into a tree sideways; the tree buckled as if it was made of paper. Will's face was completely devoid of expression, his eyes lifeless and hollow.

Gabi felt the slope quicken downward. The change in grade caused her momentum to build up faster than she could control, and she tumbled head over heels down the hill. Panic gripped her as she heard the rushing river grow closer. She threw out her arms and managed to snag a sapling. The tiny trees roots held, and she slid to a stop on her belly, just a couple of feet from a rocky precipice that overlooked churning rapids below. Above her, the bear padded down the hill, snarling and howling at its prey.

"Nowhere to run, Gabs," Will said coldly.

"Will, don't do this!" she shrieked.

Her mouth opened as the bear leaped.

A shrill scream echoed back to Gabi through the darkness as she bolted awake. One hand instantly went to her bow, the other clawed at her tomahawk. It took a moment in her groggy, panicked state for Gabi to recognize the scream as her own. Diego groaned; his tiny dark shape shifted a few feet away from her as he rolled over. Gabi sighed and lay her head back down on her pack. Only a few ragged furs and leaves stuffed inside provided any cushioning. Gabi had become accustomed to her neck and other muscles complaining about a lack of proper bedding. That part barely bothered her anymore.

But her dream was another matter. She was now fully awake, peering into the darkness around her. She could make out dark blotches that were rocks or shrubs, and tall tree trunks that were nearly obsidian in color. Arion was full and high in the sky, but the dark moon provided little light, and Persephone was a mere sliver just above the horizon. Gabi's eyes had adjusted to the dark as much as they could, though they would be a poor match for a true nocturnal predator.

She was now both the predator and the protector. Will was useless. He had spent the morning burying Caleb and Gina. The rest of the day he silently mourned his dead girlfriend. Food didn't stir him from his trancelike solitude. Even when Gabi got in his face, confronting him and pushing him to the dirt, he didn't rouse. He wouldn't speak to anyone but Kristin, and even she couldn't get him to do anything useful.

*He's got to have time to grieve, Gabi,* Kristin had said. *Just give him a little space.*

*We can't just sit around here and wait. If another of those things comes around, we're done for,* she had protested. *And if Will can't hunt, I'm the only one who can. I'm sure I could kill enough to feed everyone, but I can't help as much around camp if I do. Caleb's gone too.*

*I know, Gabi. I know.*

*So do something about it!*

The argument didn't get any better from there. In the end, Gabi promised to give them until the morning before she took matters into her own hands. Now she wondered if she'd be able to rest, much less do anything useful.

Diego whimpered again. Gabi grabbed her pillow and blanket, laying them next to him. She then put her weapons within arm's reach before settling down on the cold, loosely packed dirt. Her teeth chattered as shivers wracked her body. She reached over to draw Diego's warm body close to her, ensuring that her fur blanket covered both of them. He grumbled quietly as his eyes fluttered open.

"Gabi? Is it morning yet?"

"No," she replied curtly.

"Are you scared?"

"No," she lied. "Just cold."

"Can I tell you a secret?"

Gabi nodded in reply.

"I'm scared."

"Of what?"

"More bears."

"Yeah, they're pretty scary, alright. Big teeth, big claws. I don't like them either."

"I'm scared of how they make people go away. Like Gina and Caleb."

"I know, kid."

Diego shifted to face her. His eyes glimmered ever so slightly with soft light reflected from Persephone. He was looking at her, begging her with his sad expression. "I don't want the bears to take you away. Or me."

Gabi's stomach fluttered. The idea of death by a wild predator was always a possibility for her, and not one she relished. But she hadn't considered that possibility for Diego. He had always been protected by someone in the village, or kept close to their emergency shelter after the hurricane ravaged Camp Eight. Out in the wilderness he was completely defenseless. Easy prey for anything that wanted a meal. The very thought sickened her, even though she wasn't particularly fond of Diego. He deserved her protection.

Gabi wrapped an arm around him. He closed his eyes and whispered, "I love you, Gabi."

"Don't push your luck," she whispered back.

Diego let out a sad, indignant whimper. He fidgeted and twisted for a few minutes before settling back to sleep. The rhythmic rise and fall of his chest and the soft rush of his breath on her forearm were soothing, and Gabi soon found herself searching the sky for familiar stars. Thousands of pinpricks of light littered the darkness, and a smoky ribbon wound its way across the sky. Will had told her it was gas and matter spread across an endless expanse of the galaxy. Gabi always thought of it as a ghostly river that flowed through the night, carrying dreams along its course.

Dreams still eluded her. Not that Gabi was thrilled by the prospect of sleep. The image of Will hunting her down astride the bear was still fresh in her mind. She couldn't shake how callous and indifferent he had sounded, nor the dead look in his eyes. He had the same look in his eyes when Gabi had tried to get him to get up from Gina's grave and do something.

She sighed and closed her eyes.

*We'll see tomorrow. We'll see how lost he is.*

. . .

*Incredible.*

Darius leaned back in the chair, staring at the data rolling across the mainframe terminal screen. Layer upon layer of directories spread out like roots. Documentation files sat in support of compressed archives of images, technical specifications, and schematics. Dozens of years of technological development across dozens of industries were represented in the seemingly endless stream of files.

He flipped to the last schematic he had opened, tracing the air above the image as he followed the part's outline. It was a gear, something that had been around for centuries. But this particular example held so much more value, particularly to anyone on Demeter. It was one of the gears found inside the transfer case of a crawler. One individual spare part out of a thousand on that machine for which the colony had no spares. The directory that contained this schematic also held several dozen others. Every part necessary to build a crawler's transfer case from scratch, down to the gaskets, was included.

*So this is what you were hiding, Doctor B.*

After easily defeating the minimal security and weak encryption on the server, Darius had scrolled through thousands of folders on each of the two dozen solid state drives contained in its array. It also housed a half dozen magnetic hard drives, though those appeared to be there solely to contain the server's operating system.

The data on those solid state drives were unfathomably valuable to a fledgling colony. Technical specifications and schematics for every conceivable type of production tool, from simple machines to vehicles and advanced electronics, were neatly catalogued and distributed on the storage devices. Detailed instructions on how to manufacture nearly anything that mankind could have built in the year 2011 was at his fingertips.

*This changes everything.*

He couldn't help but grin. Sure, he couldn't piece together a cell phone from what resources the colony had to offer today, but the secret server held the keys to what would surely be a quantum leap in their development. As it stood, Concordia was on track to be on par technologically with pre-industrial America in the next ten to twenty years, with the obvious exception of the reactors housed onboard the ships, and whatever mechanical supplies survived that time span. But with such detailed knowledge at their disposal, more was possible. Darius considered the possibilities of having at least basic computers available by 16 yal, assuming they could find the appropriate mineral resources.

But as quickly as his elation rose, it was swept away by suspicion. This was an inordinate amount of detailed information, and one thing that leaped out was the fact that competing products from multiple vendors were present, particularly when it came to electronics and vehicles.

Darius disconnected the drive that he had hooked up to the mainframe. He put it back in the server, then took a moment to recall which of its siblings he was looking for. When he found the correct unit, he attached it, and began searching through the details for various microprocessors. It took him ten minutes to find what he was looking for, but the implications were clear.

*This technology is stolen.*

His surprise was only momentary. So much of Project Columbus had already been taken, either by Young, Benedict, or Kimura, it was only a minor revelation to find the entire core design of an unreleased processor amongst the many schematics. Darius sighed, deflated.

*You sold Project technology, Doc. You then stole companies' secrets? Why? To give us a head start?*

"That was mighty dangerous." Darius shook his head as he rose.

He reassembled the server and put away his tools. On his way out the door he nearly tripped on the deck plating he had taken up to access the secret compartment, so he slid the plating back into place, collected the screws, and carefully put them on the keyboard shelf of a nearby server rack. He yawned and stretched, then headed for his increasingly familiar temporary quarters in pod twelve.

Darius wrestled with the concept of Dr. Benedict's actions. The man he had worked with and admired, though flawed, had saved thousands of lives by stealing the ships. But new light cast dark shadows on the man's legacy, and Darius couldn't reconcile the need to steal so many proprietary secrets.

*We could have survived fine on what was public domain,* he mused. *This is reckless. Way too reckless. Not like him at all. At least, not what I knew of him.*

Darius stumbled, tired and brain-fried, toward the rear gallery airlock. He was so preoccupied that he didn't notice three men enter the support section from the main hall until he had almost run into them.

They were strangers, most likely from the contingent of *Mercy's* refugees that had chosen to move to Concordia. They were staying aboard *Michael* while proper accommodations could be constructed.

"Can I help you gentlemen find something?" he asked, taking a step back from them.

A slightly shorter man with pock marks all over his face nodded. "Yeah. We're trying to find the laundry room. We were told it's back here."

Darius glanced at the man's companions. One was as tall as Darius, and well-muscled. The other had a slight but powerful build, reminiscent of a recruit fresh from boot camp. None of the three carried anything in their hands. This struck him as odd, given the request for directions to the laundry room. His fingers curled up, readying for a punch if needed.

"The facilities in the support section are off limits to unauthorized personnel, gentlemen." He paused for a moment. "Besides, it seems a little late to be doing laundry."

The pock-marked man grinned wickedly. Darius brought his arms up defensively just in time, easily turning aside the man's first two blows. But he was outnumbered. The muscular man landed a square blow to his jaw, and while he was still reeling, the last assailant landed several sucker punches to his kidneys. Pain shot throughout his body, and he could do little more than try to roll over and turtle. The attackers were relentless, kicking at him furiously while he was down on the deck. His arms hurt from every blow he shielded, but he couldn't protect his entire body. He received repeated punishing blows to his gut and back. Still Darius protected himself until he couldn't hold his arms up any more. He rolled over, wheezing and coughing up blood.

"Sorry, Governor," the pock-marked man said. "Nothing personal."

The final kick was delivered to his head, and Darius blacked out.

• • •

Gabrielle Serrano
13 July, 6 yal, early morning
About 25 miles inland, southeast of wreck site
>|

Will slid from his perch atop a boulder at the edge of camp, slowly shambling over to the smoldering fire. Gabi scrutinized his every move, reading his mood from his body language, counting the puffs of fog that escaped his lips with each breath. She had done the very same thing a hundred times before with animals she stalked. Unlike an animal, Will could speak, though subtle cues in the way he carried himself spoke volumes without the utterance of a word.

He took the strips of cold bird meat that were offered to him, though he did not eat any until he returned to his perch. Even then, he consumed it very slowly. He kept to himself, staring off into the forest. Will lacked his usual razor-sharp focus, and only mumbled a short reply when Kristin came over to talk to him.

*We're not going anywhere today.*

Diego tugged at the blanket wrapped around her, breaking her attention from Will.

"Gabi, I'm hungry," he complained.

Their morning meal of leftover game bird and berries barely sated Gabi's hunger. She glanced at Gina's pack, which still rested in the same spot they had placed it after moving the camp the day before. There would be food inside, mostly dried vegetables and smoked fish. But Will was extremely touchy about Gina's pack. He threw a fit when Kristin suggested they leave it behind at the old camp, where the bear mauled two of her friends to death.

A devilish grin shot across Gabi's face as an idea formulated.

*A test, then.*

"Hang on a second, Diego. I'll get you some more."

She shrugged off the blanket. The chilling morning air left shivers running down every inch of her body. Gabi walked the long way around the fire to Gina's pack, making sure to draw Will's attention, locking stares with him for a few moments. She then opened the pack and began to rifle through it in search of food.

"Hey!" Will shouted, hopping down from his perch. Gabi continued, undeterred. "Hey, get out of there!"

Gabi found a bundle of broad tropical leaves which had been wrapped around a fillet of smoked fish. She pulled it from the pack and began to walk back to Diego, ignoring Will's shouts. He caught up with her, wrenching her elbow to spin her around. He was far stronger than Gabi, though he had never used it against her in such a rough manner. She didn't cry, though stabbing pain shot through her elbow. Gabi locked stares with Will, who was fuming and snarling.

"Put that back," he snapped.

"Diego's hungry," she replied firmly. Though the fury in his eyes made her want to shrink away, she stood her ground.

"Put it back, Gabi. Now."

"Or what?"

"Or so help me…"

"You'll break my neck?" she scoffed as she interrupted him.

Will's eyes widened in momentary shock. "What? No."

"Then what, Will? What are you going to do to me to keep from taking your dead girlfriend's precious food?"

"God damn it, Gabi!" His eyes narrowed to slits and his lip curled upward.

"I guess it's not really stealing anymore, since she can't use it."

Kristin stepped between the two of them. "Knock it off, you two."

Gabi shook her head and started to walk away. "Good to see you're up today, Will. Get your pack together. We're leaving in an hour."

"What?" Kristin gasped.

"We're not going anywhere," Will countered.

Gabi handed the package of fish to Diego, who wasted little time opening it and stuffing a fistful of fish into his mouth. Daphne had been hanging around nearby, and joined him for the extra meal. Gabi looped back around to face off with the Vandemarks.

"Yes, we are." Gabi enunciated each word emphatically.

Will's eyebrows nearly knitted together as his brow furrowed deeply. "You don't call the shots around here. I do."

"The last time you called a shot, Gina and Caleb were still alive. Your sister and I have been keeping this camp running for the past two days. Marya, too."

"I just need a little time."

"Give him some space," Kristin added, wrapping an arm around her brother's shoulder.

Gabi shook her head. "I'm not staying around here waiting for you to find your feelings or whatever crap excuse you're going to give. Every day we wait is another day one of those beasts has to pick us off. We need to move. We need to get to where we're going. Then you can go cry your ass off."

"Fuck you," he spat back.

"Will!" Kristin protested.

Gabi sniffed and shrugged. "It is what it is. Nothing against you, Will. I just don't like the idea of being prey. If I can't be the hunter, it's time to move on."

"Fine," he snarled. "Go hunt then. Come back when you're being less of a bitch!"

Gabi crossed swiftly over to Caleb's pack. She slipped it open, looking for the magazines for the rifles.

"I said go, Gabi," Will bellowed.

She slipped the ammunition out of the pack, cradling it in her arm to shield it from Will's sight as she retrieved her bow, quiver, and tomahawk. She discreetly slipped the ammunition into her game sack, then slung it over her shoulder.

"Be back in a few minutes," she whispered to Diego and tussled his hair.

Gabi slipped into the woods. She had no intention of hunting. Will had made his decision to stay clear, but she was determined not to delay any longer. Once she was out of site and sure she was not being followed, she quickly made her way to the camp where Gina died. The corpse of the bear was still there, though various scavengers had taken large chunks of flesh from its back and flanks.

Without wasting time, Gabi took the ammunition from her bag. She placed the three magazines in a neat line on the blood stain that marked the spot where Gina expired. As expeditiously as she came, Gabi left the old camp and returned to the new one.

Her early return prompted questioning stares from everyone in camp, save for Diego and Daphne, who were otherwise occupying themselves. Without a word, she rolled up her blanket and set to work packing her backpack. She then made quick work of Diego's. Gabi donned her pack, grabbed Diego's, and helped him slip on the bulky sack. When she turned around, the others were formed in a half circle around the fire pit.

"What the hell do you think you're doing?" Will asked harshly.

"What does it look like I'm doing?"

"Leaving."

She pursed her lips and cocked her head to the side, feigning deep thought. "I'd like to call it continuing the mission."

"You're not going anywhere," Will growled.

"Yes, we are. We've stayed long enough. C'mon, Diego." She grabbed her brother's hand and started walking."

"You don't know where you're going."

"Doesn't take a genius to figure it out, Will. We keep going toward the big mountains over there." She pointed generally southeast. "Then find a river that flows the opposite direction. Keep following it until it dumps into the big river, then follow that to the site."

Will's jaw slacked slightly.

"What?" she continued. "I've seen your maps a hundred times. I know your game plan. You taught me everything you know about the wilderness. You don't think we can make it there?"

"No," Kristin answered for him. "No. We need to stick together."

"We need to keep moving," Gabi retorted. She glanced around at the others, gauging their reactions. Will was shocked and furious. Kristin was concerned. Karina was hard to judge; she was probably still grieving the death of her brother. But Marya and Aidan were both intently listening to the conversation.

"We'll go in a couple days," Will promised.

"You didn't wait a couple days after the storm killed just about everyone in Camp Eight. We all went to work cleaning up and burying everyone the next day. You've never waited when something needed to be done. Not until now. Now you pitch a fit if someone dares to take Gina's food. She's not around to eat it, but you'll be damned if you let it actually go to use. You're slipping, Will. You're slipping, and you're gambling with everyone's lives."

His shoulders heaved as he let out a heavy sigh. "Fine, want to take the food from the other packs? I don't care. It's not a big deal."

"It's more than that. Every day we're out here, we could be hunted. Maybe by a bear, maybe by something else we haven't met yet." Gabi turned to Marya. "Do you want to sit here and become something's lunch so that Will can have a couple days?" Marya bit her lip and her eyes darted from side to side. "Didn't think so. I don't either. That's why we're going."

She tugged Diego's hand, and he obediently started walking next to her. They only got six paces before Marya stepped in her way.

*Damn it, Marya!*

"You've got some real guts thinking you can take over for Will," Marya said.

Gabi nodded once. "You would too, if you felt Aidan's life was on the line."

"I do, actually." Marya paused and glanced over her shoulder at Will. "That's why we're going with you, Gabi."

Gabi stuttered for a moment, unable to form a sentence. She had expected that Karina might come to her senses and follow them with Daphne, but having her rival be the first to volunteer was not something Gabi had counted on. She was thankful for the help, but not so much for the company. "Get your gear together."

Marya nodded. She and Aidan broke rank to go collect their meager possessions. A few moments later, Will growled, and stormed across the campsite. He retrieved his M4 carbine and pulled the magazine to check that it was loaded. Gabi knew that he hadn't reloaded the weapon since he emptied it into the bear. She folded her arms across her chest in smug satisfaction. Will grumbled and went to Caleb's pack, where the spare ammunition for the rifles had been stowed. As he rummaged inside, he became increasingly agitated. He dumped the contents on the ground, and when the ammunition was nowhere to be found, shouted a loud expletive.

Will was in Gabi's face in an instant. "Where is it?" he bellowed.

"Go hunting, Will. You'll find it. By then we'll be long gone."

He screamed in rage and threw the rifle aside. Gabi had only a second to react before his fist crashed into her cheek. It wasn't enough time. She toppled backward into the dirt, landing awkwardly on her pack. Diego screamed and started crying immediately. Gabi tried to recover, but Will was on her in an instant. He landed another hard blow to her cheek. She was in serious pain, and the world seemed to be fading from her vision. Then she heard the distinct metallic ping of a pistol slide.

"Get off of her," Marya shouted.

Will looked over his shoulder. He slowly got up, raising his hands in surrender. Gabi rolled out from under him and regained her feet. Marya stood ten feet away with a Beretta trained on Will. Gabi collected Diego, soothing him as she circled around behind Marya.

"Will hurt you," Diego whimpered.

"It's alright," she said. "I'll be fine in a minute."

Aidan slipped one loop of Marya's pack over her shoulder. The four oddball companions made their way out of camp, covered by Marya in the rear. They walked in silence. Gabi touched her tender cheek, which had swollen enough to hamper the vision from her right eye.

*So much for our great and shining leader,* she thought sarcastically.

About twenty minutes later, Marya broke the silence.

"Too bad Karina and Daphne didn't come with us."

"Yup."

*Karina has it coming if they fail. And Daphne's stuck with Will. Sucks for her.*

"Think he's found the ammo yet?"

"Probably."

"We should get a move on, then."

"He's not coming after us."

"Yeah? Why not?"

"Because he's lost everything now," Gabi replied coldly.

"Don't you think that might make him a little, I dunno, vindictive?"

"He's not his father."

Marya considered this for a moment. "No. No, he's not."

• • •

Andrea giggled and cooed in her bassinet. Cal stopped stirring the bubbling goo in his cauldron for a moment, stepping away to check on her. He smiled under his mask.

"Goofball. What are you up to?" he cooed back.

She gave him a toothless grin and giggled again. Cal removed his safety googles and gloves, then reached to the inner pocket of his apron for his handkerchief. After he wiped the beaded sweat from his forehead, he put his protective gear back on and resumed his work. A few minutes passed, and Andrea got bored with whatever game she was playing with herself. She whimpered for a minute, then started to cry.

*Damn it.*

He couldn't stop at this stage, or he risked losing the viability of the biodiesel component in the mixture. The glycerin would still be salvageable, but even still, the mistake would be costly. Cal hummed for a moment as he thought, then broke out singing nursery rhymes. To say that Cal was never much of a singer would be an understatement. The caterwauling that emanated from his throat pained his own ears, and he was pretty sure the local wildlife would start howling if they could hear. But after two songs, the desired effect was achieved; Andrea settled down again.

*Phew.*

He glanced up at the timer, but jumped when he was startled. Hunter was standing next to the rear shop door, accompanied by Dayton. Cal took a deep breath. When his heart settled back to a normal rhythm, he greeted them.

"I hope you didn't hear that, Hunter," he grinned from behind the vapor mask.

Hunter didn't laugh or poke fun at him. His friend's face bore a grim expression that was mirrored by the deputy governor.

"What's going on, guys?" Cal asked, feeling his nerves jitter just a little.

"We need to talk, Mr. McLaughlin," Dayton replied. "Do you have a minute?"

Cal glanced again at the timer. "I can talk, but I have to do it here."

Dayton nodded. "That's fine. Have you seen Governor Owens today?"

"No, not today."

"What about yesterday?"

"No. Why do you ask?"

Hunter and Dayton exchanged worried looks. Dayton turned back to Cal, and with a grave tone said, "He may be missing."

"Missing?" Cal blurted.

"He didn't show up at Civic Hall this morning. I checked with Devereaux to see if he was working in the square, then checked his temporary berth on *Michael*. He's not there, and no one's seen him today."

Hunter took a step forward. "This isn't like him, Cal. He doesn't just skip out. On anything. Ever."

"Are you sure he didn't just have business across the river this morning?" Cal postulated. "Or maybe a trip to Rust Creek?"

Dayton shook his head. "Roger says he was scheduled to work from Civic Hall this entire week. I heard back from Counselor Abernathy just a few minutes ago. The governor didn't go south."

"What about the farms?"

"There's a lot of ground to cover, Cal," Hunter replied. "The word is spreading to keep an eye out for him. But the last time anyone saw him was last night around seven, when he returned to *Michael* for the night. Several people saw him board the ship. No one saw him leave."

"He slipped out?"

Dayton scratched at his beard, which was now almost equally gray and brown. "I'm just hoping he's out touring farms somewhere, and that people just didn't notice him leave because they were busy."

Cal shuddered at a thought. "And what if he didn't?"

"Then he disappeared into thin air, Mr. McLaughlin. I'm not a detective, but I'm starting to wish I was."

The timer went off. Cal turned off the burner, placed the lid on his biofuel brew, and stashed his stirring paddle. He stripped off all of his protective gear except his apron, stuffing most of it in his inner pocket.

"Well, I'll let you know if I hear anything or if I see him," Cal added.

"Thank you."

Hunter and the deputy governor took their leave through the shop. Cal exhaled loudly and wiped his brow with his arm.

*The governor is missing,* he thought. *Wow.*

*And the first person Dayton comes to?* Jerk added. *You! Just like old times, huh?*

Cal winced as his inner specter cackled. He tried to think of when he last took the medication that suppressed that particular mental malady.

*Four and a half days ago,* Jerk noted. *Pretty bad that I know that and you don't. Also pretty rude that you want to get rid of me already.*

*I want to get rid of you permanently,* Cal shot back.

*Again, rude.*

*So is barging into my brain.*

*Our brain,* his double corrected. *But that's not why I'm here.*

*And why are you here? To gloat? Pester me?*

*Of course. My life would be boring otherwise.*

*Not interested,* Cal said as he collected Andrea and went inside the shop. He wasted no time in going to the stockroom and choking down one of his anti-psychotic pills.

*You're no fun,* Jerk protested.

*Good. I like it that way.*

*Fine. Just say no this time, alright?*

*To you? I always do,* Cal replied.

*Not me. Your conscience. I get the feeling you're about to try doing something gallant or stupid again.*

*Why would you say that?*

*Because you can never say no to Dayton.*

Cal sighed and began preparing a bottle for Andrea. *He didn't ask me to do anything.*

*Didn't he? Hmm. I must be slipping,* Jerk chortled.

Cal particularly hated Jerk's insanity jokes. Having a secondary personality that shouldn't exist complain about losing its mental clarity was simply disturbing and cruel in his book. What made it even worse is that it all had to do with the inner workings of his own mind.

He settled into his usual chair with Andrea and stroked her cheek. "Don't go nuts like Daddy, okay?"

*You're going to give her plenty of reasons to go insane herself,* Jerk prodded.

*Shut up.*

. . .

J.C. Rainier

Darius woke with a start as he was shoved roughly to the ground. Something in his wrist popped, and he winced in pain. The sharp stabbing of his wrist only slightly overpowered the dull throbbing from all over his body. Darius coughed and spat, trying to clear his mouth of the dirt that he sucked in upon landing. Each expulsion of air only aggravated the pain in his body. He felt like he had been run through the grain mill, and figured he probably looked about the same.

He had bits and flashes of memory from the past few hours. After taking the beating, he had the sensation of movement. Not gentle, either. There was a fuzzy recollection of being dropped as his captors carried him down the grand stairwell on *Michael*, and evanescent memories of being hauled through the outskirts of town and into the wild. But the sum of his lucid memory after being taken from the ship was a grand total of twenty or so seconds. Darius was lost; he did not need to take his bearings to know that.

Still, he rose to his feet. His movements were slow and labored, and his chest and legs burned. He looked around to survey his situation. Sparse Demeter pine was intermixed with Blue elm. The landscape rolled gently, and there were only occasional shrubs dotting the ground. Based on the vegetation, he reckoned that he was somewhere west of the town, and far enough away from the Fairweather that it couldn't be heard. Darius turned around slowly when he heard someone clear their throat.

Two of his three captors stood about ten feet away, with the last man being just out of arm's reach. All three were tired, though the man Darius presumed to be their leader still wore a smug grin that distorted the pock marks on his cheeks. He didn't appear to be armed, though his friends were. Darius found himself staring down the barrels of a pair of pistols. Any doubt left that these men were from *Mercy* vanished, as neither weapon was a standard-issue M9. One was unmistakably a Colt .45, and the other he couldn't immediately recognize.

They had left him untied. It probably didn't matter, however, since Darius was favoring his right leg. At best he could probably hobble, so he was not a flight risk. Nor was he a danger to fight, being outnumbered, outgunned, and injured. Straining his eyes, he noticed that the tree line behind the men was abrupt, and oddly linear. A few overgrown stumps in the distance clued him in to their location.

*One of the early logging areas,* he surmised.

"Well, Governor," the pock-marked man said. "You've caused a little bit of trouble here, haven't you?"

"I've caused trouble? How do you figure? You're the ones that jumped me."

His captor nodded. "True, but it didn't have to come to that. You just put your nose where it didn't belong."

"Again, I think you're confused. You went into a restricted area on the ship. Assaulted the governor of the colony you're trying to join. I'm not sure how that qualifies *me* as being in trouble."

"Well, you're here, aren't you?"

"The longer you keep it that way the more of an issue that is for you. Let me go and I'll see to it that you receive leniency."

The man chortled and shook his head, his grin disappearing. "I don't think you get how this works." He reached behind his back and pulled a gun, gesturing toward the base of the tree next to Darius. Darius obeyed the request to sit with a narrow glare. "Now, we've been up all night dragging you out in the middle of nowhere so we can talk to you in peace. I'm a little tired and cranky after all that, so you can save both of us a bunch of trouble by just answering my questions without giving me any more lip."

"And then what?" Darius scoffed. "You kill me?"

The man knelt down in front of Darius, keeping his cold, blue eyes locked on him. He reached out and caressed Darius's cheek in an oddly maternal, yet deeply unnerving way. "Oh, I'm not going to kill you, dear Governor. My boss wouldn't like that. Besides, there are so many other things I can do to you if you don't comply. You probably wouldn't want me to go into detail on that." He stood up and stepped back. "So are you going to play nice?"

Darius's skin crawled with the man's words. Though he despised the thought of giving in to his captor's demands, he didn't believe that he held any secret worth suffering for. The affairs of Concordia were a mostly open book, and the threat, though sincere, was pointless.

"What do you want to know?" Darius hissed.

"What did Doctor Benedict tell you about those servers?"

*The servers?* He thought, cursing himself for being so blind. He had been beaten just after working on the servers, a part of the ship no one knew about. *I should have known.*

"Nothing," he spat back. "I didn't know about the servers until after

*Mercy* landed."

The man nodded. "I suppose he didn't. No, they would have been pulled out and set up long ago if you had known about them. Not still scattered in pieces on the floor."

Darius swallowed hard. They had gone into the computer core after knocking him out. Likely they had taken the equipment with them as well, or at least hidden it. A hundred years of technological development, sent along by Doctor Benedict, had been lost. Darius had little time to cope with the idea.

"Did you make any copies of the data?"

Darius gritted his teeth. "No. I didn't have time."

*But I should have.*

The man nodded approvingly and put away his weapon. "What about the servers on the other ship?"

"What about them?"

"Did you take them apart?"

"What do you think?" Darius sneered defiantly.

His captor's eyes narrowed and his face hardened into a scowl. "I think that you should answer me, instead of trying my patience."

Darius's skin crawled. He still didn't trust that the pock-faced man wouldn't just turn around and end his life once he got the information he desired. Darius proceeded only on the hopes that this man had at least a shred of integrity within him.

"I haven't been to *Gabriel* since I found out about the servers."

"What about the Information Officer on that ship? Have you been in contact with him?"

"I was *Gabriel's* IO. And *Michael's* as well, after he was killed."

The man's eyebrows perked up. "So no one else has worked on the ships' computers?"

"Not since we landed."

The man tucked the pistol into his waistband behind his back. "Thank you for your cooperation, Governor." He walked to his muscular companion and whispered something in his ear, garnering a nod in response. He paused as he was walking away, then turned back to Darius. "One more thing, Governor. What exactly were you planning on doing with that data?"

Darius blinked and cocked his head, momentarily confused by the idea that there might be more than one possible use for the archive's contents. "Distribute the data as necessary to advance the technological development of the colony. Try to speed us back up to where we were on Earth before everything we brought here fails."

A wicked grin crossed the man's face, twisting his pock marks into a jagged canyon on his face. "Noble. But also wasteful."

The man walked away, fading into the distance after a few minutes. Darius stayed put, rubbing some wounds while avoiding contact with others. He was still being watched by two of his assailants, and they didn't seem keen on letting him go anytime soon. They paced back and forth, keeping both their eyes and their weapons trained on him.

"So what happens now?" Darius finally asked after ten minutes.

"We all sit here and relax," the muscular one replied.

Darius scrutinized the two men. Their fatigue was readily evident, despite their threatening manners. He couldn't fight them, but he could try to outlast them. Darius decided to settle in and conserve his energy. His best chance of escape, as he was not bound, was to wait until they could not stay awake any longer.

The two men eventually sat down and leaned up against their own respective trees, though their weapons' sights never strayed. As the two men seemed to lose energy, Darius was gaining his own. The time to escape was close at hand.

But that was as close as he got. His captors were relieved after about an hour, and their replacements were fully stocked with food, shelter, and ropes. Darius was bound at the wrists, then to the tree itself. Once his new guards had finished their work of restraining him and moved on to setting up a camp, Darius discreetly tested their handiwork. He sank into despair.

*I'm not strong enough to break out.*

"Hey, you can't leave me like this," he protested, panic starting to rise. Silence answered him. "Are you seriously going to tie me up to a tree like this? Do you have any idea what kind of animals are out here?"

His captors finished their work establishing the campsite without a word. Darius protested over and over, shouting about the danger that reaper bears posed. The warnings fell on deaf ears.

. . .

Gabrielle Serrano
14 July, 6 yal, mid-morning
About 35 miles inland, southeast of wreck site
>|

Silence was not unusual.  During their voyage from the remnants of Camp Eight, the survivors had often gone days with no more conversation than the commands necessary to sail their ship.  Gabi understood that kind of silence.  It was familiar, and it was offset by days of lively banter.  But the near deathly silence that had accompanied her since leaving the others behind was very different.  Broken only by the monotonous march of their footsteps, the soft scraping of the underbrush on their clothes, this silence felt alien.  Uncomfortable.  And there was little she could do about it.

She watched as Diego scampered ahead a few dozen yards, nearly disappearing into the lush growth on the forest floor.  It was routine for him to bound excitedly ahead of the group early in the morning, then come back and check on everyone else.  By the time the sun peaked in the sky, he would tire of the game.  That would be in about two or three hours.  She wouldn't have to worry about keeping him going for at least that long.  And at least Marya and Aidan shared the burden of herding Diego.

Gabi glanced back at the Brennan siblings.  As usual, Aidan walked with his head down.  He rarely interacted with anyone besides his sister.  Despite his seeming lack of interest in the world around him, however, Aidan could be insightful at times.  Marya brought up the rear, a few paces behind her brother.  She seemed to like it back there, and Gabi didn't mind having a little distance from her rival.

Gabi halted for a moment.  Her shoulders ached from her pack, which had slipped slightly.  She readjusted it, made sure Diego hadn't run off, then took a moment to gather her bearings.

*Looks like we're pretty close to the big mountains*, she thought, noting that she could only barely make out the dark crags through the tree line.  The more distant trees towered over the near ones.  *Slope's about to get steeper, too.*

She continued along, picking a path high enough above the stream to be safe, yet not so far as to lose sight for more than a few minutes.  The shaggy, sandy hair that crowned Diego's head was barely visible over a short bush.  He seemed intent on staying there.  Gabi grumbled, knowing she'd have to put him back on the path as she passed.

When she arrived at the bush, he turned around and smiled at her.

His lips were stained purple, and he clutched four large, purple berries in his right hand, ones that Gabi had never seen before. She gasped, and her chest thumped as her heart began to race.

"Diego!" she snapped, wrenching the berries forcefully from his hand.

His eyes widened in shock, and he froze for a second. His face then twisted into a sad pout, and he began to cry.

"What?" Gabi snarled. Diego only wailed in response. "Stop crying."

"Y-you scared me!" he finally blubbered.

"You know better than to eat strange berries."

"B-but I was hungry!"

Gabi crushed one of the berries and sniffed it. The juice was sweet smelling and slightly sticky. The flesh was rather firm, and the fruit contained a single seed, a little smaller than a cherry pit. She threw aside the fruit, which prompted another round of snot-and-tear filled protest from Diego. Marya and Aidan had heard the commotion, and had come to investigate.

"What happened?" Marya asked, snorting indignantly.

"Diego ate some strange fruit," she replied. For a split second she considered blaming Marya for not watching Diego more closely, but then remembered that it was her responsibility to watch her brother in the morning hours.

Aidan knelt next to Diego. He put his hand to Diego's forehead, then checked his pulse at the wrist, mimicking moves that they had both watched Dr. Petrovsky perform on his patients.

"Do you feel sick, Diego?" he asked. Diego shook his head and sniffed, though he stopped crying. "Does anything hurt?" Diego shook his head again. Aidan smiled warmly. "So why cry?"

"Gabi scared me and she threw away my berries."

Marya glared daggers at Gabi. "What did you do to him?"

"Nothing," she protested. "Just took the berries and tried to get him to shut up."

"And I'm sure you were as warm and fuzzy as ever."

Gabi nodded and shrugged. Marya rolled her eyes and started to walk away. "What?" Gabi asked. Her temper began to flare; dealing with Marya was never something she relished.

"He's just a kid. You need to take it easy on him."

"We're all kids," Gabi retorted. "I didn't see Will taking it easy on any of us. Diego needs to learn not to eat things we don't know about."

"That's right, he does," Marya replied. She kept walking, though at a relatively slow pace. "Just like you need to learn that he's five years old, and doesn't learn the same way we do. You've got to keep it simple and kind."

"Who died and made you Mom?"

"Your mom." The cold words rolled off Marya's tongue without hesitation.

Gabi's fury boiled over in an instant. She picked up a rock and hurled it at Marya's head, only missing by an inch. The older girl whirled around, poised for a fight. Gabi charged her, but Marya easily sidestepped, tripping Gabi on her way past. Only two seconds after she tumbled to a stop, Gabi had Marya sitting astride her chest. Gabi threw up her arms to protect herself, but the older girl didn't throw a punch.

"You don't know everything, Gabi. We're not following you because you have all the answers in the world. Only the one we need. How to get to the other landing site. We also believe that, with you, we can get there without starving. Will lost his shit, and we lost faith in him." Marya paused. She stared at Gabi with unwavering determination. "There's nothing I care about more in this world than my brother. I swear if anything happens to him because you can't handle yourself, I'll tear you apart myself."

"Why not do it now, huh?" Gabi taunted. "You've always wanted to. Here's your chance. Will's not here to stop you."

"Because I'm not done with you yet. You still have to get us to the other ships."

"Fine. Then let me do it, and stay out of my way when it's my turn to watch Diego."

Marya's eyes narrowed, and she shook her head. "I wish I could. I love my brother. It sickens me that you care so little about yours."

"He's only my half-brother," Gabi hissed in response.

"So what? Are you really going to shove him away because your mom was raped? How's that fair to him? What has he ever done to you?"

"Mama killed herself because of him!" Tears began to well in her eyes as pain mixed with frustration.

"He didn't do that to her. She did that to herself. All he's ever done to you is love you and try to be like you."

Gabi growled and rolled her eyes. "It bugs me when he tries to be like me."

Marya stood up and offered her hand to Gabi. She eyed it suspiciously, but took it, and Marya hauled her to her feet.

"Why?" Marya asked.

"Because what I do is dangerous. He could get hurt. Plus, he couldn't do it."

"Not yet, anyway." Aidan and Diego passed them, continuing along the path that Gabi had chosen. Marya took a few steps after they passed, then stopped, looking back over her shoulder. "Maybe you care for him more than I thought."

Gabi scoffed. Diego was her responsibility to watch after, but that was it. Marya's insinuation that their relationship was deeper only aggravated her nearly as much as the physical threat.

"When this is all over, I never want to see you again," Gabi growled.

"That's fine with me."

Silence again engulfed their party. This time, it was welcome.

· · ·

"Are you sure about this, Calvin?"

Dr. Taylor's pensive expression did little to mask her concern. She seemed to sense that Cal saw through her front, and diverted her attention to Andrea, who stretched in her arms.

"Why not?" he replied with a shrug.

"Because it's not your job. It's not your place."

"He's my friend, Doc. I can't just stand by."

The doctor sighed. "No, I suppose you can't. Even when you should say no, you can't."

"No one asked me to do this, so I haven't had to say no."

Dr. Taylor regarded him with a deepening frown. "Then I don't understand why you have to do this. You don't have any experience with police work."

"Neither do Dayton and Hunter," Cal added.

"Right, but they've already enlisted the former detective that came here aboard *Gabriel*," she countered.

"I know. Vaughn's doing what he can. I want to do what I can, even if that just means sweeping the farms again or knocking on doors."

The doctor grimaced and reached for the bag of baby supplies that was slung over his shoulder. He relinquished his load.

"If it's what you want to do, I'll watch Andrea for a bit. The clinic's slow right now, but things usually pick up for me around noon, so don't go too far."

He sighed in relief, though he had hoped that he would be able to devote more time to the search for Darius. "No problem. I know this was short notice."

Cal threw up a hand to shield his eyes as he stepped out of the clinic into the bright morning sun. Concordia's streets were mostly empty, as the town's residents were already settled in to work for the day. Cal stepped out of the way of a horse-drawn delivery cart as he walked down Foundation toward the Civic Hall. Monica, North Concordia's chief architect, walked slowly along the street, holding an intense conversation with a small construction crew as she inspected several buildings from the outside.

Damage from the quake still left ugly gouges in a few buildings, though most had been patched, leaving behind what Cal thought to be the structural equivalent of a scar. There was still a gaping hole in the western wall of Civic Hall's second story, and anyone passing by on Foundation Street could look directly into what was left of the Governor's Office. Cal shuddered. The missing wall was an unnerving symbol of their missing leader.

Cal made his way inside. Deputy Governor Dayton had set up temporary offices in the meeting hall on the lower floor. Though to call it an office would be generous. He had dragged out a portable table, and rearranged a half dozen chairs around it, shoving the remaining seating from the room up against one wall. Concordia's standard stood directly behind the chair at the head of the table. Dayton was slouched in the chair. He looked up at Cal, blinking listlessly. Dark hemispheres under his eyes underscored the stress and lack of sleep that was eating away at the former colonel. Hunter sat to his left, intently scrutinizing a map that dominated the tabletop. He didn't acknowledge Cal until Dayton tapped impatiently on his elbow.

"Cal?" Hunter said. His voice was a barely audible rasp.

Cal nodded at each of them. "Hunter. Deputy Governor."

"Can we do something for you, Mr. McLaughlin?" Dayton asked.

"I was going to ask the same. What can I do to help?"

The deputy governor shook his head, then looked down at the map. "I don't know. I'm beyond worried that something terrible has happened to Darius. There hasn't been a trace of him since the night he disappeared. It's almost like he fell in the river or something."

*Well, that's one way to get away from it all,* Jerk chortled, though his voice was faint and muffled. After another day or two of regular meds, he would fade into the background again.

"That wouldn't make sense," Cal remarked.

Hunter rubbed his eyes, as though doing so would whisk away the fatigue. "Of course it doesn't. He wasn't acting strange before he disappeared."

"Well, a little," Dayton corrected, "but we chalked that up to lack of sleep. Nothing that would indicate he was suicidal."

Cal thought for a moment. "An accident?"

*Wow, that's stupid,* Jerk taunted. *Even for you.*

"In the middle of the night?" Hunter snapped hoarsely. "With no trace of where he went? What, do you think he just decided to randomly do a nighttime inspection of the bridges?"

"Hey, take it easy."

Hunter rose out of his chair and ran his hand through his hair, stopping at the back of his skull as he gripped at the disheveled strands. "Sorry, man. I know you're trying to help, it's just, this whole thing has been…"

"Stressful. Troubling. I get it." Cal sighed, crestfallen. "No, maybe I should just leave this up to you guys. I tend to muck things up anyway."

"We'd appreciate the assistance," Dayton replied. "We just need some time to figure out what you can do for us."

*Probably nothing,* he thought in dismay.

Jerk was slightly amused by this. *Oh good. You're finally getting the message.*

*I won't miss you when you're gone.*

*Way to make me feel loved.*

*What was that about messages?* Cal retorted. His schism went silent.

The door swung open behind Cal, and Detective Vaughn stepped in. He was a few inches shorter than Cal, but also had twenty years on him. Like many Concordians, he had lost quite a bit of weight shortly after arrival on the planet. Cal tried to imagine him as he must have been on Earth; slightly rotund, with an appetite to match his attitude. Now he was a grim, focused machine, given a chance to showcase his skills since the disappearance of Governor Owens. He regarded Cal with a squint as he walked to the table and sat down.

"I found something," he said, though his voice was devoid of any enthusiasm.

Cal took two steps toward the table before Vaughn's condemning stare froze him in his tracks.

"Official business, Mr. McLaughlin," he grumbled.

Dayton cleared his throat and waved vaguely in the air. "It's fine, Ben. Calvin has been consulting for me off and on since before landing. He's helping us out again." The deputy governor's chair creaked as he leaned forward. "What did you find?"

Cal took the opportunity of Vaughn's presentation to take a seat at the table. The detective pulled a cell phone from his pocket. Though useless for communication, the citizens had pooled together what few phones they had amongst them when they left Earth, creating a library of sorts. The library, which resided inside *Gabriel*, kept the phones charged until a citizen checked one out for whatever purpose. With a few swipes on the device's screen, Vaughn pulled up a picture that he had taken using the phone's camera. Cal craned his neck to see, but glare from the window behind him washed out the image entirely.

"That's the loading ramp of *Michael*," Vaughn pointed out before swiping to the next image. "See this here?"

"Looks like tread marks," Hunter commented.

Vaughn's scowl shifted to Hunter. "No, look again. Figure in the scale. Trucks and crawlers have a much wider track. And there's another one here that looks a little funny." He flipped to another image. "I also didn't see any sort of tire mark pattern, so don't go thinking this was made by a hand truck either."

By that time, Cal had repositioned himself between Hunter and Dayton, leaning over the table to look at the images. "Drag marks."

Vaughn nodded. "I think so. Not sure what this mark is over here," he said as he made a circle in the air over an odd, curved mark. "I was able to follow the marks for a while. There were shoe prints every now and then on either side that paralleled this main mark. I lost it all at the road, though."

"Which road?" Dayton asked.

"Rust Creek."

"Mr. Ceretti, I think it's time for you to take a trip to go see Norris. Find out what he knows."

"Right. I'll get a horse."

Dayton shook his head, though he never took his eyes off the phone's screen. "No, tell Josephson you're borrowing her truck. I need you there today, not tomorrow." Hunter nodded and left without another word. "Detective, I want you to go over the inside of *Michael* one more time, see if you can find anything else."

Vaughn grunted as he tucked the phone back in his pocket. "I've found all I can. His bed was made, didn't look like he made it back to his berth that night. I've traced all the possible routes from the sleeper pod to the back of the ship, and there's no other trace evidence. No blood, nothing."

"Wait, blood?" Cal interrupted.

Vaughn's demeaning glare locked back on to Cal. "If my gut's right about those marks, then the governor was kidnapped."

"Kidnapped?  Who the hell would do that?"

"Assuming it's true," Dayton intervened, "it could be any number of people.  During the labor strikes he made plenty of enemies, including Norris."

Cal froze in place, his jaw slack in dumbfounded silence.  He wanted to tell Dayton that Norris wouldn't do that, nor would any of his people.

"I don't think we should rule out someone in town either," Vaughn continued.  "Or those new folks from *Mercy*."

Cal scoffed and slapped the palm of his hand into the table, making the other men flinch in surprise.  "Yeah, that's it!" he snorted sarcastically.  "I'll ask Brittany if she's seen anyone dragging around our governor.  That's what I'll do to help out."

"Mr. McLaughlin," Dayton soothed as he rose from his seat.

"Oh, so you *have* come out of your shop to meet our new neighbors, have you?" Vaughn sneered.  "I thought you were going to lock yourself away and become a hermit."

"What?  No!  Well, yes, I've met them.  Or one of them anyway.  It's a long story."

"Do you want to give me the short version, or is this going to be another boring, rambling lead that goes nowhere?"

"I thought that anything helps at this point," Cal retorted.  He was doing his best to stand his ground, but Vaughn made him feel like slinking away.  Despite his lack of stature, Vaughn was carrying himself in a very aggressive and imposing way.  It was a side of the man he had never seen before, but didn't particularly want to cross any further.

"Fine."  The detective folded his arms across his chest.  "Who is this Brittany girl and what does she have to do with anything?"

"She's an old friend from Earth."  Cal watched the other men and their stunned reactions.  "My friends were left behind when I was taken for the launch.  At first I wondered what happened to them and how they made out during the War.  Eventually I had images of how they died.  Pretty horrible shit, so I tried not to think of it at all.  So imagine my surprise when someone I thought was dead walks through my front door just days after *Mercy* lands."

"Does she know anything about what happened?"

Cal shrugged.  "I haven't talked to her about it.  I could, though."

"Have you interviewed *Mercy's* survivors, Detective?" Dayton asked.

"Not all of them.  Enough to know that no one had seen the governor."

The deputy governor slid back into his chair, which groaned under his weight.  "Would you mind at least asking this friend of yours if she knows anything?"

Cal squirmed uncomfortably.  "I could.  I'm not sure how much good it will do.  The last time I talked with her, things didn't go so well.  We pretty much pissed each other off."

"Alright, what about your other friends from Earth?"

"I don't know if any others made it.  She's the only one I've seen so far.  She came into my shop with two guys I didn't know, but they seemed to know her pretty well."

"What did these guys look like?  Did they identify themselves?" Vaughn queried.

"I don't know.  They were just guys.  They came in, bought some booze, and left."

"Please pay closer attention to details next time, Mr. McLaughlin," Vaughn rebuked coldly.  "Anything you think is minor or not worth mentioning could be something that ends up turning an investigation.  With how little I've got to work with, I need everything you can get me."

"That might be hard.  She might not want to talk to me."

"So put your big boy pants on and apologize if you have to."

Cal felt himself flush.  "Fine, I'll see what I can do."

He had to get out of there, away from Vaughn's scorn and so-called advice.  Cal's return walk to the clinic was full of self-reflection.  He wanted to help with the investigation, but he didn't trust himself with Brittany.  They had both changed so much that they seemed destined to part ways.  Cal was only beginning to realize how the resentment he still harbored for her colored their current relationship.  And there was no telling how her experiences on post-Launch Earth had done the same.

*How the hell can I even talk to her anymore?  Much less see if she knows something?*

. . .

Darius felt someone nudge his foot. He craned his head, shielding his eyes with his hands. They were still bound together at the wrist, though his captors did not keep him tied to a tree when they were awake.

The two men who had guarded Darius for the past day barely spoke at all. They seemed cautious about carrying on any conversation in front of Darius, and would only do so at a whisper beyond the range he could hear. They were, in fact, so evasive with Darius that he didn't even know their names. Darius labeled them by numbers. The swarthy black-haired man was One, and the gaunt one whose hair bordered somewhere between blond and gray was Two.

"Eat," Two commanded.

At least one of them was always on guard duty, and they took turns performing chores to keep the campsite running smoothly. Two had just finished preparing a meal foraged from native plants, and One took silent leave to eat.

Two reiterated his command by thrusting a bowl in Darius's face. Darius reached up and took the steaming bowl of soup from Two. The tips of his fingers registered the warmth of the metal bowl. It was decidedly uncomfortable given the midday heat, but the food was welcome. Darius's stomach had been growling for the last hour. He took a sip of the near-scalding broth, coughing and sputtering as it burned on the way down. Darius would have cursed if it wasn't for the fact that the scorching pain was a temporary distraction from the constant throbbing from his injuries.

The soup, though rather bland, was filling. Hearty chunks of wild potato were mixed with small, Demeter onions. There was meat, as well, though not a lot of it. It was definitely some sort of small game bird. Darius scanned the ground around the campsite, looking for signs of feathers that would give it away. He found the discarded pile of yellow and gray feathers that identified the bird as a pine ranger, an insectivore about the size of a large quail. Not commonly hunted by Concordians as they were elusive, yet didn't yield much meat for the trouble.

Darius pondered why Two would have taken out a pine ranger instead of hunting gray pheasant. There were a number of factors that he weighed, including how short a time *Mercy's* survivors had been on Demeter, the perceived marksmanship of his captor, and the time involved in finding a pheasant. The woods around Concordia were thick with pine rangers, but it took a lot more effort to find the much more rewarding pheasants.

*Are you trying to keep it simple?* He wondered. Darius glanced at Two's Winchester shotgun. It was a typical pump-action, probably 20 gauge. A small game hunter's weapon. *Not sure I want to mess with you, Two. You're a good shot if that bird was in flight. And that weapon of yours would tear me up.*

One returned from out of sight where he had taken his meal. A canteen was clutched in his left hand. On his right hip rested a holstered pistol. Another deadly weapon in the hands of a man who looked like he could put it to good use. One knelt next to Darius. He collected the empty metal bowl and poured water into it, then handed it to Darius.

"Drink," he ordered in a flat tone.

Darius obeyed. The cold water was a refreshing contrast to the hot soup and weather. He drank down the entire bowl in one breath. He panted for a moment, catching his breath, then held out the bowl expectantly.

"More, please," he asked.

One filled the bowl again without hesitation. This time Darius drank it in a far more measured manner as his captors held a whispered conversation about twenty feet away.

*They're keeping me fed. They give me water when I ask. That's good, I guess.*

Shortly after he had finished the second bowl, three men marched into camp, each with a pack on their back and a weapon at their side or in their hands. As they got closer, Darius recognized them as the men who had originally beaten and captured him. Apprehension began to take grip, and Darius clamored to his feet, scrabbling at the bark of a Demeter pine with his bound hands.

One and Two turned their backs to Darius briefly. They seemed to relax for the first time since their arrival. The pock-faced man smiled wickedly as he told them something, then One and Two scurried off and began to break camp. Suddenly, Darius was face to face with the leader of the renegades.

"Good afternoon, Governor," he grinned. "How are you feeling today?"

"Like a new man," Darius replied sarcastically.

"I'm sorry we couldn't give you a more comfortable place to rest your head. But I'm sure you understand."

"That you couldn't just walk me onboard your ship with all those eyes looking?"

"Something like that," the man replied. "Let's go for a walk here, Governor. Stretch your legs a little bit."

Darius glanced down at the gun that was trained on him, waving in the direction that the man wanted him to go. His nerves tingled, threatening to turn his stomach against him. He started to walk as directed.

*The west,* he thought. *Farther from town.*

"So it looks like you were right about the computers on *Gabriel*," the man said casually as the left the campsite. "No one's been in there since launch. That's a good thing."

"For who?"

"For you. It means that you've been telling me the truth."

"Then I think there's been a mix up," Darius corrected. "We're going the wrong way for it to be good for me."

There was a slight hesitation. "No, we're going the right way."

"Concordia is the other way."

"No, it's not." This time the response was too quick.

"Yes, it is."

"Are you calling me a liar, Governor?"

"Yes sir, I am."

Darius felt a hand yank on his shoulder. He was spun around to face the band's leader. His eyes were narrowed and he had a disdainful snarl on his lips. He raised his pistol and trained it between Darius's eyes. Darius had to fight back the grip of fear as the deadly weapon was waved in his face, with no chance of defending himself.

"Better be careful. You don't want to upset me, do you?"

"So the truth upsets you, then?"

"If you keep this up, I won't take you home," his captor growled.

Darius jerked a thumb behind him. "There's more pine the farther west you go from Concordia. To the east it thins out, and there's more larch and alder. So we're walking the wrong way."

The man stared blankly at Darius for a second, then grinned evilly. "You're very smart, Governor. I'm going to have to keep my eye on you. Keep walking."

Darius turned around and resumed the march. It was becoming clear that these men had no intention of releasing him. Turning and fighting now would do nothing but end in his death. His only hope was that they made a mistake, and that he could escape from them. That seemed to be an impossible task, if the last thirty hours or so was any indication. He had been watched like a hawk, and tied to a tree at night to prevent escape. And now they were striking out even deeper into reaper bear territory.

. . .

"That'll do it," Devereaux smiled as he crammed the last bar of soap in the small, aluminum crate. "Anything you want me to keep an ear out for once I'm back?"

"No, thank you," Cal replied. "I'm still surprised you came to see me yourself today."

The butcher's broad shoulders rolled like boulders as he shrugged. "Brayden could use a little practice running things by himself. It's a good morning to see how he handles things." Devereaux glanced down the short hallway toward the staircase and stockroom. "Where's Andrea?"

"You're not the only one who's hired help," Cal admitted.

"Oh?"

"Yeah. Well, in a way I guess. Beth decided that she wants to run a daycare. I'm her first client. She's watching over her for a bit so I can get some work done. Maybe even some errands."

"Beth as in Dr. Taylor's wife?"

"No, Dr. Taylor's daughter-in…" Cal caught himself in the realization that Devereaux was referring to Dr. Jamie Taylor, not the Dr. Taylor who taught him biostasis systems. The son who was taking over her practice at the clinic. "Yeah, I'm sorry. You're right."

Devereaux scratched at the stubble on his chin. "No kidding. Well, she's the only game in town, I guess."

"Yeah. She's not sure it will work out either," Cal added, noting Deveraux's unspoken concern about the venture's success. "It depends on how many of the moms in the colony have the luxury of staying at home with their children."

"That was my first thought. But I'm glad that you've found a solution, even if it's just to give you a little time away when you need it. So what are you going to do with your newfound freedom today?"

"I need to go shopping." Cal stood up and walked around the counter to his display rack. He selected two bottles, one of vodka and one whiskey. "I don't feel like trading favors today if I don't have to, so here's my wallet."

"You know, you could just ask me if you need something. I'm more than happy to help."

"Thanks, Frank. But I could use a trip out of the house, maybe get a little fresh air. Oh, and I have to go see how Saika is doing on that dress for Andrea." Cal looked down at the bottles in his hand. He placed the whiskey bottle on the counter, then flipped around the vodka bottle and offered it to Devereaux. "I was going to stop by your place later. It's been a while since I've had fresh meat. Find me something good?"

The butcher took the bottle with a smile. "No problem. I'll put together some choices for you. Stop by on your way home to pick one."

Devereaux departed, leaving Cal alone in an eerily quiet shop. He picked up his corn husk broom and began sweeping, listening to the rustle of the dried plant fibers with every rhythmic sweep. His shop had never felt emptier. And though it had been silent in the dead of winter, this day felt even quieter.

The silence was short lived, as Dayton and Detective Vaughn made their entry. Both men's brows dripped with sweat; Vaughn produced a handkerchief and swiped away the offending liquid.

"Anything new?" Cal asked anxiously.

"Maybe," Dayton replied.

"How much do you know about the computer systems on the ships?" Vaughn asked.

"Uh, not much. I could probably run the sleeper berths if I had to, but it's been a while."

Dayton's beard scrunched as he pursed his lips. "Sergeant Drisko didn't take you back into the core to show you the systems?"

"No. He didn't want to upset you. I was back there only once, with Hunter."

Vaughn shook his head and muttered a curse. "Another dead end. No offense, Governor."

"Still just the deputy. And none taken. Drisko's been gone a long time."

"Wait, what does this have to do with Cam?" Cal asked, thoroughly confused as to why his dead friend had come up in conversation all of a sudden.

"He was the IO on *Michael*," Dayton replied.

"Yeah… so?"

"I found something on *Michael* that I missed the first time through," Vaughn explained. "There was a floor plate in the computer core that was missing its screws. I found the screws a few feet away, on top of a…" he paused, looking at Dayton, who shrugged. "Computer thingy."

"Thingy?"

"I don't know what you call it. I'm not a techie. Anyway, there were scrape marks on the other adjacent plates, but not this one. Like something had been dragged around while this plate was missing. When I pulled it up, there were also scrape marks on the beam that the plates rest on. Something was taken from down there."

"But I have no idea what," Dayton added. "All of the servers are still there and running. All of the ship's systems are online, and there are no unexpected equipment errors, according to Hunter. Just a mess of power and network cables that don't go to anything."

Vaughn crossed his arms across his chest and shook his head. "I took a trip down south and looked at *Gabriel* also. I saw pretty much the same thing, only the scrapes weren't as noticeable, and the deck plate was screwed back down."

"That's weird," Cal said. "Why would they be screwed down on one and not the other?"

"Only one of two things. Either different people opened the compartments on the ships, or whoever did it wasn't as careful when they took whatever it was off of *Michael*."

Cal realized he was leaning on his broom hard enough that it was bowed and wobbling. He quickly put his weight back on his feet and set the broom aside. "So whoever kidnapped Darius also took something off of the ships?"

Vaughn nodded. "It at least gives us a motive. If the governor stumbled on something he wasn't supposed to, someone might have taken offense."

"Then he must have recently stumbled onto it." Cal added.

"That's right."

"So it must have been someone on *Mercy*," Cal postulated. The others regarded him silently. "If there was something there of value, someone on our ships would have had six years to take it. The strike a few years back would have been the perfect cover, too. Don't you find it weird that Darius would find whatever it is and then disappear within, what, a week of *Mercy* showing up?"

Vaughn glanced over at Dayton. "He's right, you know. I was going to tell you later, but he's hit it on the head."

"Which then makes your contact that much more important, Mr. McLaughlin," Dayton replied. "Have you had any luck?"

"I haven't even seen her."

"Make an excuse if you have to," Vaughn said in a chilling tone. "Time isn't on our side. There's no telling what might happen to the governor if we don't act quickly."

Deputy Governor Dayton took his newfound detective with him, leaving Cal again in the silence of his shop. He leaned on his counter, eyes closed with his head resting on intertwined fingers as he processed Vaughn's findings. This time he had no desire to sweep; the silence of the shop and the torrent in his brain drove him out after a few minutes. He turned back from the door only to retrieve the bottle of whiskey that he intended to use for barter and his cloth shopping satchel.

The walk along River Way did much to clear his head. By the time he passed the nearly rebuilt mill and was on the Boulevard, he was looking forward to the bustle of the market square. He went directly to Saika's clothing shop. He had a pleasant conversation with her, and she excitedly showed him a sketch of the design for her own wedding dress. This time, Cal truly did feel happiness for her, and he felt somewhat like a fool for wallowing in his own grief before. Tyler Quinn was a good man, and though both he and Saika had suffered personal tragedies since landing, they had been drawn to each other with inescapable magnetism.

After Saika promised that she'd finish Andrea's dress by week's end, Cal continued his loop around the block. The whiskey found its home with the town's toymaker, in exchange for two future toys for Andrea and two favors. The favors were spent at the baker's in exchange for a large loaf of sourdough. Cal was feeling good, having momentarily forgotten Darius and Vaughn and mysterious missing components. Until he bumped into someone on accident on his way out of the baker's shop.

"Hey," Brittany growled. Her eyes locked with his. Her eyes widened and a faint smile crossed her lips. "Cal, it's you. I'm sorry."

"No," he shook his head. "I'm sorry."

"Hey, where's the little one?"

"I got someone to watch her for a while."

She got up on her tip toes and looked over his shoulder. "Man, they have some good smelling stuff in there. Hey, you get something?" She peeked into his satchel somewhat intrusively.

"Sourdough. The real thing, not that mass produced crap you got at the store back on Earth." He noticed that her friends that came in to his store for liquor were not present.

She let out a jealous groan, and her eyes darted skyward for a second. "I'm starving and that sounds so good. Can you give me some?"

Cal looked down at his bag, and then over his shoulder into the shop. "Come here," he said as he stepped back in.

The baker's assistant greeted them at the counter. He wore a white apron that was tied loosely over his abdomen, and his brilliant blue eyes sparkled as he flashed a smile.

"Did you forget something on your list, Cal?" he smirked.

"Sort of. My friend here is new in town, and she's never had your sourdough before. Think you can hook her up with a little something?"

The assistant snapped his fingers. "I've got just the thing." He walked over to a rack of cooling bread, and plucked out a modest sourdough roll. He juggled it between his hands as he walked back, and tossed it to Brittany. She sucked in a breath of air and began tossing it back and forth between her hands for a moment before it cooled down to the point she could handle it. "It doesn't get any fresher than that."

"How much?" Cal asked.

"A friend of Cal's is a friend of mine." He knocked on the counter once. "No charge, just this time."

"Thanks," Cal grinned sheepishly.

Brittany bit into the soft roll as soon as they were outside. She stopped in her tracks and closed her eyes, savoring the moment. "God, Cal, it's been so long."

He nodded. "I know. We were eating mostly packaged food for the first few months here, and the entire first winter. I almost didn't make it past the second winter." He paused for a moment. "We almost didn't."

"The colony?" she said with her mouth stuffed full of food, her eyes bulging.

Cal shook his head. "Fifteen people died. There was a drought, and then a terrible winter. Lexi got sick and I…" he trailed off.

Brittany looked at him expectantly. "You what?"

*How could you understand just what I went through for her? What I sacrificed to save her?* He sighed. *How there was a time long ago when I would have done the same for you.*

"Nothing. We both almost died. Doctor Taylor pulled us through."

"Oh!" Brittany perked up. "I've met him. He's a real nice guy. Kinda quiet. His wife is kind of a bitch though."

Cal rolled his eyes and started to walk away, toward Devereaux's.

"What?" she asked, catching up with him.

"I dunno, Britt. Maybe it's that you just called a good friend of mine a bitch. Or that you're talking about the wrong doctor."

She cast her gaze aside sheepishly. "Sorry, I didn't know."

"There's a lot about me that you don't know. About fifty years worth."

"Hey," she snapped, grabbing his arm and stopping him. "I know we haven't seen each other in a long time, but if we're going to play games, the cards need to be the same. We've both been asleep for most of that time, so don't give me that exaggerated bullshit. It's been six years for each of us. We just spent them in different places."

"Fine," he grumbled, then turned to continue his walk. She fell in step at his side. "Let's ask each other one burning question about the last six years so we can start catching up. You go first."

"Why only one? I have a ton."

"Because I've only got time for one right now."

"Okay," she huffed. "Why'd the baker give you free bread?"

"Because I'm a good customer, and he was trying to get you to become a customer as well."

"Oh, no you don't," she hustled ahead of him, turning to face him and blocking his path. "I might buy it if it was the first time I saw something like that happen."

"Oh yeah? What else did you see?"

"The other day, at the clothing store. The woman that runs the place gave you a huge discount on your daughter's dress. Why?"

"It wasn't that big of a discount."

"I checked into it, Cal," she insisted. "It was big. Now answer the damn question."

He came to a stop and let out a heavy sigh. "Fine. When we got here, both ships were supposed to land on this side of the river. The commander of *Gabriel* broke off and landed on the other side because he had some sort of spat with the other commanders way back on Earth. He didn't want any of his own colonists to even have contact with us. At one point there was a huge fight over the whole thing.

Some people got killed, including the other commander, then we all finally agreed to be one big happy family. I was there when it all went down, sat at the negotiation table with a bunch of important people, and some people think highly of me because of it."

"Huh. So you're a hero, then?"

"Not even close. I just said that I was there. Not doing a whole lot but taking up space."

"I bet you killed the enemy commander," she smirked.

"No!" he snapped back. They had reached Devereaux's, and he stopped outside, not wanting to take her in to see what his alcohol had purchased, for fear that it would be misconstrued as more gifts from an adoring population. "Look, you're not even listening to me."

"Because you're not saying," she retorted. "I want to know what you've been up to all these years."

*Still willing to talk your head off after all this time, I see. We may have both changed, but some things don't. Well, Vaughn will be happy with that.*

"Do I get to ask my burning question, then?"

She nodded. "Fair is fair."

"Would you like to come over for dinner and a drink? I promise we can catch up on our life stories if you do."

Brittany stumbled for words for a moment, as if caught off guard. "S-sure. Tonight?"

"Tomorrow night. I'll make babysitting arrangements for Andrea."

She smiled warmly. "It's a date."

"No, it's not."

"It's just an expression," she replied, wounded.

"And I'm being clear."

She threw her arms up in exasperation. "Fine. No canned shit, though. I'm not telling my story over a pouch of fifty year-old spaghetti or anything gross like that."

*Of course not. You're going to use me, just like old times,* Cal thought bitterly. *I'm going to be kind of pissed if you can't help me find Darius.*

Cal watched her round the corner before going into Devereaux's. He sighed. *Looks like I'm eating from a can tonight if she wants something fresh tomorrow.*

. . .

Darius crested the short rise, peering at the creek twenty feet below that paralleled their path. The cool water burbled as it rushed by, taunting Darius with its song. His cracked lips felt like sandpaper as he ran his tongue over them. The forest had thickened dramatically over the past day, but the shadows provided little respite from Bravo's roasting of the earth.

"Drink, please," he wheezed hoarsely.

"Patience. We're almost there," the pock-faced man huffed, struggling for breath.

"You have no idea where you're going," Darius shot back.

"I'll know it when I see it."

"Maybe if you'd tell me what you're looking for, I could help."

Silence answered him, broken only by the footfalls of the men behind him. Two and a half days of constant hiking through the wilderness west of Concordia had left Darius's feet painfully swollen and blistered. His captors had let him take his boots off overnight, which was a welcome relief until he discovered that the swelling prevented him from putting them back on in the morning. This seemed to offend his companions, who secured the boots to his wrist bindings by their laces. Now his bruised and battered arms were forced to carry that weight in a rather awkward position. With no ability to adjust them, there was no relief from the strain.

He was directed to skirt along the edge of the precipice that towered over the stream. Farther ahead he could see sharply descending rapids. The overlook was much shorter at that point, just where the cascading water disappeared around a giant mossy rock outcropping on the far side. The pock-faced man took the lead, as he had done a few times previously, bounding hurriedly to the bend in the stream while his companions drove Darius forward. He scurried to the creek's bank at the bend, splashed some water on his face, and took in his surroundings. He then scrambled the short distance to the top of the cut, and waited for Darius with a smug grin.

"And here we are," he beamed.

Darius looked around. Nothing of particular note was present.

Hills flanked the valley, their heights scattered with pines and the occasional fir. The valley was a denser mixture of pines and alders, with countless boulders scattered like grains of rice spilled by a giant. Berry bushes—a half dozen inedible varieties—burst from every crevice, and the rocks along the banks teemed with lichen.

"Alright," Darius said. "Here we are. What now?"

"We wait."

Darius settled in at the base of a tree. He rubbed his aching feet, taking care not to touch any of the angry, swollen blisters. A few had caked over with a mixture of pus and dirt, which stung like nothing he had ever felt. He sucked in a deep breath, then pushed it out with a loud groan as the coarse rope fibers scratched one of the burst blisters.

"Would you mind not picking at those things?" his captor asked, disgust dripping in his voice. "That's a little disgusting."

"Sorry to inconvenience you," Darius shot back sarcastically.

The pock-faced man shrugged. "It's as much your fault as my boss's. I could think of a dozen other ways to take care of you that would have been easier on both of us."

The words struck Darius with an odd finality. Being kidnapped was one thing. Being kept in the dark with the promise of being unharmed as long as he cooperated was tolerable, though only barely. But to 'be taken care of,' under the circumstances, meant being silenced.

"Think I wanted to be marched all this way to have you kill me?" He choked on the words, trying to conceal the panic that was clawing at him from within. His instincts told him to flee, but that was not a possibility.

A faint smile crossed the man's lips for a moment. "No. Not at all. I tried to tell him that, but he wouldn't listen. He was pretty insistent on how we were to deal with you."

"And just how is that?"

"To make sure that you're never found. Or at least not in any identifiable way," he smirked.

The renegade glanced up and nodded at one of his cohorts, who disappeared into the woods at a jog. His other companion set his pack down, retrieving the familiar black and yellow ropes that they used to secure Darius to the trees at night. Darius tried to scramble to his feet, but found himself staring at the business end of a nine millimeter pistol.

"Ah, ah," the man scolded. "I can still make this unpleasant for you if you piss me off."

"More unpleasant than death?" Darius spat back.

His captor's head bobbed in a slow, chilling nod. "Trust me, Governor, you don't want to try me. Other men have. They thought they could stand up to me. And, well… they found out just how quickly I could turn them into little girls." His cold eyes locked on to Darius, piercing his soul with an icy lance. "Save yourself the trouble, Governor."

Darius hesitated, but backed down. He was bound tightly to the tree within a couple of minutes. In the distance he heard an off-key caterwauling that sounded vaguely like native birdcalls, though not accurately reproduced.

"So if you're going to make sure I'm never found then I'm guessing you're not going to blow my brains out. So what's with the ropes?"

"A head start," the man replied, scratching at his scarred cheek.

Darius cocked his head in confusion. "A what?"

"I've heard this place has quite the vicious predator. I'm not going to stick around to admire it, of course."

Darius kicked his legs and lunged, earning nothing but sharp pains from the weeping blisters on his feet.

"You sick bastard," he spat. "You'd leave me to die like that?"

The man shrugged indifferently. "Like I said, I tried to save you from all this. I just wanted you to *accidentally* drown in the river. You can thank my boss for this little stunt."

"Right, because this is so much better."

"You'd be dead already. Wouldn't that be better than the waiting? The horrible stench of the bear's breath before it sinks its claws into your flesh and tears you limb from limb?"

Darius snarled as he threw his weight against his bonds. "You know, I'm really starting to dislike you. Who's your boss? I'd like to file a complaint."

The man laughed. "I like your spirit. It's almost too bad that Young offered so much to have you offed. But then again, we'd probably have a serious difference of opinions at some point. It's always that way with guys like you. Too righteous for their own good. So inflexible."

*Young. God damn it.*

The mock bird calls grew closer, followed by the distant bellow of a reaper bear. His captors had attracted the attention of the living weapon that would be his end. Time seemed so short, and he had far more questions than answer. Not that he'd be able to tell anyone what he had learned. He still wanted to know, even if only for his own peace.

"So the man hires you to take me out and steal the servers, huh?" he growled bitterly.

The man took a deliberate swig from his canteen. "We were supposed to reclaim my boss's property when no one was looking. To be honest, we didn't know you were back there. It's good for us that you were, since you knew about the machines. If you hadn't been there when we took them, you would have known, and then where would we be?"

"Probably in my office, with me grilling you."

"Exactly. I'm sorry you got involved, but it's nothing personal. I've got a job to do, and thanks to you stumbling on those servers, that now includes killing you."

"Don't you think he's going to extremes just to steal a few computers?" Darius asked.

The evil smile returned to the man's cracked lips. "See, now that's where you're wrong. The items we're talking about here belong to my employer. He's quite relieved to get them back from storage."

"Bullshit. Those computers were part of Benedict's price for his technology. They became Project property when they were delivered and installed."

"I'm sorry, what computers are you talking about?" the man taunted. "Oh yes, the ones that no one's ever heard about."

"Doctor Benedict…"

"Is dead, Governor," he interrupted. "So is Doctor Fairweather. And so are you." His captor turned away and took a couple steps, then faced him again. "If it's any consolation, Mr. Young is very relieved that his property has been returned to him."

"They're not his!" Darius bellowed.

"There isn't a single soul that can dispute his claim. If it ever comes to light, that is."

*Damn it,* he cursed mentally. *If I had just told Tom. Or Roger.*

"And just what is he going to do with his so-called property?"

"Oh, that's not my business. He's the one with the eye on the bigger picture. My job is just about done. It's his turn now."

Darius narrowed his eyes. "So Young tells you to jump and you jump. No matter how much damage it does to your new home. Why does your boss want those computers so much when all they can do is help the colony?"

The laughed and waved dismissively. "I don't really care. You see, Young is a wealthy man. And this kind of job? Let's just say it comes with a very impressive pension."

"Young left all he had back on Earth. Everyone has to work for their keep around here, and that includes every one of you."

"Oh, he'll be wealthy again, now that his property has been re-turned."

Darius bit his lip. Young's plan was clear. Technological development was something that he could easily hold over the heads of Concordia's population. Though they had gone years without it, the allure of bringing back at least some of the familiar comforts of Earth might prove too strong for some people to resist, even if it was limited in availability. While Darius planned to turn the servers into public archives to kick-start technological advancement, Young was far more cunning with business. Darius now saw that, with control over the release of technology, Young could potentially gain sway over the entire colony without ever firing a shot. It represented the death of everything he had ever done in overseeing the colony, from the rationing of the early years to the construction of Benedict Square. The backbreaking work that his fellow Concordians had put in over the course of six years to build their peaceful home might all be for nothing, snatched in a power grab by a billionaire who shouldn't even be alive. It was sickening; Darius's stomach churned and he felt his blood boil.

The bear howled again, just as the man sent to lure it returned. He doubled over against a nearby tree, panting hard. The other cohort worked quickly to pack all the gear. Their leader glanced into the woods behind Darius and smirked.

"Well, it looks like we're done here. You've been a good sport about all of this. Sorry it didn't work out for you, Governor. No hard feelings, right?"

"The Lord will see you get what's coming to you," Darius seethed.

"Someday, I have no doubt. But right now I've got to be going home. I'll have a drink in your honor when I get there. Whiskey, neat. Made by that kid in town, what's his name?" Darius clenched his teeth, refusing to play the man's game anymore. He nodded once. "Well, I guess we're done here."

The three men charged downstream along the bank as quickly as they could move. They were out of sight before the reaper bear called out again. It was close by, probably within a couple hundred feet. Darius jerked in his bonds in every direction he could think of, trying to find any give in the rope, any slack that he might be able to work with.

He found that his hands could move a little bit, and that if he exhaled and held his breath, he could reach the ground. The second time he did so, he fumbled along the ground with his fingers to find anything of use. The tips brushed up against something cold and hard. Darius had to crane his neck, but was able to determine that it was a small rock with one jagged edge. He relaxed slightly, cycled two deep breaths, and tried again. His fingers again brushed over the stone, but he couldn't get a grip on it.

The bear let out a long, low noise that was equal parts howl and growl. Darius knew he had little time left. He quickly repeated his breath sequence and made one more try for the rock, but his middle finger hit it before it passed over, and the rock rolled out of reach. Darius screamed out in frustration and anguish. The beast let out its roar again. He could hear the thunderous sounds of its footfalls as it loped toward him. Darius glanced over his shoulder, and the bear was at his tree in almost an instant.

It circled around the tree slowly, bounding twice in an aggressive manner and scattering dirt into a fine cloud with one sideways swipe of its massive paw across the earth. When it growled again, Darius could smell the stench of death in its breath. Its lips curled to reveal cruel, jagged teeth, longer than anything he had seen on Earth. Darius tried to steel himself for his imminent death, but the terror that gripped him only allowed him to do one thing: void his bladder.

The reaper bear squared off to face him less than ten feet away. It crouched on its hind legs, lowering its front end in preparation for the leap that would seal the fate of its prey. As it jumped, Darius saw the left claw swipe toward his head. Instinctively, he ducked the other way and closed his eyes. He felt searing pain in his right arm and chest, and he fell to the ground.

Again, running on pure instinct, he screamed in pain and backpedaled with his feet. He got about five feet before his back ran into a tree and his eyes shot open. The bear was preparing to attack again. Next to it rested the black and yellow rope that had bound him to the tree, shredded into many pieces by the bear's claw. A trail of blood ran from where the beast stood to where Darius now cowered. A voice inside him shouted out, drowning out the world around him.

*Get up and run!*

Darius didn't have time to react fully before the terrible predator charged again. He tried to roll out of the way of its claws, but the animal grazed him across the hip. Every part of his body burned and ached, from the fresh, bloody wounds of the bear to the days-old bruises from the beating. They didn't mean a thing anymore. Darius was on his feet and running. He plunged headlong into the creek. The bear was only a couple of seconds behind him. Panicked, Darius darted to the other bank, but it was too steep and rocky to climb, so he ran further downstream.

The animal's fetid breath rolled off his skin in hot, moist waves. He couldn't chance looking back to see how far away it was. He could only keep running. That was no small chore, as the churning rapids threatened to sweep him off his feet with each stride. The creek widened and leveled out ahead, and the bank dropped to where he could probably climb out. Darius didn't give it a second thought. He plunged toward the dry shore. But as the creek widened out, it also got significantly deeper. Darius suddenly found himself without footing, and the still-rapid current dragged him downstream even faster.

Darius thrashed around, clawing for ground with both his hands and feet. His head went under at an inopportune time, and he got a lungful of water. He coughed and retched, which only made it worse, as he immediately sucked in more water as soon as he expelled it. The world began to fade, but Darius did not relent in his desperate act of self-preservation.

As he was about to get swept downstream into another set of rapids, his hands caught the trunk of a felled tree at the river's edge. He heaved with all his might, dragging himself on top, where he proceeded to spend the next five minutes coughing and throwing up. When he could breathe again, he remembered the reaper bear. He scrambled to shore and looked around for the beast. And he found it. On the opposite side of the channel, pacing back and forth. It snarled and growled at him, but made no further effort to pursue.

*What in the hell?*

That was as much thought as he gave the situation before counting his blessings and disappearing into the woods in the opposite direction.

· · ·

Gabrielle Serrano
18 July, 6 yal, midday
Approximately 75 miles southeast of wreck site
>|

Gabi kept her eyes locked straight ahead. The edge of her vision to the left was blocked out by a massive rock spire that shrouded them in its shadow. It was almost inconceivably tall, rising at least five hundred feet in less than the same span. The path ahead of them, along its base, was strewn with boulders more than twice her height. Little vegetation covered the ground; the tall fir trees had thinned out over the past few days, replaced by much shorter, gnarled species that otherwise looked fairly similar. The underbrush had also cleared out, and was now mostly composed of berries that Diego had inadvertently discovered to be edible. Unfortunately, the sparse vegetation could not mask the deep ravine that scarred the terrain to their right.

It was probably thirty feet deep, she guessed. While it wasn't a sheer drop off, the slope was hopelessly steep. If she were to tumble over the edge, the fall might not kill her. However, being stuck at the bottom with no way out was a death sentence, particularly if she fell into the ice cold creek at the bottom.

Yet ahead of them lay the singular focus of her attention; a small notch between two encroaching peaks on either side, nearly completely devoid of trees. No chasm running down the center, as it hooked to the right shortly before the pass, then ran up the side of the opposing ridge in a steep v-cut. A few large boulders rested at the notch, but nothing that looked like a major obstruction from where she stood. And all that it would take for them to get there was one last push. But that push would be over a gradually steepening incline littered with talus cast from the spire above. Time and floods had taken their toll on the ravine's channel, and at points it narrowed the path to only a few feet.

Her stomach growled, reminding her that they were hours removed from their last meal. She took a quick swig from her canteen and forced Diego to do the same, despite his protests that he wasn't thirsty.

"We won't be able to stop until we get to the top," she grumbled.

He whined once more but took two small sips anyway. The Brennan siblings followed suit without a word, then double checked that their gear was secured. They carried only the bare necessities on their backs now; even the few folding shelter panels weighed too much to port over the mountains, and had been abandoned the previous morning when camp was broken. Only food, water, weapons, flint, a section of rope, and a few thin sleeping furs were left. While they cut down on the chill at night, they did not eliminate it. Yet another misery that Gabi tried to forget.

*When we get there, it will all be better,* she reminded herself. *Warm beds, fresh food.*

She had stopped doubting that the other ships had landed, and that there was a colony to be found beyond the mountains. She couldn't afford to let herself believe there wasn't a settlement anymore. Walking through a vast, unending wilderness was taking a toll on her. She wanted to run and hide, but she would only be hiding in the very unknown she was trying to escape. There was no use taking her frustrations out on anyone else, as either Brennan would fight back, and they also had taken to protecting Diego. In any case, she knew that she was responsible for all of them now, something she hadn't quite thought through when she stormed out of Will's camp.

"What's wrong?" Marya asked, her cold voice a subtle rebuke.

"Just running through it in my head," Gabi replied, shaking away the doubt that was creeping into her mind.

"Is there something we can do to help?" Aidan's tone was far more soothing than his sister's. There was little that could rattle him. The hideous bear-like creature was one, but Gabi could not recall another time since the hurricane flattened Camp Eight that he had been unsteady.

Gabi nodded. "Follow close, and keep Diego between us."

Aidan acknowledged silently. Gabi turned for the pass, launching herself swiftly over dried grass and parched earth. The path started out as a mild slope, but the grade steepened quicker than Gabi anticipated. After only a couple minutes she was winded, and their pace slowed to a modest walk. When the terrain flattened for a couple hundred feet, she picked up the pace again, only to slow down as another rise worked against them.

"Slow down," Marya huffed in protest.

"Not until we get to the pass."

She mounted the rise and nearly stopped in her tracks. The creek had cut deeply into the ravine's bank, eroding all but two feet of the ledge. A couple trees jutted out from the side of the precipice, hooking upward near their bases.

"Damn it," she muttered.

"Now what?" Marya snapped back.

Gabi glanced over her shoulder. Her rival-turned-companion was still twenty feet down the slope, bringing up the rear. Marya couldn't see what had caused her outburst. Gabi cautiously shuffled up to the narrow ledge, tamping her foot on the ground to check its softness. It did not give at all, so she ventured farther out, with the same results.

"Nothing," she replied. "Just be careful up here."

Diego stopped at the edge and looked down, nearly causing Aidan to bump into him. His eyes widened, and he froze suddenly. A soft wail escaped his lips.

"Come on, Diego," Gabi said. "Just take it easy."

"I'll go with you," Aidan added.

The younger Brennan took Diego's hand and moved forward a couple steps. Gabi's heart raced as she considered the combined weight of the two.

"Wait!" she called out as she froze. "Wait, I don't know if it will hold both of you at the same time."

Aidan stopped in his tracks. For a moment, Gabi thought she saw his eyes bulge in shock, but he simply nodded and knelt next to Diego. "You first, little man. I'll hold your hand as long as I can. Just go real slow, okay?"

He sniffed and nodded. Gabi inched closer, flattening her back against the rock wall. Diego would have to traverse fifteen feet on his own before Gabi could reach his hand. Inch by inch he moved forward, looking to the side every couple of steps and whimpering at the gash in the ground.

"Don't look down," Gabi scolded him.

"Shh," Aidan hissed from the other side.

Diego was almost within Gabi's reach, though he moved at a snail's pace. Gabi gritted her teeth in irritation and shuffled a little further onto the ledge. Diego's cheeks were wet with tears when he looked up at her face. She could see the fear written all over his face. Suddenly, he leaped to his feet and ran for her.

"Diego!" she screamed, lunging for his hand almost too late.

Diego's foot kicked a loose rock at the rim of the precipice. He lost his footing and rolled off the edge, screaming in terror. Gabi was already on the move, and she caught his arm in her hand. But his momentum was too great. With a jerk she lost her footing, and Diego dragged her into the ravine with him. Gabi let out an ear-splitting scream as she landed sideways a few feet down from the ledge, though somehow she managed to keep her grip on Diego's arm. The impact slowed them, and Gabi threw her free hand out, clawing at the earthen wall as clumps of dirt rained down on her from above. Her hand caught something solid. Gabi yelped as her arms and wrists were stretched to their limits.

"Hold on, Gabi!" Aidan called from above.

Diego flailed around, which pulled even more on her already strained muscles. Pain like hot fire burned in her shoulders. She glanced down; his legs were dangling in empty air, unable to reach anything that he could effectively brace his feet on. His eyes were clamped firmly shut, his mouth wide open, emitting screams of pure terror. Several of Gabi's arrows tumbled from her makeshift quiver, plummeting into the creek below. Her hand clenched the exposed root of one of the trees. Her grasp held them suspended twenty feet above the rocky creek bed, though she couldn't tell for how long.

"Damn it, Diego," she bellowed. "Stop wiggling! I can't hold you!"

"Gabi!" he shrieked. "Help me!"

Gabi's head swiveled around, back to the top of the rim. Aidan was nowhere to be found. Marya's head was barely visible above the ledge, but she didn't seem to be paying attention. "Marya!" she shouted out. "Get down here."

"Hang on," Marya growled back in irritation.

Diego's arm slipped an inch, and Gabi instinctively constricted, harder. He yelped. This time his fear was mixed with pain. More dirt rained down on them, forcing Gabi to snap her eyes shut. Her knuckles ached, and she didn't think she could hold on longer than a few more seconds. With her vision cut off, she became keenly aware of the noise of rushing water below.

"Stop moving or I'll drop you!"

"Don't drop me, Gabi! Please!"

"I can't hold you. Stop it, right now!"

"No! I'll be good, I promise!"

Her eyes flickered open, and she found herself looking directly into his blue eyes. They were wide like the twin moons of Demeter, vivid and bright, streaming with tears. His lips quivered; he was out of breath. All he could do was mouth the word 'please.' The last vestiges of ill will she harbored for him eroded away, and she could finally see him for what he really was: a scared little boy, who loved her unconditionally. He needed her protection, and she was failing him.

*Don't give up on me now.*

She gritted her teeth and bore down, curling her biceps, trying to drag them both higher. The effort was nothing short of exhausting. And ultimately futile. She couldn't hope to lift them both to safety. Her hand began to slip from the root as she settled back in.

"I'm sorry, Diego," she trembled.

*I'll be with you at the bottom. And then we can both be with Papa.*

Gabi closed her eyes and took a deep breath as she waited for the strength in her fingers to fail. Moments later, they slipped, and her heart dropped into her feet.

*Sorry, Diego.*

In an instant, her momentum stopped. She heard a grunt, and felt warm breath on her neck.

"Now, Aidan!" Marya shouted, making Gabi's ears ring with the force of her voice.

Her rival's arms were wrapped around her, underneath her armpits, locking across her chest. Gabi's free arm shot to Diego in a flash, doubling her grip on her brother. She felt a yank and they moved upward a couple inches. Gabi chanced a look behind her, to see Aidan, one foot planted on a rock at the lip of the outcrop. The rope was wrapped around his waist, leading down to his sister.

"Damn it," Aidan bellowed from the ledge above. "You're too heavy!"

"Keep pulling," his sister shot back. "Just another foot."

He dug in with his heels and heaved. Veins in his neck and face bulged, and his face slowly changed from pale to a deep shade of red. As he pulled back, Marya rose, dragging Gabi and her brother with her. The process was slow, and Aidan slipped a couple times, giving them a little more of a thrill than they would have liked under the circumstances. But as soon as Marya was able to put her feet on the tree that jutted out from the cliff face, she was able to lift Gabi and Diego to the relative safety that the stalwart plant afforded. After another minute Aidan had helped each of them back to the top, and they were clear of the danger. They all collapsed in the shade of the mountain spire. Diego, still softly whimpering, wrapped his arms around Gabi. She caressed his hair and kissed him on the forehead, a gesture she would not have thought possible just weeks earlier.

Gabi locked stares with Marya, who rested with her back to a boulder, carefully rolling up the rope.

"You… you saved us," Gabi muttered hoarsely.

"Yup."

"Why?"

Marya's shoulders rolled, and one corner of her mouth twitched slightly. "We need you still."

"But you hate me."

"So? We still need you," Marya repeated in a low growl. "And Diego doesn't deserve to die."

"He's my brother, not yours."

Aidan took a seat next to his sister and offered his canteen to her. "So you'll finally admit that?" he jabbed playfully.

Gabi scoffed, but then the meaning of his words sunk in, and she grew quiet. She drew Diego closer, cradling his head in her arms as she eyed the Brennan siblings with measured suspicion.

"It's a good thing," Aidan continued, feeling the weight of her stare. "What were you thinking when you were about to fall?"

Gabi looked down at her brother, who had finally calmed down. "Don't ever leave me," she whispered in Diego's ear.

Marya looked at her knowingly, and nodded once.

• • •

*You can do this, Cal. For Darius.*

Cal closed his eyes and sucked in a deep breath of air. His stomach fluttered with butterflies, just like the first time he had met Brittany. Only this time, the circumstances were much different. Instead of being a foolish boy in love, he was preparing to ask an old friend he barely knew anymore to possibly betray her new friends. He doubted the wisdom of this gamble, as well as his ability to do it. Ultimately he had little choice. He had already invited Brittany over, and Detective Vaughn was struggling for leads in the governor's disappearance.

He fussed over the arrangement on the counter one more time. He adjusted the water pitcher to bring it into a neat line with the two cups and whiskey bottle. The dinnerware had been laid out with meticulous care. With nothing left to do he carved the pheasant, sighing with relief that it wasn't undercooked. He placed a large portion on each plate, which was then rounded off with grilled native vegetables and small rye rolls. Cal reached for the bottle of whiskey, intending to pour in preparation for Brittany's arrival, but something held him back.

*You've changed. Maybe she's changed. Let her choose.*

As he withdrew his hand, there were two soft knocks at the door. Brittany opened up the door and peeked inside. "Cal?" she asked softly.

He motioned with his hand. "Come on in. You're just in time."

She smiled and closed the door behind her. She wore a slinky red dress that stopped halfway down her tanned thighs, a garment that clearly had followed her from Earth. Her hair was pinned up in a tight bun, something that was almost unheard of for her. Cal had to remember the last time he had seen her go to such efforts to doll herself up. She smiled softly, but her eyes seemed to evade his. When he locked on to her, she just turned her head to the side, and her eyes dropped toward the floor, as if she was unsure of herself.

*It's just an act,* he told himself as she took a seat on the opposite side of the counter.

If it was an act, he shamefully had to admit that it was working, even if just a tiny bit. There was no denying that Brittany was a beautiful girl; that's why Cal fell for her all those years ago. But as a woman, she was something more. Cal felt flames of desire flicker deep inside, mixed almost instantly with guilt at having so quickly forgotten his true love.

Brittany's eyes lit up when she saw the feast on her plate. Without hesitation she grabbed her fork and took a bite. It was quicker than Cal expected. While she had never been the picture of manners on Earth, he was accustomed to her at least having a basic sense of politeness. He cleared his throat, though that didn't seem to alert her to the breach in etiquette that she had committed. Cal suppressed a grimace and folded his hands together.

"Can I get you something to drink?" he asked.

She glanced up mid-bite, then looked at the offerings that he had available. Cal was relieved that she had the decency to finish chewing her bite before answering. "That whiskey of yours is pretty good. Mind if I have some?"

Cal smiled and shook his head, then poured two fingers into her cup. He repeated the process with his own. Brittany raised her cup high in the air in a toast. "Here's to being alive," she said in a flat tone. She didn't wait for Cal to make contact with his cup before downing the contents. Her face contorted for a moment as she swallowed. Cal glanced down at the rippling brown liquid.

*I'm going to pay for this,* he thought as he downed the whiskey. Warmth slowly built into fire in his chest as the drink made its way down.

"So where's the little one?" Brittany asked just before shoveling a forkful of vegetables in her mouth.

"She's with friends. I have to pick her up in a couple hours."

She smiled and shook her head. "Man, I still can't believe it," she said, this time with a mouthful of food.

Cal made very deliberate motions as he grabbed his knife and fork, cutting into the tender slice of pheasant. "What part of it?"

"Any of it. That you're here. You've got a kid. And that you can cook. I mean, this is amazing, here!"

*Jesus, this is going to be a long night.* He poured another drink for each of them, though he took only a measured sip. Brittany took a longer draught, though this time she didn't down the whole drink in one swallow.

"Dad always said that life was strange. That it would hit you and spin you around till you couldn't see straight. And it would only be after that happened that you could figure out what you *really* wanted in life," he reflected.

She paused and leaned back in her chair. Her eyes narrowed almost imperceptibly. "So you wanted to be thrown across the galaxy?"

"No. That's what hit me. Spun me around pretty good. I guess what I'm saying is, no matter what happened, I'm thankful for what came out of it."

Brittany downed the rest of her drink and poured another.

"You should go easy on that," he cautioned.

"I'm not the one who can't hold his liquor."

Cal nursed the cup in his hand, again considering the liquid within. He took another small sip.

*If only you really knew.*

Cal turned his attention back to eating, though he kept an eye on his guest. While he consumed in a temperate manner, she consumed as if she had been starved for weeks. When she had annihilated her food, she threw back another drink before—rather impolitely—requesting another serving of pheasant. He put on a gracious front as he served her, then finished up his own meal and drink. The third filling of his cup was water, not alcohol.

"So what are you going to do now?" he asked. She stared at him blankly. "For work. Do you have any leads for work? Because if not, I can probably help with that."

"No," she replied brusquely.

"No leads, or you don't know?"

"Shit, Cal. I need some time to get sorted here. I'm not like you, I can't just drop down in some new place and be a success overnight. I'm not even any good at anything."

He smiled softly at her. "Neither was I. And trust me, it was anything but overnight. I had to put in my dues. Do a lot of crap jobs."

"You don't know what a crap job is," she snerred.

"Oh yeah?" he rose to the challenge. "Humping cargo isn't a crap job? How about living in the driver's seat of a truck for a few weeks while scientists collect samples? That was pretty boring. At least…" He paused, realizing that the alcohol was about to make him disparage the memory of someone who deserved better.

"Oh boo hoo," she snapped. Her voice began to waver. "So you had to break a sweat. Big deal. You've never really had to get your hands dirty."

"I have too," he protested.

"You didn't. You weren't there."

Cal backed off in an instant. Brittany looked up at him, her ghostly blue eyes tearing up. He could tell by the twitch in her upper lip that she was fighting back something deep within, grasping at the straws of emotional control.

"You don't get it. Your daddy picked your ass up and put you on one of those ships before the shit really hit the fan." She paused for the slightest of moments. "He left us all behind, you know. All of us. While you were asleep, we had to fight to survive. I'm not talking about grabbing a gun and shooting any damned Chinese solders either. How do you think we got food, huh, Cal?"

He just glared at her silently, trying to breathe calmly, hoping that something he did would keep his jaw from clenching tight enough to shatter his teeth.

"Rob was the first to die. All he did was knock on a stranger's door to see if they'd give us something to eat. Door didn't open, either. There was just a big bang, and Rob fell back down the stairs with a hundred holes in his chest from the shotgun."

Cal closed his eyes. Through his eyelids he could see the dead stare of Cameron looking back, as fresh in his mind as the day his friend fell over six years earlier. "I don't need to know," he muttered as he shook off the vision and focused on her once more.

"Manda was next. We thought we'd sneak into this little store in the middle of nowhere. Nebraska, I think. Only the shop owner was living inside and didn't want to share what he had. He grabbed her and put a gun to her head, told us to leave. Only when we were all outside, he shot her anyway. Supposed to teach us a lesson or something." Her stare wandered to some point off in the distance, and her voice followed. "We learned it. We never made that mistake again. The next time we came across a stash of food like that we made sure to take care of its owners first. You ever cut anyone's throat, Cal?"

"No," he replied softly.

"It's only hard the first time, when you still think of them as someone's daddy or mommy. But when you haven't eaten in three days, the cross hanging on their neck or the baby screaming in the crib doesn't mean a thing. Neither do all the prayers they say to the Lord. God doesn't make two cans of beans out of one. He can't make bread out of nothing either."

*Fuck. She's killed… no, I can't believe it. I mean, she… would she? Could she?*

"Then we heard about this guy up in Chicago who was supposed to be building his own ship. And he needed people, real people, to keep things square and to go with him when it was finished." Her laugh was slow and quiet, but it made his spine tingle and his skin crawl. "I only thought that was the end of our problems. Maybe if Mike didn't get his brains blown out on the way there, he'd have talked some sense into me. It was too good to be true. Sure, the great Harcourt Young was building his ship alright. And he was giving away the plans to smaller ships for free, so that anyone who could scrounge up some steel and a nuke could get away. But to be a part of his trip to the stars was something *special*. You had to provide for him in some way. A lot of the guys did it with their lives. They died to protect his ship while it was finished up. That's how Tae died, by the way. One of the gangs that tried to roll up and take the ship, he died taking them down."

Cal began to shake, and he wondered how much more of her story he could bear to listen to. He had taken for granted the fact that his friends would have died long ago on Earth, but the specter of each face haunted him as she listed how each of them met their end. "I don't need to know every detail…"

"Yes you do, you shit," she interrupted, narrowing her eyes until they were almost slits. "You can't sit there and judge me, or keep pretending that you've had it so hard. You don't have a clue, so I have to spell it out for your dumb ass. I have to tell you how each of your friends died because you and your daddy left them to rot on that rock. I have to tell you that I was that fucking righteous prick's personal whore for three years just to get a ride on his ship. You gotta understand every God damned thing I did just to get here. How low I had to go every day just to see the next sunrise. Now I'm here. Now I'm finally fucking free, and there's even someone here I know from before all this shit happened. But all I get from him is the cold shoulder. So yeah, Cal. Unless you can tell me what's been so hard in your life that it could hold a candle to what I've been through, you don't get to be such a dick. Ever."

"You want to know?" He snapped at her. The suddenness and volume of his growl made his throat sting almost at once. "Yeah, your life's been shit, but don't think that mine's been an easy ride."

"Try me," she shot back, crossing her arms and leveling a glare at him. The harsh tone of her voice was matched by the barrier she presented with her body language, taunting him with the preconception that he could not possibly counter her story.

He took a deep breath, cycling it out silently and slowly before drawing another in. "Did you dream when you were asleep?"

She shook her head, though the movement was subtle.

"I did. All the time. At first they were weird. The kind you'd remember for the first few minutes after waking up and be freaked out about, but by the time you had breakfast you'd forgotten them. Then I woke up. Alone. I'd ask if you ever did *that* on the ship, but I know the answer."

Brittany's lip curled into a sneer, but she did not respond otherwise.

"That's something that will creep you out. You're all alone, in space, on a ship you know nothing about. It starts to get to you after a few minutes. You start to wonder if something's gone wrong and you have to fly it somehow, but you know that you can't. That was my introduction to space. It didn't get much better from there. I chose to go back to sleep, but the dreams weren't weird anymore. They were vivid. Unimaginable."

As Cal blinked, terrible memories of all he had seen in the world of his psyche came back in a flood. Whorls of smoke drifted through his vision, accompanied by flames, and the unmistakable image of Alexis under the tree in his dreams, the field beneath her drenched in her blood. His mind recalled one sound, a whisper borne by the wind ten thousand times as he slept.

*Monster.*

"Take the three worst moments in your life. Play them over and over, minute after minute, for years on end. Then imagine you can't escape them ever, because you're in a dream, and no matter how much you want to, you can't wake up. That is what stasis was for me. A nightmare on loop that I couldn't break." Cal sighed and laughed feebly. "And the planet didn't set me free either. I've been shot at, shoved around, and watched my friend die right in front of me, and I couldn't do shit about any of it. I've starved and been frozen to the edge of death and come back, only to have my shining light, the woman I loved more than life itself, die. And I was helpless. I couldn't do a fucking thing about it. Fuck, Brittany… I didn't even get to say goodbye to her. And now every day I have to stare at *her* eyes every time I look at my child. Reminding me of what I lost." He glared at her angrily. "I don't even have an escape. You can just drink yourself stupid every night and forget. I can't. Besides the fact that I've got to be responsible for Andrea, the alcohol brings back the demons that my forty year nap so graciously gifted me with. So don't tell me that I don't understand."

"You don't…"

"Understand what it's like to sleep with someone to stay alive? You're damn right. But don't tell me I don't know about survival." He watched as she angrily snatched the bottle of whiskey and uncorked it. "We all do what we have to."

Brittany poured another drink and knocked it back. This time she didn't wince or flinch. The bottle slammed down on the counter nearly hard enough to make Cal jump. "Well you didn't *have* to invite me over tonight. You could've just let me walk away and gone back to your… your perfect life here on this shitty dust ball. So what do you want?"

Cal sighed and slumped in his chair. "I need a True, Britt."

"A what? Speak English, Cal. I'm not from around here if you haven't figured that out yet."

"A True Favor. One that may be difficult to ask of you. One that can't be repaid in money. But your return is guaranteed. If you do me a True, you get one in return whenever you want."

Brittany cackled hysterically in response. "Why? Why should I do that?"

"Because you have an old friend in need."

"I don't think our ideas of friendship are exactly lining up here, Cal."

Cal sighed and folded his hands on the counter in front of him. "Look, I'm sorry about everything I've said. I know it's not excuse, but I've been going through a pretty rough patch lately. The timing of your arrival was, let's say, not great. A month sooner or a couple months later would have made all the difference in the world. Just please, Brittany. For old time's sake?"

She scowled at him for a moment, but then the lines on her face softened. Though clearly not pleased with the idea, she nodded amicably. "What is it, then?"

Cal chewed on his lip as he composed his thoughts, clarifying them through the haze of the alcohol. "Governor Owens has been missing for a while. From what I've seen and what I know of him, I believe he was kidnapped. There's a whole bunch of stuff behind the scenes that I don't want to get into right now. The short version is this: someone on *Mercy* knows something. Either they saw something, or they're responsible. It would be really helpful if someone on the inside could keep their ear to the ground, maybe ask around a bit."

"And if it's one of my friends, you want me to tattle on them? Is that it?" she sneered.

"Honestly, yes. We haven't had any crime here in years, Britt. Squabbles and disagreements, sure, but nothing like this. If someone on *Mercy* is willing to kidnap Darius, who knows what else they'll do. They need to be stopped."

"Alright," she nodded. "I'll keep an ear out. For old time's sake. But you owe me, got it?"

"Got it." They stood up and shared an awkward moment of silence. Brittany's eyes once again found the floor, and she turned around. "Britt," he started, reaching out for almost instinctively.

She wheeled around, her eyes still bloodshot and watery. "Yeah?"

"If you ever need to talk… you know, about anything. I'm here for you."

Brittany smiled weakly, then turned and left the store. Cal dropped back into his chair, which creaked in protest. He pushed out a long, slow breath of air. The tips of his fingers brushed against the whiskey bottle's cork.

"Well, shit. That didn't go well." He poured himself another drink, raising the cup in toast to himself. "Here's to opening up old wounds."

. . .

Darius shivered and twitched, his teeth chattering together like ivory pebbles. The creek lapped gently at his knees as they sunk into the cold sand at the torrent's edge. The water was crystal clear in the middle of the channel, though the embankment that hung overhead cast a shadow that gave the illusion of an inky puddle at his fingertips. He cupped his hands together and drew a drink to his parched lips. It was cold and pure, though not nearly enough to satisfy his thirst. He bent over the creek and quickly took his fill, coughing as the nearly frozen liquid made its way down his burning throat. Icy drops rolled down his sweat-beaded chin, mixing with caked on dust and grime.

He closed his eyes and sucked in a deep breath, preparing himself for what he had to do next. *It'll just take five seconds. Five seconds, that's all.*

A stifled howl of pain escaped his lips as he lifted his right shoulder, peeling the tattered remains of his shirt over his head. His chest and shoulder burned like fire, even after his arm returned to his side. Gritting his teeth, Darius gently rinsed and scrubbed the shirt in the shallow eddy, trying to ignore the pus and blood that wept from part of the caked-over wound. The Montoya's grizzly bear—more commonly known by Concordians as a reaper bear—hadn't hit him squarely. The fact that he was still alive and breathing was proof enough of that. But it was infected, and he was on his own. He had lost his bearings long ago, and had no clue how far away civilization might be.

Once he was finished with the shirt, Darius wrung it out and meticulously laid it out on a rock. He then splashed water on his face, rubbing away some of the grit. The cold contrast against his burning skin brought his fading senses back to focus. He sighed and looked at the shadowy pool in front of him.

*Fifteen seconds, that's all. It'll just take fifteen seconds.*

Darius took a few deep breaths, then held his breath. He splashed water from the creek on his wound, which burned twice as hot as before. A sound rose in his throat that was equal parts scream and growl. He cautiously cleaned the surface of the wound, washing away dirt and yellow-red blood. The rinse also peeled away most of the herbal salve that he had applied to it earlier in the day. He repeated this task on the smaller wound on his left hip. Once the task was done, he collapsed onto his back, giving in to the spinning sensation that engulfed him. It was all he could to do shut out the pain, and the world nearly faded to black.

Darius couldn't tell how much time had passed before the wound's fire returned to a mere hammering throb. He returned to his feet and donned his shirt, which was now half-dry due to the day's heat. The gouges in his shoulder were no longer protected by the garment, and it was in danger of losing what little integrity it had left. He grumbled and walked downstream along the north bank of the creek, scanning the nearby foliage. His stiff stride left scuffs and tiny ruts in the layer of detritus that blanketed the dirt.

A couple minutes later he came across a patch of tarverberry bushes just above the bank cut. He scrambled up to them, eating the round, bitter, black berries as quickly as he could pluck clusters from the wide, squat bushes. He quickly became full, though he still choked down a few more as he had no way of carrying them with him. His stomach churned and revolted, but he managed to keep them down. After a minute's rest, he stripped the leaves off of one branch and continued on, this time staying in the trees.

*Come on,* he thought, scanning the forest floor nervously. *There's got to be some here.*

There as a flash of yellow out of the corner of his eye. He jerked his head around quickly enough to aggravate the shoulder wound. But the momentary discomfort was worth it. Darius locked on to a small yellow bird that had taken wing, and followed its course. It curved once or twice, but came to perch on a rust spruce, where the bird's sight immediately dropped to the ground below it.

*Gotcha.*

Darius made a line directly for the tiny Clark's sparrow. As he approached the tree, the bird startled and took flight again. He ignored it, interested only in the cluster of tiny white flowers on thin stalks that grew at its base. Darius dropped to his knees and tore them out of the ground, shearing the roots off and adding them to the leaves he had collected earlier. Without wasting any time he then returned to the creek's edge, where he found a large, flat rock. He placed the herbs on top, then ground them together with another rock. Every few strokes he dripped two or three drop of water into the mixture, until he had a pale, greenish-brown paste.

He dabbed his finger in the paste, then traced along the wound as gently as he could while still coating it with the salve. It burned for a moment, but then was replaced with a cooling sensation. Darius finished applying the medicine, then leaned back against a tree and sighed

J.C. Rainier

in relief.

*Thanks, Doc.*

Darius smiled and shook his head, imagining Dr. Taylor giving him a lecture about the importance of taking time to learn about the world. At the time she gave it, he couldn't imagine that he would need to know about Demeter's medicinal herbs. Now the fragments of that lesson that he could still recall were all that kept the infection in his wound from overrunning the rest of his body.

"Yeah, you told me so," he replied. He knew she wasn't there, but it felt good to say his piece. Even hearing his own voice was assuring in a way. It was a reminder that he was still alive, and that he wasn't beaten yet. It was equally assuring that he was only imagining and not hallucinating. This was a marked improvement over the past two days, when the fever had left him delirious and unable to move.

He could hear the doctor delivering a harsh rebuke, and ordering him to take it easy and rest. It was the next logical thing that she would say to him under the circumstances, though a conversation they had never had face to face.

"Sorry, Doc. I can't do that. Gotta press on. I need to find my way home and make Young and his men answer for what they've done."

Darius collected himself and continued to parallel the creek as it headed downstream. Though he wasn't sure where exactly he was, he knew one certainty about his location: this creek emptied into the Fairweather.

*If I make it there, I can make it home.*

After little more than an hour, his stomach was growling fiercely, and the light had all but drained from the sky. More tarverberries and a couple crunchy, foul-tasting beetles helped to keep the hunger away. A root-cave served as his shelter for the night. But nothing could keep out the bitter chill as the world plunged into darkness. His tattered clothes were no match for the cold, and Darius could only shiver through the miserable night.

. . .

"Shhh," Cal soothed as he gently rocked Andrea in his arms.

Her cries seemed desperate, though he couldn't figure out what it was she needed. She had already refused a bottle. He had changed her just a few minutes earlier, and she hadn't been awake for long. Yet her insistence that something was wrong split his emotions. On one hand, he felt guilty that he couldn't find the source of her discomfort. On the other, he was growing increasingly enraged that she wouldn't just settle down.

Cal paced back and forth under the cover of the shed, whispering gently to her. The exercise was as much for his sanity as it was to try to settle Andrea. It seemed to help with the former, at least. A couple minutes of wandering wore down his frustration enough to where his jaw was no longer grinding.

The break from work did nothing for his productivity. Though he could let the still idle for a while, Cal risked ruining the viability of his biodiesel if he delayed much longer. His eyes darted back and forth between the bassinet and the steel cauldron atop the larger of the stand-alone heating elements.

*Well, I guess I can let it go and salvage the glycerin if it turns.*

Cal turned the burners off and went inside to retrieve Andrea's diaper bag, which was already loaded for the day. He had hoped to be able to work through the day while still tending to his daughter, but that dream had already faded away. As he slung the bag over his shoulder he paused for a moment.

*I wonder if she's sick,* he thought. *Beth might be better prepared to handle her.*

This thought comforted him, and sealed his decision to take Andrea to daycare. Beth was the wife of the younger Dr. Taylor, and was also herself medically trained. Cal was just a hapless idiot, bumbling through the early stages of fatherhood with no support. When determining who was better suited to handle a potentially sick child, there was no contest.

The stroll in the early morning sun seemed to calm Andrea. After meandering along River Way for several minutes after it turned to Rust Creek Road, she finally settled in and stopped crying.

*Oh, sure, right as we're about to get there,* he lamented silently.

*She just wants to get away from you,* Jerk jabbed quietly.

Cal sighed as he stepped up to the door of the Taylor residence, regretting that he had taken the extra drink after dinner with Brittany. His inner twin had reared his head again, and he was low on medication.

*Guess who we're going to go see later?* Cal retorted.

*You never let me have any fun.*

The Taylor homestead was only slightly larger than Cal's. Unlike his shop, the Taylors had no commercial space in their abode; it was just a single residence, and there was an herb garden instead of a covered shed out back. The extra living space was much needed, as Beth and Jamie had two children, and the elder Dr. Taylor lived with them as well. The home was normally buzzing with energy, though this morning it was silent as he approached. Cal shuffled Andrea around so he could see the watch on his wrist. He grimaced, not realizing how time had escaped him; Steven and Hannah were already out for the day. Cal knocked on the door and waited for Beth to answer.

Beth was mid-yawn when the door swung open. Her curly brown hair had a few stray, frazzled strands sticking from it. She blinked her deep brown eyes in momentary confusion before a warm smile crossed her lips.

"Morning, Cal," she chirped.

"Busy today?"

"Not at all." Beth motioned for him to enter. "I didn't think you were coming today."

Cal stepped inside the home. Though he visited often, the cramped quarters made him thankful for the relative luxury that he enjoyed at home. While Cal and Andrea shared the loft above the shop, the Taylors had to find space wherever they could. What could generously be called a 'kitchen' was tucked in the back corner of the lower floor, but it was little more than a six foot wide countertop with a single electric burner on top. The front corner, just inside the door, was home to two hard wooden benches and a small table. Two cots lined the wall that butted up to the stairwell; this was where the elder doctor and Steven spent their nights. Jamie, Beth, and little Hannah shared the loft.

Cal set Andrea's bag on the table, then handed her to Beth. "I didn't think so either. I guess she had other plans."

"Why? What happened?"

He shrugged. "She just started screaming and wouldn't settle down. At least not until we got here."

*Because you're a horrible parent and she's got better taste than that,* Jerk quipped.

Cal ignored the schism's slight.

Beth reached a finger into Andrea's swaddling cloth to tickle her. "Guess you just like it here, don't you?" she cooed.

Cal shuffled his feet nervously and looked around. "So it's alright if I leave her here for a bit, then?"

"Of course! I'd love to watch her. Do you think she'll still be here when the kids get home?"

"I can pick her up early if it's a problem."

"No, no," Beth interrupted. "Take as long as you need. I just wanted to know because Hannah wanted to play with her."

Cal smiled, relieved that his daughter was not a burden. "I can't argue with that. Thanks again."

"You're welcome. Any time."

The return trip along the north bank of the Fairweather settled Cal's nerves, invigorating him for the day's work ahead. High, fluffy clouds drifted lazily to the east, though they were certain to burn off long before the mid-day's heat. A cool breeze blew downriver, carrying with it the scent of fertilizer from Tarver's farm. The foundry and ironworks were in full swing; the clatter and din of their operations carried well, even from the far side of the river. Jerk was jabbering away in his head, but it was nothing of substance, as usual.

Cal left the road early, opting to walk around the back of his shop directly to the shed. His heart jumped and he shouted in surprise as he rounded the corner into the shed. Brittany jumped back, equally startled.

"Jesus, Britt. You trying to kill me?" he asked, checking his pounding heart with his hand.

"Sorry," she replied. "Where have you been? I've been looking for you."

*Well lucky you,* Jerk added. *I don't know what these girls see in you.*

*I got Alexis, didn't I?*

*Only because I'm the pretty one.*

*You... I... Just shut up, will you?*

"I was just dropping Andrea off. Why, what's up?"

"I heard something. About your governor friend."

Cal's chest pounded again, this time from anxiety. News of his friend could only help the investigation. "What did you hear?"

"I've got a friend, Alan, who found something in the fields just outside *Mercy* that he thought might belong to the governor."

"What is it?"

Brittany shrugged and shook her head. "I don't know. I thought you might know what it was though. He's got it back at the ship. Come on," she beckoned.

Cal grabbed her wrist as she was about to turn away. "Wait, why didn't he bring it to Dayton?"

"I don't know, maybe he didn't want to come out here if he was wrong. He's kind of weird like that."

"So why didn't you bring it?"

Brittany sighed and rolled her eyes. "Are we going to play twenty questions, or are you going to come and look at it?"

"Fine. You're right," he said, releasing his grasp and following her back to the road.

*So much for getting work done,* he lamented.

*Yes, poor you, abandoning your boring job to go follow that.*

Cal's eyes fell to Brittany's butt as soon as Jerk's thought sank in. He glanced away, blushing with shame for how easily he had tricked himself. A few long strides put him at her side and away from temptation.

*That was low.*

Jerk was amused by this, and made a clicking noise that carried a dirty implication, but said nothing more.

They passed the market square and left the road at Benedict Square. Cal shuddered as he walked the lush fields that once filled him with joy. He glanced to his right, taking note of scaffolding being erected along the side of Civic Hall. The second story had been stabilized since the temblor struck, though the wall gaped open like a gnarled wooden maw. It was beneath that wall that Alexis had suffered her mortal wound. Though she passed away at the clinic, the ground here might as well have been where she expired as far as Cal was concerned. He shut out his thoughts and hurried quickly through the park. It wasn't until *Michael* was behind him that he allowed himself to think again.

"So this friend of yours... what was his name again?" he asked.

"Alan."

"Alan, right. So how long have you known him?"

"Three years," she replied. "On Earth, that is. He was there with Young in Chicago when we finally got there."

"So what did he do for Young?"

"Security. If you were a guy, you pretty much either worked on the ship or you worked security."

Cal thought about asking what the women did for the billionaire, but that was a wound of hers that he didn't need to pick at. Particularly not while she was helping him. Still, it made him wonder. Young couldn't possibly use that many women for his own needs. Most probably kept things running smoothly in Young's camp, but Cal still wondered just how many women warmed the man's bed to spare their lives.

*Sounds like my hero,* Jerk mused.

*Are you kidding me? It's a disgusting abuse of power.*

*Of course it is. But you should have seen your face.*

Cal grumbled to himself. His mental double kept taunting him, trying to drag him further into conflict, before giving up after a couple minutes. Brittany hiked into a grove of trees at the edge of Porter's farm, where she stopped for a rest break. She sat on a felled tree that was covered in soft bluish moss. Her fingers picked at the bark of a stout Demeter pine. The protective armor of the tree had old gouge marks that had healed in thick, bumpy ridges. Cal crossed his arms and leaned against another nearby tree, taking in the candidness of the moment. The innocent girl that he had seen glimpses of since her arrival was back, and it was an image he wanted to hold on to. It harkened back to a simpler time, far away from Demeter, before the War.

"Can I ask you something personal? About your wife?" she asked, breaking the hypnotic silence.

"Sure," he answered after a moment's hesitation.

"How do you stand it?"

He shuddered and swallowed hard. "Stand what?"

"The emptiness. The loss."

"Honestly? I don't know. I wasn't. I didn't. Losing Lexi it… it hurt. I was broken. I could barely get up, much less take care of Andrea."

"So what changed? I mean, you look like you've got your shit at least somewhat together."

The bark scraped his back soothingly as he slid to a seat at the base of the pine. The sound drowned out the heavy sigh that he let out. "Governor Owens," he replied morosely. "When I was at my worst, he was there for me. He didn't pull any punches. When others were too busy coddling me or pitying me or letting me drink myself stupid, he was there to show me just what a failure I was."

*And still are,* Jerk added.

*Shut up.*

"That's messed up."

Cal shrugged. "It's exactly what I needed. Somehow he knew. I mean, it shocked the hell out of me when he did it because it was so unlike him. It took me a couple days to understand why he did it, and I never got a chance to thank him. He's saved my life twice now."

"So that's why he's so important to you. Why you asked me for the favor."

"Yeah."

There was an uncomfortable moment of silence. Brittany nodded solemnly, sadness in her eyes. "I died inside," she said, "when Rob was killed. I don't really remember much of the month after that. Mike and Tae had to drag me around and make sure I kept walking."

"I'm sorry. He was a good friend."

She sniffed and shook her head. "It's alright. You were right, by the way. We should have all died back on Earth."

"You survived. Now you're here."

"And now I don't know what the hell I'm supposed to do with myself. I don't want to be on *Mercy* anymore. But I don't have a job or a place to live. I don't have anyone to help me." The frustration in her voice rang clear.

Cal smiled gently and turned his palms up. "You've got me. I can help you."

Brittany scoffed, wiping a tear from her right eye. "Yeah right. After I've been such a bitch to you?"

"You were right, too, you know. About how I couldn't understand what you've been through. And like an ass I've just been making things hard for you. So please, let me help."

"God damn it, Cal," her voice wavered. "Why can't you ever make it easy?"

"I'm trying to."

"No, you're just making it worse."

Cal shot her a puzzled look. She was on the verge of tears, fighting something back. His offer was innocent; a hand up for an old friend in need. Yet somehow this made the situation more complicated in her view. It was too much for him to wrap his mind around.

"Seriously. I'm sure I could get you a berth to sleep in…"

"Go!" she whispered hoarsely, her watering eyes bulging in near panic.

He stood up and slowly walked toward her, palms up, arms outstretched halfway. "Britt…"

Her lips twitched as if she wanted to say more, but no words came out. Cal heard a mechanical click come from directly behind him. He wheeled around, only to find himself staring down the barrel of a revolver. Its owner grinned wickedly, stretching the grotesque pock marks on his cheeks.

"Well, what do we have here?" he cackled. "A little something going on between you two?"

"H-hey now," Cal stuttered. "I don't want any trouble. Whatever it is you want, just take it."

"I planned on it," the man replied.

Again a noise behind Cal alerted him, this time the unmistakable sound of a pistol slide. He turned halfway around, and his heart shattered. Brittany, though a bleary-eyed mess with trembling hands, had a nine millimeter trained on Cal's chest.

"So this is Alan," she muttered, though her voice cracked once.

Cal glanced again at the menacing revolver to his right. "And is this the clue he found?"

Alan grinned wider, revealing two rows of coffee stained teeth. "Oh, he's so smart. Now I know what you see in him."

"We were never like that," Brittany shot back.

Cal turned toward her, his hands unconsciously balling into fists. "You… how could you?"

"Just an act, babe. You're pretty easy to play." She flicked the barrel of the gun in the general direction of *Mercy*, urging him to move.

"Guess she's smarter," Alan mocked as Cal began to march.

*Doesn't look like that's too hard,* Jerk noted.

There was no point in arguing with his double. Jerk was entirely right; Cal had fallen right into Brittany's hands without a second thought. Fury and hatred for his once friend mixed with despair; there was nothing he could do about it with two weapons trained on him. Only after that realization did he remember who was left behind.

*Andrea…*

. . .

Gabrielle Serrano
21 July, 6 yal, mid-morning
Approximately 100 miles southeast of wreck
site
>|

Gabi adjusted her pack with one hand, the other planted firmly on the steep, grass-covered slope. Her lungs heaved, working against the fatigue of the ascent. Sweat dripped from her brow. The drops beaded as soon as they hit the parched earth. Once her load was again even on her shoulders, she glanced back. Boulders and occasional pine trees littered the side of the mountain, but her companions were nowhere to be found.

*Damn it,* she cursed before pressing on.

The grade evened out after a couple more minutes, making the climb much easier. Gabi also altered her course to use the contour to her advantage, instead of continuing her head-on assault.

She reached the top of the ridge, her legs trembling and her shoulders sore from the biting straps of her pack. She shed the weight, resting the pack and bow against a rock that was half as tall as she was, and four times as wide as it was tall. Gabi slumped to the ground next to her supplies. The shade was a welcome relief. Her skin glistened with sweat, and the midday heat was yet to come. She took a long drink from her canteen, leaving little left for the afternoon's journey.

Once she had rested, she hopped onto the rock to take a look around. The commanding view she had over the lowlands was breathtaking. To the east, as well as near ridges such as the one she was on, the trees thinned out greatly. She could see for miles on end. Streams coursed through valleys, jamming up into small tarns and lakes where the terrain flattened. Hills rolled and jumbled together, their varied foliage weaving a tapestry of subtle colors.

Gabi grinned smugly. *You wanted to stick to the valleys, Will. Well, you never would have seen this.*

"I thought I told you to wait for us," Marya wheezed.

She turned around to face her companions. Marya was doubled over, desperately trying to catch her breath. Her face was ashen and her eyes were bloodshot. Aidan had one arm wrapped around her in support, concern deeply etched on his boyish face. Diego giggled and scrambled up the side of the rock to be next to his sister. He threw his arms around Gabi's legs, nearly knocking her over.

"I needed to see if I was right," Gabi responded. "I was going to come back for you if I was wrong."

Aidan's mouth twitched in disapproval. "We need to stay together. And you know Marya can't move that fast right now."

"I'm fine," Marya protested. She was about to pitch her case, but was cut short by a coughing fit.

"Look," Gabi said, standing her ground. "Will was wrong. Following the creek isn't the only way to get there. I can see much farther from up here."

"Great. So do you see anything?"

"Of course. I can see the creek we were following right there," she pointed back into the valley, tracing her finger along the creek's course. "I can also see another one in that valley over there. Lakes. Places we can stay and hunt while you get better."

Diego squealed in delight as he pointed out a strange, gray hawk gliding overhead.

"How much more are you going to be able to hunt?" Aidan asked solemnly. "You've only got three more arrows."

"If the game's small enough, I can hunt forever."

Aidan shook his head and helped Marya to the resting spot at the base of the rock. Gabi watched as he gave her a drink from his own canteen. She felt a little ashamed; she had gone through her water so quickly she forgot to ration some for Diego in case he ran out.

*Stupid,* she thought. She looked down the slope of the far valley to a glittering tarn. It wasn't particularly large, but it was fed by a mountain stream. The water was likely to be cold. *That would feel so good when it gets hot.*

Gabi sighed and threw her arm around Diego's shoulder to keep him close. She pointed at various features across the broad horizon, telling him about how the waters flowed downhill, educating him on how different varieties of trees grew better near water, and what places she thought would make the best hunting grounds.

Aidan clamored up the rock after a while and passed her a handful of berries. They were very tart, but edible. Yet despite their bitterness, Diego loved them. As soon as he saw them, his eyes widened, and he begged for some. She split them evenly with her brother. While Diego consumed them in under a minute, she took her time. It was a trick to make her body think she had eaten more. Hunger pangs were something they lived with every day. Keeping them tolerable was her goal whenever food was available.

She didn't have the luxury of silence as she scrutinized their surroundings. Marya gasped, wheezed, and coughed nearly constantly, and had been for two days. Gabi had to admire her rival's fortitude and drive; despite the illness, Marya had kept pace for the most part. But this morning was different. Gabi felt as if they were crawling along. They should have been another half mile or so along, but Marya kept falling behind. Even Diego could outpace her at this point.

*I'm going to have to leave her behind,* she thought. *Aidan will stay with her, of course.*

Gabi grimaced. The Brennans had both proven their worth repeatedly since their group had parted ways with Will's. Their loss might speed Gabi's journey, but it would leave her with just Diego, who was of little use other than picking berries.

Aidan returned after tending to his sister for a bit, though this time without a snack. Diego groaned when Aidan showed his empty hands.

"Why don't you go take a rest with Marya for a bit, Diego," he smirked. Diego nodded, grinned, and bounded off. As soon as he was out of sight, Aidan leaned in to Gabi's ear and whispered, "Marya can't take any more of this. We need to stop."

She spoke softly, only barely above his whisper. "How much water do you have left?"

"About half. Mar's totally out."

"Already?" Gabi hissed. She looked over her shoulder, afraid that those below might have heard her. "How much does Diego have?"

"I don't know. He was drinking a lot. Every time Mar would take a sip, so would he."

"You know we're supposed to take it easy when we're not right next to the water."

Aiden bobbed his head in agreement. "Right. But she's sick. I can't tell her not to drink."

"But we won't have enough to stay up here. We can't rest now. We have to get back to fill up our canteens."

"I don't know if she'll make it if we keep pressing on like this, Gabi. We've been keeping the same pace forever, and she's been killing herself trying to keep up. She won't let me tell you to slow down, either."

Gabi's eyebrows arched in suspicion. "Oh? Why?"

Aidan shook his head and scowled. "It doesn't matter. Please, we need to rest."

She sighed and looked out over the far valley. The tiny lake a few miles away was enticing. It would provide all the water they needed, and it would attract game for Gabi to hunt. Diego could pick the berries that would almost certainly grow next to the feeder and outlet. But it came with risks as well. Predators would likely be lurking, possibly even the horrific bear that killed Gina and Caleb.

*Well, what's it matter if Marya dies of a cold or as bear bait?*

"Think she can make it there?" she pointed to the target.

Aidan peered into the valley and nodded slowly. "I think so, but we can't go any further. Not today."

Gabi nodded in agreement and stretched. Her eyes wandered to the ridge beyond the tarn. Something just above the horizon caught her attention. It looked at first to be a thin cloud extending upward, but after rubbing her eyes and looking again she realized it was smoke slowly wafting into the air. She slapped Aidan on the arm and pointed to it.

"Do you see that?"

He narrowed his eyes, trying to pinpoint what she was looking at. "What?"

"Over there. There's smoke."

"Smoke?" He jumped to his feet.

Gabi joined him a moment later. "She can have the rest of the day once we get to the lake. Tomorrow we move out again."

"Gabi, if she's still sick…"

"Then we carry her. That's a settlement. That's what we've come all this way for, and there will be someone there to help her."

Gabi slid down the face of the rock, almost tripping over her own feet at the bottom in her haste to get ready. She called to Diego as she threw he pack over her shoulders.

"What the hell, Gabi?" Marya sputtered.

"Will was right. There are other survivors."

• • •

The absolute darkness was difficult enough for Cal to handle without losing his wits. Jerk's continuous mental berating tore at the threads of his sanity, placing the experience thoroughly in the realm of the insufferable. Cal's hands were bound behind his back, ensuring his physical safety; without them he would have clawed into his scalp until he had torn the voice from his head. In his bondage, the only defense that Cal had was to hum to himself. He tried not to think about how insane this made him look.

Jerk was his only companion, and the last one on Demeter that he would prefer to have. Since being marched onboard *Mercy* in the early morning hours, he had been locked in an empty cargo pod. Despite the appearance of poor engineering from the outside, the pod had proven to be reasonably soundproof. But from the inside, every shift of his leg or knock on the metal echoed agonizingly inside the acoustic cocoon.

When the door to the room cracked open, flooding the space with light, Cal flinched and turned his head to the side. The fixtures on *Michael* never seemed that bright, though the pain and blindness was probably the product of isolation in the void of the hold. Two shadowy figures eclipsed the opening as they walked in. One wore boots, the heavy treads clanking on the deck plating. The other person made little noise. Cal figured that they wore soft shoes.

Just as he had become used to the light from outside, one of his captors flipped on the lights inside the pod. Cal winced again, closing his eyelids instinctively. He heard the door close with a heavy clank.

"Morning, sunshine." The voice was Alan's, thin and tinny. Though it was refreshing to hear a voice other than Jerk's, his was not one that he yearned to hear.

Cal's eyes fluttered open, taking a moment to focus on the two men looming over him. Alan smirked, revealing his stained teeth. The other man was a little older, though far less repulsive than Alan. His face was clean shaven, and his brown hair was slicked back, marred by three distinct stripes of gray. Cal estimated that the man was a few inches shorter than him, but his vantage point from the floor could have skewed that perception. He was better dressed than Alan as well, sporting clean jeans and a blue button-down shirt with a matching tie.

Alan retrieved a pair of crates, setting them on the floor in front of Cal. Alan put one foot on his crate and leaned on his knee, while the older man took a seat.

"You're looking a little pale there, Cal," Alan smirked. "You don't mind if I call you that, right?"

"I'd like to call you all kinds of things, but you probably wouldn't like it," Cal retorted.

"Now that's not very friendly. I was told that you're one of the most likable people in town. But I guess that's what happens when you listen to rumors."

Cal glanced up, quirking his eyebrow.

*What the hell is this idiot talking about?* Jerk pondered.

*I was going to ask the same thing.*

Alan's grin faded after a moment's silence. His eyes narrowed slightly, as if he had been expecting Cal to react to his comment. "That's why you're here, you know. Rumors. I'm really interested in them, particularly the ones about your governor's disappearance."

Cal's lip turned up in a sneer. "Why would you need rumors about that? You're obviously the one who made him disappear."

The pock-faced captor nodded subtly. "True, but that's not what I'm after."

"Then quit playing games and get to the point," Cal snapped.

"So testy." Alan turned to the older man and shook his head. "Can you believe this?" His companion folded his arms, his body language a near mirror of Cal's. Alan sighed. "Alright, kid, I want to know about the leads in the investigation."

"If you wanted that, why didn't you take Vaughn instead of me? He knows more about those…"

"Not the ones I'm looking for," Alan cut him off. "You're the one that's been poking your nose inside of our ship, here, through that girl-friend of yours."

*She's not my girlfriend,* Cal protested silently.

*You still wanted her.*

"I was trying to help. Darius is my friend, and I needed to find out anything I could about his kidnapping."

Alan paused for a moment, giving Cal an inquisitive look. "And what made you think he was kidnapped? I mean, besides our obvious situation here, of course."

"He wouldn't disappear like that. Not on his own. Besides, Vaughn found drag marks."

Upon hearing this, the older man shot a disapproving glare at Alan, who was taken aback for a moment. A slow, methodical shake of the head hammered home the man's feelings about the revelation. Cal knew at that moment that Alan was not the one in charge, even though he ran the interrogation.

"Good find," Alan continued quietly. "So you figured out that someone took him. Then you started sniffing around on *Mercy*. Why?"

Cal sniffed. His hands began to tingle as anger began to build inside. "Why not? Seemed like a good place to start once we figured that out."

Alan took his foot off of the crate and slowly walked to Cal, kneeling close enough that he could smell the stale coffee on his breath. "You think you're a big man, don't you?" he grinned, his voice barely more than a whisper. "Even though you can't do a thing to me, you're going to play the hero. It suits you, if the rumors I've heard about you are true. But the funny thing about rumors is that there's only a grain of truth to them. Do you know how many men I've broken, Cal?"

"Should I care?" he shot back. There was something unnerving about the man's unwavering stare, but his hatred for his captor overruled the fear that the man was trying to stir up.

Jerk, however, was completely rattled. *Shut up, you idiot*, he kept screaming over and over in Cal's mind.

"I don't think it will matter in the end," Alan replied. "At least, it doesn't matter to me." He stood up and circled behind his supervisor, where he delivered the next question. "Let's just pretend that your hunch was right, and we took your governor. What's our motive for doing so?"

Cal grinned impishly, knowing that his captor had left himself open for another answer he likely didn't want his boss to hear. "Because you wanted something from the ships. Something that no one knew about. Something that Darius accidentally stumbled on."

He watched the color drain from Alan's face. His boss turned to face him; Cal wished he could see the expression that Alan had to endure.

"Who else knows about this?"

"Enough people to screw with your plans," Cal laughed.

Alan was on him in an instant. The man was freakishly strong, yanking Cal to his feet as his hand clenched Cal's shirt. Cal gasped in pain, as the iron grip also took hold of his chest hair.

"You think this is funny, kid?" he snarled.

*Oh shit, stop pissing him off. He's going to kill us,* Jerk whined in panic.

"Should I ask him if it is?" Cal winced, pointing at Alan's boss.

*Please? Please, I'll do anything. I'll stop calling you names. Cal. Your name is Cal. Not numbnuts, idiot, or stupid. Cal. Please? Please, Cal, stop it!*

"That's enough, Alan." The older man stared the two of them down. His brown eyes seemed to reflect the artificial glow of the overhead lights. His calm tone made Cal's skin crawl as much as anything Alan had said. There was power behind his smooth voice, and Cal found himself on the floor again after only a moment's hesitation by Alan.

"Whatever you say, Mr. Young," Alan grumbled as he took a seat on one of the crates.

Cal's eyes shot wide open, and an almost breathless gasp escaped his lips. "You're Harcourt Young?"

"I am."

Cal's jaw went slack. A twisted jumble of emotions slammed into him at once. Hatred, astonishment, and shock intertwined with Jerk's panic and hopelessness. He wanted to ask the man how he managed to build a sleeper ship, while at the same time berating him for using Brittany. The desire to ask him why he would have Darius kidnapped clashed with the urge to promise silence in exchange for his release. In the end his tongue was tied and lame.

"Tell us who else knows, Cal," Young insisted. "That's all we need to know."

"No," he replied weakly.

Yung's nose wrinkled and his mouth twisted. "There's no point in being stubborn. Give me the names, or I'll have Alan pry them out of you. Trust me. You don't want that to happen, not after you embarrassed him like that."

Cal took a quick glance at Alan, who was visibly shaken and fuming. His eyes were wild, and he kept popping the same joint on his right thumb over and over.

*Oh please don't add to the list of men he's broken,* Jerk howled.

"Deputy Governor Dayton," Cal sighed in shame. "Detective Vaughn. That's all I know for sure, but…" Cal bit his lip after the last word.

"But what?"

"There were others working the case. I don't know how much they were told."

"Who?"

"Hunter Ceretti. I think Traci Josephson, too."

The investor nodded once to Alan, who quickly vacated the room. Cal was hit with the sudden realization listing these names could get more people abducted. The pit of his stomach dropped, and he found himself gasping for air.

*Hunter! No!*

The door didn't fully close after Alan left before swinging open again. Brittany entered the cargo pod, wearing the same dress as the night of their dinner. She smiled, though forced and hollow, as she walked past Young and knelt next to Cal. She looked over her shoulder at *Mercy's* leader, who nodded once.

Her lips pressed against Cal's, and she forced her tongue into his mouth. Cal's heart pounded in his chest with both exhilaration and shame. Desire, anguish, and hatred roared through his veins. And yet through it all, the sensation that lingered was the faint taste of mint from the forced kiss.

She leaned in to his ear and whispered, "I'm sorry. Please forgive me."

*What the fuck?* The thought was echoed both by Cal and Jerk.

Brittany rose up and strutted to Young, exaggerating her stride slightly so that Cal got a good look at her backside. She grinned again, leaning over to give Young a tender kiss on the mouth.

"You shouldn't have rejected me," she chastised Cal, all the while smiling.

One more slow kiss was exchanged between Young and Brittany as the leader made a point of grabbing Brittany's butt right in front of Cal. He turned away, disgusted at the sight. He did not watch Brittany leave, and only turned his head back after he heard the door close. Cal was sure he was alone at that point, but Young disappointed him, leaning up against a structural beam and gloating.

"Some friendly advice, though a bit too late," he remarked.

"She was the one who rejected me, long before you met her."

Young paused for a moment. "Well that explains a lot of things, then."

"Yeah?  Like what?"

"She bolted right after landing.  Well, at least after your Militia let us go," he replied.  His words were no longer authoritative.  For the first time in their brief acquaintance, Cal heard candidness in the man's voice.  "I wish I could say I saw it coming, but reading women was never one of my strengths."

"Really?" Cal scoffed.  "You hold a ticket to the stars over her head in exchange for sex, and you don't expect her to run?  How many other women did you do that to, huh?"

"So that's what she told you, huh?  I shouldn't be surprised.  That's mostly my fault, really."

"How many others, Harcourt?  That is, if I can call you Harcourt?"

The older was seemingly at a loss for words for a moment.  "None.  Brittany was the only one, and I gave her my heart."

"Liar."

"Why would I lie to you, Cal?"

"I don't know," Cal replied sarcastically.  "Maybe to make yourself sleep better at night?  So you won't realize what a colossal prick you are?"

"Oh, I know I'm a prick," Young replied without missing a beat.  "But I'm not lying either."

"Prove it."

"Alright.  Ask me a question you think I'd lie to."

Cal searched for only a couple seconds.  "Where's Governor Owens?"

"Dead.  Somewhere in the forest.  On my orders if you must know.  Next question."

Cal was silenced for a moment.  He had suspected for some time that they might not find Darius alive, but the callous confirmation was like a stunning blow to the head.

"Am I next?"

"Unfortunately, yes."

Tears streamed down Cal's cheeks.  He had to swallow back the hard lump in his throat, and to grit his teeth to ask the next question.

"And what about my daughter?"

"Remember, I'm a colossal prick.  I don't care."

"Shut up, you sick fuck," Cal choked.

Young shrugged and returned to his perch on top of one of the crates. He folded his hands in his lap and leaned forward slightly. "Look, I know this doesn't mean anything to you, but this is all business. Things could have been very different. They *should* have been different. But Doctor Benedict and Doctor Fairweather didn't make it here, and that changes the landscape quite a bit."

"You're talking about murdering a fucking baby's parent, you shit. How do you justify that?"

"Because business is about opportunity. To say that the opportunity of a lifetime has dropped into my lap would be an understatement. This is the opportunity of the whole world. And I mean that literally. I've made an acquisition that will hand me control of the entire planet. How could I pass that up?"

Cal flailed and kicked uselessly at his captor. "You're taking away my whole world. Her world. You're going to destroy lives just so Concordia can be what, your toy? You couldn't give your heart to Brittany, you ass. You don't even fucking have one. You don't think *that* could be why she bolted?"

Young stood up and straightened his tie, then smirked. "She came back to me, didn't she? I have you and your little world to thank for that. You might want to think about that before you depart from the living. What's Concordia's motto, again? Oh, that's right. Unity and Honor. Cute, but meaningless. Look where it got Darius. Look where it got you."

Cal launched a string of vile curses and expletives at Young as he left the pod. He didn't stop until his throat burned, his voice faltered, and his lungs were left gasping and choking for air.

. . .

*Get up*, he told himself. *Get up, you need to move.*

Darius's lips twitched, releasing a long, incoherent groan. Words meant to give himself encouragement could not make their way past his leaden, parched lips. His arm flopped heavily on the ground as he rolled over. His fingers curled around a gnarled fingerling root of the towering Demeter pine, but the rest of his muscles would not respond to his will.

*Come on, damn you.*

His heavy eyelids fluttered closed for a moment.

*No, God damn it.*

They opened at once. Limbs high above danced and swayed in a breeze that he could not feel. Brown and green bled into a blurred white cloud that drifted past. Blinking his eyes only barely helped bring things into focus. His lungs heaved out a couple weak coughs. His wounds only throbbed slightly in protest. For a moment, Darius was convinced that his arm was dead, the last connections to the mauled limb finally severed by fever and infection. But he felt a gentle tickle on his hand, and managed to raise his head enough to see a beetle crawling across his skin.

He slurred an expletive and closed his eyes again. His diet of tarverberries and water was no match for the sickness that overwhelmed him. There was no warmth anywhere to be found. Even when he managed to find a patch of sun burning through the trees, Bravo's rays were not enough to stave of the icy chills that wracked his body constantly.

*Get up.*

"I'm dead," he finally managed to croak.

*No you're not. You survived your own assassination. Now move!*

Almost unconsciously, Darius heaved, straining all the muscles in his chest and left arm at once. His first attempt to right himself fell short. The second time he sat up, though the exertion left his head spinning. His stomach churned and heaved. Spasms sent him into the dry heaves; he had already thrown up what little water was left a few minutes earlier. When the convulsions subsided, he collapsed onto his back once again, panting.

To pass the time, Darius reflected on the brief history of Concordia.

The power grab by the nearly mad Colonel Eriksen had ended in the death of several crew members, and led to the formation of Concordia and Darius's eventual election as governor. The first winter, huddled inside Gabriel with the rest of its colonists and crew, eating almost exclusively ration packs. The drought of the first summer and the harsh, bitter second winter with not enough to eat. Fifteen more dead. Almost seventeen, as the McLaughlins both nearly perished.

"Why didn't we all die then?"

*Because everyone got back up,* the voice from within him affirmed, stronger than ever.

He tensed his muscles again, this time righting himself steadily. The next reflection was that of the labor strike. His own people revolted against his plans for the colony, shutting down the reactors of the ships and bringing all progress to a halt. That was followed by a sick game of paperwork designed to throw him off and slow him down.

"I should have quit while I was ahead."

*And then what? There were so many groups, and they all wanted different things. If you had walked away, then what?*

If Darius could have, he would have laughed. "It doesn't matter. It's all gone now," he whispered hoarsely. "Doc was so worried about the Chinese. And he couldn't see the enemy at his side."

To say that Darius's image of Dr. Benedict had been tarnished over the past week would be a mild understatement. His abandonment in the wilderness, much of it spent immobile and fevered, had given him more than enough time to contemplate the merits of Benedict's second betrayal: the one that allowed Young and his crew to escape Earth. The idea of nobility in Benedict's actions had worn off, and Darius had begun to view him with contempt. At best, the doctor's actions were incompetent and naïve. At worst, he was corrupt. Possibly as corrupt as the politicians that Dr. Kimura claimed Benedict was protecting the Project from.

Darius even questioned Dr. Kimura's motives. It seemed unlikely to him that the elder Kimura could have worked so closely with Benedict for so long and not known about his duplicitous nature. Ultimately, there was no proof that Kimura was anything but a fool. That, at least, was something that had been proven repeatedly.

Young was something different entirely. He should not exist on Demeter. And Darius had proven himself as foolish as Dr. Kimura by welcoming the survivors of *Mercy* into his colony. His payment for his hospitality was an attempt on his life.

*If you give up now, Young wins.*

"No," Darius muttered.

He strained again, leaning on his left arm. He winced in pain as the wound on his left hip throbbed, but his legs responded to his determination; a moment later, he was standing. Darius limped a few feet to the creek, kneeling beside it and drawing as long of a drink as his stomach could handle.

"I'm coming for you, you son of a bitch."

• • •

"Something wrong there, Prince?" Alan asked sarcastically.

Cal looked up at his captor, taking a moment's pause from stirring the red-and-white sludge in the packet that passed for pasta. He shook his head, then took another bite of the bland mixture, chewing it with utter absence of thought.

Having the company of Alan was only marginally better than solitude. Alan brought light, and the presence of another human being, even if a repugnant one. Without him, Cal would be festering in a corner of the cargo pod. It was his own personal hell, but not one that he was certain he wanted to leave. At least, not unless he somehow managed to escape. Harcourt Young had made it explicitly clear that Cal was not going to live, and that Andrea's future as an orphan was inconsequential.

Still, Cal was certain that escape would not be possible. He was only released from bondage long enough to eat, and even then only under the watchful eye of Alan. The man's witless banter was just the fetid icing on the rotting cake. He finished the ration, packed the waste inside the pouch, and folded it neatly. He then took a seated position on the floor, ankles together, wrists resting on his knees, waiting for Alan to tie him back up.

Instead, the man pulled out a clear bottle with a golden brown liquid that had been concealed behind a crate near the door. He took a seat on another empty crate in front of Cal, popping open the swing top. Cal recognized it instantly as his own product. Alan took a deep swig, wiping his mouth as he offered the bottle to Cal. Cal refused with a silent shake of his head.

"You sure? Might take the edge off your nerves there," Alan said.

"Don't think it'll help with that."

Alan shrugged and took another drink of the whiskey. "Suit yourself. I know you don't want to be here with me, but I figured you might want someone to talk to so you don't go crazy."

*That's rich,* Jerk chimed in. *You. Going crazy.*

Cal drew his knees to his chest. "I don't want to talk to you."

"I know. I'm not asking you to confess your life story. Besides, I've heard most of it from Britt. Sorry about that, by the way. But what can you do?" Alan's customary wicked grin crossed his lips. "Women, right?"

Cal looked up at him blankly. He would have loved nothing more than to wipe the smirk off of his pocked face with his fist, but he knew the effort would be pointless. Cal wasn't a fighter, but Alan was, if Brittany was to be believed. The man's cockiness suggested that he wasn't the slightest bit afraid of Cal.

"Right," Cal replied flatly. "You know how it goes. One day you're making them dinner, the next they hand you over to a sociopathic prick."

Alan *tsked* disapprovingly. "That's not a nice thing to say. If I was a sociopath, I'd be doing this for fun."

"Looks like you're having plenty."

"And it looked like your little girlfriend was helping you. See how well that worked out for you. Guess you're not the best judge of things, are you?"

Cal tucked his chin into his arms. There were many things he wanted to say in response, most of which he was sure would result in his violent end. His mind began to wander as silence crept back in. He thought about how he could have treated Brittany better, how he might have avoided her betrayal. As the threads in his mind turned dark, he wondered if Andrea would ever know the truth about his death, or if Young would somehow manipulate that as well.

Alan interrupted his reflection after a couple minutes. "You know, I think you're the quiet, planning sort of guy."

"Huh?" he replied, confused by the seemingly random comment.

His captor wagged a finger at him and squinted. "You remind me of this one guy back in Illinois. Gary Collins. He and a few of his friends showed up at the shipyard to help out. He convinced us all that they were there to help out and earn a place on the ship. Damn smooth talker. That is, when he did talk, which wasn't that much." He placed his hands on his lap, craning his neck slightly toward the ceiling. "He was a smart son of a bitch. Gary waited until he had our trust and we put him and a couple of his crew on night watch. A few weeks later, I woke up to hell breaking loose. Turns out that Gary had a couple hundred friends that wanted to hitch a ride on *Mercy*. He and his pals took out most of my detail before we could stop them."

"I'm sorry he didn't succeed."

"I bet," Alan retorted dismissively. "His little inside job did so much collateral damage to the shipyard that it set us back about three months. It actually hurt to have to put him down afterward, Cal. He knew what it took to survive in that world, let me tell you. If it wasn't for the fact that I couldn't trust him as far as I could piss, I'd love to have him here."

"So he could what, fuck up this world?" Cal spat back.

Alan considered this for a moment, his head cocking from side to side. "That could have happened. He sure could have figured out how to manipulate your governor a lot faster." He sighed heavily and took another drink. "I don't know, man. I might actually miss it."

"Miss what?" Cal asked, almost afraid of the answer.

"The excitement. The tension. The adrenaline of battle."

*Okay, this guy is definitely…*

Cal interrupted Jerk's thought. "You're sick. You got off on slaughtering desperate people?"

"You weren't there."

"I'm glad. I don't know if I would have shot you or killed myself."

Alan grinned again. "Well, let's all be thankful that you don't have to make that choice." He paused for a moment. "Speaking of thankful, Mr. Young wanted me to convey his thanks again."

Cal's stomach churned and his skin crawled. "Thanks for what?"

"Something about driving Britt back into his bed. He thought he had lost her when we landed."

"How romantic," Cal muttered.

"I guess. Bed wasn't the word he used, but I don't want to get all mushy on you. Let's just say that he's a happy man once again. The flowers are in bloom for him. Birds are singing. All that disgusting fuzzy crap."

Cal shook his head, resting it on his arm. He knew he had screwed up, and Alan rubbing it in was just pure cruelty on the part of his captor.

*Just go away and turn the lights off,* he thought.

*I don't want to be left alone in the dark with you again,* Jerk complained.

*The feeling's mutual. But right now you're better than him.*

After a minute, Alan stood up and took another drink. As he capped the bottle, he solemnly said, "Look, I know it's all gone to shit for you. I may have protected *Mercy* against people like Gary, but this is different. I got on board that ship back on Earth thinking that Young wouldn't need me any more when we got here. Have you ever drunk yourself stupid when you found out a stranger died, Cal?" Cal barely regarded him, not responding. "I did. When I found out Doctor Benedict didn't make it here. I saw what was coming. You're not the only one that's had a bad run lately."

"Why should I care?" Cal asked, growling.

Alan shrugged. "You shouldn't. Might just be the whiskey making me pour out my soul. Or maybe because you can't hurt me if I tell you."

"Why should I listen then?"

The pock-faced man ignored him. "It could have just been taking the servers back. If only your governor hadn't been there. I had to take care of him. A job that had to be done, a job I'm paid well to perform. And I did it." He swirled the bottle in his hand. "But then you got involved. Now I have to make an orphan. I've never done that before. At least as far as I know. And to top it all off, the man I have to kill is the man who makes what I need to drown out the voices from my past."

Cal looked up at him, seething with hatred. "So your big issue is that you won't be able to get wasted after you kill Andrea's last parent?"

*Shut up,* Jerk protested. *He's saying he has a heart.*

*Black and shriveled.*

Alan's brow furrowed. "I don't want any of this shit. But it can't be stopped, because it's what my employer wants. If I stood in his way, he'd just have someone else do it."

"So stand up to him," Cal snarled. "If you've got such a problem, do something about it. Even if he has you killed, at least you'll die knowing you've done the right thing."

Alan popped the cork again and took a deep draw, coughing and wiping his lips as he finished. "I don't want to die. Fuck it if my life is miserable. It already is. But at least it's a life. And maybe, just maybe, when Young is done taking over this pathetic colony of yours, I'll get to retire. For good."

The bottle was put aside in exchange for the familiar ropes Alan used to bind Cal. In a matter of minutes, Cal's ankles and wrists were immobilized, and he was once again helpless. As Alan left the pod, he paused at the doorway to give the final word.

"We leave before dawn tomorrow. I'd say get some sleep, but I don't think you will."

The words were true. Despite the all-consuming darkness after Alan shut off the lights Cal knew he could not sleep. Death had set a date with him, and he was helpless to do anything about it.

. . .

Gabrielle Serrano
23 July, 6 yal, dusk
Approximately 130 miles southeast of wreck
site
>|

Aidan paused for a moment to readjust his pack. The sweat that glistened on his forehead and the short, dragging steps that he took showed how fatigued he was. His toil under the combined weight of gear and flesh was great. Gabi shared that burden; Marya stumbled along between them, her arms draped over their shoulders.

"Stop, Aidan," Marya whispered hoarsely. "I need a break."

"We're almost there, Mar," he huffed. "Can't stop now."

"No," she rasped. Her legs faltered, dragging Gabi and Aidan to the ground.

Gabi cursed, her legs burning as she struggled to lift her stricken companion back to her feet. Diego bounded ahead of them, seemingly oblivious to their struggle.

"Diego," she snapped. "Get back here!" He froze in place, rigid as a board and eyes wide in fear. "I told you to stay close to us."

His lips curled downward and quivered. A pitiful moan rose from his throat. "But I want to see the city!"

"You can't go running off without us."

They got a few steps closer to where Diego had stopped before the load became too much. Gabi's legs buckled, and Marya collapsed on top of her. Gabi winced as she rolled the extra weight off of her and sat up. Both she and Aidan panted heavily. The muscles that she could still feel screamed with searing pain. Others had gone numb altogether, making even the simple task of opening her canteen a challenge.

Diego returned to them and helped Marya sit upright. Aidan sloughed the pack from his shoulders and drank his canteen dry. His hair was a sweaty, tangled mess. His sister coughed and wheezed. Her pallor had changed little over the past two days. Marya's strength and will to press on had diminished, however. For much of the day they had to resort to carrying her between them. Marya protested, insisting that they rest, but Gabi wouldn't allow it.

Gabi could smell the smoke of the settlement's fires. It's what spurred her on, despite Marya's complaints. What at first was a teasing odor that carried on the wind and dissipated after a moment was now nearly constant. Along with the smoke came the smells of roasting meat. They were close, but still had not seen any signs of the city. And each whiff of fresh food left Gabi's stomach grumbling and aching, adding to her fervor.

She took the party's empty canteens to the creek's edge, refilling them with cold, crystal-clear water. She splashed some on her face. At once she felt more alert, and the burning in her cheeks and forehead began to fade. Gabi distributed the water vessels as soon as she got back and checked her supplies out of habit.

*One more arrow,* she thought.

Next to Marya's health, this was her biggest concern with their situation. Her supply of ammunition had been dwindling the entire trip, but ever since she lost half of her arrows saving Diego at the mountain pass, she had to make every strum of her bowstring count. She lost two arrows in a single day through unfortunate hunting mistakes. It had cost them meat for the past two days. Gabi drew the arrow from her pack-quiver, turning it over in her hand.

*If I hunt tonight, that might be it.*

A cool breeze kicked up, bringing with it the smell of meat and fresh bread. Her hands went to her growling stomach, trying to soothe it.

*No,* she clenched her teeth, putting the arrow back in its holder. She slung the pack over her shoulder again.

"Come on, let's go," Gabi said, using her most commanding voice.

Diego bounced to his feet and was at her side in an instant. Aidan slowly got up and stretched. He reached for his pack, but Marya grabbed his wrist. Her sunken eyes burned with the crimson fire of the setting sun.

"I can't," she whispered.

"Yes you can. Here, give me your arm." Aidan knelt next to his sister, curling his arm over his shoulder again. Gabi took position on the other side. Marya tried to pull her arm away, but the illness had sapped all of her strength. Even with Gabi so fatigued, the older girl could not resist.

Slowly they trudged alongside the creek, following it downstream. Smoky haze before them confirmed Gabi's suspicion that they were on the correct track. The trip turned silent again. Marya had no barbs left for her. Aidan had mostly returned to his reclusive ways, and Gabi's solitary focus was finding this town, proving that both she and Will were right. That focus took her attention away from Diego long enough for him to slip out of their sight.

She had been in her own world for several minutes when she felt a tingle in the back of her neck, almost like a hot wind. It was something she attributed to instinct, and the instant she felt it, her eyes were scanning for what her subconscious was trying to say was amiss.

"Diego?" she bellowed when she finally realized he was gone.

Wind rustling through treetops answered her. The three companions stopped in their tracks. Sensing that Gabi was about to bolt, Aidan took Marya's weight off of her, gently bringing his sister to the ground.

"Diego?" Gabi repeated, taking a few steps and scanning the brushline.

"Gabi," Aidan said softly.

She ignored him, repeating her call. Panic began to creep in; even when Diego had wandered off before, normally he would have responded or come back if she had called to him.

"Gabi," Aidan urged, grabbing her wrist.

"What?" she spun around, snarling and yanking free of his gentle grasp.

Aidan cradled his sister's head in his lap, stroking her long, brown hair. Her eyes had nearly rolled into the back of her head, and she wheezed in shallow, erratic breaths. "Gabi, she's not going to make it," he choked.

*Damn it,* she cursed mentally.

Gabi knew that Aidan was going to stay put with Marya for the night, regardless of what Gabi wanted. Darkness was encroaching, and Diego had disappeared thanks to her inattentiveness. He couldn't survive a night in the wild without her. He didn't have any more survival skills than when Gabi was first dropped on Demeter. A faint recollection of her first terrifying night on the planet crossed her mind, followed quickly by despair.

*He could be anywhere,* she thought. *And I'm not Haruka.*

Her legs reacted before her mind fully formulated her plan. Aidan called out to her as she dashed away, but she ignored his pleas. Gabi crashed through undergrowth and catapulted her body as fast as she could in the direction of the settlement. There was a steep cut on the near bank just before the creek meandered to the left, so she hurtled up the slope. After rounding the bend, paralleling the stream channel, she came to a skidding halt. Though her vantage point was only a few feet higher than the surrounding terrain, she could see the trees thinning out abruptly, stumps littering the ground beyond. In the distance, lights flickered, and she could barely make out the dark forms of buildings. Her heart raced as she took in the sight.

*We were right!*

Gabi had no time to revel in her achievement. She barreled along toward the settlement, ignoring the scrapes and stings dealt by her reckless headlong plunge. As she neared the line of the clear cut, she realized that two of the lights were moving toward her. She stopped a moment to catch her breath and examine the source of the light. They bobbed up and down, swaying ever so slightly side to side. Shadows accompanied them—five that she could see. Four were very tall, but the one in the center was short, perhaps half the height of the others.

Then they moved close enough for Gabi to see their faces. She instantly dropped to her knees and screamed at the top of her lungs.

"Diego!"

Two of the taller shadows, accompanied by one of the lights, broke off in a run, headed directly toward her. Gabi fumbled at her shoulder, trying to ready her bow. But her fingers were so heavy and numb that she dropped it instead. By the time she picked it up, the men were on her. She fell on her rear, hands trembling as the two strangers towered over her.

One man shone a lantern at her, blinding her for a moment. "This must be one of the kid's friends," he said.

"Where are your friends?" the second man said in a deep, booming voice.

Gabi threw up her hand, trying to shield her eyes from the light and catch a glimpse of the men. The one with the lantern was solid and rugged looking; he reminded her of Will, only a little taller and older. His companion was an absolute giant by comparison, his wide, bare chest rippling with muscles.

"Jake, you're blinding her. Give me that thing," the larger man said as he snatched the lantern from his partner. He turned a knob on the side. The flame flickered for a moment, then settled at a tolerable level.

Jake stretched out his hand to Gabi. "Your friend said you and your friends were in trouble." He waited for a moment before beckoning again. "Come on, we're here to help."

By this time Diego and the other men had caught up. Diego squealed and jumped into Gabi's arms. She fell back, hitting her head on the ground solidly. There was a moment of pain, but her relief in seeing her brother safe quickly made her forget.

"Where's your sister, Diego?" asked a tall, blond man with a scraggly beard.

"This is my sister!" he exclaimed excitedly, hugging Gabi again.

The four strangers exchanged confused glances for a moment.

"Where are the others?" Jake asked.

"B-back up the creek, maybe a few hundred feet," Gabi stammered.

The barrel-chested giant nodded, then jerked his head into the darkness. "Rigger, Devon," he spit out sharply. The blond man and his companion disappeared into the woods, leaving Jake and the giant with the Serranos.

"You're safe now," the giant said in a soft voice. "I can't say we were expecting visitors tonight, but visitors are always welcome."

Gabi stood up and collected her bow, which she slung over her shoulder while eyeing the two men. The giant turned and walked toward the settlement, cranking up the lantern again to cast more light ahead of them. They wove their way through a sea of tree stumps, which abruptly stopped a few hundred feet away from the edge of the town. Jake took the lead at that point, careful to lead them down dirt paths between rows of the farm's plants. Based on what she could see of the town as they approached, Gabi was disappointed. Her initial elation at finding the settlement was erased when could see the buildings up close. While some were bigger than the Palm Palace, there were only about half as many buildings as Camp Eight had at its height.

They were led to the largest building and ushered inside. The rough-hewn timber walls were adorned with worn out tools, hunting trophies, and even a colorful quilt. A small but cheerful fire crackled in a stone hearth. An iron pot was suspended over the coals, and she salivated as soon as she walked in and was hit with the smell of the fresh cooked meal. The center of the room was dominated by a massive table, around which sat thirty chairs.

Jake hung the lantern from an iron hook driven into the wall next to the door. He offered to take their packs and Gabi's bow, but she refused. His brow furrowed slightly, but he moved on to offer them a seat at the table. Gabi did so, shedding her equipment at the foot of her chair. Diego hopped happily into the chair next to her and sat down. The giant served them bowls of steaming hot soup from the pot. Diego tried to eat as soon as the food was laid in front of him, then burst into tears when he singed his tongue. Gabi immediately gave him water from her canteen and soothed him until he stopped crying.

The two men conversed briefly by the door. Jake left the building, and the giant took a seat across from Gabi. He could almost touch the walls with his fingertips as he leaned back and stretched. He then knitted his fingers together in front of him, and began to stare at them.

Gabi tried to sit calmly and cool down her soup, but his piercing stare began to unsettle her. "So where are we?" she finally asked, hoping that conversation would ease her nerves.

"Rust Creek," he replied. "My own little slice of heaven. My name's Norris. I know your brother is Diego. What's your name?"

"Gabi."

"Where are you from, Gabi?"

"Camp Eight," she muttered, blowing on her soup.

"Never heard of it."

"It's not there anymore."

Norris nodded slowly. "That's too bad. Are there more of you coming?"

She shrugged indifferently. Her eyes closed as she savored a bite of the soup, which had chunks of chicken and carrots, and spices she could only recall in her most distant memories.

"Please, Gabi, I have to know. If your ship crashed or you have people that need help, just tell me," he insisted.

Gabi dropped her spoon into her bowl, leveling a harsh gaze at her host. "You're way too late to help."

Norris turned his palms upward, pleading with her. "I've heard about the ships. The ones that Young and Benedict gave away the plans for. I know that they're not designed for long-term survival. They're supposed to land near the town so their refugees can live in the colony."

She shook her head, furrowing her brow. "I don't know what you're talking about."

"Look, I know it was hard on Earth after we left, but it's not the same here. You can trust me."

"I still don't know what you're talking about."

He sighed and leaned back in his chair, tapping a finger on his lip as he thought. "Did your ship have a name? Maybe Young knows something about it."

Gabi glanced up at him from her bowl. With her mouth still full, she muttered, "*Raphael.*"

Norris's face went ghost white, and he nearly fell out of his chair. "Did you say *Raphael*?"

"Yeah."

"No," he sputtered. "No, it's impossible."

"Something like that," Gabi said, turning her attention back to the fresh meal.

Their host's eyes darted rapidly between Gabi and Diego, growing wide as revelation hit him. "Was he born on this planet?"

"Yup."

Jake burst through the door, slamming it against the wall. The lantern flickered with the sudden disruption of the air. Both Norris and Diego startled, with the young boy nearly spilling his soup all over himself. Jake covered the distance to Norris's side in five long strides.

"Norris! I was talking with the two other kids we found in the woods. You're never going to believe this. They're from…"

"*Raphael*," the giant man finished his sentence. "After all these years, there are survivors!"

"How's that even possible?"

The two men launched into a debate. Gabi rolled her eyes and turned her attention back to the meal. She hunched over, sipping the savory broth. As the level of the liquid lowered, chunks native vegetables poked through the surface like tiny islands. The archipelago in her bowl didn't last long against her voracious appetite. As she finished, she couldn't help but feel that the adults' boring conversation had taken a turn. There was an eerie silence, and she suddenly became aware that the two men were staring at her.

"Gabi?" Jake asked excitedly.

"What?"

"How many survivors are there? Do you know?"

"Just us."

"Just the four of you? How is that possible? How did you get here? Where did you come from?"

"We came on a boat," Diego interjected cheerfully. "Will and Gabi and Caleb and Marya sailed it!"

"Shh, Diego," she hissed.

Norris's brows arched in curiosity. "So there were others, then?"

Gabi nodded. "Yeah. Most of them died along the way."

Norris leaned back and bit his lip, nodding slowly. "I'm sorry. That's a shame."

"Everyone dies. Sometimes it's a shitty, useless death. But sometimes they make a difference."

The men's eyes bulged wide; Norris's looked as if they were about to pop out of his skull at any moment. Jake stammered, looking for the words to refute her.

"What kind of talk is that?" Norris grumbled in disgust. "You're just a little girl, what do you know about the meaning of death?"

"More than you ever will, old man," she retorted, meeting his scornful gaze head-on.

"Excuse me?"

"Don't tell me what I know."

Norris rose, his square shoulders towering over the table. He shook his head and sighed. "You must be tired from your journey. You're welcome to stay here as long as you'd like. If you'd like to go to town at some point, I'll have someone take you there."

"I can find my way around," Gabi replied, rolling her eyes. "This place isn't so big."

"This?" Jake interrupted. "This isn't the town, we're just a little village here. Mining and timber for Concordia."

Gabi bolted upright in her seat. "There's a bigger town?"

"Of course. A little less than two days' walk from here, down by the big river."

*The river! Maybe Will was right after all. If this isn't the big town…*

"Good, we'll leave tomorrow," Gabi declared.

Norris coughed, choking on the drink he had just poured and put to his lips. He recovered then said, "You just got here. And Jake says that your friend is too sick to travel. Just stick around a while and rest. You look like you could use it."

"Marya and Aidan can do whatever they want. Our deal with them is finished. We just need food and water, maybe some arrows, and we'll be on our way."

Jake and Norris exchanged glances, with the larger man frowning and shaking his head.

"You can use my bedroom in the back for tonight," Norris sighed as he walked toward the exit. "I'll be back in the morning for breakfast and to check on you." He stepped through the door into the night.

Diego softly asked for more soup, which Jake retrieved for him. The man also refilled Gabi's bowl. She wanted to protest, but her stomach quieted her. Jake took a seat across the table, next to where Norris had sat earlier. He leaned back, studying the Serranos closely.

"You know, I think my boys are about the same age as you two," he noted. "They're in bed by now, but you can meet them tomorrow. I'm sure they'd be happy to show you around the village."

"We're moving on in the morning."

Jake picked at some imaginary imperfection on his pant leg and smiled sharply. "Of course you are. Unless we lock you up."

Gabi set her spoon in her bowl, dropping her arm below the table. She leaned forward, discreetly reaching for the tomahawk looped to the side of her pack. "Lock us up? That's not very nice."

"Relax, it's an expression. My point is that we'd have to force you to stay. I know you're going to go tomorrow, no matter what I say. I don't know you, but that much I do know."

"Yeah?" she mocked. "How do you know that?"

"Well, first you've been talking nonstop about leaving in the morning. And second, Aidan told me about how you abandoned your friends. What were their names? Will, Kris, Karina, and Daphne?"

Gabi found herself lost for speech. Aidan barely spoke with anyone but his sister, but had opened up to this man. And for what?

"You've already left behind one young child," Jake continued, "and you're about to abandon two more of your friends. One who is almost dead. So what is it? Why do you need to get to Concordia so badly?"

"It's none of your business," Gabi growled.

"Important and secret. Something so critical that it can't wait a day or two for you to get your strength back. Or is it?" Jake stood slowly and stretched. "Have a good night, you two. Don't forget to turn off the lanterns before you go to bed."

Jake slipped into the night, closing the door quietly behind him. Gabi cast her stare at the dying fire in the hearth.

*Is it really that important? What's another day? It's safer here than anywhere else you've been.*

• • •

"This truly is a beautiful spot," Alan remarked. His hands were on his hips, his chest puffing visibly as he took a big breath. As he exhaled, his lips broadened into a wide smile. "There's some truly remarkable scenery around here."

Cal regarded him silently. He had no interest in engaging his captor in conversation about Demeter's sights, or any other subject for that matter. There was no reasoning or pleading with him, and despite the grim task that his employer had given him, Alan had been disturbingly chipper ever since they slipped from *Mercy*. Even the early hour of their departure, in the predawn darkness, hadn't dampened the man's spirits.

On the other hand, Cal was exhausted. His feet throbbed and pulsed, and his back and shoulders ached from sleeping on the ground. The world seemed to sway gently from one side to the other, and his eyelids felt as though they were about to lose their struggle against gravity. He was mentally taxed as well, burned out from having to listen to Alan's pointless yammering for almost two days. Despite all this, Cal could only think of one thing; a question that had been endlessly repeating in his mind for the last hour.

*Why are we on the road?*

It was a valid question, one that neither he nor Jerk could answer. Since Cal had been marched from *Mercy's* belly, Alan had been very careful to keep their distance from any established form of civilization. Understandable given the directive to murder Cal. Yet inexplicably, his captor had suddenly guided them onto Rust Creek Road, marching directly toward the tiny satellite community. Cal racked his brain on the question, trying to determine if it was a mistake, a calculated risk, or an act of sheer arrogance on the part of Alan. Even more puzzling was why Alan had stopped in the middle of the road and started spouting off about scenery like some demented tourist.

Alan's smile disappeared, replaced by a cold stare. "Are you listening to me, Cal?"

"No."

"So you don't care at all about the tens of thousands of years it probably took to create this remarkable feature? How season after season of floods and deposits shaped the channel? How they cut nearly perfectly even stairs for the water to roll down?"

Cal shook his head and shrugged; the latter motion made almost pitiful by his bound wrists. "It's just Lower Leclair Falls. If you want to talk about how it was made, you need to talk to the guy they're named after. He's a real enthusiast of that kind of stuff."

"It may be just that to you, but it's so much more to me." Alan drew his pistol—a semiautomatic model he chose before leaving *Mercy*—and motioned for Cal to leave the road. "Nature is perfection in so many ways. So many people can't look past the obvious to her deeper meaning. Here, you see the churning rapids. I see perfect death."

At once, a hard lump rose in Cal's throat. His calves, which had slowly burned for hours, went numb, and Jerk lost all semblance of control, pounding and screaming in the prison of Cal's mind.

"Get moving," Alan lowered his voice, his eyes narrow slits. "Before I make you."

Quivering, Cal stepped from the road, carefully navigating his way down the steep slope toward the roiling river. The noise was thunderous at the water's edge. Cal closed his eyes, muttering a prayer for Andrea under his breath. He felt the cold, hard barrel of the pistol jam roughly into his side. He took a breath and waited for the slug to rip through him.

A few seconds passed, but no shot was fired. The barrel was jammed into his side twice more. Cal opened his eyes and looked at Alan, who shook his head.

"Not here," the man bellowed over the noise of the Fairweather. "Up there."

Alan thrust the end of his gun upslope a couple hundred feet, where a rock precipice jutted out over the river. Cal shivered and gasped. Alan had something worse in store for him that a simple execution-style shooting.

His captor led him to the top of the rock, then urged Cal out toward the edge. The man then backed up slightly and shed his pack. He rooted around in it briefly, glancing up every couple of seconds to ensure that Cal had not tried to escape or attack him. When he stood up, he grasped a mostly empty bottle of whiskey in his hand. Alan tucked his weapon into its holster, double-checking the snaps that secured it in place.

In an instant, Alan's ugly, scarred face twisted in pure hatred. He closed the gap between them with almost unnatural speed, delivering a hard kick to the back of Cal's knee. The sting of the blow was immediately forgotten, replaced by sharper pain as his head hit the rock. Cal's mouth opened, trying to both scream and suck in air at the same time. Alan dropped his knee onto Cal's chest, pressing the precious air out of his chest. In one motion, he popped the cork open on the bottle and upended it into Cal's mouth.

Everything burned. His lungs, desperately trying to find air, sucked the whiskey down his trachea. Cal coughed and convulsed in a bid to expel the offending liquid, which burned on the way up. As he was short on breath to begin with, this process repeated itself numerous times before he had coughed it up, swallowing much of it in the process. Alan stood up and took a step back allowing Cal to roll onto his side, wheezing for air. His chest was on fire, and each breath fanned the flames.

Alan cut the ropes from his wrists; clearly Cal was in no condition to put up a fight. He lay on the ground for a few more minutes, finally catching his breath. Cal struggled to his knees. His head was swimming, and the trees seemed to rock violently. The blow to his head combined with the accidental ingestion of alcohol made him unsteady. He reached to his face and dabbed at the stinging laceration. His fingers were slick and tinted with the deep red of blood when he retracted them.

Alan shoved the bottle roughly into Cal's hand, nearly knocking him over backward. "Drink the rest if you want. It might make your end less painful."

"Than what you just did?" Cal coughed.

The man took another couple steps back and deliberately unsnapped the fasteners on his holster. "Don't forget the part you played in this. If you hadn't put your nose where it didn't belong, you wouldn't be here. You did this to yourself."

"I did what I had to. For my friend. You would have done the same."

Alan shook his head. "I can always make new ones. Besides, haven't you learned what friends are really worth? You trust the wrong one…" his voice trailed off and he shrugged passively. "You end up drinking too much, fall in a river, and drown. Speaking of which, it's time for you to do that now. Get up."

"Fuck you," Cal seethed.

Alan snatched the pistol from his side and leveled it at Cal's head. He shook his head and sneered, "You're going in the river whether you jump or I dump you in. Just remember that if your friends downstream see your body wash up with a bullet in its head, there are going to be more questions. More people like you are going to ask questions they shouldn't. More people will disappear and meet unusual deaths."

"You're a sick piece of shit, you know that? You say you want to retire from your hit man job here, then you threaten to kill more people if I don't kill myself?"

"Of course I want to retire," Alan snapped back. "But whether I get to or not is up to you. Now how much blood do you really want on your hands?" He narrowed his eyes, grinning wickedly. "I think it'll only take one person to motivate you. You know, I read somewhere that babies didn't survive very long on the frontier a couple hundred years ago. And that's about the level of medical treatment that Concordia has access to."

Cal's fingers wrapped so tightly around the neck of the bottle that it threatened to shatter. "No. Don't you fucking dare. She's just a baby, you prick. For Christ's sake, it's bad enough that you're about to kill her father. You're making my daughter an orphan. Isn't that enough for you?"

Sunlight glinted off the barrel of the gun as Alan wagged it. "It's not up to me. Now get up."

*Just do it, you idiot,* Jerk screamed. *We're already dead. Don't piss him off and make him go after Andrea, too!*

Cal lowered his head and sighed in defeat. His knees wobbled and his fingers trembled as he slowly gained his feet. Tears streamed down his cheeks, mixing with drying blood and blurring the grotesque visage of his tormentor.

"That's a good boy," Alan grinned, raising his arm a little higher to maintain his aim.

*I'm sorry, Andrea. I hope you get to grow up knowing the truth about me.*

Cal was in the process of taking a deep breath when something to the left side of his vision caught his eye. There was movement in the brush just beyond the massive boulder on which the stood. He heard a soft *thrum* just barely over the chorus of the rapids, and a blur streaked from the bush. Alan shouted out in pain and alarm. His pistol clattered to the ground. Cal blinked, barely able to comprehend what he had just seen.

Jutting about six inches through Alan's forearm was the bloody shaft and head of an arrow, its fletching protruding from the opposite side.

. . .

　　　　　　　　　　　　　　　　　　　　　J.C. Rainier

"Stay here!"

It was a directive to her brother, Diego, and all she had time to say to him as the vinewood bow clattered to the ground. She whipped the tomahawk into her hand and charged from the bush, her legs catapulting her over the uneven ground between her and her prey. A fierce, curdling sound rose from her chest. It was the cry of bloodlust, something that she had not uttered since before the storm that annihilated her people.

The man wheeled around, clutching his lame arm with his uninjured hand. His eyes widened as he recognized the danger, and his good hand shot for a knife at his hip. Gabi was on him too quickly. Her axe bit into his thigh as she passed, and he crumpled to his left in a heap, screaming and flailing. The other man—a tall, lanky blond—fell backward, nearly backpedaling into the river as she approached. He was no threat; Gabi turned from him and returned her attention to his would-be murderer. The man who would make a little girl an orphan. The man who threatened to kill that same girl.

*Take him out,* she thought, her grim focus training itself on his vital parts. *Like a jaguar. Because that's all he is.*

Bloodied and gasping, her prey managed to free a long, cruel, serrated knife from its sheath. The corner of Gabi's mouth ticked upward in glee; this opponent was no match for her. From ten feet away, Gabi hurled her tomahawk with deadly accuracy, burying its head more than an inch in his neck, just above the clavicle. He fell backward again, dropping his knife. He gurgled and clawed at the handle of her weapon, dislodging it. Blood sprayed like a fountain as the axe no longer restricted flow to the man's carotid artery. He was dead within seconds, his blood pooling under his body and enveloping the bone handle of Gabi's tomahawk.

Diego's shrill scream pierced the air, cutting through the droning of the river. Gabi cast a glance over her shoulder to make sure the blond man was still incapacitated with shock and fear, then retrieved her weapon. As a hunter, blood was nothing new to her. The fact that it was human blood was only mildly unnerving. Then again, this man had it coming. Gabi had secretly watched a couple executions, long ago. Chief Vandemark had presided over every one of them. One thing that Gabi knew is that the chief never tortured or beat his prisoners, as this man had done.

*Not an execution. Not a legal one, anyway.*

She looked back at the bush she'd come from. Diego sat huddled next to it, clutching her bow.

"Stay there!" she commanded.

Gabi turned to face the other man, tightening her grip on the tomahawk. Blood still trickled from a gash on his brow. He was frozen in place, his fingers digging into the rock like roots of a stubborn tree.

"Get up," she said sternly. He stared back at her, still as a statue. "Get up!"

He flinched on her second command, but scrambled to his feet. "W-who are you?" he stammered.

Gabi pointed her tomahawk toward a narrow game trail that led to the river thirty or so feet below. "Move it."

"B-but…"

"Move it," she repeated. The blond man complied quickly, checking over his shoulder often as he hustled to the trail.

She cast a backward glance at the bush and whistled. "C'mon, D."

Diego shuffled quietly from his hiding place. Tears streamed down his face. He squealed and nearly dropped Gabi's bow as he passed the corpse of the pock-faced man.

Gabi returned to the body, kicking it and ensuring that no life was left. "What, Diego? He's dead. Can't hurt anyone." She knelt beside the dead man, relieving him of his knife and gun. She moved on to his pack, rifling through it for a length of rope before proceeding down the slope after her brother and prisoner.

When Gabi reached the bottom of the slope she found the blond man splashing water on his face, washing away the blood and muttering under his breath. She took a moment to wash the blood from the handle of her tomahawk and the scavenged knife.

"Are you from Concordia?" she asked the man.

"Y-yes," he stuttered.

"Take us there."

"W-who are you? Why are you dressed like that?"

Gabi glanced down briefly at her fur leggings and top. She found nothing odd with the way she dressed. The man sported thin, dingy cloth pants and an equally soiled shirt. His clothing was reminiscent of what people in Camp Eight wore before the Sorrow. Before they were wiped off the map.

"You have a daughter," she said, diverting the conversation from herself.

The man's eyes widened, and again he froze. "Y-yes."

"That man was going to kill you. You said she'd be an orphan."

"That's right."

"Want to see her again?" Gabi retorted sarcastically.

"More than anything."

"Hands behind your back, then."

"What?" he gasped, eyes bulging.

"Hands behind your back."

"Why?"

"I don't know you. I don't know why that other guy had you tied up, but I'm not taking my chances."

"You saved me," he protested, complying anyway. "I owe you my life, I'm not going to do anything to hurt you."

Gabi's fingers wove the stout cord gracefully around his wrists. The bindings were secure, though likely not comfortable. Her captive grunted and winced as Gabi pulled the last knot tight.

"Show us the way," she ordered.

The man nodded and got up. He scrambled awkwardly up an embankment to the road that Gabi had departed just a few minutes earlier. She had caught sight of him and his attacker from a fair distance. Recognizing that something was amiss with the execution, Gabi had hurried Diego along. They got close enough that Gabi could hear the exchange between the two men. The would-be executioner seemed cruel, and indifferent to the fact that a little girl would be left without a father. This first lit the fire within Gabi; she recalled a memory from her distant past, when an arrogant young man by the name of Lon Carney brutally murdered her own father. Then the executioner threatened to kill the girl himself. Gabi couldn't stand by, no matter what the prisoner had done.

They walked for some time, the silence of the forest interrupted only by the prisoner's occasional attempt to engage them in conversation. He seemed to figure out that Gabi wouldn't talk to him, so he tried his hand at getting Diego to open up. Every time he did so, Gabi quickly warned Diego, and her brother remained silent, other than occasional complaints of fatigue.

After a couple hours, Diego's whining escalated to the point that Gabi called for a rest. She selected a spot near the edge of the river that was shaded by a dense grove of shorter, thin-trunked trees with bluish-white bark. She distributed hunks of bread and strips of dried meat, given to them by their ephemeral hosts in Rust Creek. Diego plopped down in the dirt and gnawed at the food hungrily. The tall, blond man smiled nervously as he took his portion, clutching it securely in his bound hands.

Her prisoner took a seat on a small boulder. He closed his eyes, seeming to absorb the sun that washed over his face. In the light, his hair shifted from a murky shade to near golden. Once Gabi had a chance to look past the grime caked on his face, he looked very young indeed. Possibly even the same age as Will.

*He's too young to be a dad,* Gabi decided.

"What's your name?" she finally addressed him.

The man finished chewing his bread before speaking. "Calvin."

"What's your daughter's name?" Gabi asked, leaving no time on the heels of his response.

"Andrea."

"How old is she?"

"Uhh… six weeks?"

Gabi furrowed her brows, and her tone was laced with disgust. "You left a little baby alone?"

"No, no, she's being watched over by a good friend," he quickly spluttered. "I only meant to be gone a couple hours. But then I was kidnapped and shoved in a cargo pod for a few days and…" he sighed and shook his head. "I don't know what the hell is going on. I don't know what day it is. By some miracle you came along and saved my life, then tied me up again and won't tell me what's going on. You're clearly not from Concordia, but I'm so confused and scared that I don't want to ask about it. I miss my daughter. I miss my home. I just want this nightmare to end."

"You were kidnapped? Why?"

Calvin stared at her silently for a moment. The muscles under his right eye twitched slightly. "I was trying to help out another friend that was kidnapped. Our governor. That man you killed, he… well, it turns out he took my friend and murdered him. I didn't know that Darius was dead at the time, I was still hoping to find him."

Diego leaned over, whispering in Gabi's ear. "What's kidnapped mean?"

She opened her mouth, about to answer, but instead simply replied, "I'll explain it later." Locking eyes again with Calvin, she continued her questioning. "So why did they take your governor? What did he do to deserve that?"

Calvin shrugged. "All I know is that he stumbled on to some secret. That man and his boss aren't from Concordia. Something that Darius found meant something to them. Something important enough that they'd kill him. Or me. Or anyone."

*Great. So I'm being led by some idiot that is trying to get himself killed.*

She chewed pensively on a strip of jerky as she tried to sort through the scenario.

"What's your name?" he asked quietly.

"Gabi."

"I'm Diego!" her brother burst in cheerfully.

"Quiet, D," she muttered sternly.

"Gabi, I can't possibly tell you how much it means to me what you did today. You're right, you don't know me, and I don't know you. I don't know how I can possibly repay you. If we get back to Concordia, just let me know what I can do for you and Diego. I'll make sure it happens."

"What could you do for me?" she scoffed. "About the only thing I can think of is shutting up."

Calvin leaned back, arching his back until his shoulders rested against a leaning tree. His hair turned sandy again as it slinked into the shade. "Something bad happened to you as a kid, didn't it?" he asked. There was a softness in his tone that was chilling. Oddly familiar and comforting, yet it shouldn't have been. "You're armed to the teeth, dragging around what, a four-year-old kid? No adults around you. You didn't hesitate to kill Alan. You could just as easily have killed me, but you didn't."

Gabi turned away and took a bite of her bread, trying to disengage from the conversation. Every word he spoke reminded her of her long-dead father, and how he used to talk to her when she was upset. Memories came to her, not of her time on Demeter, but even farther back. The faintest recollection of life on the ranch back on Earth filtered through the stone wall of her heart.

"It's okay to talk, Gabi," the man continued. "I can put two and two together. I know you're an orphan. So is Diego, I'm guessing."

"Of course he is," she growled. "He's my brother."

"And you've been watching out for him, like a good sister. All alone, trying to get to Concordia. How long have you been on Demeter?" He paused, waiting for her to answer. "What happened to your parents?"

Gabi stood up and chucked the heel of her of her bread into the woods. Her teeth clenched together, and she was suddenly aware of the tension in her forearm as her fingers flexed closed tightly. "You don't want to know."

"I asked, didn't I?"

"Mama's with God now," Diego interjected sadly.

She wheeled around, snarling at her nosy prisoner. "That's right. Our mom is dead. She killed herself five years ago, shortly after Diego was born. She was weak and couldn't take it anymore. She couldn't take the fact that Diego was born because she was raped by the man that beat my dad to death. And all of this shit happened right in front of me. Right after we crashed on this planet." Calvin's jaw slacked and his eyes widened. "I told you that you didn't want to know."

Gabi let him choke on his surprise and horror, walking to the edge of the river to calm herself down. Her hands trembled, shaken by years of anger at her cowardly mother that never seemed to fade. She took a deep breath, closed her eyes, and thought of her hero.

*You were way stronger than Mama. I just wish you hadn't gotten sick. You never would have let Will stop, would you, Haruka?*

She was startled by Calvin, who had somehow snuck up on her as she was reflecting. His voice was as calm as ever, not rattled as she expected him to be.

"You're a survivor of *Raphael*," he said. "I don't know how, but you guys somehow made it. You landed, you survived, and now you're here."

"Sometimes I think the lucky ones died in the crash," she mumbled.

Calvin chewed on his lower lip as he considered this. "That doesn't sound lucky to me. Maybe someday you'll feel different about it. Everything in life is worth it in the end. The laughter. The crying. The love, and even the loss."

Gabi shot him a caustic glance as she stepped around him. "Come on, time to move on," she deflected.

They were on the road again in a couple minutes. Diego did not roam ahead as usual; he stuck unusually close to Gabi. She accidentally stepped into him a couple times, once knocking him down before they finally settled in a rhythm. Calvin took the lead, strolling about six paces ahead of them. The monotony of marching soon set in, and she found her attention wandering.

The way Calvin tried to calm her still haunted her. When she replayed his words in her mind, she heard them in her father's voice. She shook away the distant echoes from beyond the grave.

*Keep it together, Gabi,* she assured herself. *You're almost there.*

. . .

*Get up.*

The voice inside him no longer screamed with urgency. While it told him to move, its flat tone lacked spirit and focus; it was as broken as Darius.

The fingers on his left hand twitched. Parched dirt and twigs tickled the palm of his hand. His eyelids felt like they were staked to the ground, too heavy to consider opening. Dust invaded his nose and mouth as he breathed, but he could do little but cough. After a few fits he could no longer spit out the offending dirt, and was forced to swallow his own muddy saliva.

*Get up.*

The insanity of his position might have registered if he could step back and watch what was happening to him. Face down, sprawled across the forest floor, just feet from the bank of the creek, Darius couldn't even pull himself to the edge for a drink. His lips were cracked and bloodied, and the wounds closed only long enough for the process to repeat itself. His right arm was completely limp, his injured leg nearly as lame. The nauseating stench of necrotic flesh mingled with pungent scents from bright flowers just beyond his reach.

*That's it. This is going to be your grave. He's going to win.*

Darius mumbled something incoherently. There was no one to listen. At least, no one human. Somewhere nearby, a pine ranger warbled its terse call over and over. A branch snapped in the distance; whether it was a careless Demeter deer or a scavenging reaper bear he couldn't say, nor did he care. Days of wandering in the woods delirious and starving had finally taken its toll. His spirit was as shattered as his body. Only the weak protests of his conscience remained.

The pine ranger stopped calling out. Darius strained to hear, wondering if the bird had taken flight. He was envious of that freedom; his body was now nothing more than a rotting prison for his mind. A thinking corpse.

He picked up sounds just barely audible over the babbling creek. Not the bird he sought. The tones were much too low. Nor were they as patterned as the insectivore's song. Darius cycled a deep breath, clearing his mind so he could process it better. There was definitely more than one voice, and they were moving closer. He didn't recognize the animal, though. It wasn't a bear, as the tone was too high, and not gravelly enough. Too low to be a deer or any of the known raptors. His eyes fluttered open and his heart raced when he finally identified what species could make the noises he heard.

*Humans.*

"No, don't go over there," a female voice protested.

"I have to look. I have to know," the deep voice of her male companion responded.

Darius tried to call out to them, but all that escaped his lips was a pathetic, wheezing cough.

"Why?" the woman asked. Slightly closer. They were still moving toward him. "Haven't we seen enough bodies?"

"It matters how. If this is another plague…"

"Don't say that!" The woman's voice was definitely wavering.

*Who is she? Is she crying? What plague?*

Darius could hear the footfalls of their approach, growing louder with every step. He summoned all of his strength and forced the air in his lungs past his vocal cords. Somehow he managed to groan, though not terribly loudly. The footsteps stopped suddenly.

"Holy shit, he's alive!" the man exclaimed, bursting into a run.

Darius was rolled onto his back. Light flooded his eyes, forcing him to squint. He could only barely make out the shape of a man kneeling over him. Someone moved his arms, laying them flat against the dirt.

"Hey," the man said loudly, shaking Darius's shoulder. "Hey, can you hear me?"

The response that escaped Darius's lips was so broken that he couldn't even understand it.

"W-what the hell did that?" the woman stammered, clearly agitated.

"I don't know, maybe a bear?"

Darius gurgled and tried to nod, though it wasn't clear if they could perceive the motion.

"No! No bears!" a third voice called out, whining. It was that of a young child. Frightened. Unsure.

"Shh, Daph," another woman soothed. "There's no bear here."

The man scrutinized him, probing his wounds and placing a palm to Darius's brow. He shook his head. "It looks like he's been putting on some kind of herbal paste. Maybe something to slow it down. He's got a bad infection, though. Here, Kris, help me out here."

A dark shape moved quickly through his line of vision, where he lost it in his periphery. Wrenching pain coursed through his body as he felt his torso lifted from the ground. His arms were spread wide, draped between the two people lifting him. He groaned in agony, his head suddenly swimming.

"Easy, buddy, easy," the man chirped. "Hang on for us, okay?"

*Lord, please let this be real.*

"Follow the creek. I saw the smoke coming from downstream. We can't be far now."

Darius felt his heart leap as they moved forward, lurching at first then settling into a wide, swaying rhythm. He closed his eyes. The motion made his stomach churn, and at times he felt as if his body was entirely apart from his consciousness. He tried to protest several times, but couldn't make a discernible sound. Even time didn't adhere to rationality; there was a sensation that it slowed to a crawl, or simply skipped several minutes.

Eventually shadows crept in and the forward motion stopped. He was lowered to a horizontal position again. Gone was the coolness of shade and dirt. Warmth and softness surrounded him, though something cool and wet brushed across his brow. There were voices, even more than before. Conversations surrounded him, but the words were mostly gibberish.

*Lord, what is happening to me?*

Bright light pierced through into the depths of his soul. As quickly as it came, it was gone.

*No. No, not now. I can't die.*

"Governor Owens?" A man's voice. Deep. Echoed. Distant.

*What?*

"Governor, can you hear me?"

His eyes drifted open just a crack. He was indoors. Four people stood around him, though their faces were blurs. "Yes," he managed, just barely more than a whisper.

"Governor, you're safe. It's me, Doctor Kilborne. I'm going to take care of you now, but we need to act quickly. I'm going to put you under in a second. Do you understand?"

Doctor Kilborne. A competent practitioner originally who was originally a passenger on *Gabriel*. A man he'd met a couple times in the early years, but lost contact with since he moved to Rust Creek.

"Y-yes."

"Hold up a sec, Doc," another man interjected. His voice was oddly familiar, but one he hadn't heard in years. "Governor, do you know who did this to you?"

*Jacob Granger. Calvin's former neighbor.*

"Yes." He licked his bloody lips. "Young," he rasped.

Darius felt the pinprick in his arm as the doctor slipped the drugs into his veins.

"We'll see you when you wake up."

As Darius faded into the darkness, he heard his caretakers curse Young's name.

*I'm coming for you, you son of a bitch.*

. . .

Exhaustion was her eternal enemy. More persistent than any predator she had escaped in her years as a hunter. Picking away at her consciousness as the pounding seas eroded the shore. She was so close to her final goal, yet her feet grew heavier with every step. The throbbing of her feet escalated almost in perfect harmony with Diego's increasingly urgent complaints of fatigue.

The great city, the one that Will had promised would be there, lay before them. Its heart was only a mile or two away, but a mile too far. She had seen its expanse as they came out of the hills, sprawling out in a wide circle. The city seemed to shimmer in the dying light as brightly as the river that neatly bifurcated it. Massive gray hulks, more than a dozen times larger than the pods she had seen back on Raphael Island, lay dormant on each side of the river.

But the vision disappeared as night fell, even as they pressed closer to the dwellings and shops that Calvin had spoken of. Gabi pressed on along the road, lined on either side by tall stalks of corn. Endless. Suffocating.

She had no more to give. Her feet dragged to a halt, and without so much as a second thought, she dropped her pack to the ground. Her vinewood bow, useless without any arrows, clattered to the dirt next to her. Gabi could hear her brother's sigh of relief as his miniscule load quickly met the packed earth.

Calvin stopped in the middle of the road, his outline barely visible in the moonlight. Gabi couldn't see his expression, though she knew by the tingling in her nerves that he was looking at her.

"Are you serious?" he grumbled.

"We're stopping for the night," she replied coolly.

"You've come all this way, and you're going to just stop now?"

"I'm tired!" Diego whined emphatically.

"My feet are killing me too," Gabi added. "Besides, it's too dark to see. Might break a leg or twist an ankle if we keep going."

"Sure. Spend a night in a cornfield," Calvin replied. "Sounds great. Totally comfortable. Great view of the stars." He thrust his hand skyward, emphasizing the glittering, milky multitude of lights strung in the cosmos above. He then abruptly turned toward the city and started walking.

Gabi reached to her pack and drew her tomahawk from its make-shift holster. "Hey, where do you think you're going?"

"Home. To sleep in a real bed."

She brought her arm back, ready to hurl the weapon at her prisoner's back, but stopped.

*A real bed,* she thought. *No more dirt. No more waking up in the middle of the night looking for bears.*

"Wait," she blurted.

Calvin stopped.

Gabi cursed herself silently for the moment of weakness. The idea of an actual bed was tempting. Her joints and feet ached badly.

"The town will be there tomorrow. Diego's too tired. We rest."

"Diego," he called out without a moment's hesitation. "Do you want a warm, soft bed tonight? Or do you want to sleep in this creepy old corn field."

"Bed!" Diego jumped to his feet, clapping.

"D!" Gabi snapped at him. She turned to the tall, dark form of her prisoner. "Do you want to listen to him whine the whole way there?"

"Christ, Gabi, I'll carry him on my shoulders. You too, if I have to. You have no idea how badly I want to be home right now."

Before she could react, Calvin knelt next to Diego, who scrambled up his back and perched on his shoulders. He took a few steps, wobbling awkwardly as he tried to correct his balance.

"Stop," she protested.

"This would be a lot easier if you'd cut me free."

"Don't even think about…"

"About what?" he cut her off. "You saved my life. Even though you've kept me tied up ever since, I wouldn't ever do anything to hurt you. If it's tomorrow, next week, or a month from now that I can prove myself, I can wait. Just please, I want to go home. I want to see my daughter. I want my hands to be free so I can hold her. That's the only thing I'll ever ask of you."

Gabi closed the gap between them. Her fury over his arrogance and manipulation of her brother seethed. But something else was building within her. It was subtle at first. She wondered why she didn't bury her tomahawk in the man's chest, why she hesitated. But then the similarity struck her, and it was almost too much to bear.

There, in front of her in the darkness, stood a man far too much like her own father; a silhouette in the night, with a small child hoisted on his shoulders. The gesture seemed innocent enough, but the reflection was too striking. She saw herself aloft on her father's shoulders. Taller than the world. Secure atop his broad frame, held by his sheltering arms.

Gabi dropped the tomahawk, instead selecting the dead assassin's knife to slice apart the bonds. The black nylon rope dropped in a heap at her feet. Calvin rubbed his wrists together and whispered, "Thank you."

She shook her head, as disappointed in herself as she was irritated at his ability to sway her. She went to retrieve her pack, but he followed close behind her, picking it up as she reached for it.

"Hey," she protested.

"You've done enough already. Let me do something for you now." He shifted Diego slightly as he slung the pack over his shoulder, then marched steadily toward the city.

The time passed silently, though not uncomfortably. Without the weight of her pack, Gabi felt as if she was floating along the road. They were within the city in a half hour, and Calvin opened the door to his home a few minutes later. He ushered the Serrano children inside.

Without Persephone's illumination, the inside of the home was pitch black. Gabi stumbled blindly in the darkness, shuffling a few inches at a time until her hands came into contact with something solid. A moment later, Calvin lit a lantern, bathing the room in a soft, warm glow. She stood next to a small bench. Racks on either side of the room were stocked with dozens of brown, green, and clear bottles full of liquid. Diego had been placed in the middle of the floor, rubbing his eyes and blinking.

"This way," Calvin motioned with the lantern. "Bedroom's upstairs."

He led the way up a steep wooden staircase. The room above was lavishly decorated, with a dresser full of woven baskets, a water basin, and the biggest bed Gabi had seen on Demeter backed up against the wall. She stared at it, blinking incomprehensively. It was easily large enough to sleep all three of them, and the cloth blanket that was draped over it looked as if it might keep a pleasant balance of warmth through the night.

"You two can have the bed," he said, placing the lantern on the dresser and starting for the staircase. "I'll sleep on the floor."

"Wait," Gabi blurted. He stopped, and there was a brief, awkward pause. "Won't you be cold?"

He shook his head. "Don't worry, I've got it covered."

Calvin disappeared long enough for Gabi to shed her pack and get settled under the covers with Diego. The mattress was thicker and softer than anything she had ever slept on in Camp Eight, and the blanket almost tickled her as it brushed across her chin. Diego drifted to sleep almost as soon as his head hit the pillow. Calvin returned, wrapped in a massive, dark brown fur blanket. She shuddered, recognizing the animal that it came from.

"Did you kill that thing yourself?" she asked.

He shook his head before finding a bare patch of floor to settle into. "Traded for it. I've seen what these bears can do up close. They're dangerous. Stay away from them."

*Too late for that.*

Conversation would have to wait for the morning, as exhaustion quickly overtook her.

• • •

*I'm really home,* he thought, a part of him still not believing the concept. He slowly pulled aside the massive bearskin blanket, letting the cool early morning air caress his bare chest.

Cal sat up and glanced over at his bed, where the two children slept, their features barely visible in the filtered light of dawn. The young boy, barely five years old, let out a soft, erratic snore. The older girl, Gabi, rested in eerie stillness; Cal thought for a moment that she was only feigning sleep. Even as she dreamt, she was an unsettling presence.

Gabi had been very evasive when Cal had tried to engage them in conversation. She looked to be no older than thirteen, if he had to guess, yet she dispatched Alan in a gruesome manner without a hint of remorse. She claimed that the little boy, Diego, was her brother, but they bore little resemblance to each other. Only their noses and speech matched. Everything else was different. Skin color. Eye color. Hair color. Gabi looked after him, but not in a way that Cal expected from siblings. And her short temper was particularly troublesome. Cal fully expected her to kill him the night before when he refused to stop at the edge of town. But the desire to be that much closer to Andrea, as well as to sleep in his own home, foolishly overrode his desire for self-preservation.

*At least she didn't,* he reflected.

He got up and padded silently to his dresser, shedding the tattered remains of his pants, retrieving a new pair as well as a thin, short-sleeved shirt. The change of wardrobe made him feel like he was truly free, no longer anyone's prisoner. Cal cycled a couple deep breaths and closed his eyes, listening to the river. His senses seemed to come alive at once. Soft, deep thumps from across the Fairweather told him that the South Concordia Mill was starting operations early. The pungent smell of human waste indicated that the dung draggers hadn't come by River Way recently. Varied chatter along the street heralded the colony's early risers.

*Now what?*

Cal considered the question carefully. Assuming that a relatively normal schedule had been achieved by the Taylor family in the wake of his disappearance, Beth and Jamie would not be up and about for another hour. Complicating matters was the pair of *Raphael* survivors asleep in his bed. Beyond a doubt, they needed to meet with Deputy Governor Dayton, as soon as possible, but Gabi might not like being pushed or paraded around. Then there was Young. If he wasn't already aware that Alan was dead, it would only be a matter of time before he became suspicious. Vaughn needed to know about all that had happened, both to Cal and Darius. But Cal had no idea where the detective was. He scratched at the short, shaggy beard that had grown on his face during captivity.

*Well, I guess a shave and breakfast will give me more time to think things through.*

Cal laid out his straight razor and towel on the dresser next to the ceramic washbasin. As he reached for a pitcher to retrieve water for the basin, he heard a loud slamming noise downstairs. Startled, his fingers jammed into the pitcher, sending it crashing to the floor. The sound of the shattering vessel had Gabi awake in an instant, and before Cal could react, she was up, tomahawk in one hand, pistol in the other.

"What the hell was that?" an unfamiliar man's voice echoed up through the stairwell.

Cal's heart raced as he froze in place. Gabi glared at Cal, training the gun on him.

*God damn it,* Jerk complained nervously. *Do you really have to make everyone want to kill you?*

"What was what?" another voice said, again from the floor below.

By this time Diego was rubbing his eyes and moaning, shaking off the shackles of slumber. Cal slowly drew one finger to his lips. "Shh," he hissed quietly.

"Dude, I heard something from upstairs. Someone's here."

"Knock it off, you little bitch. Alan took care of the guy. There's no one here."

"I don't like it. Where the hell is Alan, anyway? He's the one who wanted this shit anyway."

"You know how he gets when he's stressed. Probably getting plastered and blowing off steam." The third voice was too familiar to Cal, and it made his heart sink.

*Brittany. God damn it.*

He reached one hand back into the top left dresser basket and drew out his old Beretta. Gabi's eyes widened and she shifted her aim from Cal's chest to his head as soon as she saw it. Cal realized the mistake a moment too late. She pulled on the trigger.

There was no shot. She looked down at the weapon, dumbfounded. Before she had a chance to recover and sling the tomahawk at him, he set the pistol down on top of the dresser and put both hands out toward her, trying to calm her down. Her hand shook as she retrained the weapon on him.

"I'm not going to hurt you. I need your help," he whispered hoarsely as he took a step forward.

Her muscles relaxed, and she looked at him in confusion. Cal took the opportunity to gently remove the pistol from her hand. He then disengaged the safety, chambered a round, then handed it back to her, grip-first. Her confusion turned to utter shock, as she just stared blankly at him while he readied his own weapon. Cal crept forward across the floor, making sure to avoid any creaky floor boards.

He glanced over his shoulder and whispered, "Diego, stay put under the covers. Don't move unless Gabi comes back for you. Gabi, step where I step."

Cal moved forward a few more feet. Gabi didn't make a move from next to the bed. He shook his head.

*Damn it, going to have to go this one alone.*

He stalked down the stairs, taking extra caution to skip the creaky tread near the bottom of the flight. Cal took a moment's pause on the last step, taking deep breaths and calming his jangled nerves.

"No, the whiskey," Brittany directed them. "Alan wants that first."

Bottles clanked as the intruders began to clear Cal's display rack. With only Brittany talking, he couldn't tell if they were all on the shop floor or not. There was no telling how long they'd be there for, but Cal desperately wanted Brittany to answer for what she had done to him.

He stepped around the corner, keeping his back to the wall as he slinked past the kicked-in back door. Brittany caught a glimpse of him, and the bottle of whiskey in her hand came crashing to the ground. Another man was with her, loading bottles into a crate. He froze as soon as he saw Cal.

*Shit,* Cal thought. *Where's the third one?*

"C-Cal," Brittany stammered.

"Hands where I can see them," he shot back. Both of them complied without protest.

"H-How…?"

"Where's the other one?"

Brittany exchanged looks with her companion, who Cal recognized as one of the two men that was with her the first time she entered his store. He checked over his shoulder, down the hall. The other man was nearly on him, knife in hand. A single, deafening shot rang out, and the attacker collapsed at Cal's feet, howling and clutching his leg. Gabi stood at the bottom of the stairwell, her pistol trained on the crumpled assailant. Cal nodded in gratitude before turning back to the other intruders.

"Pick him up," Cal motioned to their crippled companion.

"Please, Cal," Brittany croaked, her lips trembling.

"Do it."

"Please, you've got to listen…"

"No, I'm done listening to you."

"Cal, please! They…"

"NOW!" he barked back.

The intruders scurried along to help the wounded man to his feet. Cal motioned toward the front door; they trudged along in compliance. Brittany gave him a tearful look over her shoulder. A look that might have melted his heart a week ago, but now only fueled his anger.

Gabi nodded once at Cal. "You got this?" she asked

"Yeah," he replied, though he wasn't sure that he did have full control. "Get Diego and come back down. We're going for a walk."

She retreated back up the stairs, the wood squeaking sharply as she pushed off of the loose step. A moment later the front door flew open. Hunter stepped through, his weapon trained on the three intruders. His eyes grew wide and his jaw slacked.

"Cal?" he gasped.

"Hunter! Man, I'm glad to see you."

"I heard a shot. What the hell happened? Where have you been? We thought you were kidnapped, like Governor Owens."

"I was. Long story. But these three need to pay a visit to Detective Vaughn."

"Alright then, let's go." Hunter stepped out of the building and motioned for the prisoners to follow, never turning his back to them or letting his aim waver.

By this time Gabi and Diego had come downstairs. The girl fell in beside Cal, her weapon squarely aimed at Brittany's back. Diego peeked out from behind her, eyes locked on the pool of blood at his feet. He was clearly not used to the violence that he had seen recently, and it pained Cal.

*Too young to see this. Too young to understand.*

Hunter was not the only one attracted by the fight's commotion. As they led their prisoners down River Way, dozens of Concordians joined, gawking and gossiping amongst themselves. Frank Devereaux met them at Benedict Boulevard, his M4 ready. He pulled Cal aside as they passed.

"I thought you were dead. What's going on?" he whispered.

"They were behind the governor's disappearance. Mine, too. We're taking them in."

Frank clapped his hand on Cal's shoulder solidly. "I'll take it from here. Go get your daughter."

Cal watched the procession for a moment. Gabi was a couple paces behind Hunter. She had tucked the pistol into her waistband. He cringed, wondering if she had figured out how to engage the safety.

"Those two kids there, they need a place to stay. They need to talk to Dayton. Make sure they don't wander off, alright?"

"Of course. But why?"

Cal sighed deeply. "It's a long story. One we'll be talking about for years to come."

He left Devereaux to ponder the thought, and quickly caught up with Gabi. She regarded him indifferently as he approached.

"Did you put the safety on?" Cal asked.

She nodded. "I forgot about that before. Lucky you."

"My friends will watch over you for a bit until I come back."

"I don't need to be watched," she shrugged.

"No. I guess you don't. But they'll be around if you need anything."

"Where are you going?"

Cal smiled warmly, the heaviness of his ordeal melting away like ice in the sun. "To hold my daughter again. To bring her home."

Cal could have sworn he saw the corners of Gabi's mouth twitch upward in a fleeting smile. "Good. She needs you."

"Thank you, Gabi. For everything."

With a shrug, the young *Raphael* survivor marched away, flanked by her brother and Devereaux.

. . .

The city of Concordia was breathtaking. Not only did it completely dwarf Camp Eight in every aspect, it felt truly alive. Perhaps that had something to do with dozens of people rushing from their homes to witness Cal's prisoners being paraded to a large building next to a vast, lush field. Still, without the crowd of gawkers, the sprawling settlement was impressive. Nearly every building was at least two stories tall. Streets knitted together, serving as the fabric that held the clusters of dwellings together. Beyond the town sat a massive gray hull, many times larger than the pod that sheltered the storm survivors back at Camp Eight. On their march, Gabi had been able to look across the river. Still another half of the city lay on the far banks of the wide channel, just as grand as what she had already seen.

And yet, she wanted to take Diego by the hand and run away from it all. The ultimate goal of Will's personal crusade surrounded her, and all she could think of was how alien it all felt. How much she wanted to escape in that moment.

The thick padding of the chair in which she sat supported her body well, but she still could not get comfortable. Diego could not settle in to a chair either, though for different reasons. His eyes were wide with awe as he moved around the room, examining everything within reach with blind curiosity. He had spent no less than ten minutes scrutinizing the massive desk before them, and rummaging through its drawers. The bookcases had occupied him nearly the entire time since.

Gabi glanced through the open door, down the second floor hallway. Cal's friend that had escorted her to this building stood a few feet away, out of earshot, holding a muted conversation with another man. He was a little shorter, with a full head of hair and beard, their deep chestnut tones marred with silver.

Their conversation ended, and Cal's friend gave the other man a salute before disappearing down the stairs. The older man turned and slowly walked toward the room, keeping his eye on Gabi the entire time. She glanced over at Diego, who was bouncing on the chair next to her.

*When he comes in. That's when we'll go. I'll grab Diego and we'll run,* she thought. A moment later, the voice of reason kicked in. *And where would we go? There's nowhere else. We left Will behind. There are no other cities.*

The man closed the door behind him as he entered, then took a seat behind the desk. He folded his hands in front of him. The weight of his stare made Gabi squirm. After a minute of awkward silence, he finally spoke.

"Are you hungry?"

"Yes," Diego blurted. Gabi shot him a glare, and he sat still, shrinking away into the chair.

"Good," he continued with a smile, drawing his hands into his lap as he leaned back in his chair. "Breakfast is on the way, and I'm not sure I can eat it all by myself."

Gabi slouched in her chair. Her eyes wandered to the slatted frame that covered the windows. The city was out there, full of strange people. The lands beyond were almost completely unknown to her; their travels had taken them through only a tiny fraction of the surrounding area. She had made it to Will's paradise without her mentor by her side. In that moment, his absence was keenly felt. He was supposed to be in her place, explaining their journey. He was to be the face of the survivors, not her. She bit her lip nervously.

"Is something wrong?" the man asked, bringing Gabi's focus back to him.

"No." Her response was curt.

"Just not sure about me, are you?"

Gabi nodded after a moment's pause.

"I don't blame you. You don't know me. But I know that Calvin wanted to make sure someone was watching over you. He and I go back for years. I'm more than happy to help out. My name is Tom." He waited a moment, biding the awkward silence by tenting his fingers. "What are your names?"

"Gabi." She tilted her head slightly toward Diego. "This is my brother, Diego."

Her heart jumped as the door creaked opened. Her head swiveled around to meet the source of the disturbance. A smallish, slender man limped toward them, bearing a tray full of food. Gabi began to salivate as soon as she smelled the fresh bread. When the tray was placed on the table, she could see heaping plates of fruit and scrambled eggs, as well as several slices of toast.

"Please, help yourself," Tom beckoned.

Diego squealed with delight, though he looked expectantly at Gabi.

She nodded, and he snatched a large, pale green fruit. Gabi was a little more reserved and polite, thanking their host under her breath as she loaded eggs onto her toast. Warmth spread through her chest and stomach as she consumed the fresh, steaming food.

"Glad to see you like it. So tell me, how did you meet Calvin?"

"She saved my life," Cal's voice came from behind her.

Gabi turned her head toward the door. He had just stepped inside, and he cradled a tiny baby in the crook of his arm. Her bright blue eyes were wide open, and her fingers curled and relaxed slowly, grasping at something unseen in the air. Cal wandered to a chair opposite from Diego and sat.

"I'm very glad to see you, Mr. McLaughlin," Tom beamed. "We all feared the worst when you disappeared. It was like losing Darius all over again."

She could see Cal's jaw clench as he ground his teeth together. "Well, I guess we can call off the search for him."

The older man's smile evaporated. "Then he's…" Cal nodded silently. "I see. And the group that was herded in here this morning, they had something to do with it?"

"I'm not sure how much they had to do with Darius, but they were cleaning out my store this morning. The girl…" his voice trailed off, and for a moment Cal seemed very distant. "Brittany was the one that lured me into the trap."

Tom sank into his chair, nodding solemnly. The room grew eerily quiet as the men pondered some connection to the female robber. Something that she wasn't privy to as an outsider. Yet there was an underlying message that only Gabi understood; Camp Eight wasn't the only place that had problems. Even Concordia had its criminals. Criminals were always punished, but it had been nearly four years since Gabi had witnessed justice in action.

*I wonder, how do they handle executions here?* She considered this for a moment as she finished the first slice of toast and reached for some fruit.

"So Gabi and Diego have a bit of a story themselves," Cal said, shattering the silence. "And it's just as unbelievable as everything else that's happened lately."

The older man's eyebrows arched. "More incredible than saving your life?"

"They're from *Raphael*."

Tom's jaw dropped, wavering slightly as words escaped him.

Gabi shook her head and bit into the sweet fruit. She knew an onslaught of questions was about to be launched. Will should have been in her place. When Gabi took charge and pushed forward, she had done so only with a vision of the town they would reach. The aftermath never crossed her mind.

"How?" Tom coughed.

"I don't know. I still can't wrap my head around it."

"You're sure you were on *Raphael*, Gabi?"

"Yeah," she shot back.

"How long ago was this?"

"Six years."

Cal smirked and shrugged as Tom gave him an incredulous look. "What do you remember about the ship?"

Gabi sighed and leaned back, trying to think about the craft that brought her to Demeter. Only a couple minor details came to mind. "We left Earth on rockets. That's when we got to the ship, I think. I remember it being really big when we first got off the rocket, but after we crashed and it was on the beach, it looked really small."

"Beach?" Tom asked. "Where was this beach?"

"We came from an island. The beach was close to where the town was."

Cal leaned sideways toward his companion. "ESAARC?" he muttered. Tom nodded in agreement, though he held up his hand to stem further comment from Cal.

"Where the town was? Did something happen?"

Gabi nodded and hushed her voice. "It was destroyed by a hurricane about a year ago."

The older man's excitement dissipated, and a slight frown formed at the corners of his mouth. "I'm very sorry to hear that. That must have been terrifying." He paused slightly. "How many more survivors are there, do you know?"

"Just me and Diego, and two more that we left back at the other town. Marya and Aidan."

"Town?" Tom asked, slightly puzzled.

"Rust Creek," Cal clarified.

"Four? That's it?"

Gabi thought about this for a moment. She knew that at least one of the other two ships that had left Camp Eight had foundered. Though bodies hadn't been found, the debris had been found far enough offshore that survival would have been impossible. The second ship was farther ahead of them, but could have taken a different route. With no trace of their journey, Gabi had no idea whether they were alive or dead, and without knowing which ship was destroyed, who might possibly be left. Then there was Will.

"Maybe another four," she guessed, assuming that Will had come to his senses.

"Where are they?"

"I don't know. We… we got separated," she lied. "Just a few days away from Rust Creek."

"I know this is a hard question, but I don't want to make any assumptions. What happened to your parents? Did they survive the landing?"

Bursts of memories flashed through her mind, though clouded as if they were glimpses of an interrupted dream. Terror. Fire. Running. Then the first clear post-Earth memory she had hit her. It was the image of Lon Carney standing over her father's body. A stout branch was clutched in his right hand, dripping with blood, and a cruel smile twisted his lips. Gabi wanted to scream, just as she had done as that defenseless girl six years earlier, but her lungs felt paralyzed. She dug her fingers deep into the arms of the chair and took in a huge, gasping breath.

"Gabi? Are you okay?" Cal asked, concern written on his face.

She sprang from her seat and bolted for the door. "Gabi!" Diego called after her as she flung it open and hurried down the hall. Her lungs heaved as she drew in breath after breath. The walls seemed to close in on her as she scrambled to the top of the stairs. She stopped there, hearing the excited jabbering of dozens of strangers down below. A hand closed gently around her arm. She tore away from the grip, spinning around and backing up to the wall.

"Hey, hey," Cal soothed, pulling his hand back. The commotion seemed to disturb his daughter, and she began to whimper softly. Diego arrived just a second later, taking his place at Gabi's side. He threw his arms around her, squeezing as tightly as he dared.

"Don't touch me," Gabi warned, glaring at Cal.

"Take it easy. Tom didn't mean anything by it."

"Why does everyone want me to remember all the bad shit that's happened to me?"

Cal sighed and knelt in front of her. "We don't know what all has happened to you. When we got to the planet, *Raphael* was gone. All that was left was its landing beacon and a distress call. No emergency transmitters. No follow-up radio contact. All these years it's been assumed that the ship blew up on entry, and that there were no survivors."

"But we *did* survive," she growled. "And no one came for us. We had to come to *you*."

"If we had known, we would have sent help. But you're here now, and Tom's going to want to know what happened. If you want to take it a little at a time, that's fine. If you'd rather talk to someone else, I can make that happen too."

"I don't want to talk to anyone!" she shouted.

The din coming from downstairs subsided somewhat. Gabi shrank against the wall; her careless outburst had attracted the attention of the people in the main hall. She slammed her fist into the wall in frustration.

"Come back to the room with me," Cal smiled warmly. "I'll make sure Tom doesn't ask you any more questions. You can sit and relax. Eat more if you need to. It's a nice quiet place to spend some time while we figure out all the messes going on today."

Gabi nodded hesitantly. They returned to the room and took their seats again. Cal leaned over the desk and whispered a few sentences to Tom. The older man glanced at Gabi a couple times, then nodded.

"My apologies, Gabi," Tom said. "We will discuss this at a later time. Please let me know if there is anything I can get you."

She grabbed some more fruit from the platter and curled one knee to her chest as she began to eat it. Diego quickly got bored of his chair and resumed his thorough inspection of the room. She found herself lost in thought, wondering if Will had actually snapped out of his funk. After considering the worst possible outcome, she wanted nothing more to do with contemplation.

"Did he give you any idea why Young wanted those computers so badly?" Tom asked Cal in a hushed voice.

"There's something big on them. Young himself said it was the opportunity of a lifetime. Controlling the world," Cal replied. "And he'll kill anyone to have it."

Tom nodded and scratched his beard. He took a pen from one of the desk drawers and began to scratch something down on the paper in front of him. "This man is a threat. A renegade. Having him on the loose isn't good. For anyone."

Cal cast his gaze down at the paper. "What's this?"

"Devereaux's orders. And an arrest warrant for Young. Last I heard he's still onboard his ship. The CVM marches as soon as they're mustered."

"Good. The sooner he's brought in the better."

"Who is this Young guy?" Gabi asked.

The two men looked at her, unaware that she had been listening in on their conversation. Tom stumbled for words, but Cal beat him to the punch.

"The man who wanted me dead. He's a criminal."

"So you're going to stop him?" Gabi returned.

"Yes."

She smiled weakly. "I hope you get him." She considered telling them that Young was a cornered animal, and that he would fight like one. But it wasn't her fight.

*I hope their hunters are good*, she thought.

• • •

Only a sliver of Persephone hung in the sky. Barely enough for the CVM to distinguish *Mercy* from the surrounding plain, it was not enough to reveal their movements as they closed in. At least, that's what they were counting on.

*Too late to go back anyway,* he thought.

Another heavy boot was planted in his hands. He heaved upward, even as his knee ground painfully into the dirt. Private Inouye pulled himself upward, gaining a foothold on the emergency ladder built into the side of the ship, and he started the climb that his squadmates had completed before him. Next up was Sergeant Josephson. She was to be the last of the Militia members to climb to the top. More importantly, she was in command of breaching *Mercy* from above, with the bulk of the platoon. Without fuss, she accepted the boost onto the ladder and began her scramble.

Frank sighed. *Godspeed, Sergeant.*

He turned to the darkness, away from the ship. He had one squad with him for the second breach. Frank could only see a couple of the men—Private Smith and Corporal Wright—but he instinctively felt the presence of the others. There was something else he felt. It was an almost palpable sensation of fear. He could feel it shroud him and cause his fingers to tremble ever so slightly. And that bothered him almost as much as his orders.

*These kids aren't ready for battle,* he thought. *They've only fired at targets, not enemies.*

The veteran of the Battle of Laramie had no choice but to shrug off his concerns. The time for action was at hand. He clicked his tongue three times; it was a signal to his squad to stay close. Frank lowered his M4's aim toward the ground and clicked on the flashlight attached to its receiver rail. They moved swiftly through the darkness, moving forward from the flank of Pod Four. His heart thumped harder in his chest with every beat until he thought that Young and his men could hear it inside *Mercy's* walls.

The ground dropped away suddenly, exposing a dark pocket underneath one of the cargo pods. Frank clicked once and motioned his light toward the depression. Corporal Wright turned on a flashlight before scrambling head first into the hole. The others followed him in quick, silent procession. Smith. Hamilton. The Brandt twins. Eight men plunged into the darkness underneath the ship before Frank slipped in behind them.

Unevenness in the ground led to tunnel networks of varying sizes and lengths underneath any ship on Demeter. The colony's children called them "rabbit holes", but until this day they had been little more than nuisances to the parents of adventurous youth. And while both *Michael* and *Gabriel* had settled into the ground far enough for the rabbit holes to mostly disappear, *Mercy* had not had the time to do so. It was this detail that Frank was hoping to use to his advantage.

When the tunnel reached the main hull of the ship, the raised centerline under the hull allowed them more freedom of movement. They could stand up, albeit hunched over. Frank led his men toward the front of the ship.

Gunfire erupted above, deadened by feet of air and steel. Josephson had made her breach, and was fighting the renegade crew. Her platoon would be exposed to fire on their way in, and casualties among the Militia were sure to be high. Frank shoved aside thoughts of his men being slaughtered. They would do no good if he failed in his mission.

Moments later they reached their target, just behind the forward cargo ramp. Frank reached up, jamming his fingers into the crack of the emergency airlock access port. He grunted and wheezed as he tried to part the two halves of the access door. His first bid was unsuccessful, but he was joined by Wright for the second try, and the panel jerked and slid open. Just inside the access port was the outer airlock door. Its locking wheel turned slowly, though the protective outer panel had managed to keep it from seizing during the journey. After a few turns, the door dropped suddenly, knocking Frank off his feet and sending him tumbling.

"I'm alright." He shrugged Wright off as he regained his feet. "Get the inner door."

"Yes, sir!"

Frank assembled underneath the airlock with the rest of his men. The inner airlock door creaked open, and was followed almost instantly by two loud blasts. Wright cried out in pain, and dropped to the ground. His flashlight came to a rest next to him, shining its light on the wounded soldier. He clutched at his shoulder, which leaked blood from a gunshot.

"Hamilton," Frank barked as he dragged his squadmate away from the opening. "Get up there. Use the hatch for cover and clear the hall behind it." He turned back to Wright. "Stay low and don't move. We'll come back for you."

Frank had his M4 over his back and was climbing the ladder into the belly of the ship before any of the other soldiers reacted.

"Come on, Bravo Squad! Move out!"

Hamilton discharged a short burst from his carbine down the hall then heaved his body up into the hallway. He ducked around the cargo hatch and took cover just as an unseen assailant rattled off three more shots, narrowly missing Frank's head as it emerged from the airlock. Hamilton's weapon belched in response, and a body fell to the floor a few feet away.

"Clear sir," Hamilton shouted, though the ringing in Frank's ears nearly drowned out the report.

Frank pulled himself onto the lower gallery floor and quickly took up a defensive position behind a structural brace. "Move it, Bravo, move it!"

The Brandt twins were the next ones through the airlock, taking their position at the next set of beams. Private Smith barreled down the hall toward the main stairwell, but was cut down by enemy fire just beyond the Brandts.

"Damn it! Covering fire! Move it, Hamilton!"

Echoed gunfire from farther aft was shortly overpowered by staccato bursts from the Brandts' weapons. Hamilton charged past them, coming to a stop at the first turn of the stairwell. He raised his carbine and let loose a barrage, which was returned in kind. Frank gritted his teeth as Hamilton's body jerked twice from hits. One of *Mercy's* crewmen fell over the deck railing above, slamming into the stairs and rolling to a stop at the bottom, motionless.

"Hamilton!"

"Shit," he bellowed. "Fuck, I'm hit!"

Frank glanced behind him. No more squad members were left in support.

"Trask, Elliott, Jacobs, get your asses up here on the double!"

No response came from the airlock. Frank had little time to process that he was down six men; three casualties, and three that were likely cowering under the ship. The mission was getting out of hand and he needed to press forward with force, but he couldn't ignore the wounded men.

"Damn it," he cursed, his eyes returning to the front. "Sean, get

Hamilton out of here. And send those useless pricks up here if you find them. Steve, you're with me. Take point."

The twins moved swiftly. Sean made his way to Hamilton, looping his arms under the wounded man's pits to drag him away. Frank followed Corporal Steve Brandt closely, keeping his M4 trained at the top of the stairwell the entire time. They emerged into the upper gallery and made for the protective cover of a bulkhead. Shouting and gunfire burst out every few seconds in the rear section of the ship where Josephson's platoon had made their breach. Their target was in the opposite direction; whatever trouble the sergeant and her men were in, he could not help them.

The two men hustled toward the bridge, stepping over the bodies of both renegades and civilians, checking the connecting corridors of pods one and two. Each connecting corridor hid one of Young's men, but Frank and Brandt weren't so easily fooled. They took down the crewmen, then pushed forward toward their objective. They paused outside the bridge airlock for just a moment.

*Remember the mission,* he told himself, cycling a deep breath.

Frank nodded at Brandt, who crossed the threshold first. Frank was on his heels, mounting the three short treads to the top of the bridge's stairs. Harcourt Young was waiting for them. The billionaire's eyes only squinted slightly as the light from Frank's tactical flashlight fell on his face. The teenage girl whom he held tight in front of him, however, had eyes wild with fear. Young's pistol was held up to her chin, its barrel glinting menacingly.

"Drop the weapon!" Brandt commanded.

"Ah, ah, ah!" Young warned. "One more step and you get to clean her brains off the walls."

The sounds of fighting grew closer. The disgraced billionaire must have heard it too, as he licked his lips once and glanced quickly behind the two Militia members. A wicked grin crossed his face.

"You're smarter than I thought," Young continued. "Not just a brute force attack. No, your main attack was a diversion. You somehow found a way in, didn't you?"

"Drop it and let her go, Young," Frank ordered firmly. "You can't escape."

"No? No hope at all?"

A massive explosion ripped through the belly of the ship. Frank was caught off balance for a moment, and Brandt reeled from the shock. Young fared little better, and he was only able to steady himself and reposition his hostage in front of him.

"Drop it," Brandt repeated as the pistol returned to the girl's chin.

"I see your men found the servers," Young sneered. "Too bad. I wonder if any of them survived, or if you're all alone now."

Frank lowered his weapon's sight a couple inches, drawing its angle in slightly. His eyebrows arched as his thumb discreetly moved the selective fire switch to full automatic.

*Remember your orders.*

The renegade's eyes darted between the two men. His smile waned for a second before he flashed it again. "You know, there is one saying you guys have that I like. Dum vita est, spes est."

"Don't do it," Frank growled.

Frank read the billionaire's intentions even before he moved a muscle. Harcourt Young retrained his weapon on Corporal Brandt, but never got off a shot. Frank squeezed the trigger on his rifle, tearing the desperado and his hostage to shreds as the rifle's magazine emptied completely.

Without thought or hesitation, Frank reloaded his weapon. He stepped forward, nudging Young's lifeless body with his boot.

"Captain!" Brandt shrieked. "Captain, you killed the hostage!"

"I did," he murmured.

He dragged his feet down the stairs, put his back to the wall of the airlock bulkhead, and slid down the wall until he was seated. A short burst of gunfire echoing through the halls barely registered through the post-adrenaline haze.

Brandt paced over to the opening, towering over his commanding officer. "What the hell? You totally blew her away. You didn't have a clear shot. Why the hell were you on full auto?"

"I did what I had to do," he croaked. His throat constricted as he met the condemning gaze of the corporal. "Go help Josephson. If any of these bastards are left, flank them."

"Yes, sir," the younger man sneered as he stepped through the airlock.

Frank placed his rifle on the ground after Brandt left, burying his face in his hands. His closed eyes could not block out the terrified face of the blonde girl as his rounds tore into her chest. She was innocent. She deserved better than instant condemnation. He didn't need to read the orders that were in his breast pocket again. He had memorized all the words, but they were of no comfort.

CAPT. DEVEREAUX-

IN LIGHT OF NEW INFORMATION REGARDING HARCOURT YOUNG AND THE CREW OF MERCY, MY PREVIOUS ORDERS ARE NO LONGER VALID. THE COLONIAL VOLUNTEER MILITIA IS NOT TO BE MADE AWARE OF YOUR NEW ORDERS. AS FAR AS THEY ARE CONCERNED, WE ARE STILL PROCEEDING ON PLAN.

HARCOURT YOUNG IS NOW CONSIDERED AN IMMINENT DANGER TO THE PEOPLE OF CONCORDIA, AND HAS MADE CREDIBLE THREATS TO THE SAFETY AND LIVES OF OUR CITIZENS. IT IS FOR THAT REASON THAT YOU ARE HEREBY ORDERED TO EXECUTE HIM AND ANY CREW ON MERCY WHO BEAR ARMS IN HIS DEFENSE.

WHILE I IMPLORE YOU TO FIND A WAY TO MINIMIZE CIVILIAN CASUALTES DURING YOUR ASSAULT, THE ELIMINATION OF YOUNG TRUMPS ALL OTHER CONCERNS, AND MUST BE COMPLETED AT ALL COSTS.

YOUR SECONDARY OBJECTIVE IS TO RECOVER THE SERVERS STOLEN FROM GABRIEL AND MICHAEL. THE DATA ON THEIR DRIVES IS OF IMMEASURABLE VALUE.

GOD HAVE MERCY ON US FOR WHAT WE MUST DO.

THOMAS DAYTON
ACTING GOVERNOR
CONCORDIA, DEMETER COLONY
ALPHA CENTAURI


*At all costs, Governor,* he thought as he retrieved the orders and a lighter from his chest pocket. A moment later the orders were ablaze, only dropping to the deck when his trembling fingers could no longer handle the heat of the flames. *At all costs.*

· · ·

Tom folded his hands on the desk in front of him. His thumbs jousted and pressed together, doing little to help him mask his concern over what the report contained. The papers were formed in a crisp, uniform stack just beyond his fingers. It contained some thirty pages of accounts from a dozen men and women of the CVM, as well as the commander's personal report. And it was a sickening read, if ever there was one. No detail of the gruesome battle was left out, and it left his heart and mind heavy.

Tom glanced up from the pile at the Militia's commanding officer. Devereaux maintained the rigid posture of a man at attention, even though he had been asked to sit at ease. Dark circles ringed his eyes, his hair was a tussled mess, and his skin was almost ghostly pale. Devereaux looked as if he hadn't slept in days, and yet he was going through the motions of his service. Habits that had been drilled into him throughout his military career. Inside, there would be no ease for this man, Tom knew. Not after reading the final details regarding the Battle of Mercy. He had to wonder if Devereaux was avoiding sleep because of the nightmares that were sure to torment him.

"Thank you for your report, Captain," he began. "I have some questions for you."

The commander nodded almost imperceptibly, remaining silent. Tom sighed and grabbed the stack of papers, thumbing through them until he found the start of Devereaux's personal report.

"Can you explain to me your decision to split your command?"

"I felt that a second squad would meet less resistance on its way to the primary target. I believed that the main force would draw the defenders toward them." Devereaux's answer was delivered in a cold, almost clinical manner.

"And why did you leave Josephson in charge of the main force?"

"You know why, sir."

Tom tossed the papers down in front of him, sending them sliding in a disheveled mess. The commander reacted with only a momentary glance at the desk.

"That's right, Captain. I know why. You wanted to make sure your primary objective was completed. That bastard knew we were coming, and he played us. We walked right into it, too."

"Sir, he didn't survive," Devereaux protested.

"No." Tom straightened up and tented his index fingers together. "No, he was cornered. Young knew he had nowhere to go, so he set it up for a bloodbath. Now eighteen of your men are dead, along with dozens of innocent civilians."

"That wasn't our fault!"

"No, but we're still going to catch hell for it. All of us."

Devereaux leaned in slightly. Hints of silver in his scraggly beard glinted in the window's light. "*Mercy's* survivors will set that straight. The ones who got away from Young's men. They'll let the world know that sick bastard tried to use them as human shields. That Young's men shot their own people as they tried to run from the battle."

"I know, Frank. But who knows how long it'll take before the people believe them. That other black mark doesn't help things either."

Tom could see the other man's Adam's apple bob as he swallowed hard. "I did what I had to do, Governor."

"In cold blood. That's how Corporal Brandt described the way you gunned down a fifteen year old girl. Cold blood. Those are words that aren't so easy to forget."

"I neutralized my target."

"You murdered an innocent girl!" The legs of Tom's chair screeched hideously as he shot out of it in an instant and leaned over the desk.

Devereaux met his level just as quickly. "You told me to complete my mission, whatever the cost. That was the cost, Governor."

The men glared at each other for a minute before Tom drew his chair back to the desk, sitting down with a measured sigh. He pinched the bridge of his nose as he considered the brutality of the incident. Rumors of the vicious sort were already circulating through the small community, and it felt like he and the CVM had been damned before being given a chance to explain what happened.

"What about the servers?" he asked softly.

"They should be back onboard *Michael* in a day or two. I still don't know why you sent Josephson back to get them. They were completely blown to hell in the explosion."

"It's a long shot, but I'm hoping someone out there has enough computer or electronics experience to recover some of what's on them. Mr. McLaughlin told me that what's on them could control the whole colony. I have to know what it was that Young wanted so badly."

Silence passed between them, interrupted only by the precise ticking of Devereaux's watch.

"Is there anything else you need, Governor?"

"No, Frank. You're dismissed."

Devereaux snapped his body to attention then bowed slightly. Tom nodded and waved him off, which prompted the captain to leave the room. Tom stared off into oblivion while chewing on his thumbnail.

*How much will it all cost in the end?*

He heard someone clear their throat, which startled him back to the real world. Roger Miller had entered the room, though it was unclear how long he had been standing around waiting for Tom's attention. The deputy governor motioned for his liaison to have a seat.

"Do you have the reports I requested?"

Roger shook his head. "No, Governor. I was trying to get them from Doctor Taylor, but he wasn't available."

"Did he say why?"

"I never got a chance to speak with him. Or the elder Doctor Taylor either. They were too busy. I… I don't think you're going to believe this."

"What is it, Roger?"

"They had a patient transfer come in late last night from Rust Creek. Tom, it… it was Darius. He's alive."

Tom didn't waste a second. He was on his feet and halfway to the door before Roger stepped into his path, blocking his egress from Darius's office.

"Get out of the way, Roger. I need to see him."

"You can't. He's resting. They had to do surgery on him as soon as they got him."

Tom stepped around his subordinate and through the door. "What kind of surgery?"

"They had to take his arm."

He stopped in his tracks, his fingers curling into tight balls that bit into the palms of his hands. His hatred of Young coursed through every synapse in his body. If the billionaire had still been alive, Tom would have made him regret that detail. When Darius had been presumed dead, there was a preconceived notion in Tom's mind that the deed had been relatively quick and painless. Whatever had transpired had left the governor alive, but severely maimed. That callousness and lack of mercy didn't sit well with Tom.

"I'm still going to the clinic," he growled. "I want to be there when he wakes up."

"I understand. Is there anything I can do for you?"

Tom narrowed his eyes and nodded slowly. "Contact Abernathy and Hausner. See which one wants to defend those three pieces of shit from *Mercy* that Mr. McLaughlin caught in his shop. And figure out where we're going to hold their trial. I want to show the world exactly what *Mercy* brought here."

· · ·

*No room for Mercy,* Darius pondered as he examined the silver seal of Concordia emblazoned on its blue background. *There could have been. There should have been.*

Darius let the supple fabric of the flag slip through his fingers, allowing the banner to go limp. He sighed and turned the corner, slowly ascending the stairs to the second floor. His hand glided over the smooth, polished bannister. An odd sensation echoed in his nerves, and he could have sworn that the touch was mirrored exactly in his right hand. Darius paused and closed his mind, gritting his teeth.

*It's not real.*

The fact that his right arm had been amputated at the shoulder didn't make the sensations feel any less real. Every bit of twitching, pressure, or pain that came from below the surgical cut was a construct of his brain. It was a cruel, torturous reminder of his ordeal. He much preferred the physical pain as the wound healed; at least he could dull that with pills.

His office resided at the end of the hall atop the stairs. Yet as he walked toward it, it seemed somehow alien. He knew that Deputy Governor Dayton would not have moved any of the furniture, and that the order of the books on the shelves would not have changed significantly. Even minute details such as the scratches on the desk were static from his life as governor. A life that looked distorted and distant.

Darius pushed gently on the door, which swung open with its familiar soft creak. Dayton glanced up from behind the desk. He froze in place for a second, then stood up quickly, pushing aside a stack of papers on which he had been writing. A moment later he had rounded the desk, and was motioning Darius toward the chair he had just abandoned.

"Darius, I wasn't expecting you to come by. I would have had everything ready for you if I had known."

Darius ignored the deputy's prompts and took a seat in one of the four chairs on the near side of the desk. Chairs reserved for those who would meet with the governor.

"It's alright, Tom. I'm not here to work. Thought I'd stop by for a bit."

Dayton's eyes darted between Darius and the governor's chair, unsure of what to do next. He timidly returned to the chair and sat. "You've been cooped up in the clinic so long. I can't blame you for getting a bit restless."

Darius nodded slowly. He sank deeper into the chair, a soft smile crossing his lips. "It'll be good to finally go home."

"When does the doctor think you can go?"

"Tomorrow morning. I told him I was ready today, but he wouldn't have any of it. Gave me a long lecture about the importance of following his advice."

"And then he let you go for a walk?" Dayton asked impishly. "You could just slip the leash and go home yourself."

Darius chuckled softly. "He'd tell his mother. Then I'd be a wanted man, hunted down by the medical community and their vast army of nosy neighbors."

"It would be a short search. Everyone knows where you live."

The cheer suddenly drained from Darius's disposition. He glanced down at his missing limb. Softly, he added, "Anyone could point me out in a crowd, too. I don't exactly blend in."

Dayton chewed on his lower lip pensively, leaning back in the governor's chair. "I'm sorry, Darius. It's over, though. Harcourt Young is dead, along with most of his men. The trial's just about to start for the last three."

*Young. His men. A couple dozen innocent civilians. All dead, thanks to Devereaux's raid,* he though bitterly.

Despite the loss of innocent life, Darius didn't believe that the assault could have ended with significantly less bloodshed. Both Dayton and Devereaux were seasoned commanders. After hearing of the battle a few days after he lost his arm, Darius had come to the conclusion that things probably would have been worse if he had been in Dayton's position instead. He would have marched the CVM to the ship to demand surrender. Right into an ambush. It would have been bloody, and Young just might have escaped.

"Are you going to testify?" Dayton asked expectantly.

"No. I don't have anything to say about their particular crimes. I never met any of them, nor were they there during my captivity." There was a brief pause. "To be honest, I don't want to be there either. I have a lot to put behind me. That's just one more reminder that I don't need."

"I understand."

Darius heard someone rapping softly on the door to the office. He craned his neck just in time to see Roger enter, limping over to the desk. Darius briefly recalled the day that his liaison suffered the crippling injury that gave him that limp. Six years earlier, at the hands of another callous enforcer. One who wore the same uniform and once stood shoulder to shoulder with them as comrades in arms.

*How does trust begin?* Darius mused.

"Governor," Roger nodded. "Good to see you out and about." He turned his attention to Dayton. "I have a follow-up on that report from earlier. We confirmed it's another ship. We believe it landed about four miles south of the town. Captain Devereaux is already out investigating the first one. What do you want to do about this one?"

Darius shifted uncomfortably in his chair. *Ships?*

"We don't have many more men to spare for this," Dayton replied, scratching at his beard. "Sergeant Brandt just earned a new stripe, time for him to see how it fits. Have him take the rest of the CVM to check it out. Tell him that if he knows of any volunteers who want to go with, he's welcome to have them tag along. Only as reserves, though. I don't want them up front if something goes wrong."

"Of course, Governor." Roger paused, his face draining of color. He acknowledged Darius. "My apologies, Governor."

Darius waved his hand dismissively, waiting until the man left before reacting.

"More ships? What the hell is going on?"

"The beginning of Doctor Benedict's legacy," Dayton sighed heavily. "At least that's my guess. The first one overflew the eastern edge of town late last night. It's tiny, by any standard. Probably as big as an ESAARC pod. We think it landed halfway between here and *Mercy*. Then we heard rumors of another one early this morning. It didn't fly over us, but Porter saw something last night when he was in his fields. Word took a little while to reach us."

"The size of an ESAARC pod," he echoed, the words almost hollow and numb.

"That's right. Sounds about like Doctor Benedict's design for the masses, doesn't it? Escape pods for the lucky. And desperate. The last thing I want running around here is another Harcourt Young. So that's why the Militia is going. To secure the ships and their passengers."

"And then what, once they're secure?" Darius responded mockingly.

The response came with a broad shrug. "Hopefully integration.

Any ideas on how to go about that, Governor?"

Darius's heart began to beat against the cage in his chest. He stood up, taking a moment to steady himself as his balance hadn't fully returned. "It's your problem now. You're the governor."

"What?" Dayton gasped, rising to his feet and meeting Darius's gaze.

"I came here today to resign. My time behind that desk can't be measured by achievements. It can only be measured by the heartbreak that Concordia has suffered. Year in and out, time and again we've been struck by tragedy. We keep working through it somehow. But I can't. Not anymore."

"Darius, please think about what you're saying. You're the one who has guided and shaped this town into what it is today. You've had difficult calls to make that no man should ever have to. You have been the one to bring us through these challenges to make us stronger."

"I have no more left in me. I can't keep giving Concordia what it needs. What it deserves."

"Of course you can," Dayton shot back as he rounded the desk. His hand fell on Darius's good shoulder with a firm grip. "Give yourself the time to heal and rest. I'll keep everything running for you. When you're ready to take the helm again, it's yours."

Darius gently grabbed Dayton's wrist, pulling he hand off his shoulder. His tone was sober as he replied, "I was never ready for it in the first place. I see that now that I've paid the price myself."

"That was Young that did that to you," Dayton growled.

"And that's something I expect to hear for a long time. Maybe forever."

Dayton paused, still taking in the suddenness of Darius's move. After a few moments he nodded, then returned to his seat. Concordia's new governor gazed at his hands as they slowly glided over the armrests, as if the piece of furniture was suddenly new again. He glanced up. "So what will you do?"

"Continue my service to Concordia in the way I was always meant to. Tomorrow, when I return home to *Michael*, I'm going to get to work recovering data from the drives that Young tried to blow to bits. That is, with your permission, Governor."

"Of course," Dayton replied with a nod. "What's on them, anyway?"

"Technology. Our future. I'll keep you up to date with the progress." Darius turned toward the door, stopping just before he reached it. "Keep us safe, Governor. In Honor and Unity."

• • •

The door to Civic Hall swung open with a loud creak. Frank's lantern cast a dim, yellow light into the meeting room that danced and flickered with even the slightest breeze. The lamps inside had all been extinguished; Frank sighed in dismay.

*I swear I saw light in the office window,* he recalled.

He stepped through the door and made his way past the podium, carefully avoiding haphazardly arranged chairs along the way. Every other stair creaked under the weight of his boots as he climbed to the second floor. His legs were tired from the return trip, and with each step his feet felt heavier. He kept his feet moving even as he let out a great yawn, intent on reaching the room at the end of the hall. A soft glow highlighted the top and bottom edges of the door. Frank smiled weakly; he hadn't imagined that the governor's office was lit after all.

Frank rapped softly on the door. He waited a minute, but there was no answer, and no sound from beyond. Slowly he turned the knob and pushed the door, which complained a little more quietly than its counterpart downstairs. Deputy Governor Dayton was slumped over the desk, his head resting on folded arms. Every few seconds, Dayton let out a snore that sounded more like a trapped bee. Frank froze for a moment, unsure if his intrusion would be welcome.

*Don't be stupid. He needs to know.*

Frank knocked on the door a little louder. Dayton startled awake with a loud snort. He rubbed his eyes and stifled a yawn before scrutinizing the source of his rude awakening.

"Captain, you're back." Dayton motioned to a chair. "Please, sit. Tell me what you found."

Frank wasted no time in accepting the offer. It didn't matter that the seat wasn't well padded; he welcomed any chance to get off of his feet after hours of marching. His soles throbbed and pulsed even after being relieved of their burden.

"It was as you suspected, Governor," he started. "A single pod with a small reactor and an automated guidance computer. Sleeper layout almost identical to ours."

"Then Young was right," Dayton sighed, leaning back into his chair. "Doctor Benedict really did design another ship. And Young released the plans, just as he promised."

"As ordered, we secured the craft and searched for weapons. Nothing to speak of. Two rifles and a half dozen pistols."

"Nothing you couldn't handle, I trust?"

Frank cleared his throat, squirming slightly in his seat. "It wasn't necessary. They surrendered on sight. Sir, they're Chinese. Not military, either. Just civilians. They're pretty beat up and weak. Forty nine total. They double-bunked some of their younger children."

"Chinese?" Dayton repeated incredulously. "How the hell did they get the designs?"

Frank could hear heavy footfalls coming up the stairs, as if someone was taking them in giant leaps. He glanced over his shoulder once, but the far end of the hall was still dark.

"I haven't a clue. I tried to get it from their leader, but I couldn't quite follow. He was talking a mile a minute, and begging us for mercy. That's about all I could get from him. He didn't speak much English."

The footsteps had reached the top of the stairs. Frank looked back again to see Sergeant Brandt walking down the hall clutching a lantern, panting hard. He came straight in and dropped into the seat opposite from Frank, exhausted.

"Sergeant, you're back sooner than I expected," Dayton remarked.

"Thought you needed to know," the sergeant gasped. He held up one finger as he doubled over to catch his breath.

"Back?" Frank asked curiously.

"There was another ship, Captain. I sent him with the remainder of the CVM to investigate."

*Another ship. Two in as many days. Have the floodgates opened?*

"It was a small ship," Brandt continued, having found a second wind. "I counted forty berths. A lot of young children doubled up. Fifty three survivors, two casualties." Brandt shook his head sullenly. "Both kids. Their berth failed at some point during the spaceflight."

"A shame," Dayton nodded. "Were they armed?"

"Pretty heavily, but they gave up their weapons without argument. They were just relieved to have found us. We're a long way from Detroit."

"Detroit?"

"Yeah," Brandt affirmed. "And that gets us to the part you'll really want to know. There are more ships coming. The group's leader told us about the ones he knew about. They're part of a larger group of survivors who started gathering in the Detroit shortly after plans for these little ships started popping up all over the place. They took over an old auto manufacturing plant. Converted its floor to build sleeper ships. There were at least six more on the line when this one was launched."

"So we're looking at a steady stream of refugee ships, just from this one location. And who knows how many more from other areas."

"Yes, Governor."

Dayton craned his neck slightly and scratched at the full beard that adorned his chin. It didn't take long for him to finish absorbing the sergeant's report.

"Very well, gentlemen. I want a full manifest of both ships, including occupation and skills of all of the adults. I will make sure that the support section of *Gabriel* is sealed before any of them arrive. Assign them temporary quarters in pods one through four until we can give them work assignments."

"And if they refuse to come?" Frank asked.

"They have no choice. Any sleeper ship that lands on Demeter is the property of Concordia as far as I'm concerned. That includes any assets contained within. Go get some rest. We start in the morning."

*They come or they starve.* Frank suppressed a disdainful sneer as he dragged his exhausted body from the room. *Welcome to Concordia.*

• • •

The statue was easily three feet taller than Will. Standing on the tips of his toes, his hand could only barely touch the bridge of one of the sleeper ships it immortalized. Seeing that he was able to perform the feat, he immediately returned to a more dignified stance. His hand slid down the bronze body, his fingers tracing the spine of the ship's upper deck.

"Why are there only two?" Gabi asked.

The silence that answered her spoke volumes. Will ignored her entirely. Kris looked away, losing herself in the distant horizon. Karina simply shook her head.

"There were three ships that left Earth, right? Ours, and the two that are here."

"Gabi," Karina said softly, pointing at a thick metal plate affixed to the statue's heavy stone base.

She knelt next to it, trying to make out the words. Reading only came to her with great difficulty; it was something that Will had tried to get her to learn after his arrival in Concordia a month earlier. Her teacher in school was insistent that Gabi was very far behind in her reading skills, and that she work on it twice as hard as the other children. But Gabi found it, as well as school in general, tedious and maddening.

"Deh… dead. Dead catted."

"Dedicated," Will corrected.

"Damn it, Will, just tell me what it says," she snapped.

He sighed, kneeling next to her. "Dedicated to the founders of Concordia, Earth's first extrasolar colony. With their homeworld dying, these intrepid men and women crossed the treacherous void of space in order to survive, with no knowledge of what their future held. In this place they shed much blood and many tears. Their labor and sacrifice has built the cornerstone of a new world, and a place for humanity to flourish in Unity and Honor." He cleared his throat. "The fine print below is the important part. It says that this monument marks the site where the refugee ship *Michael* landed, and that *Gabriel* landed on the other side of the river."

"So this hunk of rock and metal is only for them," Gabi seethed.

"Kind of short-sighted, looking back." Cal's voice made Gabi and Will flinch in surprise.

She sprang to her feet, regaining her composure. He stood behind their small group. Andrea was secured in a cloth sling draped across his chest, one of her hands jutting out from her perch and clinging to her father's crimson shirt.

"We didn't forget *Raphael*, though. Ever." Cal pointed at a large stone that stood upright just outside the paved ring that circled the statue.

Gabi and her companions slowly made their way to the marker, which had two plaques on it. She checked to her right for a moment, making sure that Diego and Daphne were still in sight. The young children seemed to be occupied hunting for bugs in the grass.

"I take it none of you have been here since the monuments were repaired and put back?"

"No," Will responded. "When was that?"

"Last week."

Will nodded as he placed a palm on the large, domed rock. "I just got back to town two days ago. I head out again tomorrow. This was the only day we could all get together."

"What does this one say?" Gabi butted in.

Cal replied before Will could open his mouth. The way the words rolled off his tongue, he must have had the verse memorized. "Dedicated to the lives lost aboard the refugee ship *Raphael*. A catastrophic accident aboard their ship claimed the lives of over two thousand men, women, and children seeking a new life on a world far from their homes. Grief from their loss is shared by everyone in the community. Our hearts and homes will be ever open to them, and their pioneering spirit will be eternally joined with ours in Unity and Honor."

*I guess they really didn't forget us. They just didn't know.*

"There's more," Will noted. "There's a second plaque here."

Cal nodded as the others crowded around close, trying to get a better view. "That was just added, as part of the repairs."

"Six years after landing, a small group of six refugees from *Raphael* arrived in Rust Creek. Having survived the destruction of their ship, the crash landing of their emergency pods, and the subsequent years in isolation, they sought to find and join the Concordia colony. Against all odds, their journey was successful." Will's jaw slacked after the last word, and he was suddenly speechless.

Gabi felt a lump rise in her throat, and her eyes began to water.

Karina continued the next part, her voice shaky. "In addition to these six survivors, two young children, born on Demeter, accompanied their guardians across land and sea. Their story of determination serves as a testament to the resilience of the human spirit."

"Th-they've put our names here," Kris gasped. She began to read their names from the bronze plate, but choked up halfway through. Will took over when his sister could not continue.

Gabi turned away, trying to force down the knot in her throat that threatened to strangle her. Try as she could to hold them back, a pair of tears rolled down her cheeks. She took a few steps away from her companions, hoping that she could keep her emotions in check enough for them not to notice.

"Caleb's name should be up there," Karina croaked.

"So should Gina's," Will added, his voice distant. "So should Nick's. And Dan's. And Mom and Dad's, and about a thousand others, too."

*No more Sorrow, Will. It's over. For good this time.*

Gabi wiped the tears from her eyes just as Cal appeared at her side. "You okay, Gabi?"

"Yeah," she lied.

"I know adjusting to life here hasn't been easy for you. I've heard about the problems you've had in school, and how you sometimes butt heads with your foster parents."

"They treat me like a child," she protested.

"You never really got to *be* a child," he retorted. "You've got all the time in the world to grow up and be an adult. You can go back to being a hunter if you want; no one is going to stop you. And if that's what you want right now in your life, I don't think anyone can stop you. But you don't have to take care of anyone right now. Please at least think about slowing down and letting life happen. Be a kid once in a while."

"Being a kid is stupid."

"I don't think they think so," Cal nodded toward Diego and Daphne, who were busy chasing each other and giggling.

Gabi shook her head vigorously. "That's not me. I'm going out with Will when he leaves tomorrow."

"Does he know that?"

"He won't care. We've hunted together hundreds of times."

Cal smiled nervously. "Of course. But if things are different in the morning, I'd love for you and Diego to come with me to the harvest festival tomorrow. Tons of food, music and games."

*Music,* she thought, remembering better times that had long since passed. *It could… no, what are you thinking? Just go with Will.*

"Well, I have to get going," Cal added. "It was good seeing you again. Just think about what I said, okay?"

She nodded tersely as they shook hands. Gabi watched as he walked the path down the hill toward the arbor promenade, a part of Benedict Square that Gabi found particularly beautiful. As Cal disappeared into the tree line, Will made an appearance at her side.

"Promise me that you'll work on your reading, Gabs."

She rolled her eyes and turned to face him. "What's the point, Will? It doesn't do me any good out there."

A hard scowl formed on his face. "Out there isn't for you anymore. You need to read to have a shot in school."

Gabi opened her mouth to protest, but she knew from his expression that this was set in stone. She hung her head, realizing that a part of her life was over. That it was unacceptable for a twelve year old girl to be roaming the forests alone, hunting. And if Will would not go with her, no one would.

"Hey," he said softly, lifting her chin with his finger. "I know it feels like your world is being turned upside down again. This time it's for the best. Trust me."

She smiled weakly. "I always have."

"It's getting late. You and Diego should go home."

"Yeah, we should," she muttered under her breath.

Gabi took a long glance backward as she collected her brother. The four companions, chatting and hugging next to the memorial stone, had mostly scattered to the wind since arriving in Concordia. But in that brief moment, they looked as they had just before leaving their cursed island. Bathed in the orange glow of Demeter, this time they reminisced about friends and loved ones, rather than planning their futures. Somehow, Gabi knew that this reunion would not be repeated for a very long time.

The image was not complete, and there were absences that could not be filled. Notably absent from the image were troublesome Marya and her brother Aidan, whose company she could only now admit was sorely missing. Their new lives had been established miles away in Rust Creek. There were other holes in her heart that could not be filled.

Holes created by the deaths of their other companions, Gina and Caleb. Holes created years earlier by her father's murder and her mother's suicide. The tears flowed again, and she could not stop them this time.

Gabi sprinted down the hill to Diego, skidding to a stop in front of him, falling to her knees, and throwing her arms around him as tightly as she could.

"Gabi? What's wrong? Why are you crying?" His tiny, innocent voice soothed as he wrapped his arms around her.

"I love you, Diego," she whispered through her tears. "I'm sorry I haven't been a better sister to you."

"It's okay. I love you too. It'll be alright."

*Can it ever be?*

. . .

*It's quiet,* he thought, closing his eyes and drawing in a deep breath. Andrea cooed softly in her sling, reacting to the rise and fall of his chest.

A moment's calm was something he needed, and there was no better place to accomplish that in the city than the arbor promenade. Pine rangers flittered from treetop to treetop without a care as to the plant's origins. To them, a Demeter pine or blue elm was just as fine of a perch as a wild Earth cherry, as long as there were insects to catch. In a few minutes the sun would dip below the horizon, and the small birds would retire for the night. Glow hawks would take to the sky, assuming the duty of sky patrol.

Cal's nerves settled somewhat, though his stomach was still in knots. There was a goodbye to be said. It was not to be a bittersweet affair full of hope for future reunification. There would be plenty of emotion, however, anger and disappointment being the primary drivers. It wasn't Cal's first choice in how to deal with the situation, but he needed closure, and his hand had been forced to a degree.

He wandered slowly along the promenade, paralleling the length of *Michael's* hull. A slight breeze rose as he neared the cargo ramp, bringing with it the faint smells of fertilizer and dried waste. Not exactly the most pleasant smells, but certainly familiar. Except during the winter, Concordia always smelled at least faintly of these, and it was a reminder that he was home. The home he never wanted to leave again.

Governor Dayton had looked truly shocked when Cal declined an offer to join the Colonial Volunteer Militia. Shorthanded after the Battle of Mercy, the CVM had been on a recruiting spree. In another lifetime Cal would have signed up without hesitation. Dayton was a man he held in high esteem. But Lexi's death and his abduction had changed everything. At long last he had learned to say 'no' to Dayton, something that Lexi worried that he could never do. Even Jerk, the mental schism silenced by medication, had expressed the same concern. They were ultimately right. And saying no, despite disappointing Dayton, felt oddly liberating.

Cal's pace quickened as he climbed up the ramp into *Michael's* belly then ascended the rear stairwell to the empty upper gallery. It had been years since he last walked the corridors of the ship that carried him to Demeter. Other than faded paint chipping off of the walls, little had changed. He paused and took a deep breath at the top of the stairs, shaking his hands at his sides in a final effort to calm his nerves.

*It's time.*

His feet carried him swiftly to the entrance to pod twelve. Having his old pod reassigned as a prison was surreal, and it made him shiver slightly as Hunter ushered him through the airlock.

"They're waiting for you," his friend stated. "Alpha corridor. Better hurry."

Cal nodded, wasting no time in moving toward the front of the ESAARC pod. He passed the door to the pod's cockpit, a place he had spent countless hours studying and stargazing during the journey. A short climb had him in Alpha corridor. His eyes took a moment to adjust to the bright light inside.

As his vision came into focus, he could see the broken, sorrowful look on Brittany's face. Her lips trembled as tears coursed down her face. Behind her stood Governor Dayton, arms folded across his chest, lips pursed. To her right stood Sergeant Brandt of the CVM, his hand firmly locked around her arm just above the elbow. Brandt stood motionless, his gaze fixed on some point on the wall behind Cal.

"Cal," Brittany sobbed. "Thank God you're here. You have to stop them from doing this. Please."

He spoke softly in response, shaking his head. "That's not what I'm here for. I need to know why."

"Damn it, I'm your friend! The last one from home. Don't do this to me!"

"We stopped being friends the second you set me up. Nice of you to warn me about that, by the way."

"I tried," she choked through her tears. "But it was too late. Alan was already there."

"And what about breaking into my store? My home?"

Brittany looked away, too ashamed to meet his eyes. "The damage was already done. I had to show them I was still with them."

"Well, I guess that sums up how you really felt about me, friend." Cal's voice was ripe with condemnation.

"I didn't mean for any of this to happen!"

"You could have stopped it at any time. You could have just walked away, Britt. Faded into Concordia. Did you really think you were worth enough to Young for him to hunt you down?"

"You don't understand. He loved me."

"What a perfect pair you made, then."

A scream rose from Brittany's throat, a mixture of anguish and rage. The noise startled Andrea, who immediately began to wail. Cal reflexively stroked his daughter's cheek and soothed her.

"I didn't love Harcourt," Brittany shrieked.

"What about Rob?"

Shocked silence answered him. "I... I..."

"Yeah, that's what I thought." Cal could barely contain his disgust. "Young was in love with you, and you spurned him. Rob literally went to the end of the Earth with you, and you couldn't even fathom giving him your heart, could you?"

"That's not fair!" she protested.

He ignored her and continued. "So I guess that's why you threw me aside, Britt. I loved you, once. Back on Earth. It seems like forever ago. At this point, it might as well have been. But it fits. You use a guy for what you can get from him and move on. And now that you're in trouble you're playing whatever card you can to get away."

"Cal..."

"Just stop." Cal paused long enough to draw in a deep breath. He puffed up his chest and straightened his posture, giving him an extra two inches over Brittany's diminutive figure. "You're going to sleep now. When you wake up... when they move you to a proper jail, I'll be an old man. Andrea will probably be older than you. Certainly wiser. And there will be one thing you damn well know she'll understand better than you. What *true* friendship means."

Cal nodded once at Brandt, who stepped behind her and took firm hold of both of her elbows. She called out for mercy, struggling against the sergeant in futile defiance. Governor Dayton opened one of the upper sleeper berths.

"The stasis portion of your sentence begins today," Dayton boomed, addressing the prisoner. "Upon completion of a proper incarceration facility, you will be revived and relocated, at which point you will serve the prison portion of your sentence. You will be eligible for parole not less than ten years after the beginning of the prison sentence."

"Cal!" Brittany begged one final time, though it fell on deaf ears.

Brandt hoisted Brittany into the air like a sack of flour. Dayton guided her feet into the berth and held them steady as Brittany was secured inside the sleeper. The door closed with a resounding click. A second later, Brittany started pounding on the berth from the inside.

Dayton walked slowly over to Cal, pressing a darkened button on the computer console next to him. "It's all ready, Mr. McLaughlin. You know what to do."

Cal retrieved Andrea from the sling, snuggling her close to his chest to help calm her from the ordeal. He did not make a motion toward the computer screen. "It doesn't feel right. Even after all she did to me, it still feels like I'd be betraying her if I turned on the sleeper. How could I explain to Andrea that I pushed the button?" He sighed. "It would make me no better than Brittany."

"You have every right to after she turned you over to that psychopath. No one would think any less of you."

"I would. That's enough for me. Thank you for the offer, but I can't be the one to do it."

Dayton's arm fell to Cal's shoulder. He squeezed once gently, then said, "I understand."

A moment later the governor activated the sleeper berth. Brittany's thrashing ceased after a minute as the gas placed her into a deep sleep. Cal felt a momentary pang of guilt as the sentence was carried out. For him, Earth officially died in that moment. Concordia was all that remained. His life with Andrea.

Cal stumbled numbly out of Alpha corridor, and out of a habit from years past, ended up in the pod's cockpit. He situated himself in the left seat, curling Andrea in the crook of his arm. His neck craned upward, looking through the top canopy windows. There his gaze remained fixed on the sky as Andrea fell asleep and the night sky was painted with the glitter of endless stars.

• • •

"Where did I put that manifest?" Tom grumbled, flipping through the mass of paper on his desk. After a moment's panic, the missing folder was set down in front of him.

"In my hands, Governor," his subordinate replied softly. "Sorry, I wanted to get a peek for myself. Maybe help you assign the new arrivals."

Tom was still unsure of his new deputy. It was a shock to the entire city when the previous deputy governor, Roger Miller, passed away suddenly in January. Cardiac arrest, according to Dr. Taylor. Not comforting in the least, since Roger was only forty five years old. Tom had more than a decade on the deceased deputy, but still felt as strong as the day Concordia was forged.

Roger's replacement was younger, taller, and stronger. Not to mention that his family was as close to royalty as existed in Concordia. That may have played a small role in his landslide victory during the special election in March.

Whereas Roger would listen to Tom's endless explanations and offer quiet counsel when sought, Deputy Governor Tyler Quinn was not a man to sit idle for a long speech. The man had ideas, and the passion with which he executed his job grew day by day. In another time, Tom might have sought such a trait when promoting officers. After six years in the governor's seat with a more passive voice of reason at his side, Quinn's exuberance sometimes teetered on the edge of upsetting.

"Well?" Tom retorted with thinly veiled sarcasm. "What are your thoughts on the fresh crop?"

Quinn's lips distorted in an apathetic grimace. "This group looks more like scavengers than survivors. No real usable skills that I can see. Makes me wonder if they stole the ship, or if Earth is starting to scrape the bottom of the barrel at this point."

"It could be either. It's been six months since the last pod touched down. They're getting fewer and farther between. I don't think we'll see many more in the future."

"Kind of a shame. Only a few people will be able to escape that hellhole anymore. No hope for those left behind."

"Where there's life, there's hope, Tyler."

The younger man shook his head. "I'm not going to fly there and ask them if they believe it. In any case, there's still the problem of these thirty-six new arrivals. There might be a good candidate or two for the CVM, but that's all I see."

Tom picked up the folder and scanned through the list of names and occupations, adjusting the thin glasses on his face when he couldn't read a line. On first glance, Quinn seemed right. Among the survivors were a bartender, an interior decorator, and a delivery truck driver. Their occupational skills weren't exactly in demand in Concordia.

"Maybe another approach. Let's give them some hope and see what they do with it. See to it that they attend Unification Day."

"You think they might take issue with the Chinese settlers? I don't think they're quite up to speed on what's happened."

"I don't see a huge problem unless Devereaux didn't do his job in disarming them when they landed. And as much as I hate to say it, it's a quick way to weed out undesirables. If anyone picks a fight, it's back to stasis for them."

Quinn rolled his eyes, though he still confirmed the governor's orders. Tom checked his watch after the young man left. He had a few minutes left before his next appointment, so he set to organizing the paperwork on his desk. That task was finished with a couple minutes to spare, which he used to polish up his Unification Day speech. Soft rapping on the door broke his concentration as he neared the end of the speech. He glanced up at his visitor.

"I'm here for my annual report, Governor," Darius said as he stepped into the room.

"Please," Tom smiled softly as he offered a seat.

Six years had passed since Darius lost his arm. Yet every time he came into the room, Tom had a moment of uneasiness. Every visit triggered a disturbing, ephemeral image of what life would be like if his own limb had been taken. The moment passed quicker with each year, though Tom still felt ashamed of his childish reaction. Darius was maimed by a reaper bear and, whether he knew it or not, he served as a living reminder of the creature's danger.

That grave injury was the final straw that broke then-Governor Owens. The reins were passed to Tom, and Darius became as close to a hermit as one could get sitting in front of screens all day. After he was able to recover some data from the phantom servers that Young had sought, Tom had jokingly given him the title of Technology Minister. That joke evolved into a legitimate position in Concordia, and Darius's personal calling.

Incredibly, the ex-governor managed to recover nearly eighty percent of the information from the wrecked drives. Concordia was poised for a technological explosion. At least, once the issues of resources and manufacturing were ironed out. Much of modern Earth technology relied heavily on plastics, and the colony lacked the raw materials or methods to refine them. It was up to the Technology Minister to safeguard the data for Concordia's future.

"I've completed an integrity test of each ship's arrays, Governor. I'm afraid it's not pretty this year."

Tom's stomach knotted up. *More issues.*

"What seems to be the problem, Minister?"

"Another two blades on *Gabriel* have failed. System boards in both cases, so I can't even combine them to make one good one. I'll pull the rest of the parts that are good, but that leaves us with only seven good blades left until we have to take her redundant array offline. If they keep dying at this rate, *Gabriel* will have no backup in two to three years. *Michael* won't have redundancy much longer, either."

"After all the sacrifice and the work to recover that damned information, it's just going to fall apart." The governor sighed heavily and rubbed his brow. "What can we do?"

Darius shook his head, concern etched deeply in his ebony features. "Unless we magically find a way to manufacture replacement computer parts in the next two years, the only thing I have left is a complete gamble. Take *Gabriel's* servers offline now. Patch up *Michael's* and strip what's left for parts. We can probably squeeze a decade or more out of it."

"And if something happens on *Michael*, say a fire or explosion," he replied, instantly spotting the flaw in the plan.

"Then we lose it all. We go back to only the knowledge in our books."

"And get set back who knows how many years. Decades."

"Maybe even centuries," Darius added, biting back his frustration.

"Two years," Tom repeated, sinking into his chair. "There's no way we can build you new parts that soon."

"I know."

Tom turned his chair to the side, casting his gaze out the window. The grounds of Benedict Square were being prepared for the Unification Day celebrations. Celebrations that would draw thousands together the next day. Original colonists, survivors of *Raphael*, and post-War refugees of a dozen Earth nationalities, all sharing a holiday that held different context, yet the same ultimate meaning: healing and unity. Perhaps the refugees from the latest pod didn't understand yet, but they would, in time.

*So what do we give them? Hope, resting on chance? But what hope do we have of regaining Earth's technology, if we can't maintain the data banks?*

"Do it," he muttered. "It's as good as gone if we don't at least try to keep it together. After tomorrow, I'll gather the geologists and prospectors again. We found coal, right? Maybe we'll find something else useful."

Darius nodded, exiting wordlessly. It was for the best; Tom might have tried to have the minister dissuade him from the course of action. It had to be right, despite his misgivings. The difficult, dangerous choices always were. It didn't make it any easier to swallow.

The air in his office seemed stifling, and the walls dark and confining, so he decided to go for a walk. The mild, filtered sun felt good on his skin, and the breaths he took were invigorating.

As he strolled down Foundation Street, signs of the colony's expansion could be seen everywhere. Fresh dirt packed over a recently filled trench ran the length of the street, with short, perpendicular spurs running at regular intervals to buildings on either side. Just beyond the town, halfway to River Islands, sat the first concrete building on Demeter: a small waste treatment plant. Farther upstream was a purification facility. Both had come online within the last two years, and their service range was steadily increasing.

*I guess it's not all that bad,* he thought. *Even without Benedict's servers we're not living in the stone age. We have electricity as far out as Rust Creek. Running water and sewers are becoming more common.*

Tom reached River Way and circled back west, taking time to enjoy the view of South Concordia from the far banks of the Fairweather. The walk did him much good, and the troubles of his earlier meetings melted away. The smells of fresh baked bread mingled with sawdust as he passed industrial buildings of several flavors on his way. All the while, he considered how he would pass the evening. He ended up at a small two-story shop a few doors from Benedict Boulevard.

Andrea McLaughlin giggled and smiled when she saw Tom walk in. Her blue-green eyes twinkled brighter than the red bow that held her sandy hair in a neat ponytail. She stopped coloring for a moment and shouted, "Daddy! Governor Tom is here!"

A second later, Calvin emerged from the back of the shop, carrying a wooden crate full of soap in his arms. He slid his load onto the counter and came to greet the governor with an outstretched hand.

"Good to see you," Cal grinned. "It's been a while, how have you been?"

Tom shrugged indifferently. "Another day, another challenge."

"That ship that landed the other day?"

Tom nodded slowly.

"Well, I don't think they'll be any worse than the rest," Cal added.

"You're probably right," Tom agreed. He wandered over to the sales counter, where Andrea was hard at work drawing something that vaguely resembled her house. "That looks really good, Andrea."

"Thank you!"

"It wasn't that long ago that you could barely scribble."

"I don't know where the time goes," Cal remarked. "Did you know that she's starting school this fall?"

That was a measure of six years that hadn't registered before, and it made him acutely aware of his age in that moment.

"Has it really been that long?"

"It has." Cal smiled weakly. "So what brings you in today?"

"Do you have another bottle of your private reserve? I ran out a couple weeks ago and haven't had a chance to get more."

"Of course." The younger man reached blindly under the counter and produced a clear bottle full of rich, dark whiskey. "Four favors. On your tab?"

"Please." He took the bottle from Cal, rolling it over in his hand as he examined it. "Will I see you tomorrow?"

"I wouldn't miss it for the world. Andrea would never let me hear the end of it if we didn't go."

"What's that, Daddy?" the little girl asked, looking up from her drawing.

"The picnic tomorrow, sweetie. Just telling Governor Tom that we're going."

"And that we're going with Katie and Luke?"

Cal stuttered, and the color drained from his face. His loss for words was telling. The fact that it was over spending time with a single mother from one of the Detroit pods was nothing short of damning.

Tom smirked. "Katie and Luke?"

"Please, please don't get the wrong idea," he pled. "I love Lexi. I always will. But she's been gone for so long now, and Katie… well, we've really connected."

"No one will get the wrong idea, Mr. McLaughlin. No one will question your love, either. No matter what your mind tells you, you can't shut out love forever just to hold on to a memory."

Cal reached inside his shirt and fished out his necklace of rings. He looked down, his fingers tracing the original aluminum wedding bands. "I know. It's just hard to let go."

"No one ever said anything about letting go. Look at it this way; do you think Alexis would have wanted you to be alone if it meant misery?"

"No," he admitted after a moment's thought.

"So enjoy the day, and the company."

Cal grinned halfheartedly. "Of course. See you tomorrow."

The governor saw himself out and made his way back to Civic Hall. After he prepared and consumed a light dinner in the kitchen, he took the bottle of whiskey and a small glass up to his office. Tom settled into his chair and poured a stiff drink. He read through his Unification Day speech. With a disgusted sneer, he crumpled it up and threw it away, retrieving a single, blank page from his stationery drawer. He downed the first glass of whiskey, and waited as the warmth spread throughout his body and his mind loosened up.

*What are we?*

The question had no simple answer. While most Concordians had immigrated on the original sleepers, waves of fresh refugees had infused new life and experiences over the years. Citizens of a dozen countries on Earth found their way across the void using Dr. Benedict's illicit sleeper ship plans. The more recent additions had lived a nightmare on Earth, but their time on Concordia, with the exception of the survivors of the *Mercy* incident, had been peaceful and prosperous. The opposite was true for the original colonists; they left Earth before the worst atrocities occurred, but struggled during the early years on Demeter.

*But we have all survived, against all odds. That is what we are, and that is what we do. No matter what is thrown at us, we survive and then we thrive.*

He poured another drink, and set to work preparing his speech.

Words flowed from pen to paper, shaped by movement of phrases and concepts. His vision of what Unity and Honor meant came to life before his eyes. As the ink dried, he finished the second glass of whiskey. In the morning, his fellow citizens would hear his words, and Concordia would be set for another year of history. It would put one foot in front of the other, galvanized against tragedy and misfortune, as it had always been.

. . .

>END PLAYBACK|

Credits and Acknowledgements
24 March 2014
The real Earth, somewhere in Washington State

Spring 2014 is here, and it's time for another release. This is the milestone of my fifth book. But more importantly, this is the end of Project Columbus.

This is a series that I first started envisioning in late 2011. Something that I was never sure would ever see the light of day, even as I laid down the words for all fifty chapters of *Columbus: Flight*. Something absolutely extraordinary happened in September 2012. My words became available to the public.

And for those of you who have followed me from the beginning of *Flight*, I have no words to describe what an honor it has been to tell my story to you. So in the simplest terms possible… From the bottom of my heart, thank you. Each and every one of you.

As always, I need to give special thanks to my beta readers Sarah, Karie, and Rob. *Columbus: Mercy* is a mixture of elements written back in the days of *Flight* woven with the story that progressed and changed as recently as *Winter*. Their guidance through the maze of story arcs has been phenomenal these past two years.

I would like to profusely thank Mathew and Bridgette Reuther of Oakenbrand Press. Their continued support and encouragement is of immeasurable value. I am proud to have Bridgette's beautiful artwork gracing the cover of my book yet again.

Of course, continued thanks to my wife Megan and our three boys for keeping me sane throughout the writing process. With *Mercy* wrapping up, we're looking forward to a little quality time together before I launch my next project.

On the topic of projects, I would like to remind my readers that, since the release of *Winter* a few months back I, joined forces with local artist Anastasiya Kochetova to produce a web comic series, titled The Sorcerers. This urban fantasy series can be viewed at **http://sorcerers. manyhatsonline.com** and updates (currently) once a week on Wednesdays. Also, keep an eye on my blog for updates on what stories I have on the horizon.

Thanks once again, everyone. Project Columbus will be available in an Omnibus edition later this Summer, and I hope to have a new series ready for you all in the not too distant future!

## About the Author:

J.C. Rainier is product of the Pacific Northwest, born in the Seattle area in 1978, and living in the Puget Sound area his whole life. He is the younger of two children in his family, and his older brother proved to be a giant pest up through his teenage years (as siblings tend to be).

J.C.'s parents were both educators working at the middle school level, and he married into another family of educators. In his family, counting in-laws, there are now two retired principals, two retired teachers, a retired school counselor, and an active science teacher.

In his youth, J.C. read quite a lot. The Call of the Wild was one of his early favorites, and into middle school he began to devour other books such as Anne McCaffrey's Dragonriders of Pern series. Unfortunately, J.C. developed a form of dylexia that made reading from the page of a book difficult. It was later discovered that the curvature of the page itself caused the issue, and the advent of the eReader (with its perfectly flat screen) has allowed him to once again enjoy reading as he used to.

He enjoys both indoor and outdoor pursuits including computers, cars, and camping. J.C. and his wife enjoy hockey, and set aside time several times each season to watch the local WHL franchise.

J.C. and his wife are raising three boys, including a set of twins. If his blog ever fails to make sense, he's probably had a very long night just prior to writing it. If said writing is just a random set of characters similar to "adsk,wr3.1", then one of the children has managed a surprise attack on his laptop.

. . .

www.ingramcontent.com/pod-product-compliance
Lightning Source LLC
Chambersburg PA
CBHW061559170626
46811CB00001B/261